ChangelingPress.com

Omega Wolves

Will Okati

Omega Wolves
Will Okati

All rights reserved.
Copyright ©2022 Will Okati
Second Edition

ISBN: 978-1-60521-839-7

Publisher:
Changeling Press LLC
315 N. Centre St.
Martinsburg, WV 25404
ChangelingPress.com

Printed in the U.S.A.

Editor: Margaret Riley
Cover Artist: Bryan Keller

The individual stories in this anthology have been previously released in E-Book format.

Table of Contents

Lost And Found
Will Okati

Years ago, the Wasp Lake pack forced Matthias out after he dared fall in love with the Packmaster's Omega son, Bree. Now Matthias has made his fortune on the sea and returned to claim his mate. But the world he left behind isn't the one he finds.

Bree has become an outcast and been lied to from the start. He's been told Matthias left because he'd fallen out of love with him. He hasn't mated with any other wolves or borne them cubs, but the struggle against his Omega nature has taken its toll. He knows he can't hold out much longer, even if he does have a secret den to hide in when he's in heat.

Matthias takes shelter from a blizzard in Bree's bolt-hole just as mating fever consumes the Omega, and the former lovers are reunited just in time for their world to change again -- for keeps.

Chapter One

Matthias

Find shelter -- or die.

Matthias tilted his head back, pointed his muzzle at the sky, and howled. He held his breath during the silence that followed, ears pricked erect and quivering as he listened for any sign of the pack.

At first he heard nothing but the screaming of the blizzard and the rush of snowfall that'd trapped him out in the heart of the storm. He'd meant to hunt and find a den before night fell, but the blizzard had had other ideas. Matthias bared his teeth at the blinding torrents of snow that meant to kill him if they could. Let them try! They wouldn't find it that easy to finish him. He'd spent years working his way back home, and he'd be damned if he lay down now.

Then --

Wolves howled faintly and far away. *Who calls? Who calls?*

Son from away come back, Matthias called back in his wolf voice. *Hunting on Wasp Lake.*

Snow bad there, snow bad. Three or more wolves sent him that message. *Find shelter.*

Matthias growled to himself before howling his reply. *Shelter where? Where, shelter?*

Their answer took long minutes to come, but when it did it was in a strong, clear call. *Cabin, east side of Wasp Lake. Omega's bolt-hole.* They sounded grudging. *Packmaster says, you shelter there now.*

A pause.

Away-hunter! After the storm, you answer challenge, or you go. Understand?

Matthias drew his lips back over the gleaming fangs he boasted in his wolf form. He'd been an orphaned adolescent boy the first time the pack cast him out, and he'd had no choice but to take to his heels -- but he hadn't spent his time away idly. He was an Alpha now, one who'd earned the fortune he'd set out to make, and who didn't mean to leave the Wasp Lake pack before he'd gotten what he'd come for.

That would have to wait. For now.

Understand, he called back. *Going now, to cabin.*

No answer came to that. Guessed that meant he was on his own. Matthias shook himself good and hard to rid his thick timber-gray coat of the snow that'd gathered while he stood still, and with a leap forward pushed his powerful muscles into a long-legged gallop.

He'd forgotten how winters could be so harsh this far inland. Where he'd lived, the seas never froze and snowstorms were never worse than mild squalls. Nothing like this. Inland, the snow fell so heavy and dense it blocked out the world past the end of his muzzle, and so cold his body begged him to stop, to rest, to sleep.

No. Matthias gritted his teeth and forced himself forward. He didn't think the pack would have sent him on a wild goose chase. They'd want to know who he was and why he'd entered their territory before they decided what to do with him. The Omega's cabin he'd been promised would be there.

Though it did occur to him to wonder if an Omega lived there just now or if they had an Alpha ready and willing to defend his territory.

If there were, then so be it. Matthias wasn't any stranger to fighting for his life. He knew how to survive.

His keen sense of smell while in wolf shape picked up the signs of habitation long before his eyes would have been able to. Smoke from a wood fire, tilled earth, and goats kept in a warm winter enclosure. Not far ahead now. *Almost there. Keep going.*

Another burst of energy brought Matthias to the edge of a clearing, and when the winds broke momentarily he saw the blessed yellow halo of lights shining through windows of heavy, opaque glass. He shook more snow off his coat and loped toward the steps of the small cabin -- only to scrabble to a hasty stop when the Omega wolf he'd been warned of burst through the cabin's door with his teeth bared in a mighty bark.

Matthias deflected the attack and feinted a bite at the Omega's neck. *Shelter-claim. No fight.*

Fight! No shelter, the Omega insisted. *You go.*

Matthias bared his teeth. *Packmaster orders.*

The Omega wolf scoffed at that. *Packmaster not here. I am. You go!* He tried to dodge low and snap at Matthias's underbelly.

Enough of that. Matthias seized the Omega's scruff in his teeth and shook him until he yelped. There was something strange about his scent. Something almost familiar. A spicy sort of fragrance that tickled his nose and sent a frisson of mixed irritation and heat up his spine. Had they fought before? Matthias couldn't be sure, his blood too hot for rational remembering.

Without letting go, Matthias growled. *Shelter-claim. Nowhere else. I stay.*

Any other Omega would have given up at that, but not this one. He got in a lucky nip at Matthias's shoulder and bolted for it when Matthias let go in his surprise. Scrambling on the longest legs Matthias had ever seen on a wolf, it had almost reached the door of the cabin by the time Matthias caught up. One mad leap brought him on top of the wolf, and their momentum carried them indoors.

The Omega turned, snarling.

Enough! Matthias reached deep inside himself for the ability to change his shape, shook off his wolf form, and rose to stand on two feet. He kicked the door shut and secured the latch. The wolf's scent surrounded him inside, dizzying him briefly.

"I'll bite you again if I have to, and I promise you won't like it one bit." The warmth of the cabin threatened to overcome Matthias. He planted his feet firmly on the split log floor and raised his chin. "Stand up! Who are you?"

The Omega wolf stopped mid-lunge, staring at him. Though they balked, no Omega could resist an Alpha's command, and when he spoke they had no choice but to cast aside their animal form and stand in man shape. The Omega's legs were even longer as a human, his body slim, and his face heartbreakingly lovely. His wide blue-gray eyes focused on Matthias in startled shock. "*You.*"

Matthias's lips parted in equal surprise. This wasn't just any wolf, but the man Matthias had loved once and had to leave behind. The Omega he'd come back to the Wasp Lake Pack to find and claim for his own.

"Bree," Matthias said, his heart leaping. "*Bree.*"

* * *

Bree

Am I dreaming? Bree backed away from Matthias, though there wasn't far to go inside the cabin. It'd been his father's, used as a way station during hunting trips, and was little more than a box with storage cupboards built into the walls. A handful of steps brought his shoulders to the far wall, which made his skin prickle with cold from the chill leaching through the logs.

The Alpha wolf -- Matthias -- stared at him with his lips parted and his eyes huge. "Bree."

Bree shook his head stubbornly and said nothing. He had to be dreaming. Matthias had left him years ago without a word, not one word. Bree had given up hoping Matthias would come back after the first winter gave way to spring. Even if his subconscious betrayed him every now and then, Bree knew better than to think miracles really happened.

Matthias shook his head as if in wonder. "Look at you. You haven't changed at all."

"Right," Bree scoffed at that because yes, he had. He'd been the son of the former Packmaster when Matthias left, and sibling to the Packmaster's Alpha heir. They'd wanted for nothing, not even in the cruelest weeks of winter. He'd been padded with supple flesh and clothed in the finest and warmest that money could buy.

That had been before the old Packmaster went hunting bear and didn't come back. Before a challenge for leadership of the pack sent Bree's sibling away with his tail between his legs. The Pack had let Bree stay on the outskirts, but only because he was Omega.

And they'd never let him forget that.

Matthias hadn't heard, or had chosen to ignore, Bree's reply. He walked forward as steady and sure on two legs as he would be on four paws, his gaze fixed eagerly -- hungrily -- on Bree's face. Oh, he'd changed. No longer a skinny stripling adolescent, he'd grown into a real man, thick with muscle and tough with sinew. His face had matured, the strong bones finding their shape. The eyebrows were still the same, one permanently bent in an arch.

The sight of him kindled a fire in Bree. His body didn't care that this wolf had walked away from him before. It wanted Matthias now.

"You're as beautiful as the day I lost you. Bree, my pretty Bree," Matthias murmured as he came closer, steady and sure and just how Bree remembered him. "Did you miss me?"

He wasn't dreaming. But how --

It didn't matter. Matthias had *left* him. Bree shook his head so hard that his long red hair whipped against his cheeks. "Go away."

"I'm not going anywhere." Matthias was so close now that the Alpha scent of him flooded Bree's senses.

Naked as he was -- as they both were, after changing shape -- there wasn't any hiding how his body had reacted to Bree. When he closed the last bit of distance between them, his cock pressed thick and hard against Bree's belly.

Bree moaned. He couldn't help it. He'd forgotten how good it felt, to have a man desire him so plainly. It'd been months -- no, years -- since he'd let any man or Alpha near him. Packs always needed more breeders, and Omegas were too precious to cast out, but Bree had sworn he'd be damned before he'd spread his legs for any wolf at Wasp Lake.

So far, he'd been lucky. He'd always managed to hide when he felt his heat cycle coming on and rode it out by himself. Why the new Packmaster allowed it, Bree didn't know. Maybe he thought time would wear his resistance down.

Maybe he was only giving Bree enough rope to hang himself with.

And now this. *Matthias.*

Matthias's warm hands rested on Bree's ass. When had that happened? Bree moaned again, shaking with the effort it took not to grind forward. His body wanted this. It'd gone soft and open, eager for Matthias's cock, the lubrication an Omega's body produced to ease the way already trickling down the soft skin of his inner thighs.

"You smell..." Matthias nuzzled the juncture of Bree's neck and scraped it lightly with the edges of his teeth. His hands tightened on Bree's ass, kneading the taut muscles there. When he rolled his hips, the delicious friction drew groans from both of them, a noise that Bree sharpened to a cry as Matthias slipped two fingers inside him. "Wet."

Bree struggled against himself, panting in sharp short bursts. "No. You left."

"I'm here now." Matthias spread his fingers. Pressure and heat and lust made Bree want to sob with the hunger they roused for more, *more*. "And you're still mine."

The words were a shock of cold water.

Bree found the strength somewhere, somehow, to push hard against Matthias and shove him away. Not far, but far enough to catch his breath. He pressed his thighs together and made himself ignore both the fierce clamor of his body and the burning ache in his heart. "I am no one's Omega. I belong to me."

Matthias's gaze, dark with lust, lingered on him. Bree could feel him taking in every detail, every piece of him that had changed. Matthias wasn't anyone's fool. He would see how thin Bree had gotten, how low poverty had brought him. How desperate he was.

Bree held his head high, though his eyes stung with unshed tears. "I belong to *me*," he said again. "You can stay as long as the storm lasts, but then I want you to go. Do you understand?"

Matthias hadn't stopped drinking him in. No less hotly but more calmly, more thoughtfully. "I understand."

"And you agree?"

"If you want me to go after the storm ends, and after I'm sure you can make it safely home, then I'll agree." Matthias stepped back, still hard, but showing himself not to be a threat. Mouth quirking up at the corner when he saw how Bree's eyes were drawn to the rigid length of his cock. "And if you change your mind, then I'll agree to that, too."

"I won't." Bree hugged himself as the first warning wave of heat ebbed away, leaving him wobbly in the knees but in control of his head again. Had Matthias noticed the change in his scent? Bree couldn't tell. "And that's not the bargain I offered."

"No, it's not." Matthias let his gaze drift hungrily over Bree one more time. "I'll be a gentleman. I won't force myself on you until you ask me to."

Bree squeezed his thighs together against fresh lubrication. His body liked that idea far more than he wanted it to. But though his face burned hot, he stood his ground. "I won't."

"Even so." Matthias brushed the backs of his knuckles against Bree's cheek. "Just one more thing."

Before Bree could ask, Matthias had put both strong arms around him and enfolded him in an embrace that sent a shock of gentle warmth straight down to his bones. A hug that made him feel safe, protected -- cared for.

"I missed you, Bree," Matthias murmured in his ear. "So much. I dreamed of you every day I was gone, and I've wanted this every night. More than I know how to say."

Prickles of electric excitement seemed to burst across Bree's skin. He drew in a sharp breath and struggled against the need to wrap his arms and legs around Matthias and let Matthias do what he would. He held out, but only just, and panted with the effort when Matthias let go and looked down at him, mouth tilted in the smile that used to be Bree's favorite.

"Do we have a deal?"

* * *

Matthias

Matthias's stomach growled.

Bree blinked up at him, wide blue eyes dazed. Just as Matthias had hoped, and just as he'd remembered. Bree always had been a spitfire. He should have recognized an Omega so ready to fight right away. The only way to calm Bree when he got good and worked up was to kiss the mad out of him, and he doubted Bree would leave his balls intact if he tried it now.

He was tempted to try anyway. All those years apart had seemed to last forever.

Matthias thumbed at Bree's soft mouth and made himself step back. Just as well to take a breather. Let his mind catch up to his body and heart. "If there's anything to eat, I'd be obliged."

Bree licked his lips where Matthias's thumb had been. "I… There might be something. I don't know. I don't live here all the time. I just come when it's…" He shook his head briskly and pressed a hand to one rose-red cheek. "I'll look."

"If there's nothing, I'll go see if I can scare a rabbit out of its den."

Bree wrinkled his nose. "They're awfully skinny this time of year."

"Skinny's better than nothing at all." Matthias propped his hip against the wall and crossed his arms, watching Bree thoughtfully as the Omega moved about. He walked a little more awkwardly than Matthias remembered; the Bree in his memory was graceful as a dancer, his muscles lithe and fluid.

Except when he was in heat.

Matthias's nostrils flared as he caught the scent that'd been teasing at him since he shut the cabin door behind them. *Ah, that explains it.* The first time he'd seen the change come over Bree, they'd both been too young to have any sense, and it'd scared the devil out of them.

Only the first time. The second time…

Matthias's mouth curved, recalling how he and Bree had spent hours wrapped up in one another, discovering the new differences in their bodies -- the things that made them Alpha and Omega, and that would tie them together for the rest of their lives. An Omega in heat was an amazing creature. His body opened, wet and slick and hot, eager to be filled. His ligaments looser, giving him a swaying gait; his nipples tight; his body temperature higher. His scent, intoxicating.

Oh yes. It'd been worth it, even if they had to hide their mating from the Packmaster and his heir, and dunk Bree in an icy stream to alter his scent before he returned to them.

Matthias clicked his tongue. As many times as they'd brought each other to orgasm, it was a marvel Bree hadn't gotten pregnant before they figured out how to avoid the problem with a sachet of silk soaked in tansy oil.

Now there was a thought. Matthias's groin ached and throbbed as the images of Bree full to the brim with his cubs passed over his mind's eye. They weren't wet-behind-the-ears teenagers anymore. They were men, full-grown, who could raise a family of their own if they chose. Far from here, and away from the memories of bad times.

And Matthias did choose.

But that would have to wait. Matthias's focus shifted, his mouth changing its shape to a frown, as he studied Bree. If he looked past the allure of an Omega on the cusp of going into heat, he didn't like the apparent changes in Bree at all. He'd gotten taller, but no heavier; thinner, in fact. His legs should have been willowy, not bony, and while his hair was the same heavy sweep of cinnamon silk that Matthias remembered, it looked dry and rough. His hands were reddened from work and marred with the sorts of small scars a man alone tended to gather chopping wood and butchering meat.

What had happened to him? Matthias scented the air carefully but couldn't detect any traces of family scent on Bree. *So, then.* The Packmaster who had cast him out for daring to take his Omega offspring's virginity and claim his heart wasn't around any longer. Nor the heir, either.

Good, in one sense. Less fighting in his future to claim Bree, though he would have if he'd needed to.

Bad in that the mate of his heart had suffered.

Well, I can fix that. He'd made his fortune for Bree, and if he could only get them both back to the coast, where life was kinder, he'd soon fatten Bree up again.

His body liked that thought. The only question was -- would Bree allow it?

"You're staring at me." Bree stopped in mid-reach for a high cabinet shelf. He clutched an oiled-paper packet of what smelled like truly ancient jerky to his chest with one hand and held another of something that might once have been maple sugar candy in the other.

Matthias made himself shrug casually. "Was I?"

"You know you were." Bree lay both packets down on the countertop that held a basin for washing. He turned his back to bring down a tin pot from the high shelf and glanced over his shoulder. "You're still doing it."

"Is that a fact," Matthias murmured. Since he'd been caught, he didn't bother trying to hide it. "I spent a long time looking at you only in my memories. I'm making up for lost time."

Bree pressed both hands to his face. "Don't. Please don't. I can't think when you do that."

"Do what?"

"Look at me as if you want to eat me alive. You make me want to..." Bree moaned, shifting his hips. "And I can't. I won't. You *left* me, Matthias!"

"Yes, I did. Because I had to." Matthias's frown deepened. "I told you all of that in the letter I left you. How I had no choice but to go. I couldn't fight the whole pack then. I told you in the letters I sent you from the coast."

"You -- what?" Bree lowered his hands and shook his head. "I never got any letters. Not even one."

The Packmaster. Matthias shut his eyes and stifled a growl. He should have known. It would have been just like the possessive old bastard to forbid them so much as a civil goodbye.

When he opened his eyes, Bree had pressed one hand to his throat and the other to his heart. The blue of his irises swam with unshed tears. "I thought you stopped loving me."

Matthias's heart couldn't help but yield at the sight. *Poor thing.* "I could never stop loving you," he said quietly. "I still do."

Bree shook his head mutely. His lips moved but without sound.

Outside, the wind howled and lashed against the walls of the cabin. Matthias cocked his head to listen. "Sounds like the storm's picking up. They always do, before they're over." He made up his mind. Bree had been through enough shocks tonight, and from the smell of him his Omega biology was about to take charge. "Turn the lamp out, Bree."

"But you said you were hungry --"

He was, but not for food. Soon enough, neither of them would have a choice. Best that Bree gather his strength first. "No," Matthias said, and blew out the lamp himself. "Get some rest. I'll keep watch."

Chapter Two

Bree

"I can take care of myself," Bree said into the sudden darkness. Without a chance to adjust, his eyes strained to keep track of Matthias. He could smell the Alpha wolf, could hear his movements, but he couldn't tell where Matthias was.

Not before Matthias's sturdy warmth settled at his side and lips brushed his cheek. "I know you can. But you don't have to, tonight."

Bree raised his chin. "I always take care of myself. There isn't anyone else."

"There is now." Matthias touched his mouth to Bree's temple, laid his hand on Bree's shoulder -- then, reluctantly, let go. Bree heard him pace to the other side of the small cabin and settle against the wall, standing. When he spoke, it was with an Alpha's command. "You'll need your strength later. Rest."

Bree's body obeyed without his mind's permission, bringing him down into the tangled nest of blankets he'd cast aside earlier. He kept them in this cabin for no other purpose; they were soft, freshly washed, and soothing to his bare skin.

He closed his eyes and listened to the sound of Matthias's quiet, steady breathing.

Rest. As if that made any kind of difference to the frenzy of a heat cycle. As if it ever stopped an Omega from begging for cock and spunk to put out the fire inside him. Bree bit his lip savagely and curled his hands into fists.

Maybe it wouldn't be so bad. He'd managed on his own before. If he could keep the fever quiet, and the shakes hidden, and lie still so that his scent didn't carry...

Across the cabin, Matthias sighed. "Stubborn Bree. Go to sleep."

Bree's body acquiesced.

* * *

He woke with a start, and a stifled scream, with fire licking at his limbs.

Oh. Oh, he'd forgotten. Every time, he forgot what this felt like. Bree rolled onto his stomach and thrust a corner of the blanket between his teeth to bite on. His limbs shuddered, racked with tremors, and were so slick with sweat that his knees slid on the floor. Not just sweat, he realized. His body had opened and released the chemical mix that made him wet enough for beads of slick to drip down his thighs. He could smell himself, and he stank of pure animal lust.

He bit down on the blanket to muffle his keening cry and spread his knees, thrusting his hips up, his body presenting itself.

Came back down as quickly, moaning around his mouthful. He knotted his fists and banged his head against the floor.

He needed to be *fucked*. His body roared with the demand for it. His cock jerked helplessly in spontaneous orgasm that provided only a spike in the fever with no relief.

"Bree."

Bree stiffened. *Matthias*. He shook his head and ground his fists into the blankets, but his body opened and another gush of lubrication wetted his thighs.

"Oh, Bree," Matthias said on a long breath. "It doesn't have to be like this."

He didn't wait to be told to go, or to come, but with a few quick steps settled at Bree's side. He laid his hand on Bree's back, his touch so blessedly cool Bree almost sobbed with relief. If he let himself, he could love Matthias again -- love him as if he'd never stopped.

And if he lost Matthias a second time, which he *would* -- he didn't get to keep the things he loved -- Bree knew he couldn't survive that again.

He tried to shake Matthias off, but Matthias wouldn't go. He pressed down instead, bearing Bree flush to the floor. Fresh sweat beaded on Bree's limbs, and he couldn't stop himself from spreading his legs and moaning.

Matthias hesitated, but only briefly. He pressed his mouth to the back of Bree's neck and grazed the skin lightly with his teeth. "I can help you, if you want. All you have to say is 'yes.'"

Bree shuddered. He'd forgotten how gentle Matthias was. Even when they knew nothing about sex, and almost nothing about the biology that drove them to reproduce on this lonely planet, Matthias had always been -- sweet. Kind.

He left you, Bree reminded himself.

But he'd come back. And he'd sent letters.

That you never got.

That wasn't Matthias's fault. It might not be true, but if it was... the old Packmaster would have been happiest if he'd been able to lock Bree up in a cage and hide the key until he'd found just the right political match for his Omega child. He'd been so white with fury when he found out Bree had given himself to Matthias, Bree had briefly feared for his life.

It made sense.

The fever abated briefly, then rose to a crescendo. Bree's cock had never gone soft, and it surged again, driving him to rut against the blanket. His second climax ripped through his belly and made him push his hips up in desperate need.

"Is it usually this bad?" Matthias asked, drawing soothing strokes over Bree's back.

Bree could only shake his head in mute denial. He spat out the blanket and began to pant, high thin noises escaping him with every breath. "Don't. Please, don't."

If you let him have his way with you, he might stay, a voice coaxed inside Bree's head. *If you bore him a child, he'd stay.*

Bree snapped his teeth in maddened frustration and pushed the thought away. He wouldn't do that to himself, or to a cub. Not ever.

"Bree, I'm sorry." Matthias rubbed his shoulders. "If I could go back in time and find a way to take you with me…"

Bree shook his hair aside and looked back over his shoulder. His eyes had adjusted to the lack of light at last, and he could see Matthias's face clearly. His strong bones showed boldly through his smooth skin, making him look as if he'd been carved from stone. His eyes glittered with a darkly-burning fire barely held in check, and when Bree glanced down the length of Matthias's body he could see Matthias's cock jutting up dark and hard and eager.

Matthias could give Bree what he needed. Bree wouldn't be able to bear it if he risked his heart and Matthias left, but neither would he survive this kind of heat fever if it wasn't quenched.

And Matthias was gentle.

Bree licked his lips, though his tongue was dry and his mouth parched as cotton. "Don't breed me," he whispered, startled at how rough and ragged his voice sounded. "Just help me."

* * *

Matthias

Poor wolf. If Matthias's heart hadn't already been moved to pity by Bree's struggle, any resistance would have melted now. He stroked Bree's back, ignoring the beads of sweat that stood out over his trembling muscles. "All right. Shh now, shh. I'll take care of you."

Bree still had the wherewithal to glower over his shoulder. "That wasn't an answer."

"It was implied, but if you need to hear it in words, I'll do what I can to keep you safe." Matthias carried on rubbing gently at Bree's taut back and kept his voice to a low murmur. Soft, soothing, and it gave him time to think.

He stilled Bree when Bree bucked beneath him and keened out a wordless whimper. Omega biology could be cruel, but he'd never seen someone so affected by his body's chemistry -- and he'd been around other Omegas in heat, even if he didn't take advantage of what they offered. Bree shivered and dug his fingernails into the blanket, almost tearing at it.

"You said you would take care of me," he pleaded.

"I am. You need to relax first," Matthias said, still stroking Bree's back, his flanks, his hips. "It's been a long time for you. Hasn't it?"

Bree didn't want to answer that, but after a moment's wrestling with himself he nodded grudgingly and muttered, "Since you left."

Part of Matthias exulted fiercely at that. Another part marveled at the strength of will that made that possible. Another part still frowned at what that meant for how hard it might be to win him over again.

The last part winced in empathy. The urges that drove Alphas and Omegas weren't meant to be denied. Bottling anything up for months -- even years -- worked for a while, but only made the inevitable explosion that much messier. No wonder Bree's body had rebelled so intensely.

He took Bree's hips in his hands and tugged, guiding him over. Bree obeyed, but with a frown of confusion. "What are you doing?"

"I'm not going to mount you from behind, shove my dick in, and be done with it," Matthias said. "Did you think that's what I had in mind?"

Bree groaned and covered his eyes with his palms as he settled onto his back.

He had thought it, then. Truth be told, Matthias wouldn't have minded. His body chemistry responded to Bree's with a powerful, raging hunger and thirst. He could have taken Bree like an animal and fucked the heat out of him, but --

No. He'd be damned before he treated Bree as less than human, and he'd spent years learning how to control himself. He would fuck Bree, no doubt about that, but he'd make it good for Bree. For both of them.

Bree had begun to writhe, subtly at first and then more desperately. He parted his legs and panted. "Please. Cover me. I need -- I can't --"

Matthias shushed him again, but willpower was one thing and being made of stone was fully another. He crawled between Bree's legs and helped Bree raise them to clamp around his hips, giving him something to hold onto. Then, he bent his head to Bree's chest and pressed his mouth to the dent between Bree's collarbones. He swirled the tip of his tongue in the small hollow, then scraped it lightly with his teeth. Giving Bree his scent and taking Bree's for his own.

Bree moaned and wound his arms around Matthias, clinging tight.

Good for a start, but he wasn't anywhere near finished yet. Matthias moved slowly over Bree's chest, pausing everywhere that looked good to him and marking it with his mouth. He lingered longest at the soft spot beneath Bree's ear, where his jaw began, and used his fingers to slowly stimulate the rest of Bree's body. Taking both Bree's tightly knotted nipples between his callused fingertips, he rolled and pinched the nubs until he could almost feel the breast tissue growing heavier, firmer, fuller. His skin burned hot and dry with fever, no longer sweating. Lubrication wetted his thighs, and Matthias's too.

Matthias grunted; he couldn't help but press his cock down, nudging it at the rim of Bree's opening. The feel of it almost made him lose control. He reached between them to squeeze himself and felt the slight swelling of his knot starting to form.

Careful. He meant to keep his promise and not give Bree a belly full of pups he didn't want. That meant keeping his knot to himself, and not locking them together.

Easier said than done. Matthias gritted his teeth and used his fingers instead, sinking them deep inside the Omega and thrusting -- two, then three, and Bree's greedy body admitted four with the barest resistance.

But it wasn't enough to satisfy him. With a low, ragged sob, Bree rocked his hips upward, straining to bring himself in contact with Matthias's hard-on. "*Please.*"

Matthias's hips jerked without his mind's permission, almost penetrating the Omega. He held back by the barest of margins. "You told me not to."

Bree tossed his head on the blankets and sank his teeth into his lower lips. "I know, but it's not --" He caught his nipples between thumbs and forefingers and pinched hard. "It isn't enough. Can't you -- something, anything, please."

Matthias groaned and dropped his head hard on Bree's chest. Bree's eager fingers, shaking slightly with the fever, carded wildly through his hair. Lust clouded his mind, making it impossible to catch any clear thought, but if he was careful not to let them lock together...

Chances were only fifty/fifty at best, but it was better than nothing.

Matthias started to raise his head, to ask Bree for his consent, but he didn't get a chance. With an impatient growl, Bree locked his knees around Matthias's thighs and canted up *just* so, bringing their bodies together. It was too much. No one could have said no, and Matthias had missed Bree for years. He caught Bree's hips again and held them hard, keeping them still, as he slid deep inside.

Bree's nails scored stinging lines down Matthias's back as he keened his pleasure, and Matthias knew he left bite marks on Bree's slim, pale shoulder, but that didn't matter a damn. All that he cared about was thrusting deep and hard, so hard they shifted back inch by inch over the blanket, both slick and sticky and drunk on the heady smell of sex.

Bree felt so *good*, so hot and tight and eager, his inner muscles clasping Matthias and only reluctantly letting him go. Small orgasms made the Omega ripple with pleasure, but desperate for more.

"Matthias," he chanted, thrusting up to meet Matthias's pushes down. "I need -- I don't -- I *need*. Please, please."

Matthias raised his hips and, with the greatest effort of will in his life, held them still. The tendons in his neck stood out and burned with the strain. He was almost there, he could feel it, and Bree's scent demanded he bury himself deep and tie them together.

"Matthias, *please*," Bree begged, out of his mind with heat.

No. Shaking with the effort of it, Matthias slid slowly into Bree, so slowly that the friction nearly drove him mad -- and that was the point. Just before he was fully inside -- almost, but not completely -- he put his hand between them to be sure his angrily swollen knot didn't penetrate, and his own touch -- or Bree's desperate clawing at him -- was enough.

He groaned deep in his chest as he came, the kind of ball-squeezing orgasm their bodies were made for, emptying himself deep inside Bree. He made himself pull out before he'd finished, and though his muscles didn't want to cooperate he sat up and brought Bree with him, a shaking mess in his arms.

Gravity would help, though this wouldn't. Matthias couldn't leave him wanting, though. A firm hand around the Omega's cock, stroking hard, and he flew to pieces. His come decorated Matthias's stomach, thick as cream, hot as molten silver. Bree keened his completion, a raw shout that made Matthias's ears ring.

Bree crumpled forward and into Matthias's arms, collapsing against him. Matthias had been ready for that, and though his groin still burned with aftershocks he was sated for now. Bree too. The fever faded, racing away from his body.

Matthias wrapped them both in the blankets Bree had tossed on the floor and let Bree curl tightly into him. He could keep them both warm. "There," he crooned, letting his senses fill with the sight, sound, and smell of his mate heavy and solid in his arms as Bree drifted off into a light sleep. "There. I said I'd take care of you, Bree. I meant it, and I always will."

He would go back to the coast when he'd finished here. He'd known from the start that he would, but now he was sure of one more thing. Whatever it took, no matter what he needed to do to make it happen, he *would* take Bree with him.

He'd find a way.

Chapter Three

Bree drifted languidly from sleep to wakefulness, so slowly he couldn't track the difference as he floated upward. He was warm, swaddled in blankets, cozier and more comfortable than he'd been in years. Though he couldn't tell whether it was night or day, the soothing flicker of firelight and crackle of wood burning told him he was safe inside.

Without opening his eyes Bree indulged himself in a long, luxurious stretch that pointed his toes and eased the stiffness out of his back, his neck, his arms. He came back down with a sigh and tucked one hand beneath his cheek. So strange, to feel so good. Bree made small murmuring noises to himself in appreciation. His muscles were usually drawn tight with tension and knotted with stress, but everything had relaxed until he felt loose and easy.

He drew one knee up to ease the only small ache he felt -- a slow, lazy pull between his legs that ebbed and peaked in slow pulses.

Between his --

Bree's eyes flew open, and he caught his breath. *Matthias*. Had he dreamed it?

No, he hadn't. When he blinked his vision clear Bree's gaze landed directly on the man, who'd made himself a nest by the cabin's bare-bones fireplace and busied himself with a paring knife and a stick of kindling. Curls of shaved wood littered the floor at his feet. He'd found clothes sized to fit him; he must have gone rooting through the old things Bree's father and brother left behind back when they used this cabin for hunting.

Matthias glanced sideways and down at Bree with a quiet smile. "There you are. I was starting to wonder if you were going to sleep all day."

"What time is it?" Bree reached up to try and untangle the mass of his hair, which had tied itself in hopeless knots from sleeping on it unbraided. He cocked his head. "Did it stop snowing?"

"It's nearly ten o' clock, and it's stopped snowing heavily for now." Matthias tapped his palm lightly with the stick he'd been carving. "From the looks of the clouds, the storm's not done yet. We'll get another wave of heavy snow before it's dark."

Not enough time to make the run back to town, even in their wolf forms. Bree bit his lip in frustration.

Last night had been... Bree didn't have the words for it. He remembered it all, though he wished he didn't. His face burned hot with embarrassment over how desperate he'd been, how he'd begged Matthias to fuck him.

But Matthias had been so gentle. So patient and kind. Bree took a carefully discreet sniff and couldn't discern any change in his personal aroma. If Matthias had bred him, his keen sense of smell would be able to detect minute differences even this early.

He hadn't. And Bree didn't know what to do about that. About any of this. He'd spent the past few years hating Matthias or grieving him. Then Matthias had come back, and he'd treated Bree as if Bree were more than just an Omega, as if he were special.

The way he used to, before he left.

When Bree pressed his now-cold hands to his hot face, Matthias made a sudden sympathetic noise. "You'll feel better if you wash off last night's sweat. I brought some water in to melt; it won't be hot, but it's warm enough, and I tore up an old shirt to use for a sponge." He made a rueful grimace, the kind Bree used to love for the way it crinkled the corners of his eyes. "No soap, but I like the way you smell."

Bree kept his face covered, too humiliated and touched to speak for a long moment. Finally, he managed a nod.

"Ah, Bree," Matthias said. He rose gracefully to his feet. Bree heard a few muted noises, and then Matthias was next to him, gently tugging the blankets off and laying down a wooden bowl filled with water, makeshift sponge floating inside. Matthias smoothed down his hair. "Go on. I'll keep my back turned if you want."

Bree nodded again, stiffly. He kept his head down until he was sure Matthias had retreated to the far corner of the cabin, crouched on his heels and patiently waiting. In profile, not quite with his back turned, but he fixed his gaze on the wall and kept it there.

The water was almost hot, just shy of steam curling off the top. Bree moaned at the first touch of the warm, wet cloth against his skin. He couldn't help it; the more he woke, the more sensitized his nerve endings seemed. Not as electric as the night before, but he was still in heat and his body craved any kind of caress.

Matthias shifted, as if he wanted very much to look sideways, but held himself in check. His hands opened and closed slowly where they rested on his knees. "Good?"

"Good," Bree whispered. He drew the cloth up his arms, swallowing down the noises his body wanted him to make at the sensation. "You didn't have to."

"I know. I wanted to."

When Bree ran the cloth down his chest, he could see -- and feel -- how his breast tissue had changed slightly, from flat to slightly swollen. It always happened when the heat was nearing its peak. He squeezed his thighs together to hold back his reaction to their exquisite sensitivity. He didn't dare wash there. Heaven only knew what he'd do if he gave into that urge, but once he'd thought of it the heat flashed through him. He rocked until it passed and rubbed the cloth hard over his arms with shaking hands.

His body cried out for what it wanted. Matthias to cover him, fuck him, love him. From that, a cub to love and raise.

It could be easy, so easy. He could at least try. And if he couldn't keep Matthias, then a cub…

Bree shook his head hard and pressed his hands to his eyes.

Matthias's nostrils flared at Bree's changing scent, but he said nothing. "This isn't how I imagined us meeting again," he said idly. "I had all kinds of scenarios cooked up. It was how I soothed myself to sleep those first few months."

Bree hesitated. "You did?"

"Mmm. Then I picked the ones I liked best, and I carried those with me all day long." Matthias chuckled. "My favorite was the one where I kicked down the door to your father's house, tossed you over my shoulder, and carried you away with me. Even in my dreams I knew you'd probably take a few bites out of me if I tried that. I still wanted to, though."

Bree almost smiled but didn't. He lowered the makeshift washcloth into the bowl and shivered, then wrapped his arms around himself in vain effort to keep warm.

Matthias went on, sobered. "If I'd taken you then, they would have come after us. Probably would have killed us both, or just me, and then they'd have made your life too much of a hell to endure. I couldn't do that to you."

All true, but it hurt no less to hear. Bree drew a deep breath and licked his lips. "Matthias?"

"Hmm?"

"Is it this cold on the peninsula? Does it snow?"

"Some," Matthias said, sounding curious. "Not this much. I mostly see it from the water."

"You do?"

"I do," Matthias said, proud now. "I own a fishing boat, Bree. Bought and paid for with the money I earned crabbing and doing cod runs year-round. It's small, but I have two deckhands who work for me. It's only the start, Bree. I'll get a bigger ship, more hands, and then a second ship. I'll make something of my life."

"I believe you," Bree said, though his heart sank. So. Matthias would go back. He had work that he loved, and a home to return to, and a dream to chase.

And Bree would be left on his own. Again.

* * *

Matthias

Matthias sighed. Because he couldn't resist the urge, he reached out to take a long, still-silky lock of Bree's hair and wind the strands around his fingers. Bree bent his head and pushed into the touch. He didn't say a word, didn't look any less conflicted, but he did it and that gave Matthias hope.

"I can't change the past," Matthias said. He slid his fingers through Bree's hair and cupped the side of his head. "If I could, I would. I'd go back in time. Believe me."

Bree didn't answer but let out a quiet breath that tickled Matthias's wrist.

Matthias stroked the fine molding of Bree's skull, soaking up the warmth of his skin and reveling in the bliss of touch. It'd been a long, long time. Maybe for both of them. This close, he could smell the heat still had Bree in its grasp. He'd expected no less, but for a small mercy it seemed to be in a lull phase. Lulls were a necessary part of the cycle, and a man only had to go through the entire business once to recognize the importance of eating, drinking, and resting while he could.

Rest, they'd taken care of. Bree had slept almost six hours. As for food and drink, Matthias hadn't been idle while Bree dozed. He tugged gently at Bree's hair to be certain of having his attention. "Are you hungry?"

Bree blinked sleepily, as if he'd been on the verge of dozing off again. A good sign. He trusted Matthias more than he wanted to. "There's nothing in the cabin except what I showed you last night. Jerky, hard candy, odds and ends." His stomach rumbled. He bit his lip as he pressed a hand to it. "But I am hungry."

"Good." Matthias stood and held out a hand to help Bree up. "Come on. Follow me."

Bree frowned and hesitated but took the offered help. "Where?"

"Not far. Just to the hearth." Matthias grinned broadly and beckoned, allowing Bree the dignity of following on his own once he'd satisfied himself he could manage. He led the way to the fireplace and picked up a hooked poker to uncover a Dutch oven he'd half buried in the ashes. When he flipped its cast iron cover off with the poker, the smell it released made his mouth water.

Bree's lips parted. "Is that rabbit?"

"I told you I'd go hunting, if need be. Found a nice fat one in a den not far from here." It'd been an easy catch, and Matthias had thanked it for its sacrifice, burying its heart so it could return to the earth. He'd kept the skin, though, tacked up outside to freeze solid for later. Soft and white, it would make a fine set of gloves for Bree to keep his hands warm.

Bree peered over the edge of the pot, clearly not quite believing what his nose told him until his eyes confirmed it. "There's more than rabbit in here."

"Potatoes and parsnips," Matthias said, thoroughly enjoying Bree's surprise. "I dug to the very back of the shelves, and those had rolled into a corner. I found some flour to thicken up the broth too. Even a little salt."

Bree frowned at the pot for a moment, then -- just before Matthias would have started to wonder what was wrong -- he glanced up with his lips quirked. "That's all well and good. But did you find anything to eat the soup *with*?"

Matthias laughed. "Sorry, no luck there." He crouched again and took up the piece of wood he'd busied himself with while the stew cooked, handing it to Bree. "But I made us a spoon to share. You go first. It's good, I promise."

Bree looked at the spoon, so simply carved Matthias wouldn't be surprised if they got splinters in their tongues, as if it were something rare and special. "Oh, Matthias."

"It's just a spoon," Matthias said, to spare Bree his pride, though his heart ached all over again. Had no one been kind to him since Matthias left? "Go on and eat. You need the calories and the salt."

Bree tucked his hair behind his ears, dipped the spoon, and blew on a mouthful until it was cool enough to eat. His eyes flew open wide, then he moaned at the taste and went back for more right away.

Watching Bree fill up made Matthias warm with pleasure. He sat back on his haunches to watch, not bothered about the notion of there being none left for him. He'd had enough to keep body and soul together these past few years, and suspected it might not have been the same for Bree. Bree ate quickly but neatly, spilling barely a drop of gravy, and made contented noises around each mouthful.

Matthias propped his chin on his hand. "There's a public house back on the coast that always made me think of you. They make this fisherman's pie two ways. One with shellfish, a lot of pepper, a lot of rough-cut vegetables, and a thin broth. The other way is delicate, with whitefish and parsley and cream. Your favorite."

Bree shot him a frowning look but didn't stop eating to interrupt, and he seemed to be listening. He swallowed and said, "You love it there. Don't you?"

"The winters are mild, and the summers actually get warm. What's not to love?"

Bree snorted quietly.

Matthias laughed. "Yeah, I didn't believe it until I saw it either. There's so much to see, Bree. The sea frightens some people with how big and endless it looks from the shore, but I never got tired of watching it."

Bree had nearly emptied the pot, and scraped up the last scraps without looking at them, his gaze trained solely on Matthias.

Matthias could drown in his pretty eyes. *My Omega. My mate.* He licked his lips before going on. "I built a house there, on the peninsula," he said as quietly as the crackling of the fire. "With windows that face the sea, and a kitchen big enough to cook whatever you want to eat. And a bedroom in the coziest spot, where it never gets cold. The bed is big enough to burrow in, and soft with furs I trapped myself."

"Matthias…" Bree laid the spoon aside and covered his face again.

Matthias wasn't about to stop now that he'd finally started. He took Bree's wrists gently in both hands. "What's wrong?"

"Matthias, you…" Bree twisted his wrists to free them. "Please."

Matthias let go reluctantly.

Bree raked a hand through his hair, looking helpless. He shivered once, and when Matthias scented the air he caught the returning rise of pheromones and hormones that signaled the lull was nearly past. An hour, two hours, and Bree would be as wild and desperate as he had been the night before.

Watching him could break Matthias's heart. He exhaled slowly, letting his hands fall loosely between his knees.

Bree shivered again and shook his head. "I don't..."

Poor man. Matthias knew what he wanted to do, and what Bree needed for him to do. He hoped.

He stood, holding out his hand again. "Run with me."

Chapter Four

Bree

"What?" Bree stared up at Matthias.

"I need to hunt again to provision us through the rest of the storm," Matthias said. He still held his hand out for Bree to take and waited patiently for him to make up his mind. "Rabbits or ptarmigan are all we're likely to find, but I don't mind that. It'll do you good to get out for a little while."

Bree wasn't too sure about that. He'd never tried leaving the cabin while he was in heat. Why would he? It would have been like waving a red flag for any Alpha who cared to try and chase him down. And yet...

Now that he thought about it, Bree wanted to run. His limbs ached from inactivity, and the air in the cabin seemed too stuffy, too still, too close. He bit his lip, hesitating.

"It will help. Trust me, I've seen it." Matthias grinned ruefully. "Well. Not up close and personal. I haven't been with another Omega since I left. But the mated men I fished with always had stories to tell, and there were a couple of bonded pairs who worked the sea together."

Bree barely heard the last part of that. Matthias hadn't been with another Omega since him? Truly?

Matthias must have seen the wondering in Bree's eyes. He inclined his head. "Not one, and not once, Bree. They couldn't compare to you. I didn't even want to try."

Bree shut his eyes. He ached to shed his human form and take to four legs. To run and burn off some of the mad energy that drove him.

It was just...

"Come on," Matthias coaxed. Since Bree hadn't taken it, he laid his hand on Bree's shoulder and squeezed gently. "If I'm wrong, you can take your best shot at me afterward. No reprisal. But I'll bet you anything you want to wager that I'm right."

Bree opened his eyes.

* * *

He was right.

Melting into his wolf shape felt -- orgasmic wasn't the right word, nor strong enough, but Bree couldn't think of a better one. He arched his back and panted with the sheer rightness of the feeling, then shook himself so hard he nearly knocked himself off his paws.

Nearby, Matthias laughed at him as wolves did, with his tongue lolling and tail wagging. He bounced on his forepaws and yipped at Bree.

Bree wrinkled his muzzle at Matthias, then shot forward and nipped at his flanks -- and ran the way his wolf form wanted to, fast as the wind, free as the air. His limbs stretched in an agony of exquisite sensation and the ground flew past beneath him.

From behind, he heard Matthias's delighted bark and a scrabble of paws as he bound forward. Bree glanced back once and saw the Alpha keeping just behind him, guarding his six. He feinted as if he too were going to deliver a play bite, but clashed his teeth together on the air instead.

Bree couldn't help it. He laughed too, inside his head and in the body language of the wolf.

He wheeled around a hundred and eighty degrees, spraying freshly fallen snow in a broad arc, and thumped his forepaws together on the ground before him. He stretched in a play bow, tail up and wagging, and barked at Matthias.

Matthias barked back, then tilted his head and howled loud and long and exuberant. Bree couldn't help joining him. He looked ridiculous all covered in snow, as square and sturdy in his wolf form as he'd be in man shape, and so happy.

Padding forward, Matthias nuzzled at Bree's jaw. He licked, though not as a submissive wolf would do, and before Bree realized what he meant he'd taken Bree's throat gently between his teeth, as gently as if Bree were made of glass or eggshells. He growled quietly.

The wolf wanted to claim his mate as much as the man did.

Bree froze. He wanted -- he did -- but he couldn't --

He snapped his jaws at Matthias, not in play this time, and bolted for it. Closing his ears to Matthias's startled bark, he ran with all the strength and speed his long limbs could bring to bear, and faster than he'd known he was capable of.

Matthias followed. Bree could hear him and could tell he didn't mean to stay just far enough behind to play. This was a serious gallop, his broad paws slamming into the snow, and he broadcasted the scent of stubborn determination.

Bree ran faster, jaws wide, eyes wider, pelting across the frozen Wasp Lake and doubling back to throw Matthias off his scent. He kicked up snow wherever he could and hid behind it. And even underneath the wildness of the wolf, Bree the man could feel his fever starting to spike.

He'd been afraid this would happen. Burning off energy, that was all well and good. Trouble was that heat cycles didn't give a flying fuck about what shape an Omega was in, and an Omega's instinct was to bow to a dominant Alpha. His body demanded obedience. It told him to change shape, to kneel and present, and to let himself be taken over. It wanted to be fucked until they were both raw and drained of all strength.

It -- he -- wanted to be Matthias's, entirely and without reservation. It begged him to give in.

Bree howled and ran faster.

Not fast enough. Matthias was right on his heels, snapping at him. He'd tackle Bree to get him to stop, Bree knew it. He dug deep for more strength, and --

And collapsed under the weight of a full-grown timber wolf landing atop him. Matthias took Bree's neck in his teeth and shook him, not gently this time. He growled around his mouthful of skin and fur, then let go to bark so loudly it made Bree's ears ring in protest. Coming around front, he took Bree's neck from the front and snarled, a deep rough rattling sound.

Too focused on Bree to see what lay just beyond him. But Bree did. He froze, utterly silent, absolutely still, not even breathing. Matthias noticed *that*. He let go at once, and looked over his shoulder at the bear that stared back at them.

It wasn't possible. Bears weren't awake at this time of year. They were all in their dens, hibernating away the winters, and yet there he was. Skinny, Bree noted, far thinner than a bear should be, and his fur was patchy with mange. Scrape marks showed where he'd been trying to chew through the bark of a tree for nourishment, so desperate for food he'd eat anything.

And they'd run right into his jaws. Slow and stupid with cold, the bear hadn't thought of attacking them yet, but he would. He'd have to, to survive. Kill or be killed.

Bree summoned up his last drops of strength and darted in front of Matthias, baying his deepest warning. He kicked backward to drive Matthias away, but as for him, he snarled at the bear and stayed put. It could *try* to bring them down, but Bree damn well meant to be as tough a mouthful as possible.

Matthias didn't run. Of course he didn't. Bree despaired of the stubborn wolf, but Matthias crowded in beside him and loosed another thunderous bark. He bared his teeth in a growl that promised the same thing Bree had.

The bear had to be starving. Anyone could see that. But when faced with two wolves baying for his blood, it only settled back on its haunches and sighed. Then, it held one paw up in the clumsiest possible sign for them to stop.

Bree did, far too surprised to do anything else. Was he a shifter? There were no bear shifters in the Wasp Lake territory. Were there?

Too late to ask, even if he'd dared. The bear dropped to four paws and loped away, back stiff with pride.

Matthias was on him right away, scolding for all he was worth. Though Bree tried to dodge the licks and nuzzles, Matthias had greater strength and in the end simply pinned Bree down. His quiet whimpers were only noise at first, but then...

Then, Matthias laid his muzzle next to Bree's and crooned a wolf song. Relief. Love. Deep, abiding love.

A man might lie. A wolf couldn't.

He loves me, Bree thought, dizzy with it and with a sharp, roaring spike of fever. *He loves me that much. Even if he's going to leave me and go back to the sea, he* loves *me.*

Bree knew what he wanted now. No matter whether it was right or wrong or safe or sane, he wanted it too much to say no.

Surrender.

* * *

Bree didn't remember how they got back to the cabin. He didn't even remember running there or dropping his wolf form. Adrenaline, fever, or both made it all a blur for him, and even when he came back to himself in human form inside the four fitted log walls, his mind didn't clear.

Matthias. All he wanted, all he needed. *Matthias.* If he had nothing else but this before Matthias left him again, it would be enough.

Matthias slammed the cabin door and threw the latch with shaking hands. When he turned to Bree, his eyes were huge and dark, and his teeth bared.

Bree panted, staring back at him. His skin burned as if he'd caught fire, and his thighs were soaked. He reached between his legs to stroke at himself and cried out at the brush of his fingertips against sensitive flesh.

Matthias stared as if he'd been struck by lightning.

Bree raised wet fingers to his mouth and sucked at them. Salt and earthiness exploded on his tongue, and he moaned. "Please, Matthias. *Please*."

Matthias licked his lips. "How?"

"I don't care. Please. Fuck me, Matthias. I'll die if you don't." He would. Or so it felt. The fever would eat away his bones and crumble his skin to ash. Bree made himself walk forward on shaking legs. He wound his arms around Matthias's neck and pressed their bodies together, skin to skin, cock to cock, breath to breath. "*Fuck me.*"

With a groan that seemed to come from somewhere so deep inside it couldn't be mined, Matthias gave in. He seized Bree by the hips and lifted him. With his back to the door, Bree had just enough room to lock his legs around Matthias and hold on, desperate for whatever Matthias could give him.

Matthias thrust up, and in. Deep in, girth burning and length seeming to go on forever, filling Bree. He set his teeth hard against Bree's shoulder and growled low in his throat, helpless. "Bree. Oh God, Bree. You feel…"

Bree's body clamped down around Matthias, trying to draw him deeper. It wasn't enough. He rolled his hips to try and draw Matthias deeper still, impatient keening cries pouring from his throat. "More, Matthias, please more."

Matthias set his jaw and shook his head, but though his head said no, his body began to move. He held Bree's hips too hard, just right, and drove up into him. No resistance. Bree's body opened to let him inside;

Bree let him go only reluctantly and cried out with every stroke up.

It wasn't *enough*.

Bree could feel Matthias holding back, and could tell how much it cost Matthias to do so. He couldn't focus on anything else but that. Dragging his head up, even though a curtain of wild red hair blocked his field of vision, Bree met Matthias's eyes to plead with him.

Matthias shuddered bone-rackingly hard. "I can't. You said not to."

Said not to *what*? When? Bree couldn't think past the need to have Matthias deep as he could go, and the desperate drive to put out the fires inside him. He rolled his hips and moaned, begging without words. He could feel the half-swollen knot in Matthias's Alpha cock bumping him every time Matthias thrust up but not slipping inside. A hard ridge that would finally be enough to satisfy him.

Matthias pressed his hips back, away -- but not for long. He held Bree as if Bree weighed nothing at all, though his muscles quivered with electric tension. He wanted it too, didn't he?

Why didn't he take it?

Bree couldn't think with the fever consuming his brain, but he could act. He swallowed down the water that collected in his mouth at the thought, and he waited until Matthias gave in to the animal need to fuck, until he drove up once more.

Then, Bree came down and took Matthias inside him. All of Matthias. He cried out, high and thin, as the knot lodged inside him and swelled hard, tight, fast.

Locked together.

Bree met Matthias's wide, stunned stare, and held tight.

"Oh, Bree," Matthias breathed. "I'm sorry."

Sorry didn't matter. All Bree gave a damn about was quenching the flame. He rocked his hips, begging, and Matthias's resistance crumbled.

Somehow they were on the floor, though Bree didn't remember getting there, on the blankets that still smelled of last night's sex. Outside, the storm finally came home to roost. Winds howled, if not louder than Bree and Matthias, and a barrage of snow battered the fitted log walls of the cabin until they groaned in protest.

They didn't matter. Not even climaxing mattered, Bree's orgasm lost in the furious rush of chemicals flooding his body. Matthias was in him, fully in him, and his knot sealed them together. He strove against Bree, every limb slick with sweat and his mouth hot, eager, hungry. He lifted Bree's legs and tightened them around him so he could fuck deeper still.

Bree held on tight, and when Matthias shuddered to a stop with his back arched and mouth open, he threw his head back and keened through a second climax. One that didn't feel like any he'd known before. One that went on, and on, until he'd lost himself, flown into as many pieces as the falling snow.

Matthias's seed filled him and cooled him, blissful relief that made him sob for gladness.

The world went gently, peacefully dark as Bree fell.

Chapter Five

Matthias

Though Matthias was sure he'd slept as soundly as Bree, he still woke first. Still muzzy-headed, he turned to lie on his side and pillowed his cheek on his hand, all the better to watch Bree peacefully at rest.

"One little orgasm, and you're out like a light," Matthias murmured, tracing the elegant line of Bree's neck and shoulder.

Not that he minded. He got to look at Bree all he liked now, after all.

Woken by his touch, Bree stirred and mumbled. He blinked his eyes open, ginger lashes so long they tangled together and made shadows on his cheeks -- but the dark shadows beneath those eyes had faded, and his creamy pale skin had a healthier warm glow beneath it. He smiled shyly at Matthias. "What are you looking at?"

"You," Matthias said. He ran the backs of his knuckles lightly over Bree's chest, pleased when he moved into the touch. Then he nodded upward. "The eye of the storm finally came home to roost."

Bree laughed into his makeshift pillow. "That's the worst mixed metaphor I've ever heard."

"If the shoe is applicable, don't fix it." Matthias gave in to the impulse to bend over and press a kiss to Bree's temple. "How are you feeling? In a lull?"

"Another lull," Bree agreed as he stretched and yawned. He snuggled back down in seeming contentment.

Outside, the winds whirled and howled, beating against the wall of the cabin. Matthias listened to it in awe before turning back to Bree. "I'd say it was too bad we didn't get any meat while we were out, but all things considered... I'm not complaining."

Bree's cheeks went apple red. He hid his eyes, but he was laughing too. "You're awful."

"I know." Matthias caressed his once and hopefully future mate's hip and assayed, casually so that Bree could take it or leave it as he wished, "I think we've got the day."

Bree glanced up -- and without a complaint at being trapped with Matthias, nor even a glimmer of regret. His lips curved into a smile, and the hope that filled Matthias's chest at that was a nearly tangible thing. "Maybe so. What do you want to do with it?"

* * *

"Matthias, stop!" Bree pounded at his shoulder. He'd wrapped himself up burrito-style in not one, not two, but three of the blankets, but left his feet bare. "I haven't excavated that cabinet in years. All you're likely to find are mouse skeletons and moldy bread crusts."

Chuckling, Matthias let him land the blow. He only wore one, toga-style, but it was enough to keep him warm. "If I do, then we can make soup."

Bree pretended to *tsk*, but he waved in a faux-magnanimous gesture. "Go ahead then, knock yourself out. Just no comments about my housekeeping."

As if that were likely. Matthias regarded Bree for a moment without bothering to hide his admiration. Bree still wouldn't open up about what his life had been like these past few years, but Matthias knew enough of what an unmated Omega went through to be sure it hadn't been easy. To run and hide -- successfully -- here every time he went into heat, and to ride it out alone without relief, well. Only the strongest would survive that.

Bree blushed and ducked his head, pushing his hair back over his shoulder. "Don't."

"Can't stop me," Matthias murmured, but he let his gaze wander back to the storage cupboard he'd opened. He'd had to force the wood, swollen shut for who knew how long with the humidity, and he doubted they'd find anything edible in there. Still, no harm trying. He could manage a day or two on an empty stomach, but he'd rather see Bree well fed.

Inside, the cupboard was a nearly cavernous thing, far colder than the rest of the cabin. Matthias stuck his head inside and rooted around, then came out with a noise of triumph and two withered but still sound apples, one in each hand.

"Those have to be at least a year old," Bree protested, though he stared lustfully at them.

"They're well aged," Matthias corrected. He found the knife he'd used to butcher that morning's rabbit, washed clean in the snow, and sliced both apples in half. He pressed the whole kit and caboodle on Bree. "Go ahead and eat. I need both hands for rooting."

Bree eyed him. "Don't think I don't know what you're doing, Matthias. Just like the stew. I'll save you your share, and I want you to eat it too. Okay?"

Caught, but Matthias couldn't complain. He looked over his shoulder. The lull in his heat cycle was treating Bree more kindly than before, giving him a warm glow to his cheeks and a healthy sort of relaxation in his limbs. His eyes seemed almost luminous, and his smile genuine.

What if Bree really had forgiven him? The thought made Matthias catch his breath. If Bree was willing to let the past rest in the past, and to make a future with him… It would be more than a dream come true. It would be a wish fulfilled.

"Matthias," Bree said quietly but firmly, nudging him.

Matthias grinned at the Omega. "I won't say I'm sorry for liking to look at you. Or that I can help it." He turned his back to the cupboard and held out a hand. "On second thought, I think I'll take my share now. Give me a quarter."

Bree rolled his eyes, but indulgently, and passed over half of a half of one apple. When Matthias bit in, he found it was still juicy and that the mealy flesh crunched satisfyingly between his teeth. Sweet-sour flavor filled his mouth, making him moan.

At that, Bree nodded in approval. "Good. Keep doing that." His blush deepened. "You're going to need your strength too."

Fair point, actually. Matthias took another quarter when Bree pressed it on him. A memory struck, and made him smile. "Do you remember the time we tried growing our own garden?"

Bree snorted. "You mean the time we tried digging a shallow pit in the woods and chucking in seeds, thinking they'd grow? Because I remember *that*."

"And coming home covered in mud," Matthias said. "Absolutely plastered in it. All I could see was the whites of your eyes."

"Ooh, I got whipped for that. Did you?"

"No one to whip me," Matthias said. It was only a partial lie. Bree's Alpha sibling had tried to beat the tar out of Matthias for sullying the family's Omega. He hadn't been as successful as he'd planned. As Matthias remembered, that Alpha went home with a blackened eye and a split lip.

Bree probably knew all that. He gave Matthias a thoughtful, nearly shy look as he ate the rest of his apples in neat bites. "It wasn't a bad idea, though. Do you remember why we did it?"

Matthias did. They'd both been on the cusp of adolescence, each aware of the other in ways that were new and frightening and exciting. Matthias had only had vague ideas of what mating involved, but he'd known even then that his heart belonged to Bree. Alphas provided for their mates. He'd figured that a garden first could help supply a homestead later. That it would be the start of his taking care of Bree.

"I do," Matthias said. He took Bree by the hand and drew him slowly closer, nuzzling in at the curve of neck and shoulder he'd admired before. "It was a good idea. We just lacked the experience to make it work then, that's all."

To his delight, Bree tilted his head back to give Matthias room to work. His skin was cool -- no fever yet -- but his body supple and soft and willing. "Do we have the experience now?" he asked, laying a hand at the back of Matthias's head. "Do we, Matthias?"

More than, Matthias meant to say, but the words got lost along the way. With his nose pressed to Bree's skin, Bree's scent had flooded his senses, and it was --

Different.

He sniffed again, trying to pinpoint the changes. They were subtle, so incredibly minute, but there all the same.

"Matthias?" Bree had gone still. "What's wrong?"

With the spike in emotion, the scent intensified. Matthias breathed deep at the exact right moment, and the pieces fell into place.

Nobody's fool, Bree. Bree breathed through his mouth, chasing the same scent as Matthias had. Matthias knew he'd recognized it when he froze in mute horror.

No wonder the "lull" had been so kind. It wasn't a lull at all. That was the scent of a bonded -- and pregnant -- Omega.

Oh God.

Matthias halted the panic before it could begin. Time enough for that later. "Bree." He tried to rub some life back into Bree's suddenly stiff shoulders. "Bree, talk to me."

Bree brought up both arms, heedless of the blankets sliding off him to pool on the floor. All the good, healthy color had drained from his skin, leaving him paler than milk. "Don't."

"Bree --"

Bree said nothing. He turned his back on Matthias and made for the corner, as far as he could flee in the confines of the small cabin. Stopping there with a start of surprise, as if he'd forgotten the limitations of the storm, he brought one hand to his mouth and clamped it there. His hands were shaking.

Matthias let out a long, quiet breath. The tension in Bree's back made him ache in sympathy. If he touched Bree now, he thought Bree would shatter apart like a glass figurine.

With the blankets gone, Bree's scent seemed richer and stronger, filling the cabin and even drowning out the icy bite of the blizzard winds. Matthias could taste it on his tongue. It wasn't like any other fragrance in the world. Some combination of honey and cream and earthiness. It made him think of walking into a real home to find someone baking fresh challah, with tart cherry jam tucked inside the braided layers.

Bree wasn't actually pregnant -- just yet -- but he'd been fertilized, and his body knew it. Pregnancy was just a matter of implantation and time. The Omega part of his biology couldn't have been happier.

As for what the rest of Bree thought, Matthias couldn't make out anything past the paralyzing wave of terror and numb shell shock. Considering that, maybe he didn't need to try and push past them. They were plenty enough.

The minutes ticked on, inexorable in their passing. Bree didn't speak or move. He barely breathed. His eyes were wide and wild, with long beats going by between blinks. When he swallowed, the rough movement of his throat pushed Matthias past what Matthias could bear.

"Talk to me," he said, still on his side of the cabin. Once he'd spoken, the ice splintered and his next words came easier. "Bree. Talk to me."

An Alpha's command would break through the most stubborn Omega's defenses. Usually. Bree glanced sideways at Matthias, but kept his hand firmly pressed to his mouth.

Still, it was a start. Matthias locked gazes with Bree, not letting him look away. This was too important. "I didn't do it on purpose. You know that."

Bree said nothing and did nothing, save for tracking Matthias's every move and gesture.

"I didn't," Matthias said again. "Because you asked me not to, at the beginning. I would have let you walk away from this place unchanged, if that'd been your choice. But..." He stopped to gather the courage of his convictions. "But I'm not sorry."

Bree's eyes went wide. Indignation? Shock? Matthias couldn't tell.

He went on. "I dreamed about this too, while I was away. Having children with you. Making a family. It's what I've wanted ever since we were kids digging a garden. I am sorry it happened without your say-so, but Bree... You always dreamed about that too. I know that. I know you."

Still, Bree said nothing. His hand drifted slowly down away from his mouth to cover his heart instead.

"This is my fault, and it's my responsibility," Matthias said. His mind had been working furiously all the while, and he thought he had a plan in place now. If Bree would agree to it. He came two steps closer, hand out in a soothing gesture. "I meant to go back to the coast after leaving here."

Bree brought his head up sharply. "And now?"

"And now," Matthias said. He'd come close enough to take Bree's hand, and Bree allowed it. His fingers were ice-cold. Matthias chafed them gently, trying to warm him again. "And now it's up to you, Bree. The coast is a long way. You may not want to come with me.

If you don't, then I'll stay." He rested his other hand against Bree's cheek. "I'll be your protector, and I'll be as good a father as I can to the cub if you'll let me be a part of its life. If you tell me to keep my distance, I'll try, but I think I'd fail. I don't ever want to leave you again, Bree, and nothing on this earth is going to make me do that."

Bree's lips parted. "Why?"

That was the easiest question of all. "Because I love you," Matthias said. He still couldn't read Bree, and it made a knot of tension twist in his stomach. If Bree said no… Matthias tried again to convince him, taking his biceps in both hands and shaking him gently. "I love you. Do you hear me? I always have, and I always will."

Bree slowly blinked, his eyelashes sweeping his cheeks, and said nothing.

On the fine edge, Matthias pushed that little bit further. He had to know. "I won't leave again unless you order to me to go, but I don't want to. Not ever again. But it's your choice, Bree. What do you want? What are you even thinking right now? Tell me. Please."

* * *

Bree

Tell Matthias what he was thinking? Bree shook his head slowly, baffled. The man offered him everything he'd ever wanted dressed up on a silver plate, and then asked that question?

Didn't Matthias know?

No, Bree realized in the next breath. Matthias didn't know. He held Bree's arms tightly, but not so tightly that he couldn't have escaped if he'd wanted. Seen this close up, his strong bones seemed to stand out starkly beneath his skin. A muscle ticked in his jaw when he swallowed, and he searched Bree almost desperately with his gaze.

He's afraid I'll say no.

Almost not believing it, Bree searched him right back, hunting for any hint -- any chance -- that Matthias might be lying, telling the pregnant Omega what he thought Bree would want to hear. But he wasn't, was he? Matthias meant every word he said. Bree was sure of it.

And that meant...

That meant he'd been just as honest before, didn't it? The reasons why he'd left Bree behind, and why he'd come back now. All true.

He was right about another thing as well. How much Bree wanted this.

Bree brought one finger up abruptly to press it to Matthias's lips. "If you want me to answer, then you have to let me do the talking now. Do you understand?"

Matthias looked taken aback, but he had willpower enough not to ask "why" or say "yes." He nodded once, roughly.

"Good." Bree freed his arms, only to give Matthias a gentle push backward. Maybe not so gentle; Matthias nearly stumbled but caught himself in time for Bree to push him again. Step by step, Bree walked Matthias across the room, speaking in brief bursts. "Say it again."

Matthias frowned in confusion.

Push. "Tell me how you feel about me," Bree insisted. "Please, Matthias. You can speak when I say. Tell me."

"I love you," Matthias said without hesitation. "You're the one good thing in my life. You're my true North."

A rippling shiver ran through Bree's muscles. "Do you want me for your mate? Forever and ever. Tell me."

"I've never wanted anything more."

Push. "Do you want this child?"

"Yes," Matthias said, steady and true. "I want to watch you carry it, and I want to be by your side when you bear it, if I can."

Bree had to gather his strength to keep going. "Would you still want me if there wasn't a cub?"

"More than life," Matthias said. "More than breath."

They'd almost reached the far wall of the cabin by then. Discarded, forgotten blankets tangled around their feet, and Bree had to stop walking lest he make them both fall. He licked his lips once and asked, "Will you promise never to leave me again?"

Matthias cupped Bree's jaw, his hand tough from hard work, but his caress gentle as a kiss. "I will never leave you, Bree. Not until death parts us. I swear."

He meant it. All of it.

Bree let his eyes flutter closed, then opened them again, and gave Matthias a deliberate, hard push that did knock him down. He landed on his knees, but he looked back up at Bree as if Bree really *was* his North, and nothing could jar the compass off true.

"Good," Bree said. He came down too, into Matthias's lap, guiding him down onto his back. When Matthias lay fully on the floor, Bree smoothed his hands over Matthias's broad chest and the pounding of his heart. "I believe you."

Matthias's smile could have outshone the sun.

Bree had positioned them deliberately so that his knees rested on either side of Matthias's hips. His legs were long enough that he hadn't made contact yet, and he had room to reach beneath and take Matthias's cock in hand. Half hard, but Bree could do something about that. He stroked lightly, teasingly, watching Matthias's face for his reaction.

Matthias's eyes slammed shut, and he bit back a groan. "You don't have to."

"But I want to," Bree said. He trailed his fingertips down Matthias's shaft, then came up again, closing his fist loosely. "I think you want me to."

"You're not wrong." Matthias brought his hands up to rest lightly at Bree's hips. He'd gone hard under Bree's touch, stiff and ready, and a warm red flush started to spread down his chest. "Beautiful Bree. But you're not in heat anymore. Are you?"

Bree shook his head. He'd never known what to look for before, but he understood his body now. The heat fever had faded into a full-body glow, as if he'd basked in the sun for hours. His limbs were loose and his muscles soft, not shaking with need, and his mind was clear. His cock hardened slowly, drawing Matthias's gaze.

"And you want this?" Matthias asked, taking Bree in hand as lightly as Bree had taken him.

Bree moaned at the touch and rose up involuntarily. He was wet but it came easily, with no throbbing in his head and no twist in his guts. Slippery as silk between his legs. When he touched it, rubbing his fingertips together, it stoked gentle fires that had nothing to do with Omega body chemistry and everything to do with his heart. He wanted Matthias inside him. Craved it more than shelter and bread. Wanted this for its own sake. For his sake. For Matthias's.

It felt like coming home, to spread his thighs just that bit wider, and to slide down. His body accepted Matthias so easily, the stretch and burn just enough to make him cry out in pleasure, and it was reflex to take Matthias's hands in both of his as his ass nestled against Matthias's groin.

Bree opened his eyes then and found that smiling came far more easily than it had in years. With Matthias inside him, surrounding him, at his mercy, Bree had all the power in his hands... and it was easy, it was good, to give Matthias his equal share. "I want this. I want you. If you want me -- have me."

Matthias surged up to meet him and captured Bree with a hard, hot kiss. "Always."

He kissed Bree again, and then once more for good measure, thrusting gently, rocking them together; he took Bree's cock in hand and stroked him without mercy but with kindness, knowing what he needed. He shushed and soothed Bree as Bree rose higher, sharper, never stopping until Bree had flown apart.

Bree's orgasm came as suddenly as a flash of light, simple and sweet as a candle's glow; Matthias's as slowly as the tide, rolling to shore one thrusting wave at a time, so softly that when it came Bree had both hands on Matthias's face, murmuring to him, coaxing him to let go. He cradled Matthias's head to his chest afterward, too full for words.

But Matthias wasn't done. Not just yet. "You're mine, Bree," he said, meeting his eyes openly. "As I am yours."

And that was true too. Bree believed it.

"Good," he said, running his fingers through Matthias's hair, pressing a kiss to the top of his head. "Now. Tell me more about living by the sea."

Epilogue

Matthias

Home at last.

Matthias eased the bushel basket he'd carried from the dock down into the nest of spiky grass that grew by his back doorstep. It'd been Bree's idea to keep a good-sized rock handy there, perfect for placing on the lid of baskets like these so their contents couldn't pull off a prison escape.

He crouched to make sure his cargo was secure and nodded in satisfaction. A fine, feisty specimen of a king crab crawled about inside, one that Matthias had caught in the bay himself. The season had just opened, and as far as Matthias knew Bree had never tasted crab fresh from the sea before. It might tempt his appetite. He hadn't been hungry for the past few days, but as big as he'd gotten, he needed to keep up his strength. Matthias could do the cooking himself. All he needed was a pot of boiling water and a scoop of drawn butter.

With the basket secure and his stomach rumbling, Matthias knocked on the doorframe three times. "Bree? I'm back."

He didn't get an answer, but Matthias had learned not to be alarmed. Bree had fallen as much in love with the sea as Matthias had, almost at first sight, and sometimes he drifted into a trance while he watched the waves from their front window.

Or maybe he'd taken a nap; sleep was another thing that'd come hard for Bree lately. The nurse practitioner who lived nearby and had taken to checking in on them every day had assured Matthias that was normal, when an Omega was due any time.

Bree had rolled his eyes when Matthias questioned that, and kicked him smartly out to "go put all that energy to good use instead of hanging around here and fidgeting; you're not the pregnant one, are you?"

Matthias chuckled. Bree had kissed him goodbye and given him a long, sweet hug at the end of that order. He didn't mind that kind of farewell.

Once inside, Matthias kicked off his messy, muddy boots and shed his coat. "Bree?"

Nothing, but he could sense a quiet, living presence in the front room. He'd be by the window then. Matthias flipped the suspenders of his oilskins off his shoulders and made for the room where he was sure he'd find his mate, one hand on his belly, his gaze fixed on the sea. When he came in, it usually brought Bree out of his reverie; he'd turn, then, and give Matthias one of his brilliantly beautiful smiles.

He poked his head around the open door, scanning it. Just as he'd thought, Bree sat at the window with his arms gently cradling himself. He turned right away to focus on Matthias with a radiant curve of his lips. "There you are. I've been waiting for you."

The pleasure of it warmed Matthias from the inside out, driving away the last of the cold sea air. "I brought home a king crab. Feeling hungry?"

Bree's smile widened, as if something had tickled his sense of humor. "I think I could eat, actually."

"Good." Matthias cocked his head, wondering what Bree thought was funny. "Do I have seaweed in my hair?"

At that, Bree laughed out loud. "Matthias."

What on earth... Matthias walked fully into the room, hands on his hips, frowning.

And promptly fell with a crash that rattled the windows. It was a hell of a noise, but Matthias barely noticed over Bree's laughter -- and the sudden, startled cry of a newborn.

"You..." Matthias said. He climbed to his knees. "When?"

"This morning. You'd barely been gone three hours." Bree rocked the bundle he held, shushing and soothing. "I would have sent someone to come get you, but it was all so fast. If the nurse practitioner hadn't come by to check in, he'd have missed it as well."

Matthias finally managed to balance himself on his feet. He couldn't stop staring, drinking it in. Everything he'd ever wanted. His home. His mate. His *family*, now. All his dreams come true.

Bree looked back up at Matthias with his gaze luminous.

All the love they shared between them was written in his face. Matthias could see it all, every mile of the journey from Wasp Lake in their wolf shapes, and every nail they'd driven into the boards that built their home. All the nights spent awake telling each other their wishes for the future, and all the dreams they'd put into this cub that'd become true.

Matthias hoped his showed the same. He thought it did.

And it must have. Bree held out one hand, waiting for Matthias to take it, and smiled widely at him. Welcoming him, heart-whole. "I love you too, Matthias. Now, come and meet your son."

Safe and Sound
Will Okati

Ivoire, the packmaster's Omega cousin, has gone and gotten himself in a family way. Abandoned and alone, he and the pup he carries are in need of sanctuary.

There's not much packmaster Lewis can do about Ivoire's situation beside busting heads and making the bastard responsible pay. And -- while he's away -- making sure the young Omega finds himself safe in the hands of Zachariah, a widowed Alpha who's turned his back on the rest of the world.

Zachariah is everything Ivoire needs, and Ivoire is nothing Zachariah thought he'd ever want again, but nothing good was ever gained from playing by the rules...

Chapter One

Zachariah

Wolf howls split the evening, so loud they fairly made the air reverberate, and very nearly cost Zachariah his right foot.

He managed -- just -- to swing his ax wide and instead divert the blade into the side of his barn with a splintering *thwack*. The blow reverberated clear up his forearms and made his skin tingle.

Zachariah glowered first at the ax, then up at the source of the racket. With that much commotion, it had to be the Wasp Lake pack's deputies. *Deputies, hah!* A fine and fancy name for a group of roughnecks who liked nothing better than to lay down the law as they interpreted it. They weren't bad when taken one or two at a time, but with three or more they tended toward mob madness.

Every now and then they tried to recruit Zachariah. They liked his size, his Alpha status, and his stoicism. Would have been better off saving their breath. Zachariah wanted nothing to do with them. With any wolf, come to that, and for good reasons. He lived at the very edge of the pack's boundaries, and he kept himself to himself. Their troubles were none of his concern.

Still, unless Zachariah stuffed his ears with cotton wool he couldn't help hearing the wolves howl and yelp, and though he wasn't in wolf form he could still understand their yammering.

Hunt! Smell! Smell here? Smell there?
No smell here. Want them, want them. Trail by lake?
Must find, must find. Smells good, want him --
Want him, want him, yes! Take him --

Zachariah rolled his eyes. So they had mating on their minds, and an Omega in their sights. Too bad for the Omega, but whoever he was, he sounded smart enough to lead the deputies on a decent goose chase.

Godspeed.

He shrugged the intruders off, knowing they'd pass through his land and be out of his hair soon enough, and scowled at the ax sunk into his barn wall. Tugging it free was relatively easy, but the hole it left behind would be a bitch and a half to repair. He poked at the splinters with a grim scoff, wondering if the Packmaster would hear a demand for restitution. He was a young man, this new Packmaster, and supposedly fair minded.

Maybe so. Zachariah would believe it when he saw it.

He sank his ax into the chopping block to get it safely out of the way. Like the barn wall, it gave way far too easily. Zachariah hadn't built either cabin or barn. He'd bought them from an Alpha moving north to join a Barrow pack. They must have been good in their day. Well-loved.

Too bad for them. Zachariah wasn't the man or wolf to give love to anything. How could he, when his heart had died the day his mate and pup did?

He might be better off tearing down the barn and building a new one, he decided after a moment's thoughtful rubbing at his chin. He had no need for such a large outbuilding anyway, since he didn't keep goats or cows, and if he got rid of the barn then he could tear down the thickly overgrown herbs that surrounded it, too. Someone must have put a great deal of care into that garden once upon a time, though their choice of planting had always baffled Zachariah. Lavender, lemon basil, rosemary -- and peppermint, that last choking everything else half to death.

Zachariah kicked carelessly at the peppermint, releasing a cloud of nose-blinding reek, then drew up short in surprise.

He wouldn't have been surprised at anything taking root there, but the last time he'd checked he hadn't had any Omegas growing in his garden.

Zachariah looked again, but his eyes hadn't deceived him. An Omega had hidden himself in the heart of the peppermint tangle, crouched and ready to run at a split-second's notice.

He froze when Zachariah looked at him, his blue eyes wide with alarm behind the tangle of soft brown curls that tumbled over his face. He was all but naked, dressed in tatters that barely covered his dignity.

Zachariah blushed and looked away, but the face lingered in his mind's eye, tempting him until he glanced back. The peppermint drowned out any hint of Omega scent, but as dainty and sweet-looking as the young man was, he couldn't be anything else.

Two and two came together in Zachariah's head. *So you're the one they're hunting, hmm?*

The Omega raised a finger to his lips and gave Zachariah a pleading look.

Pretty smart to hide in the peppermint. Zachariah hadn't smelled a thing.

Not his problem. Still…

Zachariah raised one shoulder and turned away, back to the barn.

A good thing, too. Seconds later, one of the deputies barreled into his yard, nearly knocking himself unconscious on the chopping block before he tumbled to a stop and shifted into man shape. He sneezed mightily once he got a whiff of the reeking peppermint and scrubbed irritably at his face. "Have you seen an Omega come through here?"

Zachariah gave the deputy a sideways look and pulled his ax free of the chopping block.

To give credit where credit was due, the deputy had balls. He took a step back at the sight of the ax, but didn't tuck his tail between his legs and run. "Well? Have you?"

Zachariah chose a hefty chunk of wood and braced it on the chopping block, then split it neatly in half before he answered. "Nope."

"He's the packmaster's cousin," the deputy went on, either brave or stupid or both. "Packmaster got called out to a territory dispute, and he'll be gone at least overnight. The cousin was supposed to have come in today, but he didn't make the meeting point and no one's seen him."

Zachariah scoffed quietly. He chose another section of firewood and set it up for the strike. "That a fact?" Arm raised, he aimed. "I don't know about this Omega. But if it were me, I'd probably run like hell from all that 'take him'."

Thwack! He hit the log dead center with his ax.

The deputy's face went ghostly pale. "Fuck it, man. Just let us know if you see him."

Zachariah raised the ax in what could have been either agreement or warning. He didn't much care how the deputy interpreted the move so long as he got his mangy hide shifted and off Zachariah's property.

Which, Zachariah was grimly glad to note, the deputy did. Pretty damn fast, too. Zachariah stacked firewood while he waited to be sure the whole gang of them were well away, and didn't make a move toward the peppermint before he was certain.

Then he stalked to the overgrown garden patch and parted the weeds with two hands to glower down at the Omega still hiding there.

The Omega grinned up at him. "Thanks. Mind giving me a hand up?"

"I don't need your thanks," Zachariah grumbled, stripping off the flannel-lined coat he wore to toss it at the Omega. "Cover yourself up." He waited until the Omega was done with that before he took the Omega's hand and pulled, helping him to his feet. Good God Almighty, he was heavy for such a small thing. He --

As the Omega stood upright, Zachariah saw the reason why. No wonder he was heavy, with a belly like that on him. Not just an Omega, not just pretty --

No, not pretty. Beautiful, rather, lovely in a way that Zachariah had thought he'd forgotten how to recognize, a way that sent a punch of hungry wanting through his guts.

Beautiful, and plainly unmated, and pregnant as all hell.

And hiding in his peppermint. Zachariah dropped the Omega's hand as if it'd burned him. "What the devil are you playing at?"

* * *

Ivoire

"What am I doing? That's the million dollar question right there." Ivoire put both fists to the small of his back and arched to ease the strain at the base of his spine. *Oh, that's better*. He hadn't realized before he got pregnant how the weight up front would pull at his bones -- and he had three months to go.

The Alpha wolf who'd saved Ivoire's bacon stood as if someone had nailed his feet to the ground. *Grim-looking, isn't he*? Too bad. He had the kind of face that could be handsome if he knew how to smile.

Of course, that could be circumstantial. Ivoire cocked his head to one side, considering. The Alpha had fixed his stare on Ivoire's belly the way a munitions expert might size up a suspiciously ticking package in their afternoon mail.

Ivoire decided not to mention that. His sense of humor had always been a little off-kilter, and he'd learned when to keep his observations to himself, though he refused to stop thinking them. If you weren't able to laugh, sometimes you wouldn't be able to do anything but weep.

Anyway, it wasn't a new sort of reaction. Ever since Ivoire's pregnancy had started to show, he'd gotten plenty of that. Faced with a pup in the oven, Alphas tended toward either ball-clenching terror or salivating while they eyed Ivoire up like a rare steak.

"It's a good question," the Alpha said gruffly. "You didn't answer."

"That I didn't." Ivoire tried to pat discreetly at his eyes, stinging from overexposure to mint. "Mind if I come out and join you? And what's your name?"

The Alpha wrinkled his nose but took a grudging three steps back to give Ivoire room. He watched as intently as a hawk until Ivoire had freed himself, then grunted. "Zachariah."

"A man of few words, Zachariah?" Ivoire held out a hand. "I'm Ivoire. The packmaster's cousin, in case you were wondering. The same one those bully boys were chasing."

"Figured that." Zachariah frowned at Ivoire's hand, but finally, briefly took it. His was so large that Ivoire's disappeared inside his grasp, but firm and warm and dry, rough from hard work.

Ivoire approved. His back didn't, especially after the run those deputies had given him. He kneaded the base of his spine through the flannel-lined jacket and glanced about. Looked like the only place to sit was the chopping block, which struck him as just a hair too much in the way of poetic irony, but beggars couldn't be choosers. He pointed. "Do you mind?"

Zachariah grunted again but stepped out of the way. Ivoire supposed that meant no. Or maybe yes, he did at least mind the interruption, but he'd allow Ivoire to sit anyway. At least for now.

It wasn't a bad seat, actually. Almost comfortable. And seen up close, Zachariah did have a nicer face than his scowl would have a casual observer believe. Angled cheekbones, lovely firm jaw, Roman nose. Something about the eyes that suggested he could be kind, if someone taught him how. Something heated, and... appealing. Yes, appealing.

The urge to make him smile overcame Ivoire's better judgment. "Do you want the whole story, or just the Cliffs Notes version?"

He almost got what he'd been looking for. Just a tug at the corner of Zachariah's mouth before he pressed his lips together. "Just the facts."

"They're pretty simple." Ivoire turned both palms upward. "My pack is based outside Whittier. When I went into heat I chose an Alpha who said all the right things -- he was a charmer -- but who did all the wrong things. He promised he'd marry me if I got pregnant, and I believed him. I shouldn't have. So here I am."

Zachariah's mouth twitched again. "About that."

Ivoire tried to neaten his hair, which felt like it had exploded into a halo of tangled curls and reeked of mint. "That's a little tougher. My cousin must have sent that group of idiots to escort me back here, and their hormones took over." He propped his chin glumly in his hand. It'd happened in Whittier, too -- more than once. "I gave them the slip, and I was lucky enough to find your garden."

"Risky."

"Worth it." Ivoire rested a protective hand on his belly. He might be alone in this pregnancy, but he wanted this pup. He hadn't chosen his Whittier Alpha on a whim. Ever since he'd presented as an Omega, he'd yearned for babies of his own to love and care for. At twenty-three, he'd been so tired of waiting for that to happen that he'd *made* it happen. Come what may, and no matter what, he could never -- would never -- be sorry about the pup. "Do you think they're gone?"

"I think you smell like a jar of mentholated chest rub. Even if they're not gone, they'll run the other way if they catch a whiff of you coming."

Surprised, Ivoire laughed out loud -- and was delighted to see Zachariah's twitch bloom briefly into a real smile. It did wonders for his face. Indefinable, but whatever it was seemed to tug Ivoire toward him. To make him...

Want.

Oh. Ivoire sat up straighter, focus turned abruptly inward. He hadn't felt desire in months, not since his last heat cycle -- and all things considered, figured it was a case of good riddance. He'd thought perhaps he wouldn't have an interest in anything below the belt until after he gave birth, that it was part of the process. But this? Oh, this was different. Warmth kindled inside him, a low simmering heat that tickled at his nerve endings and woke them from their long sleep. He shivered, his skin suddenly over-sensitive.

He pressed his thighs together to relieve the need for friction and returned Zachariah's narrow look with a frank one. He couldn't smell a blessed thing over the mint, but to his fascination he saw Zachariah's pupils dilate. He felt it, too, then.

What is it about you? Ivoire wondered. *Why are you different?*

Zachariah's focus sharpened. "You okay?"

Embarrassment warmed Ivoire's face. *For heaven's sake. An Alpha's the last thing you need right now, kiddo.* "Me? Fine. Just fine." He boosted himself back to his feet -- but too quickly. The weight of his front overbalanced him, and he stumbled.

"Careful!" Zachariah had quick reflexes and caught Ivoire before he fell, taking him by the elbow. As Ivoire struggled for balance, the only thing he had to catch himself against was Zachariah's tall, solid torso.

Ivoire bit back a whimper at the feel of Zachariah's muscles, hard as stone. His body heat radiated through Ivoire, and squeezing his legs together against the rush of arousal barely helped.

Zachariah stared down at him, eyes dark and deep enough to drown in.

"Thank you," Ivoire said when he could trust himself to speak. The urge to lay his hands on Zachariah was almost more than he could bear, and he had to make himself go on. "Can you point me toward my cousin's homestead? He said it wouldn't be far past the old overgrown barn, which I assume this is."

To his surprise, Zachariah's frown took on a new angle. He stepped back, tucked his hands in his pockets, and shook his head.

Ivoire missed his warmth right away. "Something the matter with that plan?"

"'Not far' doesn't mean the same thing here as it does outside bigger cities," Zachariah said. "He's a good ten miles off."

"Oh, no." Ivoire's heart sank. "And it's getting dark."

And the deputies were still out there. They might not be too put off by the mint if they laid eyes on him. Ivoire wrapped his arms protectively around himself, then bit his lip. If he ran for all he was worth, then maybe...

No. He'd never make it. Ivoire raked his hand thoughtfully through his hair. There was only one thing he could do, and he'd just have to hope it didn't come back to bite him too sharply.

"Sanctuary," Ivoire said, planting his hands on his hips. No Alpha could deny an Omega safe haven if he asked for it. Not even if he hadn't been the packmaster's cousin. "I claim sanctuary."

Zachariah growled low in his throat. "I was afraid you'd say that."

"Is that a yes?"

Ivoire thought he spied a glint of reluctant -- very reluctant -- admiration in the Alpha for his nerve. "You're a piece of work, Omega," Zachariah said. "All right. Since you ask so nicely. Just until Packmaster's back. Understand?"

"Deal," Ivoire said, putting out his hand. "Shake on it, and we'll call it good."

Chapter Two

Zachariah

He'd shaken the Omega's hand. *Why did I do that?*

Zachariah shoved his armload of wood into the hearth far too haphazardly to be of any use. Grumbling under his breath, careful not to burn himself, he jabbed at the wood with an iron poker until the logs settled into place. With his luck he'd cast sparks on the piles of boxes he'd never unpacked and burn the place down from rafters to railings.

Fool. Damn fool. Why hadn't he escorted Ivoire to the packmaster's cabin himself? He could have made the offer before Ivoire claimed sanctuary. That would have been easy enough, and the deputies probably wouldn't have gone after him.

If they had, though. If they had. And if they'd taken Ivoire...

No. He'd had no choice.

Zachariah dropped his head forward and rolled his neck until it popped. That helped with the tension in his back but didn't do a damn thing to ease his mind. Or the rest of him, for that matter. Zachariah had long legs, and crouching before the hearth put enough pressure on his groin to strangle his cock. A good thing, too. One touch of the Omega's hand and he'd gone abruptly, blindingly hard for the first time in -- he couldn't remember when his body had woken up like that.

A long damn time ago, anyhow.

The fire had started to catch, flames licking up the sides of the logs. Zachariah leaned forward and inhaled their scent. Anything to drive out the overpowering mint. Though that might have been a good thing. Had he gotten a nose full of Omega hormones, God knew what he would have done. Maybe thrown Ivoire on the ground and gone at him right there, no better in the end than any of the deputies.

He closed his eyes and breathed in deeply, despite his mind's eye casting up picture after picture of Ivoire. Round and ripe, almost glowing, and despite everything he'd been through, still smiling. Still brave.

Hell.

"Zachariah?" Ivoire called from the room just beyond. "Do you have any towels?"

Zachariah opened his eyes. Steam drifted through the open doorway. Ivoire must have been standing directly behind it, with the bathroom door open. Hot running water was a luxury in the interior of Alaska, but the previous owners had installed a system fit to make the hardest Alpha weep. Just about efficient enough, in fact, to take care of a mint-drenched Omega before the smell made the house unlivable.

If Zachariah looked closely, he could just make out the silhouette of Ivoire's shape on the wall.

He turned his head and stabbed his poker at the burning logs. "Under the sink."

"Why would you -- never mind." Ivoire sounded amused. "Zachariah?"

Blast the Omega and his playfulness. Zachariah's cock throbbed with denied lust. "What?"

"Do you have a robe I could borrow? The coat's wonderful but might not be good to sleep in."

The mental image of Ivoire's naked body flooded Zachariah's mind and hit his groin like a shock of lightning. He shifted his weight and growled to himself, trying to argue away the urge. Didn't help. It'd been the same way with his mate. When they'd been with child, he'd turned into the worst and most insatiable kind of beast. Couldn't help himself.

It felt wrong, and it felt right.

"Use the robe hanging on the door," he said, biting off each word. He pressed his hands to his face.

Use the robe, and don't speak to me again. Not until I've got control over myself.

Merciful silence followed, but it wasn't as much help as Zachariah had thought it would be. With no commentary from Ivoire, the only way Zachariah could be sure he was all right was to watch his shadow on the wall.

He'd done that with his mate. He remembered that now, among all the other things he'd tried so hard to forget.

So beautiful, his Jace had been. Tall and lean and narrow-hipped. He'd joked about looking like an alder tree with one great big bole growing out of the center, but Zachariah couldn't get enough. He'd gone to his knees and worshiped Jace's changing body every chance he got. And so sensitive -- he'd barely had to breathe over Jace's cock to make him go off -- but he would beg for more, and more still, all Zachariah could give him.

And then. *Then.*

Time was meant to heal wounds, but it hadn't. Zachariah pressed his fist to his chest, the heart inside still raw as a skinned rabbit when he thought of his mate. Sweet Jace, narrow-hipped Jace, too narrow to give birth to a big wolf's pup. Things like what had befallen him weren't supposed to still be possible in this day and age. They weren't.

But they did. They had.

And here Zachariah was, alone in a house he'd meant for his family. He opened his eyes and gave the fire a savage jab with his poker.

After he'd lost Jace, he'd promised himself *never again*. No Omegas. No pups. No broken hearts. He admired Ivoire's spunkiness and liked his friendly manner, but Zachariah's brain knew better than to lust after an Omega -- any Omega -- for any reason. If his body didn't want to listen, then he'd batter himself with memories until it lay down and gave up. He would be his own master.

"Zachariah?"

It was automatic reflex to look up when spoken to. When Zachariah raised his head, his gaze landed on Ivoire fresh from a hot shower, wrapped from neck to toes in his robe. He rested one hand lightly on the broken-down ladder Zachariah kept propped in a corner, meaning to use it for kindling one day. Damp hair curling in a halo around his head, skin radiantly pink and scrubbed clean.

Barely a trace of peppermint left. Nothing but pure Omega scent radiating from him. Musky and salty, earthy and sweet. Ripe as late summer plums hanging heavy off their branches, begging to be plucked. Lips parted, eyes luminous. A temptation no man could resist, no matter how wrong. No matter what he might have promised himself.

A wave of loneliness and longing took Zachariah's breath away, and nearly knocked him flat. He swallowed around a knot in his throat, and it ached.

"Zachariah," Ivoire said -- gentle, so gentle that it hurt him. "Zachariah. Can I come dry myself by the fire?"

* * *

Ivoire

So that's how it is.

Ivoire held himself back, at the very edge of the room. If he was going to be invited in, it had to be Zachariah's decision.

He hoped Zachariah chose to say yes. Poor man. Ivoire saw now that what he'd perceived to be gruffness, standoffishness, was more along the lines of loneliness and some deep sorrow that weighed heavy on his shoulders. Ivoire didn't know what had happened, but from the way Zachariah looked at him it wasn't hard to guess. Zachariah's scent wavered from strong and pheromone-rich to abruptly nil, then back again as he fought with himself.

It made Ivoire's heart ache for the Alpha. His cousin had given him a brief précis of all the pack members. Zachariah had lost his mate, who'd been pregnant with their first child. He'd moved up here and kept strictly to himself since then.

And it was a shame. From what Ivoire saw, there was a good, kind man in there who needed waking up.

He'd been told before -- often -- that he couldn't keep handing pieces of his heart to anyone with a sad story, and Ivoire did see where his critics were coming from. Trusting the wrong man had left him pregnant and alone.

But he couldn't see kindness as weakness. Or rather, he didn't want to. Ever. If that got him hurt, then so be it. He stroked his belly, feeling the pup turn. Rewards were sometimes worth the risks, after all.

After what seemed like half of forever, Zachariah swallowed roughly and nodded. He turned back to the fire, deliberately away from Ivoire.

Best to tread gently with this one, Ivoire decided. He pulled the robe, deliciously imbued with Zachariah's everyday male scent, tighter around himself and was pleased to find it large enough to swaddle him completely. Hands in the robe's pockets, he padded casually to the fire and sighed with contentment as the heat enveloped him.

Zachariah cut his eyes sideways at Ivoire and opened his mouth as if he meant to speak, then shook his head. He jabbed his poker at the fire and laid it aside.

This wasn't going to be easy. Well, Ivoire had never let that stop him before. He tilted his head, noticing now that he'd come to a stop how blank and bare the cabin's walls were. Stacks of unpacked cardboard boxes blocked the window. "Have you lived here for long?"

Zachariah looked up with a jerk. "What?"

The Alpha wasn't used to conversation, was he? Ivoire had seen that before with other lone wolves. Lonely or not, they'd forgotten how to keep company with their own kind.

Ivoire held his hands out to warm them. "I think I told you that I grew up in a pack near Whittier, didn't I? This house reminds me of where I was raised. Not fancy, but it had lovely bones."

Zachariah kept his gaze fixed on Ivoire, but his forehead crinkled as if he wasn't sure what to make of him.

Still, there was longing in his eyes. Ivoire caught the thread and wound it gently in. Though Zachariah had as little furniture as he did decoration in his home -- which was to say, none that Ivoire had seen unpacked so far -- he had spread sheepskins in front of the hearth. Real ones, from the fluffy Dall rams that roamed the mountains. Ivoire suspected Zachariah usually slept on those.

He laid his hand on Zachariah's shoulder and only smiled when Zachariah's muscles went abruptly tense. The Alpha wouldn't be used to touch, either. "Help me kneel down? I want to dry my hair."

As Ivoire had hoped there was a well-trained gentleman underneath Zachariah's hermit ways. He didn't speak, but let Ivoire use his arm to lever himself onto the sheepskins. They were as soft as he'd imagined, and he indulged his whimsy by stroking them.

"You like those?" Zachariah's voice was rusty from lack of use. He touched the fluffy fleece as if it were the first time he'd ever thought to do so.

Good! A good start. "I do. I've never been much of a hunter, so they're the first I've seen up close."

"Most wolves hunt. Out here."

"Then I suppose I will, too, once I've settled in." Ivoire ran a hand over his belly, watching Zachariah watch him hungrily. His hands flexed, as if he, too, wanted to touch. "I've always been more of a gatherer. A gardener. Tomatoes, beets, carrots. I've even kept bees."

Zachariah shook his head, his gaze darkening briefly. "No hives around here."

"There could be. You never know about anything until you try."

Zachariah grunted thoughtfully. He poked at the fire, then said, "You ought to have family to help you."

"Well, that's the point of coming to live with my cousin."

Ivoire turned his profile to the fire and began to finger-comb his hair, watching Zachariah all the while. He could see faint trembles running through Zachariah's limbs, and how he would start to lean toward Ivoire but then remember himself and draw back.

Touch-starved for sure. Not good. Ivoire had read accounts of how infants suffered when they weren't held enough, and wondered how nobody thought the same likely to happen to adults. He leaned closer to test that theory and wasn't surprised when Zachariah unconsciously mirrored his movement.

Better, but still…

Best think for a moment, Ivoire, he cautioned himself. *How far do you want this to go?*

A good question. He bought himself some time by braiding his hair loosely.

The arousal he'd felt earlier when he first caught Zachariah's scent hadn't faded. Ivoire could still feel it simmering away inside him, making his skin too warm and his breath short. He pressed his legs together and felt that they'd gotten slippery with beads of the lubrication his body produced. Far less of it than when he was in heat, but give him a little encouragement and Ivoire knew his body would open so easily for Zachariah.

Thinking that made him catch his breath. A burst of hunger heated his blood. His scent must have changed, gotten thicker. Zachariah's nose twitched and his lips parted to draw the fragrance over his tongue. His hands shook from the effort of keeping them still, fisted on his knees.

"Oh, Zachariah." Ivoire touched the big man's face impulsively.

Though Zachariah's eyes flew open wide, he didn't pull away. He swallowed instead and kept his gaze fixed on Ivoire the way a drowning man would fix on a rescue line. "What are you doing?"

Ivoire trailed his fingertips along Zachariah's jaw, amazed at the tension he carried just in his face. Ivoire wanted to ask how long it had been but kept that to himself. Zachariah needed this -- yes, and Ivoire needed it, too. The comfort of another's touch. Kindness. A reminder that they weren't alone after all, at least not now.

Zachariah drew in a sharp breath and turned his face, but not away, instead pressing his cheek into Ivoire's palm. "You shouldn't."

"But I choose to." Ivoire moved his hand to Zachariah's shoulder, and used it to boost himself up not quite onto Zachariah's lap, but very nearly. He pressed his forehead to Zachariah's, and then his lips to the corner of Zachariah's mouth. "And I think you want to choose this, too."

* * *

Zachariah

Oh, God. Zachariah went still, so still he could hear the beating of his heart above the low crackle from the hearth. Ivoire nestled onto his lap as if he hadn't noticed, his slim arms sliding warmly around Zachariah's shoulders, his small hand cradling Zachariah's nape.

His eyes fell shut at the touch of Ivoire's mouth against his. "I don't understand."

"It's all right. Here." Ivoire took Zachariah's hand and drew it gently lower to rest on his hip.

Zachariah's breath rasped in his throat, and he flexed his hand involuntarily. God, Ivoire's skin was smooth and soft, the hair so fine he could barely feel it with his rough fingertips. Ivoire made a murmuring sound of approval and cuddled in closer.

"You don't --" Zachariah had to stop when his voice gave out. His hands had started to move without his permission, gliding underneath the old robe and up bare flesh, admiring the elegance of Ivoire's back, the curve of his pert ass... "You don't owe me this."

"I know that." Ivoire touched his mouth to the corner of Zachariah's. Zachariah knew if he looked at the Omega just then, he would find those pretty lips curved in a teasing smile. "It's not about owing, Zachariah. It's about feeling good for a change."

Zachariah stilled his hands, but didn't open his eyes. "I don't understand."

"I know that, too." Ivoire nuzzled at his jaw. Zachariah could feel the brush of Ivoire's eyelashes on his cheek. "We've had our troubles lately, both of us, haven't we?"

Zachariah couldn't deny that. He opened his hand slowly, so slowly. Wanting. Aching. And yet...

"I want us both to feel better," Ivoire said. He rolled his hips in a slow, gentle wave. "I'm giving you myself tonight, Zachariah. All you have to do is take it." He guided Zachariah's hand between his thighs. "All you have to do is take me."

Every man had his breaking point. Zachariah was only human, only wolf, only Alpha. He could *hear* the line snap as he stepped across it, but it hardly mattered when he had a lapful of warm, willing Omega overwhelming his nobler intentions, drowning him in sweetness and scent.

He surrendered.

"There you go," Ivoire murmured as Zachariah's arms tightened. "Oh, yes."

Zachariah didn't need the encouragement, and he barely heard the words. He found Ivoire's cock and held it briefly in his palm, amazed at the sleekness of the velvet skin, then he slipped behind it and brushed his fingertips through the moisture slicking Ivoire's thighs. The Omega wanted this. It wasn't just words.

God. Zachariah needed skin. He tugged at the belt of Ivoire's borrowed robe until it came free, and impatiently shoved at the thick terry. Ivoire helped, rolling his shoulders and shrugging the cloth away. It fell in a pool behind him, leaving Ivoire naked and hard on his lap. Not content with that, Ivoire worked busily at Zachariah's belt and zipper, managing to slide his jeans down far enough to free his cock.

Zachariah hissed at the shock of the cooler air, and looked up then to see Ivoire gazing down at him. His eyes were wide and his lips parted, his cheeks and chest flushed a pretty pink with arousal. He did want this, and yet he looked -- uncertain.

It'd been too long for finesse. Zachariah took Ivoire's hand and brought it down to wrap around his aching cock, glorying in the gasp of surprise and delight that drew from the Omega.

Oh, but that was almost a mistake. The touch of another hand on him -- Zachariah slammed his eyes shut and strangled a groan that seemed to start in his core. Ivoire's hands were small but clever, and they knew what they were doing. He stroked Zachariah with a firm grip, gentle but hard, crooning words Zachariah had lost the ability to distinguish. He could feel the slow, steady beads of Ivoire's lubrication pattering on his thighs.

When he thrust two fingers inside the Omega, Ivoire rolled his hips and cried out.

It went to Zachariah's head. He'd forgotten how it was to make love to an Omega. How hungry they were, how much their bodies demanded, the lengths they could take. His hips jerked, cock seeking the friction their position denied him. Best he managed was to rub against the softness of Ivoire's inner thigh, but oh, that was almost enough to drive him wild.

"Zachariah," Ivoire gasped, coming to a shuddering pause. "Kiss me. Please, kiss me."

He couldn't have said no, and he didn't want to. Holding Ivoire by the nape, Zachariah found he could meet and match the Omega there. Ivoire parted his lips to let Zachariah plunder his mouth, surprised at how sweet he tasted.

"Like mint," Ivoire said with a shaky, bubbling laugh. He bit lightly at Zachariah's chin. "You, too. But you can't reach. I didn't think -- it's been a while, I -- Here. Like this."

Ivoire started to slide off Zachariah's lap. Zachariah knew what he meant to do, that he planned to get on his hands and knees, that he would kneel and present himself. And that would have worked better, maybe, but --

"Don't," Zachariah gritted out. His face burned at Ivoire's questioning look, but he'd gone too far, and he *wanted*. Slowly, bashfully, he brought his palm up the roundness of Ivoire's belly. He breathed in sharply through his nose at the feel of it. He hadn't even let himself think about this since losing Jace, about how it had driven him mad with lust back then, but the ripeness of this Omega filled his mind with white-hot fire.

He groaned with appreciation he couldn't hold back and prayed Ivoire would understand.

Ivoire went briefly still, then seemed to melt on Zachariah's lap. "Oh," he breathed, coming back in. "Oh, yes. Please, Zachariah." He pushed at Zachariah's shoulders until Zachariah got the idea and eased them both down, Zachariah on his back and Ivoire straddling his groin. His cock nestled into the slickness of Ivoire's cleft, so hard he thought he might burst.

"Not before you're inside me," Ivoire said, soft and low. He reached between his legs to help guide Zachariah, and took both his hands for leverage as he slowly, slowly lowered himself on Zachariah's cock.

They both cried out. Zachariah couldn't help it, watching the Omega take him deep. Lovely Ivoire arched his neck and sank his teeth into his lip, fucking himself on Zachariah's cock, taking him in so easily, fitting their bodies together.

Zachariah knew he should have let Ivoire keep both hands, but he couldn't deny this hunger. He let go of the right and rubbed Ivoire's belly, amazed at the tautness of the skin, the fullness of him.

If that were *his* pup in there, making Ivoire bloom... "Oh, God," he groaned, taking Ivoire by the hips. He thrust up, hard and fast, almost too hard. Ivoire cried out, but came back to meet him, body demanding all he could give. "God, God in heaven, God..."

"More." Ivoire brought Zachariah's hand back to his belly and kept it there as he rose and fell. Faster, slower, tighter, squeezing him, his cock rubbing against Zachariah's stomach with every stroke. His breath grew short and jagged.

Almost there, almost there. Zachariah brought them both up, just high enough to press his mouth to Ivoire's belly.

Ivoire cried out as he came, his mouth in a tight O and his eyes shut, a flood of warmth spreading between them. Zachariah couldn't hold out against that, against the muscle contractions that kneaded his cock and brought him over the edge with a shout so loud and hoarse his throat burned.

Zachariah fell back -- nothing in the world could have stopped it -- it was as if his ligaments had come loose -- and caught Ivoire as Ivoire came tumbling after, all damp curls and belly and Omega scent. He'd slipped free without noticing, only realizing it when Ivoire curled one leg to bring his knee gently to rest at his groin.

For a moment all Zachariah could do was try to breathe, to remember how to speak.

Ivoire's kiss startled him, soft at the edge of his jaw. "Thank you."

Surely he hadn't heard that right. "What?"

"I said thank you." Again, a kiss, then Ivoire rested his head on Zachariah's chest, right over his pounding heart. "I'm glad this happened before I stopped believing in nice men."

Zachariah wasn't a nice man, and he knew it. Sanity had started to slide back in through the cracks, and with it came pure dismay. A nice man wouldn't have done that. A nice man wouldn't be capable.

"I can hear you thinking, you know." Ivoire butted his chin against Zachariah's collarbone. Around a yawn, he said, "And you're wrong. Since I'm the only one here, and I think you're nice, you are."

Zachariah threw his arm over his eyes in despair -- but the other had found its way across Ivoire's back, as if to shelter him. He was so warm, and already his breathing had started to even out in sleep.

He'd move in a minute, he thought, keeping his eyes shut. Make a bed for Ivoire out of the boxes. He knew where things were, even if he'd never unpacked them.

Yes, that was the right plan. Make him a bed, a separate bed, and sleep the madness off.

And in the morning, he'd make sure Ivoire knew this couldn't happen again.

First he needed to pull up his pants. He'd rest a moment first. Just a moment...

Chapter Three

Zachariah

A few minutes' work with a pair of scissors and an old T-shirt, and Zachariah had something that wouldn't win any beauty contests but *would* serve well enough as a mask that'd cover his mouth and nose, and tie behind his head. Add a pair of sturdy work gloves from the same box the T-shirt had been in, and he was all set to tackle the mint patch.

Funny how he'd never thought to do that before, only wrinkling his nose every time he had to work near the overgrown vegetation and moving on as quick as he could. But that morning, while half listening to Ivoire pattering around in his kitchen, he'd glimpsed the box in his peripheral vision and the idea just... came together.

Not that it had anything to do with Ivoire. He'd slept well, that was all, and rest rejuvenated the mind.

Zachariah glanced back at the cabin. He couldn't see Ivoire, who was still wearing his old robe -- claimed it was too comfortable to lay aside -- but could hear the Omega through its open window. Singing some radio hit, or trying to. For all his other virtues Ivoire couldn't carry a tune in a bucket with both hands. A particularly discordant note made Zachariah wince, then lift the corner of his mouth.

Lord, what a handful.

No word had come from the packmaster yet. On the other hand, none of his deputies had come around overnight, so might be he ought to count his blessings there.

Ivoire would be gone soon enough.

The knowledge griped at Zachariah's guts, but he shook his head stubbornly and double-tied the knot on his mask. What had happened between him and the Omega the night before had been something else, for sure, and he couldn't deny it'd done them both some good. Ivoire had slept at least as soundly as Zachariah, and still been snoozing when Zachariah woke at dawn. Nor could he claim his house didn't feel more welcoming with an Omega in it.

But Ivoire wasn't *his* Omega. The packmaster would have other plans, and what did he want the hassle for anyhow?

He didn't. Nope. No more than he wanted this mint. Zachariah crouched, all the better to deal with the roots, and gave them a good yank. They came free easily enough, though a few broke off before they cleared the ground.

As he scowled at the ragged roots, Zachariah recalled suddenly and vividly an older wolf's bemoaning the mint that'd infested her backyard.

"Toss one sprig of mint over your shoulder and let it touch the earth, and you're done for," she'd said. "In the end I just decided to move before it could take over my whole garden!"

Inside Zachariah's house, Ivoire started doing something that clanked and rattled. Zachariah lifted his head and narrowed his eyes at the window. Try though he might, he couldn't make out any details. The angle was wrong. Sounded like pots and pans coming out of boxes.

Well... there couldn't be too much harm in that, could there? He'd started the unpacking himself that morning. Ivoire was saving him some time and effort. Decent payback for sanctuary.

And if you believe that, my son, I've got a bridge to sell you. Zachariah scoffed at himself and bent back to his task with a will.

He'd gotten halfway through the first patch, tossing everything aside on a pile he'd either compost or burn later, when a distant wolf song made him prick up his ears. Listening intently, he identified three separate wolves moving in a triangle formation. They sounded older than the pups who'd been on the rampage yesterday -- old enough to be worth listening to.

Seeking, one of them belled. *Seeking Packmaster's kin. Where? Where?*

Zachariah rubbed thoughtfully at his chest. He didn't think Ivoire had heard. The Omega hadn't stopped his cheerfully tuneless mangling of the entire Top 40.

Packmaster sends word, another, nearer wolf howled. *Seeking. Where?*

Zachariah hesitated. On the one hand, he wasn't inclined to trust any of the wolves in his pack just then, and yet if they weren't trying to pull a fast one, it was his duty to respect their packmaster, and it'd be his hide if he obstructed the man's justice.

He still didn't care for the idea of handing Ivoire over.

Well, he wouldn't. Not until he knew for sure Ivoire would be well taken care of. Answering the call didn't equate tossing Ivoire off his land.

It'd been a while since Zachariah had tried a partial shift, and he was sure he looked like a caricature of himself, but with a wolf head and neck on a man's body he could communicate and fight dirty if need be. He tilted his head back and howled his reply. *Answering seekers. Who asks? Why?*

A pause, and then the deepest of the wolf howls replied. Zachariah recognized it as the packmaster's second in command, a former Ranger who no one doubted could be relied upon. *There? Where?*

Zachariah, he replied reluctantly. *Sanctuary. Safe.*

The second pause went on long enough to make Zachariah knot his fists in readiness. *Good*, the deep-voiced wolf answered at last. *Keep there. Packmaster returns in one-day, two-days, soon as possible. Keep safe until.*

Zachariah curled his lip. *Safe from deputies, too?*

The wolf's answer was as dry as a howl could be. *Deputies scruffed. Packmaster will punish, has sworn it.*

Huh! Well. Good enough, Zachariah supposed. Would have been better to muzzle them in the first place, but perhaps Ivoire would get a chance to witness against the lot and teach them a lesson. Zachariah grinned again, surprising himself. Ivoire didn't have a vicious bone in his body. He'd need someone to take his part there.

Zachariah supposed he wouldn't mind volunteering, if called upon.

Agree, he called back at last. *Will keep here. Will keep safe.*

Had Ivoire understood any of that? Zachariah shifted back to fully human shape and undid his mask, craning his neck while he did to get a proper look through the cabin window. Now he saw what Ivoire had been up to. Not pots and pans, but -- a ladder? Hell. Yes, a ladder. Specifically that rickety-ass old ladder he'd meant to burn. It wouldn't support a mouse's weight, much less that of a pregnant Omega, but even as he watched Zachariah caught a glimpse of Ivoire's sleek calves, climbing the rungs.

Oh, it'd be a fine thing if the Omega broke his neck just when Zachariah had promised to keep him safe, wouldn't it?

If Ivoire hurt himself…

Cold chills rocketed through Zachariah's spine and set fire to his feet. He'd started running faster than his mind could process it, and jerked back in surprise when his body barreled through the cabin door.

"Ivoire, *stop*!"

* * *

Ivoire

Ivoire caught the ladder rungs to keep himself from falling. Once he was sure he wouldn't slip, he held on to the top rung and turned as best as he could from what had once been his waist. "Zachariah, what on earth?"

He'd *been* annoyed -- any kind of fall was dangerous for a pregnant Omega -- but at his first sight of Zachariah's face, Ivoire's irritation dissolved. White to the lips and eyebrows, his hands were shaking on the doorknob.

Terrified. For him?

Ivoire eyeballed the ladder carefully. "This isn't meant to be used, is it?"

"I kept meaning to chop it up for kindling," Zachariah said, voice hoarse. He swallowed hard and stood up straight, shoving his trembling hand in his jacket pocket to hide it. "Get down from there. Now."

Ah yes. Ivoire recognized this kind of mood. In some ways, Alphas were all the same. Give them a good scare, and they'd rage the walls down to conceal how frightened they'd been. God forbid anyone think they were capable of worry.

But no, that wasn't fair. Ivoire sighed and rubbed at his belly to try and soothe his pup, who hadn't liked being shouted at. Zachariah was likely just out of practice. Besides, whether it stemmed from anger or alarm, Ivoire rather thought he liked the way strong emotion livened Zachariah right up. It suited him far better than the gruff, stoic mask he'd worn the day before.

And besides, this situation gave him an opportunity waiting to be taken. "If it's that dangerous," Ivoire said mildly, waiting, "Then come and help me down."

Zachariah narrowed his eyes, but if he knew what Ivoire was up to he didn't choose to call him on it. He stalked to the ladder and steadied it with one strong arm, his barrel chest pressed against Ivoire's back. "Turn this way. Put your arms around my neck. I'll lift you to the ground."

Ivoire bit back protests that he was pregnant, not helpless, and gave the man his way. Why not? He liked how his arms fit around Zachariah, and how even as heavy as he'd gotten, Zachariah could lift him like a handful of feathers.

Even better, Ivoire liked the way Zachariah paused ever so briefly to press his nose against Ivoire's neck and breathe in his scent. The touch gave him a good shiver that went straight to his toes and made them curl.

You are dear, aren't you? Ivoire thought fondly. *Hide it though you might.*

He would have enjoyed a chance to ruffle Zachariah's hair in response, but once Zachariah had plunked him more or less gracefully on the cabin floor, the Alpha let go and stepped back.

"Just so I'm clear, was it the ladder or was it any kind of messing with your stuff that got you hot under the collar?" Ivoire asked, teasing him a little. He wanted to keep that spark of Zachariah's burning. "Either way, you have cobwebs in the corners up there."

Zachariah shot him a dour look but plucked a cleaning cloth off the ladder rung where Ivoire had left it, stretched his arm to its fullest extension, and did away with the offending spider webs in three brisk swipes. "Happy now?"

"Ecstatic," Ivoire assured him. "No, really. I don't mind that the spiders got a free show last night, but I'd rather you didn't have them for roommates in the long run."

Zachariah almost chuckled at that. "Me neither." He caught himself and went stone-faced. "Word came through from your cousin the packmaster."

Ivoire's breath caught in his throat. He scolded himself -- his cousin's protection was what he'd come there for in the first place, for heaven's sake -- but he couldn't alter his body's reaction. "And?"

"And you stay here for now." Zachariah crossed his arms. "Under my protection, until your cousin's back in town."

For the life of him, Ivoire couldn't tell whether the idea pleased or displeased the Alpha. "All right," he said slowly, searching Zachariah's face. On impulse, he took Zachariah's hand. "Thank you."

Zachariah looked down at Ivoire's fingers, so small and delicate compared to his, and -- blushed. Red blossomed in his cheeks.

Ivoire's heart melted. He patted Zachariah's arm, then took pity on him and let go. "Okay then. If I'm going to be your roommate for a day or two instead of the spiders, then I want to earn my keep. What can I do that's more useful than dangerous?"

Just as he'd imagined likely, Zachariah argued that. "You don't have to."

"Yes, I know. That's why I said I *wanted* to." Ivoire lifted his chin. "I can unpack boxes. I can clean, if you have a broom or a mop."

"Uh-uh." Zachariah dug in his heels. He gestured awkwardly at Ivoire's middle. "Not... like that." He saved himself by grinning, a quick flash of humor, and adding, "How would you even see where you were sweeping?"

Ivoire roll his eyes, but an answering smile tugged at his lips. "Carefully, and with patience. I mean it, Zachariah. I'm not going to stand here twiddling my thumbs all day. That's not me."

Zachariah blew out a breath. "Stubborn, aren't you?"

"Absolutely yes." There was a fine line between standing one's ground and crossing the line, and Ivoire thought he'd just about reached it on this point. Besides, now that the pup was awake it'd started beating on his insides like a tympani band, and Ivoire could only divide his attention for so long. He laid his hand on Zachariah's arm without thinking. "I won't push myself too far. I know my limits. But I need to be busy. You understand that, don't you?"

He thought Zachariah would keep right on going, but the Alpha surprised him with a thoughtful gaze and a nod. "Yeah. I do."

Ivoire raised one shoulder and waited. *Well then*?

"Unpacking," Zachariah decided. "As long as you don't try and lift heavy things. Or -- no, wait. Do you know how to draw?"

The non sequitur startled Ivoire. "What?"

"Draw," Zachariah repeated. "I can't do straight lines, but I was thinking it's about time I got my plans for this place properly worked out. It'd help if I had them down on paper, too."

Was he inventing busy work just to keep Ivoire occupied? Ivoire couldn't quite tell. He wouldn't put it past Zachariah, and yet -- well, it was sweet, wasn't it? And he wasn't running in the opposite direction, nor slamming up another set of defensive walls.

Ivoire supposed he could compromise. "I don't know about straight lines, but I guess I'll find out. Do you have a paper and pencil somewhere in here?"

Zachariah's grin took his breath away. "Guess I'll find out."

* * *

Half an hour later found them perched on the edge of Zachariah's front porch, their legs dangling over the side. Ivoire nibbled at the barrel of the pencil Zachariah had found for him and sharpened with a jackknife. "So you'll have a shed for the goats here on the right? Or did you mean left?"

Zachariah leaned into Ivoire's space to study the line drawing taking shape. "Which side is the well on? Away from that."

"Left it is, then." Ivoire penciled in a rough square. He hadn't been wrong -- he couldn't do straight lines -- but it didn't matter so much to either of them. Holding the drawing up, he turned it this way and that in admiration, not of form but of content. Goats, chickens, woodshed, smokehouse, and even a sauna for when the plumbing froze, as was wont to happen during Alaskan winters. "Look at this. It's amazing."

Zachariah rubbed the back of his neck. "It'll do."

"*It'll do.* Listen to him. *Tch*! All you're missing is a good garden, and this place would be nearly self-supporting," Ivoire marveled. He tickled Zachariah lightly in the side. "No green thumb?"

"Never met a plant I couldn't kill." Zachariah frowned at the drawing. "Shame. Would be handy to grow what I need." He hesitated. "Where would you put a garden plot? If it was your land to plan as you pleased."

Wistfulness tugged at Ivoire's heart. He hadn't had a really good garden in years, and the soil seemed beautifully rich on Zachariah's land. Mint certainly thrived, but he could tell the previous owners had loved to grow other things, as well. If it was his, not just in daydreams, the things he could do there!

Zachariah took his silence the wrong way. "I might give it another try. Why not? Can't do worse than salting the earth. Maybe I'll do it right this time." He poked at the paper, nearly jabbing a hole through it, and growled at himself. "Where would you put a garden? Go on. Show me."

"You really want to know?" Yearning gave way to the excitement of a challenge. Ivoire drew an X over the barn that currently stood across the way, and then a circle around it. "Right here. You can gravity-feed a drip irrigation system. That's how most people kill plants. Not enough water, or too much."

He handed the paper triumphantly back to Zachariah for him to study, but almost dropped it. His pup had snoozed away most of their conference, but he must not have cared for jolts of adrenaline. He woke up now and delivered a stern kick to Ivoire's kidney that made him yelp.

"Shit!" Zachariah tossed the paper to one side and reached out, stopping before he made contact with Ivoire. "The hell was that?"

Ivoire pressed both hands to his back. When he looked up, he saw that Zachariah had gone stiff as a board and alert as a hunting cat. It made him laugh, though slightly breathlessly. "Normal, Zachariah. That was normal. I think he's going to be a soccer player. Or she."

Zachariah didn't look anywhere near convinced. His beard, neatly trimmed though it might be, nearly bristled with concern.

Bless his heart, the big -- Alpha, Ivoire thought, amused. He took Zachariah's hand. "Come here and feel for yourself." Ignoring Zachariah's instinctive resistance, he called on his own wiry strength to get the man positioned. For heaven's sake, they'd been far more intimate than this before. "There."

"There what?" Zachariah eyed him warily. His palm barely made contact -- at first. Then, the magic of it drew him under its spell. Ivoire had seen it before. He brought his other hand around to hover just above the right side of Ivoire's belly. "It's... hard."

If he kept looking at Ivoire like that, then yes, it certainly would be, but Ivoire thought he might want to keep that to himself for the moment. He didn't dare break Zachariah's concentration in any case. He moved Zachariah's hand slightly, using it to nudge the contrary pup until it stirred and turned, gentler now.

"Oh, God," Zachariah whispered. "Oh, *God*."

Ivoire cradled both of Zachariah's hands in his own, guiding him. "There. It's all right. You see? It's just fine."

He wasn't prepared for Zachariah's abrupt lean forward, nor for the big Alpha to press his head hard against Ivoire's chest. Quiet, almost choked-off breaths followed, and the shaking of Zachariah's fists pressed against his hips.

This wasn't repayment of thanks, or making each other feel good. This was affection. This was his heart, held in his hands.

"It's all right," was all Ivoire could say, stroking Zachariah's back in confusion. "It's all right. I promise."

But it wasn't. Holding the Alpha in his arms, the plans they'd drawn up for this place still fresh in his mind, Ivoire knew one thing suddenly and for certain.

He wanted to stay. To be Zachariah's Omega.

Could he have that? He didn't know. What did Zachariah think, behind his stoic bearing? What did *he* want?

Chapter Four

Zachariah

Finally, the flood of emotion eased. Though his bones ached like an old man's, Zachariah found he was able to sit up and give Ivoire his shoulder back.

Ivoire made a small humming sound and pressed his cheek briefly to Zachariah's. A small gesture, yet it encompassed so much more. Forgiveness -- understanding -- acceptance -- affection.

So strange that such a little thing could make such a big difference. But that was Ivoire, wasn't it?

Zachariah rubbed tiredly at his face. He couldn't remember how long it'd been since he cried. Probably not since just after he lost Jace. "Sorry."

"You don't have to be," Ivoire said. He picked up the paper they'd cast aside and pretended to study his drawing. "I never have understood why Alphas aren't supposed to have emotions. Aren't you human, same as the rest of us?"

"It's different."

Ivoire snorted quietly. "I have a penis and a womb. *That's* different, Zachariah."

To his own surprise, Zachariah laughed. It sounded horrible, a sharp and ragged bark of a thing, but Ivoire crinkled his nose and grinned back.

Zachariah rubbed at his chest, wondering what the sensations there meant. They weren't the familiar icy numbness he'd carried around with him since Jace's passing. Nor were they hot like anger, or prickly with wariness. More... empty. Yes, empty, but not forlorn.

More like a sense of waiting for something to happen. But what?

Zachariah let out his air in a long, slow puff as he watched Ivoire fold the map they'd made in half, but when Ivoire started to struggle to his feet, the only thing he felt was a sudden surge of not wanting that to happen.

He pushed himself off the edge of the porch and held both arms out. "Don't do that. I'll help you down."

"Are you sure? I'm pretty heavy."

"You keep asking that. You don't feel that heavy to me."

"Hmm. Wait a couple of months." Ivoire reached down to grasp Zachariah's arms, and let Zachariah help him down. His feet touched the ground with still-light agility.

Only seven months? Less than Zachariah had thought -- but he remembered, with an inner chuckle, how unwise commenting aloud to an Omega about that kind of thing could be.

Ivoire gave him an unimpressed look, as if reading his mind, and swatted his arm. "After all that, I think I've earned a nap. Do you mind?"

No, Zachariah didn't, and yet -- he couldn't be certain, but he didn't think Ivoire really wanted to sleep. Now that he'd composed himself, he thought Ivoire's demeanor seemed the slightest bit off. Less cheerful, and more pensive.

It didn't suit him.

It'd been a long, long time since Zachariah made any sort of impulse decision, but they seemed to come naturally these days. He held out his hand. "Do you have any of those power bars left?"

Ivoire blinked at the non sequitur. "Sorry?"

This kept happening, too. Zachariah shrugged it off. "I was thinking if a power bar's enough to keep you fueled for a while, you might go for a walk with me."

Frowning, Ivoire gathered his hair together, pushing it over his shoulder and tucking wisps away from his face. "I might. Why are you asking?"

Zachariah shook his head slowly. He didn't know. Could only take his best shot, and say what was in his heart. "You didn't get to see much of the homestead before. If you're going to live here, you ought to know the land. I can show you, and I can keep you safe."

And he wanted to see what Ivoire thought of his place. He wanted to be the one to introduce him to this world.

"I'm not dressed for it," Ivoire said, biting at his lip.

"I'll find you something." Zachariah hadn't opened any of the boxes with Jace's old clothing, but he knew where they all were. They would do for Ivoire if he rolled up the sleeves and cuffs. It'd be hard to see them worn again, but the Jace he'd loved would have preferred to see them get some use instead of being left to molder.

Hand still out, he waited for Ivoire to take it or decline -- and knew he hoped, so much, that the answer would be yes. He smiled at the Omega. "Will you come?"

* * *

Ivoire would, and he did.

Zachariah stopped with one foot on the gentle rise leading them up from the creek that cut across one corner of his acreage. It ran low this time of year, easy enough to step across, but maybe not so easy for a pregnant Omega. "Need a hand?"

"No, but I'll take one anyway." Ivoire's mouth quirked. He took Zachariah's hand lightly, but even so his touch made Zachariah's palm tingle. Once across the creek, he stopped to gauge the rise. A hooded, zipped sweatshirt that had once belonged to Jace hung tent-like on Ivoire's smaller frame, except for across the belly, where it was almost too small.

Zachariah could barely keep his eyes off the Omega. "It's not much further."

"So you keep saying."

Despite his teasing, Ivoire wasn't even winded. He managed the rise and fell into place at Zachariah's side easily, naturally, as if he had always walked there. Ivoire was just the right height for Zachariah to rest an arm across the Omega's shoulders if he wanted.

Maybe. Maybe someday.

He eyed Ivoire in silence as they walked. Ivoire had a nice color to his cheeks from the exertion, but his muscles were lithe and capable. A walk like this would have been more than Jace could handle. Before he'd been half this far along, his ankles had swollen terribly and his blood pressure risen too high for doing much. Their pup hadn't been nearly as active either.

Jace hadn't been well all along, had he? Only neither of them knew enough to understand it.

Ivoire, though. Ivoire glowed with health. With happiness, too, under the thin layer of pensiveness -- and with hope that peeked out every now and then.

Hope for what? There was the question.

Zachariah lifted a low-hanging branch for Ivoire to slip under. "If this hadn't happened to you," he started suddenly, needing a second then for his mind to catch up with his mouth. "What would you be doing with yourself now?"

Ivoire drew his eyebrows together in a delicate point. "There's no sense in asking that. I can't change things."

"Humor me."

"I don't know." Ivoire rubbed at his belly. "I wish I'd made a better choice for my pup's father, but... I'd probably be doing the same thing, Zachariah. I wanted this. It's what I was made for."

"No regrets?"

Ivoire took the question seriously and mulled it over for a few minutes, keeping pace with Zachariah as he did. "I don't think so," he said at last. "Because I don't mind the consequences. I welcome them. I'm capable, Zachariah, and I'm willing. I might be small, but I'm strong. I can do this. I know it. So how can I be sorry?"

He meant every word of that. Zachariah could hear the truth in Ivoire's voice, and it made his heart squeeze tight in his chest. He cleared his throat and lay his hand on Ivoire's shoulder -- slight, slim, and so very strong. "You're a fine wolf, Ivoire."

"You're not so bad yourself," Ivoire replied. He stopped to smile up at Zachariah. "And you're getting better."

Zachariah thought Ivoire meant that, too. And more, that he was right. The emptiness that'd filled his chest after he'd poured out all that old grief seemed to change as he drank in the Omega. His heart grew warmer, and fuller.

Slowly, he brought his hand up to cradle Ivoire's face, his thumb tickling lightly at Ivoire's mouth. Ivoire's pupils dilated, and his lips parted a fraction.

"You are so beautiful," Zachariah whispered. "How are you so beautiful?"

"I..." Ivoire shook his head, seemingly lost for words. He covered Zachariah's hand and let his eyes fall closed.

The urge to kiss him nearly overcame Zachariah, but -- no, not just yet. He glanced up to confirm what muscle memory of his land's boundaries told him, and nodded in satisfaction.

Brushing the pad of his thumb just under Ivoire's eyes, he said, "Keep them closed for a minute. Can you turn around? I'll help you if you need."

Ivoire's mouth curved into a smile and he didn't speak, but he allowed Zachariah to manhandle him as gently as possible. Zachariah turned him in a half circle, facing outward, moved in close behind him, his chest to Ivoire's back. They fit as if they'd been made for each other.

"Now," he said, hushed. "Look, Ivoire. This is what I wanted you to see."

* * *

Ivoire

Ivoire opened his eyes.

"Zachariah." His hand flew to his mouth. "Oh, Zachariah."

Behind him, Zachariah's chuckle vibrated gently against Ivoire's back. "You like what you see?"

Ivoire shook his head in silent amazement. *Like it? How could anyone not?*

Zachariah had brought him to the very edge of a precipice. Three feet forward and they'd have tumbled off the side of the cliff, but Ivoire didn't feel the slightest chill of fear. Zachariah's arms were warm and steady around him. Zachariah wouldn't let him fall. And if they hadn't come so close, the view would have been lost.

A little risk was worth a great reward.

Below them, the entirety of the valley spread out like a picture in an expensive photography book, casually turned open to just the right page. Mountains jutted up tall and proud and eternal, sloping gradually down. Fluffy white dots of sheep wandered those precarious slopes as casually as if they were on flat land, weathered evergreens keeping watch. The dark slate blue of Wasp Lake cut through the bottom, winding in and out between homesteads that were no more than colored squares from this height.

Ivoire breathed in greedily. The air was clean and sweet, if thin, and tasted wild. "Oh, Zachariah."

Zachariah hadn't moved away. He kept a secure hold around Ivoire, careful of his hands -- perhaps a little too careful -- but becoming less so. One warm palm cupped Ivoire's hip, and he nestled his chin in the crook of Ivoire's shoulder. "Guess you didn't get to see this side of the place, running from the deputies."

"Not half." Ivoire reached out toward the clouds. They looked close enough to touch. "It's... I don't have the words, Zachariah. Whittier is beautiful, when you know it, but not like this."

Zachariah's warm breath tickled the back of Ivoire's neck, making him shiver deliciously at the sensation. He smoothed his hand down Ivoire's arm, stopping when he braceleted Ivoire's wrist. "Thought you'd like it. Hoped you would."

Ivoire was drunk on it, and on the hard line of Zachariah's body nestled against his. "I could fall in love with it."

"Ah," Zachariah breathed against Ivoire's ear. Slowly, almost shyly, he trailed his hand back up to rest over Ivoire's belly. "Could you, now?"

Did he mean... Ivoire swallowed. Warning chimes pealed in his ears, but they seemed distant, far away, not mattering. Recklessness fueled his blood instead. He covered Zachariah's hand with his own. "I could, if I chose to."

"Mmm." Zachariah nosed behind Ivoire's ear. His lips brushed the soft skin there; when he spoke, his voice had dropped into a deep bass. "Would you choose?"

Definitely dizzy, and utterly drunk, and Ivoire didn't care. He stretched his arm up and back to brush his fingertips along Zachariah's jaw. "I might. I... Oh, Zachariah." The Alpha had slipped his hand beneath the hem of the voluminous sweatshirt he'd loaned Ivoire, and stroked him slowly, skin against skin. "*Zachariah.*"

"*Shh*, now, *shh.*" Zachariah pressed his head briefly and hard against Ivoire's. "Trust me?"

Though he trembled, Ivoire nodded. Zachariah's body ignited his, lighting him up from the inside. He didn't know precisely what Zachariah had in mind -- well, he hoped, and he could make a good guess -- but if he was wrong, he didn't care. He could trust this sweet, gruff Alpha.

And if that Alpha was falling in love with him, too...

Wanting him, for certain. Ivoire rolled his hips curiously, gratified when he rubbed against the evidence of that desire. Zachariah grunted, but brought his own pressure to bear with shallow grinds and easy thrusting. He held Ivoire close to him so he couldn't move, and stroked harder.

Ivoire's cock filled more slowly, but no less surely. His lips parted on a moan of anticipation. "Zachariah. Please..."

"I've got you." Zachariah applied pressure to Ivoire's hip, as if he meant for Ivoire to turn around.

Ivoire resisted the motion. "Don't. You won't be able to reach if I'm facing you."

"I'll think of something." Zachariah nudged him gently. "Please."

"I'm just trying to help."

Zachariah kissed Ivoire's temple. "You already did."

Ivoire's face warmed. He pressed a hand to his cheek, not knowing what to say.

Zachariah's low chuckle made his skin sing. He tugged again, gentle but inexorable. "Turn, Ivoire."

Curiosity and hunger both made Ivoire do as he asked -- and once he had, Zachariah moved quickly, if still with that all-consuming gentleness. He lifted Ivoire across the rough footpath and put him with his back to a strong young tree away from the cliff's edge. Reverent, he drew down the zipper of Ivoire's borrowed hoodie and pushed the fabric aside to expose his belly and chest.

Slowly, he went to his knees.

"Zachariah?" Ivoire slid his fingers through Zachariah's hair, hoping.

Zachariah's eyes glittered up at him as he undid the tie on Ivoire's borrowed sweatpants. His calluses brushed against the so-sensitive skin inside and made Ivoire gasp. "Told you I could reach."

Zachariah nuzzled at the soft skin of Ivoire's thighs, found a secure hold on his hips, and bent to take the Omega's cock into his mouth.

Ivoire moaned, startled and eager. He tugged at Zachariah's hair harder than he meant to, but Zachariah didn't protest. The Alpha cradled Ivoire on his tongue and took him deeper, instead, not stopping until there was no farther he could go. Zachariah's breath warmed Ivoire's groin, humid and heavy, and his hands kneaded at Ivoire's legs.

A sharp tug arrowed through Ivoire, seeming to come from breast through belly and to groin, making him cry out in ecstasy. Zachariah -- an Alpha -- was *good* at this -- at nursing Ivoire's cock as if he loved it, as if he would have done it for hours.

Ivoire's knees wouldn't hold him up for that long, but he wished they could. He tugged Zachariah's hair again, reckless now, as pulses of heat and electricity rolled through him. Building higher, hotter, they peaked and plateaued as Ivoire widened his stance.

Zachariah drew off, briefly, to lift Ivoire's leg and brace it over his shoulder. Ivoire had no choice then but to reach up and steady himself by taking hold of a tree branch -- and once he'd done that, Zachariah took Ivoire's other leg over his back. He was strong enough to brace Ivoire's hips, and his shoulders wide enough to bear the weight without a tremor.

"Zachariah," Ivoire gasped, rocking his hips. The wet, tight heat of Zachariah's mouth filled his entire world. He could feel himself coming, almost there, almost --

Zachariah let go. When Ivoire cried out in disappointment, he gave a low, rumbling laugh. "Still got you."

As carefully as if Ivoire were made of glass, Zachariah lowered Ivoire to his feet. He undid the waist and twisted his hips, sending his jeans down, then reached between them with one big hand to catch both of their cocks in his grasp. The shock of sensation made Ivoire gasp, but Zachariah caught the noise with his mouth and kissed the words out of him.

Ivoire threw both arms around Zachariah's neck and hung on for dear life. He drank in the scent and musk the Alpha gave off, and offered back what he could. His orgasm built again, quick-pulse-fast as the pounding of his heart, in time with the rhythm he could feel in Zachariah's shaft.

"Zachariah," Ivoire panted into the Alpha's mouth. "Zachariah, *Zachariah*…" He dug his nails in and raked Zachariah's back, which made him groan and thrust forward harder, sending shudders of sensation through them both.

"Again," he ordered, tightening his grip. "Ivoire, more, harder."

Ivoire sank his teeth into Zachariah's lip. Excitement sparked through him. He hadn't played rough in too long, and it felt so good, so good --

His back arched when he let go, his shout tumbling over Zachariah's lips, broken between Zachariah's panting for breath, and catching in turn Zachariah's strangled groan. Wetness burst between them, thick and creamy, and Ivoire couldn't tell which belonged to who -- but it didn't matter.

Ivoire knew it now. He could love Zachariah.

And if Zachariah could love him, too…

That would be happiness.

Zachariah's limbs shook, fine tremors running through his muscles, and his breathing still came in quick puffs, when he eased his arms away from Ivoire. He gulped on a dry throat and pressed his forehead to Ivoire's.

Do you love me? Ivoire carded his fingertips through the shorter hairs on Zachariah's nape. *Do you? Could you? Will you?*

As much as Ivoire had liked that, his pup hadn't. Indignant, it delivered a solid kick that made Zachariah startle back -- but with a laugh, and he returned right away to stroke Ivoire's belly in that endearingly shy way he had sometimes. "Strong," he said, drawing thoughtful lines with the pad of his thumb. "Real strong. Ivoire..."

He stopped there, shaking his head.

Moved, Ivoire cupped his cheek until Zachariah looked up and met his gaze. "It's all right."

Zachariah's grimace said otherwise, the stubborn Alpha. He sighed, then set his shoulders -- but laughed when the pup told him again, in no uncertain terms, to back off or put his dukes up. "All right, all right," he said in that low baritone burr. "Only because you asked nicely."

He took a step back, and that might have been all right, but Zachariah had long legs, and his stride was long.

And the cliff's edge was there, just there.

Panic bolted through Ivoire, a slap of pure terror. He flung his arms out and caught hold of Zachariah's shirt, yanking him forward. Zachariah roared in surprise, and then in equal horror when his foot encountered nothing. For a terrible moment, Ivoire thought he wouldn't make it, that he couldn't be strong enough --

Zachariah fell forward, rolling away from Ivoire as he did, but they were too tangled. They went down together, safely away from the cliff's edge, but so hard that Ivoire yelped with the shock of impact. His head buzzed and his eyes wouldn't focus when he opened them to see Zachariah scrambling over the top of him, face slack with fright.

For one second, two seconds, three, all they could do was breathe, short gasps of alarm.

The pup protested, beating at Ivoire's liver, and he shut his eyes with a moan. "Zachariah."

"Ivoire," he said, ragged. "Oh, God. Ivoire." He shook like an aspen, but despite that he was already standing, trying to help Ivoire up. "Are you hurt?"

"No." Ivoire checked himself, but he didn't think he'd damaged anything. Well. Not anything physical. Terror still made his blood run cold. "I'm all right."

Zachariah didn't look as if he believed Ivoire even a little. His jaw set in a grim line. "You almost weren't."

"Me?" Ivoire found the strength to stand. "Me? You were the one who almost fell off the side of the cliff, and you're worried about *me*?"

He might as well have saved his breath; Zachariah wasn't listening. Slowly, and so clearly Ivoire could track its progress, those stone walls of his ground mercilessly back into place.

"Zachariah," Ivoire pleaded, reaching up to touch his face.

Zachariah stepped back before Ivoire could make contact. "You're all right now," he said as if to himself. "That's all that matters. Come on. I'll get you back to the homestead."

Before Ivoire could protest, Zachariah started walking, leaving Ivoire no choice but to follow.

He almost didn't, too indignant and still shaky with alarm, but -- no. He wouldn't let Zachariah do this again, to himself or to -- to -- whatever they could be, or could have been.

Ivoire picked up his feet and followed.

They moved faster than Ivoire would have liked, too quick to stop and speak. It was all he could manage to keep going without running out of breath, though every time he thought Zachariah paused to look over his shoulder, he opened his mouth to try.

No luck. By the time they reached the cleared land below, near the half-uprooted patch of mint, Zachariah still hadn't said a word, and Ivoire had had enough. He planted his feet in the mangled earth and swiped at Zachariah's elbow.

Zachariah evaded him. "Not now."

"Then when?" Ivoire pushed his way in front of the Alpha. "You're shutting me out. Don't. Please don't."

Impatience flashed across his face. "Even for your own good?"

"Don't you think I know my own good?" Ivoire refused to budge. He thought he saw a crack in the wall and pressed his advantage. "I'm all right. I'm still strong. The pup is, too. And you're safe."

Zachariah didn't answer him. His hands flexed, as if he recognized he couldn't fight this but still wanted to. "Ivoire --"

"Well now," an unfamiliar voice came, making both Zachariah and Ivoire jump.

Ivoire looked over his shoulder to see an Alpha propped against the edge of Zachariah's porch. He didn't recognize them at first. Not one of the deputies, but an older man with an athlete's muscle layered over tough bones, a lean face with a Roman nose, and power written on every limb and feature. His mouth tilted crookedly up on the left.

"Good thing I came home early," Packmaster said. He nodded to them. "Zachariah. Cousin Ivoire."

Chapter Five
Zachariah

Zachariah bristled. The Master of the Wasp Lake pack had propped himself against the edge of Zachariah's porch as if it belonged to him, and Zachariah's first reaction was to throw himself at the man and knock him down.

He held himself in check -- just barely. His fists tightened as he nodded to the man. "Sir."

Packmaster's given name was Lewis, but no one ever used it, not even Ivoire. He inclined his head slightly to Zachariah in acknowledgment. That, and nothing more.

How long had he been there? Had he heard anything? No way to tell. There were cool customers, and then there was the packmaster of Wasp Lake. His eyes were pale as Arctic ice, chilly and opaque. He made an improvement over their old packmaster, who had been as irascible and temperamental as Lewis wasn't, but sometimes Zachariah wished for a leader with blood in his veins instead of frost.

Looked like Ivoire did, too. He hesitated between them, looking first at Zachariah, then being drawn back to the packmaster. "Cousin," he said at last, brushing strands of hair away from his face. "You've changed."

Packmaster didn't so much as shrug. "I have. Are you hurt?"

"I -- what? No," Ivoire faltered. He laid a hand on his belly. "We're fine."

"Hmm," Packmaster said, canting his head slightly to one side.

His way of speaking began to grate at Zachariah. Too precise. The packmaster said exactly what he meant, and nothing at all of what he felt, and they were two different things. "Ivoire's unhurt," he said shortly. "I'll vouch for that."

Unhurt for now, at least. Who knew what might have happened if they'd had even another hour together? Zachariah couldn't risk it. He wouldn't.

Packmaster didn't acknowledge Zachariah's statement but regarded Ivoire calmly as he said, "The deputies who gave chase will be punished. Was that conveyed to you?"

Ivoire gave up the attempt to keep his wind-tossed hair in order; the breeze seemed particularly determined to keep his curls dancing. "Yes, sir."

"Good. So will the Alpha who defaulted on his intent and left you in this state." Packmaster gestured simply at Ivoire's midsection. "I've entered into an agreement with the Whittier pack. Your former paramour will be fined a quarter of his yearly income as child support."

"But --" Ivoire lifted his chin. "I don't need it. I can take care of myself."

The corner of Packmaster's mouth lifted, but no one could have called his expression a smile. "Are you questioning my decision?"

Ivoire went stiff. "Yes!"

"Hmm." Packmaster remained unruffled. "Be that as it may, the decision has been made, and the word become law. He won't be allowed to mate with any other Omegas for five years, to make sure he's learned his lesson."

Secretly, Zachariah approved. The Alpha who'd betrayed Ivoire deserved worse, but this wasn't bad for a start.

Ivoire, on the other hand, had gone rosy red with fury. "I should have been allowed a say in this."

"You weren't there." Packmaster turned his cool gaze on Ivoire. "I was, and I take care of my own. Whether they like it or not. Go and get your things. I'll escort you to my cabin."

"But I don't --"

"Ivoire." With that one word, Packmaster cut him off in mid-sentence. "Go and get your things. We're leaving."

"But..."

Ivoire looked at Zachariah in a way that would have melted the hardest of hearts, and oh, it nearly did Zachariah in. It took all the stubborn strength he could bring to bear to not let Ivoire see how he'd been moved.

Zachariah hardened his heart. Packmaster would keep Ivoire safe and sound. He wasn't an affectionate sort of man, but neither was he reported to be cruel. Ivoire would be all right under his care. That was the only thing that mattered.

It's for the best. Deliberately, Zachariah looked away from Ivoire's pleading.

He'd said nothing, but Packmaster had taken all of that in. He transferred his focus to Ivoire and said, with an Alpha's command, "Go."

Ivoire didn't have a choice. Alphas and Omegas alike obeyed their packmaster, unless they were willing to fight to the death. With a cry of dismay and anger, Ivoire ran up the cabin steps and slammed the door behind him.

Packmaster didn't even blink. "He'll get over it."

Zachariah wasn't so sure. He rubbed at his chest, amazed at how Ivoire's upset hurt his heart. He didn't mean to speak, but words came out nonetheless, a gruff bark of demand. "What will happen to him?"

"To Ivoire?" Packmaster's mouth twitched again. Casual, he tucked his hands in his pockets. "He's an unclaimed, unmated, fertile Omega. He'll stay at my cabin until he's delivered, and then I'll find a mate for him."

Zachariah's hackles rose. "Does he get any say in who?"

Packmaster gave him a cool, remote glance. "He didn't choose wisely the first time."

No, but he doesn't deserve to be punished for that. Zachariah couldn't help grinding his teeth. "And you think you can do better?"

"I am Master of this Pack." He looked away. "I know what I'm doing."

"Ivoire deserves someone who'll love him, and be a father to that pup."

Packmaster shrugged unconcernedly.

If Zachariah stayed put another second longer, steam would start pouring from his ears. Lewis might be packmaster, but by God the man had icicles in his heart. "I don't --"

"Do you have any better suggestions?" Packmaster asked without looking back.

"Me," Zachariah said.

The single word rang out as loud as a gunshot. Blood roared in Zachariah's ears. Had he really said that out loud?

Yes. He had. And by God, he didn't regret it.

"Me," he said again, facing Packmaster directly. "I'll take care of him."

"You?" Packmaster gave him an unimpressed once-over. "Tell me. Why should I trust my cousin to you?"

His resistance made Zachariah feel mulish and all the more determined. "It's worked out well enough so far. There's room for him and his pup."

"You would willingly shelter, feed, and care for the both of them?" Packmaster cocked an eyebrow. "Why?"

Zachariah struggled with himself, but he needed to say this out loud. "Because I care for him. And he cares for me. That's more than most ever get, and it's a good start. I'll give you my word, Packmaster. If he'll have me, I'll have him."

Packmaster chuckled, nearly inaudibly, and shook his head. "About damn time."

What?

"To be honest, I thought I'd have to sweet-talk you around some more. You've been a bachelor for so long," Packmaster said. His gaze went from cool to frank. "I know my cousin, and I know my pack members. It isn't always straightforward, taking care of my own, but by God that's what I do best."

Why, that sneaky... This was a setup? Zachariah's mouth fell open, but after a moment he shut it. Given the givens, and what he'd gotten, well...

He couldn't complain.

Looking pleased as punch with himself, Packmaster tilted his head toward the cabin. "How much did Ivoire bring with him?"

What? Zachariah frowned. "Not much. A few bits of ragged clothing."

"Hmm. He's taking a while to get that together, then," Packmaster said. He gestured faintly toward Zachariah's cabin. "Go see what's keeping him. I want us home before sunset."

Zachariah's hackles rose. He wanted nothing more than to tell Packmaster exactly where he could shove his orders, but... He pricked his ears up and couldn't hear a single sound from inside the cabin.

Hell. Did Ivoire make a run for it when we were both distracted? Zachariah wouldn't put it past the Omega. He'd been lucky as hell to get there safely in the first place. There weren't any more mint patches for him to hide in, and even with the threat of punishment there were always randy Alphas ready to try their luck.

Forgetting Packmaster entirely, Zachariah bolted up the steps and into his empty cluttered cabin. His heart pounded a frantic tattoo against his ribs. If he'd lost the Omega...

If I've lost the Omega… If I've lost Ivoire's love…

It'd been too late from the beginning, hadn't it? And he'd been too blind to see -- when he wasn't willfully blinding himself.

Lord in Heaven, what a fool he'd been.

* * *

Ivoire

Ivoire pressed both hands over his ears to block out his cousin's cool voice and kept his head bowed. He'd gotten as far as the sheepskins he and Zachariah had slept on, but his legs wouldn't carry him any farther. Not when he could hear every word of Lewis's plans for his life.

What had happened to Lewis? The Alpha cousin that Ivoire remembered had never been effusive, but he wasn't frozen through and through. He'd come hoping for sanctuary, not judgment and management.

Well, he'd found sanctuary. Just not where he'd expected it.

Ivoire knuckled his ears when new shouting made him flinch. Had he been so wrong about Zachariah?

He didn't think so. He would have sworn otherwise.

Maybe he'd been a fool. Lewis wasn't wrong. He'd been a fool before, and he'd given his body if not his heart unwisely.

But with Zachariah…

A solid hand on his shoulder made Ivoire startle upright. When he raised his head, he saw Zachariah drawing back. Relief mixed with helplessness, both written clearly on his face and at war with his stoic mask. "Ivoire. You're here."

"For now," Ivoire said with a snap of his teeth. "Did you think I was already gone?"

"I…" Zachariah swallowed hard and shook his head. "You're here."

That was the last straw. Ivoire pushed himself to his feet, angrily swatting away any attempt to help before it could be made, and launched himself directly into Zachariah's space. "Yes, I am, and so are you, and do you know what, Zachariah?" His voice broke. "I've had enough of this."

Zachariah's eyes went wide. He took a step back.

Ivoire pressed forward, too angry to care about nicety of manners. "From the moment I saw you, Zachariah, I knew you were different. You're as unlike the Alpha I chose as night and day. I didn't know how until I saw how lonely you were."

Zachariah frowned, his eyebrows coming together.

Ivoire refused to acknowledge that. "And I realized how lonely I was. How lonely I had been. But then we fit together, Zachariah. Just like puzzle pieces, we came together and it was good. It is good! Only you can't see that."

Zachariah said nothing.

"And I'm done with waiting for you," Ivoire went on, jabbing Zachariah's chest with his forefinger. "I don't want to go with my cousin. I don't want to give birth alone, without someone who loves me. Not while you care about me."

"Ivoire…" Zachariah said, shaking his head.

"No! You love me. I know you do, and don't you dare say otherwise." To Ivoire's dismay, his voice broke and a salty tear fell down one cheek. "Don't you?"

"Ivoire." Zachariah's lips parted, curving into a gruff smile. "You love me? Really?"

Ivoire wrestled himself for control but couldn't grasp it. He wiped at his eyes. "I do. And you can't stop me. I'm going to be your mate, Zachariah. Your Omega. We've both earned a second chance, and I'm going to take it whether you like it or not."

At first, Ivoire couldn't identify the rough sound Zachariah made, but when he realized it was a laugh he stopped and stared at the Alpha in disbelief. "This isn't funny."

"Don't I know it," Zachariah said. He put his arm around Ivoire, sturdy and warm and safe. "Are you sure? Tell me."

Ivoire held his head high, gaze locked with the Alpha's "I'm going to be your mate, Zachariah, and you're going to be mine. No matter what comes, I'd rather do it with you than alone." He swallowed. "So there."

His quiet Alpha didn't answer in words, but in deed. Zachariah bent his head, and brought his lips gently down against Ivoire's.

Oh. Before that moment, Ivoire had doubted what Zachariah's answer to his claim would be, but not now. There couldn't be any mistaking this. He wound his arms around Zachariah's neck and pulled him lower. Parting his lips, he welcomed the Alpha in to stake his claim. He even crooked one knee around Zachariah's to hold him that way.

"My cousin…"

"Is gone, if he knows what's good for him." Zachariah tilted his head. "Hear that?"

Ivoire listened, too. All he heard were footsteps walking leisurely away. He licked his lips. "Good. Take me to bed, Zachariah. If I'm claiming you and you're claiming me, I want to put the seal on it."

"I don't have a bed," Zachariah teased.

Ivoire punched him lightly in the bicep. "Then take me to the floor, Alpha. I don't care, as long as you take me."

"You're going to be the death of me," Zachariah told him, grinning. "But somehow I don't think I'm going to mind." He bent to get his arm under Ivoire's knees, and with one agile lift had Ivoire in his arms.

Ivoire squeaked and threw his arms around Zachariah's neck, then smiled so broadly his cheeks hurt. "Is that a yes?"

Zachariah nuzzled his jaw. "Well now. What do you think?"

* * *

The house was cold, and Zachariah insisted on taking the time to build a roaring fire in the fireplace before he nestled them down, naked, in the sheepskin rugs that were as soft and welcoming to a wolf as a proper feather bed, though Ivoire had plans to make sure they acquired one of those, too.

For now, this would do. Oh, this would do.

Ivoire braced himself on Zachariah's sturdy lap, mouth open as he sank down on the Alpha's cock. "*Oh.*" Zachariah filled him to the point where he could feel a delicious stretch, a heady burn, and it made him feel as if his blood was on fire. "Oh, Zachariah. Yes."

Zachariah's chest glowed with sweat, and his hands shook slightly as he fought for control. When Ivoire bent to kiss him hungrily, he murmured against Ivoire's lips. "You are strong. Strong as the earth."

"You're damn right I am," Ivoire replied, his mouth touching Zachariah's with each syllable. He sat up and guided Zachariah's hands to his hips. To be filled was good, but to move was better. He rolled his hips until he found a rhythm that pleased them both, shallow thrusts and deep grinds. "*Mmm.* You feel so good, Zachariah. Don't stop."

"Won't," Zachariah promised. He kneaded Ivoire's hips. "God, you are lovely. Don't leave."

Ivoire moaned at the sensations inside him. "I won't. Try and make me go, and I'll come right back. Both of us."

"Good," Zachariah hummed. He rocked his hips up, sliding deeper, and let his hands roam over Ivoire, stroking his belly in seeming fascination, in definite appreciation. "Hot. So hot."

"The next one will be yours," Ivoire promised. He twined his fingers briefly with Zachariah's, then leaned back to display himself for Zachariah's pleasure. His muscles clenched deep inside, a sort of pulling at his bones that made him cry out. "And soon."

Zachariah growled. His hips jerked, fucking Ivoire deeper, harder, as if he were already trying.

Ivoire fisted his hair as he rose and fell on the Alpha's cock. "Soon as can be. Soon as I'm in heat again."

And Zachariah -- snapped. He lifted Ivoire off him and rolled forward. Too hot and eager for grace, he manhandled Ivoire about until somehow Ivoire was on his hands and knees, with Zachariah behind him.

"Oh yes," he breathed, spreading his legs. "Zachariah, *yes*."

With a growl of dominance and possessiveness, Zachariah slammed into Ivoire and slid home. Ivoire cried out in shocked pleasure. He hadn't known how good it would feel from this angle, or how *deep* Zachariah could go. Though he couldn't get a hand around his own cock, that hardly mattered; he came hard, rolling pulses that wrung him dry.

Zachariah cupped Ivoire's belly in one hand, fucking Ivoire as deep as he could. "Mine," he growled. "Mine, mine, *mine*. Ivoire --"

He shuddered and howled when he came, the sound enough to wring a second, dry orgasm out of Ivoire. His groin jerked with the effort, almost painful, utterly electric. He turned as best as he could in a desperate search for Zachariah's mouth and managed a clumsy kiss full of shaking breath and willing heat.

When Zachariah slid out, slick with his own spunk, he guided Ivoire down to lie beside him on the soft sheepskins. Without needing to be asked, the Alpha let Ivoire pillow his head on his chest to listen to his heartbeat. He stroked Ivoire's belly until Ivoire could breathe evenly again.

It didn't come a moment too soon. The second he could speak, Ivoire looked up to catch Zachariah's gaze. "Just in case it was in question -- at all -- it isn't now, Alpha. I'm staying with you. I'm making this a home for both of us, and I'm going to grow a garden to feed us. Love me, and I'll love you. Deal?"

Zachariah laughed quietly, still a little breathless, but he drew Ivoire up to kiss him. "Done," he said. "And done."

Ivoire's heart swelled. "If my cousin makes any trouble --"

"He won't." Cameron snorted. "Lewis knew exactly what he was doing. I'd bite him if he wasn't Packmaster."

Sudden understanding filled Ivoire's mind. *Not far past the overgrown barn, indeed! It was a setup from the start, wasn't it?* If he hadn't been wrapped up in Zachariah's arms he would have face-palmed. "Oh, that rat."

Zachariah let Ivoire go long enough to breathe, but didn't let him go far. He stroked Ivoire's back. "It's official if we say it to each other now, Ivoire. I'll be your mate, if you'll have me. I'll be a father to your pup, and to any pups we might have together. Will you? You have to say it."

So many words from his quiet, gentle-hearted Alpha. Ivoire's face didn't seem big enough for the width of his smile, but he didn't try to hold it back. He gave Zachariah everything he had, and his heart, too, when he said, "Yes. Oh yes, Zachariah. I will." Their first kiss as a mated couple made his heart sing.

Epilogue

Zachariah

Alpha fathers generally stayed with their mates during delivery, especially with home births, but the midwife had told Zachariah firmly that for every rule there was an exception before showing him the door.

Left without any way to distract himself, he paced the floor instead and bit his nails down to the quick. The sounds coming from the bedroom were muffled, but not nearly muffled enough.

Ivoire, he thought, as if he could send his brain waves through the securely shut door. *Ivoire, remember you're strong*.

Strong enough to tame him with the steel daintily hidden in his velvet glove. Despite himself Zachariah almost chuckled, remembering how the Omega had given him what-for the day their Packmaster poked his muzzle into their business.

I know you love me. And Zachariah did. Even more since then. Ivoire showed it in everything he did. Witness this hallway, for one! With Ivoire at his side, helping him, the boxes Zachariah had put off unpacking seemed to almost melt away. Cobwebs disappeared, and windows were washed to let the sunlight in. He wasn't pacing on bare boards, but on braided rugs that absorbed the shock of his footsteps.

He stopped to wince at the sound of Ivoire's groans from inside the room.

Remember you're strong!

Zachariah paused, holding his breath, but the noise had stopped. He pressed his fist to his forehead. Midwife be damned. Five more seconds and he'd break that door down, see if he didn't! He --

One door opened, if not the one he'd hoped for. The front door, without so much as a knock or a by-your-leave, admitting a gust of frozen air and freshly fallen snow. Packmaster Lewis stepped through, dusting a coating off the shoulders of his voluminous coat. Zachariah had made it for him out of ram's hides in thanks for his meddling -- if he hadn't threatened to take Ivoire away for good, Zachariah knew it might not have sunk in, how much he wanted Ivoire to stay.

He wouldn't say they got along, Packmaster and himself, but they respected each other.

"Anything?" Lewis asked tersely, head cocked to listen before Zachariah could answer.

Zachariah gnawed at his thumbnail. "Nothing."

No one who didn't know him would be able to read Packmaster Lewis's concern in his cool expression, but Zachariah had learned better and could hear the subtext in his quiet, "Hmm." He raised an eyebrow. "Going to barge yourself in there?"

"Thinking about it."

"Think harder," Lewis said. He unbuttoned his coat and held it open wide. "Well? You're safe inside. Let go of my legs and go latch onto your father."

Two pups clung to Lewis, one attached to each of the packmaster's legs. Three years old, there wasn't a shade of difference between them. Each had their Omega parent's curly dark hair and wide blue eyes, but while Lachlan was shy down to his bones, Kieran boasted the most mischievous smile a pup could get away with. Though Zachariah had looked, he couldn't spy a trace of their biological father in mind or body, and was savagely glad of it.

He knelt and waited, arms open, for the pups he'd adopted as his own to run to him. They looked at each other in the way twins had, giggled, and barreled toward him on their short chunky legs.

Lewis watched with that not-a-smile of his, the one that -- if you knew him -- betrayed his hidden amusement. "I'd thought it would all be over by now, or I'd have kept them out a while longer."

The reminder made Zachariah tense with worry, but he shook it off lest he frighten the children. "Ivoire's tough."

"That's a fact," Lewis replied. He lifted his head, and smiled faintly. "There. You hear that?"

Zachariah rocketed to his feet, ears straining. Was it -- no -- *yes*, yes, he did. It grew louder as he listened, a whimper that became a full-throated roar. Kieran and Lachlan stared, wide-eyed.

He thrust the pair of them at Lewis and seized the doorknob the second his hands were free, giving it a fierce twist that all but tore it off the hinges.

Inside, Ivoire was laughing at him, the sweetest sound he'd ever heard. The midwife had propped him up against every pillow they owned, and though white with strain he'd never -- never -- been so beautiful.

Zachariah sagged against the doorframe in relief. "There you are."

Ivoire's eyes crinkled with the width of his smile, with appreciation of the words Zachariah had said to him the day they mated. "Here I am," he said. "And there you are. Strong as can be. And here's our new son, Zachariah; come and meet him."

"Damn right I will." Zachariah's heart couldn't have been any fuller. He crossed the room and knelt beside the bed, taking Ivoire's hand in his and kissing the back. "Because he's mine. As are you, Omega. And I'll never let you go."

"Good." Ivoire pulled Zachariah in to kiss him. "As it should be, Zachariah. My Alpha. My sanctuary, safe and sound."

Here and There
Will Okati

As the captain of a fishing vessel, Alpha wolf Dominic considers himself married to his work. That's always been enough for him -- he's never been interested in a family. Until he meets Sawney.

Though he's always wanted pups, Omega physician Sawney is committed to his practice and his patients. He's never made time for a mate. But as he gets older he's finding it harder to resist the demands of his body. When he meets Dominic, his urges catch fire and breeding with the Alpha is all he can think about.

Dominic proposes they strike a deal. He can give them both what they want, no strings attached. One pup, a good friendship, and all parties satisfied.

Only it's not quite that easy. Passion and friendship are one thing, but what happens when the "single parents" realize they're in love?

Chapter One

Dominic

Dominic ran toward the neatly kept cabin as fast as his legs could carry him, knees churning, arms pumping. His jeans were zipped but not buttoned, his belt flapping loose at both sides, and one bootlace had broken when he stepped on the trailing end. He'd somehow managed to put both coat and sweater on inside out, and he absolutely did not care.

He avoided the necessity of steps by vaulting from packed earth to neatly split pine boards, and pounded the freshly painted front door with one fist.

No answer.

Of course. Dominic lambasted bloody hell out of the door with his other fist. If need be, he'd add a kick or two. A man in his position couldn't be too proud. And if the doc wasn't at home --

The top half of the door swung open, while the bottom half stayed latched. Standing behind it, a tall, slim Omega blinked at Dominic through pale green eyes set like jewels in a piquantly angled face, taking him in and not looking overly impressed. At first.

Then, the Omega chuckled and propped one elbow on the inside doorframe. "Who's in labor?"

Dominic couldn't find his tongue at first. The Doc, if this was the Doc, was definitely a wolf. Dominic's Alpha nose wouldn't deceive him. But Dominic would be damned if he'd ever seen another human being look quite so much like a cat -- or if he'd ever had such an instant urge to stroke a man until that man purred. He stayed as clear as he could of entanglements, thanks.

He shook his head briskly and tried again, this time using actual words. "Labor. Henry Call. His Omega, Oliver. How'd you know?"

Doc's smile widened as he coughed delicately. "Well, there are only a few reasons why Alphas knock on my door with quite that sense of urgency. I don't smell fresh blood or gunpowder, so it's not a hunting accident."

"Could have been a regular household mishap," Dominic suggested, forgetting his urgency briefly in his fascination with the Omega. "Maybe someone fell down a well."

Doc crinkled his nose. "I suppose anything is always possible, but there's nothing like labor and delivery to induce an Alpha panic. I know Oliver. I've been seeing him for the past three months. My name's Sawney, by the way. Please wait here."

He shut the door.

Dominic boggled at the impenetrable wood, then raised a fist to tap at it. "Hello?"

"Just a minute," Sawney called back. "I need to get my kit."

Made sense, but..."And you're going to leave me standing out here in the cold?"

"You're a big tough Alpha wolf," Sawney replied, a smile evident in his voice. "I think you can handle it." He relented far enough to crack the door slightly ajar. "And I'm not in the habit of letting Alphas I don't know into my den."

Hard to deny the sense in that either, but Dominic couldn't figure why it only piqued him more. Clever and careful usually weren't turn-ons.

Go figure. Dominic craned his neck for a better peek around and then inside as Sawney moved away. From what he could make out, the inside was as neatly ordered as an operating room. Not so the outside, with evidence of half a dozen tasks started and left unfinished. Probably didn't have much time for the busywork of a homestead between calls.

Interesting. He'd be a petite wolf, good at speed and distance, and probably an efficient hunter with that sort of focus. *Wonder why he went into medicine?*

Hell, Dominic wondered why anyone would, but he'd always known he was born and meant and made to captain a fishing vessel. He wanted nothing more, and he loved it with all his heart. For him, shore leave was an occasional necessary evil. Stuck in town overnight while his ship's engineer fixed a fault in their hydraulic system, he'd planned to toss his bag in a corner of his old buddy Henry's place, help keep him distracted lest his nine months pregnant Omega throttle him for being too underfoot. They'd planned to go hunting shore-side.

Didn't happen. Dominic had barely set foot in Henry's yard before a hell of a racket assaulted his ears. Henry had stuck his head out of an upstairs window and begged Dominic to run for the Doc. *Fast.*

So he'd done his part. It'd be great if the Doc could do the same.

Dominic raked a hand through his hair when Sawney, still safe inside, set his kit down and pulled a phone out of his pocket. "Doc. Get your ass in gear, would you?"

"First babies take their time," Sawney replied, implacably dialing. "Oliver isn't due for another two weeks, though, and while I know *of* you, we haven't properly met before, so I'll just make sure of the situation."

"About that --"

"Five more minutes won't hurt."

Dominic gritted his teeth and waited for the call to *not* complete, as he would have warned Sawney about had he been allowed. When Sawney frowned at his phone, Dominic cleared his throat. "Their phone's out. That's why they sent me running down here. Can we move already, please and thank you?"

Sawney sighed and tapped one foot on the floor. "Did you happen to hear how far apart the contractions were?"

"Two minutes. I have no idea what that means, but he said two minutes."

Sawney's eyes widened. He picked up his kit and made straight for the door. "How fast can you get me there? I assume you brought a four-wheeler?"

"About that," Dominic said. He gave Sawney his best crooked grin, the one that'd gotten him in and out of trouble ever since he'd hit puberty. "I got off a boat half an hour ago, Doc, and I've spent ten minutes of that arguing with you."

Sawney groaned. "You ran over here in wolf form, didn't you?"

"Carrying my clothes in my mouth," Dominic confirmed. "He said run. I didn't think, Doc. I just ran."

Hard to tell, but he would almost swear Sawney tried not to smile at that. "Alphas," he murmured, finishing with a click of his tongue. He pointed sternly at Dominic. "I'm only doing this for the sake of my patient. No funny business. No sniffing beyond the rib cage. And you're carrying my kit for me. Deal?"

Dominic's intrigue ripened into full blown fascination with the doctor. One cool customer, wasn't he? And handsome. Couldn't forget that. He stuck out one hand. "Deal."

"Hmm," was Sawney's only reply, but that definitely was a smile he tried to hide. "Turn your back while I change forms."

Dominic obeyed, calling back over his shoulder, "I'm not in the habit of assaulting Omegas I've never met before." *No matter how pretty they are or how sweet they smell.* The scent grew stronger once Sawney exited his house, and almost overwhelming to the senses when his clothes hit the deck.

A shiver rippled through the air. Dominic turned away, as promised. When he looked back, a neat black wolf chuffed at him around the set of scrubs it held in its muzzle. It darted past, feinting a nip at Dominic's knees. *Well? We're in a hurry now. Let's go!*

A grin split Dominic's face. Well now. He usually didn't find much of interest on shore leave, but he had a feeling this particular trip might be a touch beyond the pale.

Bring it on.

* * *

Sawney

Sawney let himself out of Henry Call's square red cottage and closed the door carefully, quietly behind himself. Standing on the front stoop, he placed both hands at the small of his back and indulged in a luxurious arch as far back as he could, then left, then right.

Crack! Pop! Crack!

Ohh, that was better. Sawney moaned in relief, then startled at the sound of a single man applauding. He cracked one eye open and found the dark-haired sea captain parked on an old stump used as a chopping block. In the different light, Sawney saw those deep brown waves were ticked with silver, as they had been in Dominic's wolf form. He brought his hands together in a one-man round of applause and showed Sawney the best side of his most roguish grin. "Nice work, Doc."

Sawney relaxed into his own smile, slower and wider, and twisted left to get the last bit of stiffness out of his spine. "You were here the whole time?"

"I was," Dominic said, looking frankly impressed every time Sawney got a good *crack!* out. "Damn, Doc, how do you do that? Every time I come back from a long trip out I'm knotted up like old rope and it takes days to work the kinks loose."

"Practice."

Dominic accepted that with a shrug. "'Course, I didn't mean just the spine thing. Like I said, I was out here the whole time. Got a few good earfuls of the whole business." His grin tipped up at one corner. "And again, nice work. You know what you're doing."

The praise warmed Sawney's cheeks, but he was too satisfied to be embarrassed. "It was a good birth. Quick, but letter-perfect. A healthy Omega, a healthy pup. I can't ask for more."

"How about an escort home?"

Sawney blinked at Dominic. "Are you volunteering?"

"No reason why I shouldn't," Dominic said as he stood and dusted wood chips off the tight curve of his ass. "And it seems fitting. I dragged you out, so I should see you safely home again."

Oh really? Sawney arched a curious eyebrow. True, it wasn't the safest thing in the world for an unattached Omega to take a late night stroll by himself, but everyone in the Harbor knew Sawney and his worth as their physician. No one would bother him, and even if they did, Sawney was quite capable of defending himself.

And yet... He closed his eyes and let the warm sense of quiet exuberance flood through him again, the reflected rush of adrenaline and excitement that always followed a good birth.

No, he wouldn't mind an escort home.

Sawney stepped off the porch, and gestured to the empty space at his side. "Let's see if you can keep up with me."

A flicker of challenge glinted in Dominic's eyes, and his crooked grin turned wicked. "I think I can manage whatever you throw my way, Doc."

Oh, Sawney didn't doubt that.

At first their trip was a quiet one. Dominic hummed to himself while Sawney tucked his hands in his pockets and let his eyelids fall to half mast, feeling more like he was floating than walking.

Dominic chuckled. "You always react like this to a job well done?"

"Mmm," Sawney said with a contented sigh. He could feel Dominic watching him, his curiosity tempered with something warmer, something that mixed well with his own euphoria. "There's nothing like it -- bringing new life into the world, being there to see it happen."

"I can tell. Feels like I'm walking a young god home from his temple." Dominic cleared his throat hastily. "Anyway."

Sawney crinkled his nose as he laughed on the inside. Who'd have thought a fishing boat captain had such a sense of poetry?

He liked it.

"It's much the same for me as well," Dominic went on thoughtfully. "When I'm out at sea and I've got the bottomless Bering under my feet. Never feels like work, even when I've been at it for thirty hours and I'm dying for food and sleep. Always feels like…"

"Like joy," Sawney murmured. "Like flying."

Dominic made a rumbling sound of agreement. "Not that it doesn't have its drawbacks, I suppose," he went on, his gaze drifting to the water always on their left. "Some men say they're married to their jobs, and so I am, but the sea's not an easy lover. Tries to kill you every other day and twice on Sundays, and I keep coming back for more."

"I asked Henry about you, you know. Oliver put his two cents in soon as he had a chance," Sawney remarked. "They spoke well of you."

Dominic acknowledged that with a rumbling noise.

Gruff, but you couldn't ask for a better man, was Oliver's verdict. Henry had said simply, *I'd trust him with my life.*

Their commendations made Sawney curious. "You never mated?"

Dominic shook his head. "No. Plenty of fishermen do have mates and kids and they make it work, but it never seemed the right fit for me. Leaving my mate alone nine or ten months out of the year with no guarantee I'd come back home again, or in one piece? It's a lot to ask of anyone." He let out a breath. "Still. Sometimes I think I'd like to leave something good in this world when I'm gone from it."

Sawney knew the feeling. He also knew what Dominic was going to ask next, because everyone did. The difference was he thought Dominic would actually understand. "I want a baby," he said. "One of my own. I always have." And the older he got -- thirty-two now -- the stronger the yearning became, until it was a never-ceasing hunger. "But if I'm going to help others, to use my skills, I can't be tied down to a mate. It would never work."

Dominic made another rumbling noise.

Was it Sawney's imagination, or had Dominic slowly moved closer as they walked? Sawney didn't think it was wishful thinking. Dominic's elbow nearly brushed his, and his steps had fallen into sync with Sawney's. He moved with a deliberate, rolling gait, probably learned at sea. A fluid motion that should have been at odds with his tough exterior, but fit him to a tee.

Hips that rolled like that would give him a delicious advantage in bed.

The warmth in Sawney's cheeks suddenly blazed hot. He could feel the heat all the way to the tips of his ears, and he could smell the rush of pheromones wafting from himself. His skin felt suddenly too sensitive, the ground too hard and his knees made of rubber. It wasn't time for his heat cycle, but he knew better than anyone how the only thing to expect there was the unexpected.

He heard Dominic's sharp, surprised inhale, and felt a ripple of tension roll through the Alpha. Felt, too, how he brought himself under strict control a half second later. He even came to a stop.

When Sawney opened his eyes to find out why, Dominic only nodded to the right. "We're here," he said simply, though his shoulders were drawn tight as wires with the effort of restraint. "Safe escort home, just as promised."

And so they were. Sawney couldn't believe it. The trip back had gone so quickly. He touched the tip of his tongue to the bow of his upper lip, thinking as fast as he could. He knew what he wanted, and knew too that it would be playing with fire.

But he'd been so cold for what seemed like so long, and he wasn't ready to let go of the warmth yet.

Dominic reached up to tug at a lock of his hair. "I'll be on my way."

Sawney touched Dominic's wrist to stop him. "You don't have to. Come inside. You walked me home, and that means it's my turn. Let me offer you a drink."

Chapter Two

Dominic

Well, now. Dominic hadn't expected an offer like that. Some Alphas would; others would expect it as their right, but he'd deliberately steered his mind away from any testosterone-laden thoughts. Especially after learning Sawney was as wed to his vocation as Dominic himself.

And yet here they were.

Sawney hesitated, keys in hand, halfway to the door. "That is, if you want to," he said. "It isn't obligatory."

Damn. Sawney must have taken his surprise for lack of interest, and that wouldn't do. Dominic weighed him up for a moment -- there was heat there, as well as hope -- but unless he was mistaken, Sawney wasn't altogether sure about exactly what cards he wanted to lay on the table. A one night stand? A kiss goodnight? Or more, much more.

He'd like to know the answer to that himself. "A drink sounds like just the thing, Doc," he said, letting his gaze drift up and down over the Omega. "After you."

Sawney ducked his head almost shyly. He fumbled the keys on his first try. So, he *was* nervous. Probably didn't do this too often. Dominic didn't either, but God help him, he found Sawney's lack of experience endearing. Almost as appealing as his tight, sweet body and the fragrance that enveloped him. Sweet, salty, Omega.

Dominic caught a whiff of his own stronger Alpha musk as he followed Sawney into his home, and was struck by the differences between them. Beeswax and leather. Honey and iron.

Sawney stole the occasional peek over his shoulder at Dominic as he made for what proved to be a tiny galley kitchen. Must not do a lot of cooking, Dominic decided, which made sense for a man so engaged with his work.

He stretched on tiptoes to retrieve a bottle of brandy from a high cabinet, blowing dust off as he brought it down and presented it to Dominic. "I don't have any proper glasses," he admitted, catching his lip between his teeth. "Do you mind teacups?"

Dominic didn't, but he had a better idea. He tilted the bottle back and shot a mouthful, savoring the way the liquor burned on its way down, enjoying it almost as much as the way Sawney's gaze fixed on him, mouth slightly open, while he drank.

Extending the bottle, he rapped Sawney's hand lightly with the side. "Your turn."

Sawney swallowed quickly, but he was man enough to rise to any challenge, as Dominic had thought he might. He took a larger gulp than Dominic and came up with his eyes glittering in the low light. He licked his lips clean, and was hoarse when he spoke. "I like it your way."

Then, as if confused by his boldness, he turned his back to rummage in the cabinets. "I think I've got some crackers in here. Or trail mix, maybe... Yes." He emerged with a sleeve of cheddar crackers and thrust them at Dominic. "Here. They go well together."

"I expect they do." Dominic popped a cracker into his mouth and bit, but he didn't taste a thing. In taking the offering he'd come close enough to Sawney to breathe him in, his Omega scent stronger now, almost narcotic. He bent his head and nuzzled beneath Sawney's chin, seeking more of that fragrance.

Sawney bit back a moan and jerked forward slightly, pressing his knees together. A wave of scent eddied between them. If Dominic had him naked already, he knew what he'd find. Slick readiness, wet willingness.

If it had been any other Omega, he'd -- but it wasn't.

Dominic made himself draw back. Not far. Just enough to capture Sawney's attention, to open those eyes and get them focused on him. He waited for that before he spoke. "I don't think either you or I are usually big on beating around the bush. Am I right?"

Sawney's pupils were huge. He shook his head slowly. "I wouldn't normally do this," he said. "It's the night. The good birth. It makes me… It drives me. Makes it hard to deny myself."

Dominic nodded. Much as he'd suspected, then. He cupped Sawney's cheek and drew in a sharp breath as Sawney pressed into the touch. It couldn't be helped; he had to have his hands on the Omega. He stroked them down Sawney's sleek sides, the elegant curve of his back, the full sweetness of his hips, the humid dampness at his inseams.

He only just managed to stop.

"Is something wrong?" Sawney looked torn between worry and arousal. "I know I'm older."

"Older? Thirty-two, that's not old. Maybe to risk a first pup," Dominic said frankly. Then, raised a finger to Sawney's lips. "Unless that's the idea."

It certainly was his. Inspiration came in a rush, dizzying him.

He could see Sawney didn't understand; he frowned and started to speak despite the barrier.

"Listen to me, now." Dominic chafed Sawney's biceps as gently as he could, though being this close made him so hard that finding words wasn't easy. "I never mated because I'm married to the sea. You never mated for the sake of your independence. I'm not looking for a mate now, either. But you want a child, and the sea is dangerous."

He took his finger away, and Sawney licked the place where it'd rested. "What are you saying?"

Dominic couldn't hold back from touching the Omega any longer. He slipped his hand beneath the hem of Sawney's shirt and glided it over his bare stomach beneath, imagining things he'd never dared to before. Then, he slid it down to cradle Sawney's cock, just as hard as his own, and was rewarded with a soft cry and a surge forward.

"I'm saying I can give us the best of both worlds, Doc," he whispered in Sawney's ear. He bit the lobe, then drew it into his mouth, and held Sawney up with an arm around his waist when the Omega's knees would have gone. "A pup for you. A legacy for me. No strings to tie us down, and everything we ever wanted."

"That's if you want it." Dominic let go of Sawney. He had to make this choice standing on his own two feet. "If you do, then say so, and I'm your man."

* * *

Sawney

Oh, this was madness. It was -- wasn't it?

Sawney pressed his hand over his heart, which beat as hard and fast as a caged bird's wings. He licked his lips, trying to think. If he wanted to, he could do this. Henry wasn't given to false flattery. If he said Dominic could be trusted, then Dominic could. End of discussion.

And -- would he ever have a better chance? Even if anyone local had been willing to engage in a no-strings affair, the inevitable breakup could make life in a small pack terribly awkward.

But Dominic spent almost all his time at sea. That wouldn't be a problem.

Sawney's body pleaded for him to give in. To satiate the craving to mate and breed. He'd been made for it, after all, and he wanted to. Wanted so much that his skin warmed, and he felt himself begin to open. The shock of it and the accompanying head rush made him draw in a sharp breath. He rocked forward on his heels and nearly lost his balance. So strong. So good.

He made his choice.

Looking up at the Alpha, Sawney reached for the hem of his shirt, pulling the entirety of the thing over his head. It'd been a long time. A long, long time since a man looked at him the way Dominic did now, leaning forward with his lips parted. Hungry.

"Whoa there," Dominic murmured, gaze riveted to Sawney in a way that made Sawney not want to "whoa" at all. "I take it that's a yes?"

His willingness made Sawney bold. "It's a 'close the curtains and follow me'."

Deliberately he turned his back and walked away. He was gratified by the abrupt shadows that blanketed his cabin, Dominic doing what he'd asked.

When he looked over his shoulder, he could feel how the atmosphere of the room had changed and moistened his lips in response. "I'm not in heat. Yet. It might not work."

"We'll see." Dominic replied absently, eating Sawney alive with his eyes. The sea captain's hand drifted down to his lower stomach, settling there just above the growing bulge between his legs. "Worth a try, anyhow. Don't you think?"

Sawney inhaled sharply. That erection was for him. Dominic had gotten hard thinking about the two of them. A wave of warmth rushed through Sawney, bringing with it a light sweat and another spin to his equilibrium.

He wanted more.

"Stay there. I want to…" Sawney had to drink that in. He opened his belt slowly, then drew down the zipper of his jeans. Eased the denim down his hips, and let it fall once it reached his knees. He stepped lightly out of the tangle, bare as stone save for his tightly fitted shorts.

Bold, he cupped himself. "Is this what you want?"

Dominic's eyes glittered. He'd stood rapt, but now he was on the move, a predator's slow prowl. "That's close," he said, his voice deeper, more animal. "Take those off."

Sawney eased the cotton down his hips, and kicked them away. He turned in profile, teasing. "This?"

"Almost." Dominic was nearly close enough to touch. His nearness made Sawney's skin prickle, damp with new sweat and rolling waves of heat, and drew a moan from his lips. He felt oddly as if he stood at the very edge of some great precipice, and one good push would send him over. He grasped Sawney's hips and kneaded the curve of his ass, sliding his fingertips boldly into the cleft, already wet with arousal. "There," he rumbled, deep and low. "That's what I want."

They were only words, but at the sound of them, Sawney fell. His heat usually came on slow, creeping up on him, and regularly as clockwork, but not here. Not now. It hit him with the force of a hurricane, his body on fire and the pulsing, pounding need in his groin all that he could think of. He moaned, spreading his legs to give Dominic more room, and tilted his head back.

"Kiss me," Sawney begged. "Please. Please kiss me."

Dominic obliged, his mouth fierce and unrelenting, but seemingly no less eager than his fingers as they delved into Sawney. Spread him open, slid inside. He brought their hips together and rocked them, grinding hard and slow and deep.

Sawney cried out. His arms came up, wrapping around Dominic's neck, cradling his head, bringing his hands into contact with as much skin as he could. He dug at the offending barrier of Dominic's shorts until they fell away, and wrapped one leg around Dominic's hips to give him all the room he wanted.

Dominic's lips were darker and shiny when he tore away. "Heat?"

Sawney could only respond with a whimper, and a push toward the Alpha. Closer. He needed to be closer, to have more. Eager moisture dripped down his thighs, slick and clear.

"How about that," Dominic murmured. As easily as if Sawney weighed no more than a sack of feathers, he lifted Sawney and let him wrap both legs around his waist. "Oh, you are hot for me. You want my cock. You want me to give you a pup. To get round and full with my son growing inside you."

Sawney could only moan, too lost for speech, and too hungry to think. *Yes. Yes, I want all of that. Everything.*

Dominic eased Sawney onto the bed, coming along for the ride, and settled between his legs, pushing his fingers in. Three at least, or maybe four. Sawney couldn't tell, but they weren't enough, they weren't enough. He tried to draw them deeper, to make them thrust harder, but he couldn't.

"Ask me," Dominic muttered, his mouth busy at Sawney's neck, his chest. He stroked Sawney's stomach in fast, feverish circles, his Alpha scent as thick as smoke. "Tell me what you want."

Sawney didn't think he could. Was sure he'd gone past words, but he needed Dominic's cock in him *now* and if this was the only way..."Fuck me," he breathed. "Fill me up. Don't stop until you come."

Tendons stood out in Dominic's neck as he squeezed his eyes shut and swore, but apparently the captain could follow orders when they pleased him. Lifting both of Sawney's legs, he hooked them over his shoulders one by one, then raised Sawney's hips to rest on his knees. Sawney covered his eyes, as astonished at himself as he was eager, and pressed his heels into Dominic's back. "*Please.*"

Dominic pressed a quick, hot kiss to Sawney's knee, and slid home.

Sawney's heart pounded, beating so fast that it would have killed anyone who wasn't a shifter, wasn't an Omega. Deep liquid pulls made Sawney moan and arch beneath Dominic.

Sawney's mind knew what was happening -- his body opening, preparing for fertilization -- but his body was overwhelmed with delight.

Dominic moved inside Sawney, thrusting deep. His breath was warm and damp where he panted against Sawney's throat. "More?"

Sawney groaned in affirmation and rolled his hips. He clawed at the sheets, at whatever of Dominic's skin could be reached. *More. Yes.*

And yet more wouldn't be enough to satisfy a ripe Omega. His own orgasm surprised him, but didn't satiate him.

Sawney clutched at Dominic, begging incoherently, saying things he was glad he wouldn't remember, but knowing they needed to be given voice. Dominic's sweat dripped onto his skin as the Alpha spread his legs wider and plunged deeper, harder, faster.

He could feel it starting to happen. Canted his hips up and squeezed with his legs. Bit at Dominic's shoulder, tasting faint copper and bright salt.

Bore down, trapping Dominic's cock, and sank his nails into Dominic's legs.

"Ah, fuck!" Dominic swore, shuddering to a halt.

The Alpha ground his teeth audibly, then stroked so slowly, so deeply, that Sawney arched his neck and his back as one. Though even in his state he could feel how much the effort cost him, Dominic held still, as deeply seated as he could go. Taking Sawney's cock, still hard, he stroked slowly, working him past what he could bear, waiting until Sawney could take no more and begged him.

Dominic pressed his mouth to Sawney's thigh, groaned, and came.

Sawney's vision went supernova, filled with the flares and sparks of his blood pressure soaring, and his ears filled with static. His body drank Dominic in, ground kept dry and barren for so long that it struggled now.

Yes. Oh yes.

It might not work, Sawney remembered himself saying, as well as Dominic's reply of *We'll see*.

Shouldn't he know? Shouldn't he be able to tell? Some Omegas could, right away. As if their bodies were so attuned that they sensed fertilization long before implantation. It wasn't supposed to be possible, yet he'd heard it over and over again.

Sawney splayed his hand open wide on his stomach, closed his eyes, and held his breath. He couldn't tell. He wished, he hoped, he wanted, but...

Sawney startled when Dominic pressed a lazy kiss to his jaw and interlaced their fingers together. "You all right?"

Was he? On the whole, questions aside, Sawney thought so. Sore in the best possible way. His limbs felt heavy, languid, and his heat had receded enough to be a pleasant warmth. Glad to be distracted -- maybe it wasn't meant to be -- Sawney turned on his side and draped one leg over Dominic's hip.

"I'll take that as a yes," Dominic murmured. He caught a lock of Sawney's hair and wound it idly around his forefinger. "Friends, then? Come what may."

"Come what may," Sawney agreed. "It's a deal. Friends." He liked the way that felt.

"Good. And, Doc?"

Sawney blinked in response, a slow sweep of eyelashes, and found himself tickled into warmth in response to Dominic's cheeky smile.

"It's likely to be a couple months before I'm back this way, and I'll be leaving tomorrow." He winked. "But there's plenty of hours between now and then. Want to help me fill 'em?"

Sawney broke into a smile.

Then, instead of saying so, he showed Dominic his yes.

Chapter Three

Dominic

A couple of months? Try closer to four, nearly four and a half.

Not by intention. Dominic had planned it out before he so much as set foot on his boat the morning after leaving Sawney's bed. He'd go after blue crab, maybe do a cod run, then check back in. Should have been no trouble.

Except blue crab took longer than Dominic had planned; they were wily bastards. No time for cod before red crab, that had to wait for after. Then he had to go for snow crab, and then cod again. Days slipped past like sand through his fingers, dropped by handfuls into the Bering.

Once in a while, Dominic would find himself with a quiet moment, with his face pointed toward shore and a single thought drifting to mind. *Did it work?*

He had no idea. Sure, he could have asked but only if he wanted to kick-start the gossip chain, and he was sure Sawney would rather keep his private life private.

Safer that way. Still, not knowing nearly drove Dominic out of his mind, and the only thing that eased him was fishing.

Even now, he could have been out to sea. He'd hired a deckhand for snow crab who usually fished lobster in Maine and tuna off the Outer Banks, a genuinely crazy bobcat shifter called Painter who loved fighting, drinking, and telling whopper yarns about fucking. Half the time Dominic had wanted to dump him over the rails, but it'd be a damn shame to waste a storyteller like Painter on fish food.

Painter had offered Dominic a spot on his East Coast boats during the summer months, one good turn deserving another. Tempting. Truly tempting.

But he had to know. Before he cast another line, he had to know.

Dominic turned himself and his boat toward home.

Two solid days' travel later, and the harbor town where Sawney lived was close enough to smell. Dominic leaned into the wind and sniffed eagerly, his wolf senses catching hints of dry land. Earth, concrete, and green, and the scent of people who weren't saturated with fish-stink after months on board a ship, a blessed relief and novelty. Enraptured by the difference, Dominic leaned so far over the rail he risked losing his balance.

A solid arm tugged him back and set him safely on his feet. "Careful, Captain."

Embarrassment made Dominic gruff. He socked his first mate, Matthias, on the arm instead of saying a proper thank-you.

Luckily, Matthias was a good-natured kind of soul who captained his own ship when going after salmon, and only grinned at him before leaning companionably on the rail too. "Smells like home," he said, beatific. "I'm about ready to get there myself. It's been months since I saw Bree or the pups."

Despite himself, Dominic pricked up his ears. "Pups, plural? I thought you just had the one."

"Nope. Well, maybe," Matthias amended. "The second one's due right about now. Might be here already, but I hope I haven't missed it."

Dominic wondered if Sawney would be the one to deliver that pup. If it would leave him floating on adrenaline and bliss this time too. "You should have said. I'd have figured a way to shave a couple days off the trip. I give my fathers-to-be their fair share."

"Yeah?" Matthias arched an eyebrow. "Most don't. I'll take you up on that next time."

"Lord help, man, the second one's not even here and you're already talking about a third?"

Matthias laughed. "I promise you I'm not the only one. Bree says most Omegas are like that, and Alphas are missing out. As long as he's happy, so am I." He took a deep breath and sighed with satisfaction. "Almost there. You have someone waiting for you, don't you?"

The question took Dominic by surprise, and before he knew it he'd answered. "Yeah. Well, maybe." He snorted quietly at his unintentional echo of Matthias's words. "It's complicated," he finished, and hoped that wasn't giving away too much.

"Always is," Matthias said. He slapped Dominic on the back. "Good luck to you, Captain. If you do have someone, then good for you and about damn time."

"You're not such a fine fisherman I can't tip you overboard here and now."

"If you did, I'd just swim to shore," Matthias said with a broad grin. "Bree's my other half. Come fire or rain or snow six feet deep, I'll find my way back to him."

Looking at the man, Dominic knew that Matthias spoke the truth. He wanted to ask how, or why, but he didn't. He kept his mouth shut and his gaze fixed on the shore, willing it to come closer, faster.

He had to know.

* * *

Far too much later for his taste, though by the clock it had only been six hours, Dominic found himself nearly frozen to the path that led to Sawney's neat little home. He clutched a takeaway cup of cold coffee in one hand; he'd taken one sip and realized what a bad idea caffeine was. The word would have spread by now that he and his boat were back on shore.

Sawney would know.

The house looked dark to Dominic. No lights on. Hard to say if anyone was inside -- long residence made sure Sawney's scent permeated this bit of real estate. What if he was out on a delivery? Pups waited for no man. Could even be at Matthias and Bree's. Bree had greeted Matthias at the dock, enormously pregnant.

Dominic gnawed at the inside of his cheek, then felt a sudden surge of impatience. Like he'd said to Sawney before, neither of them were natural wafflers.

Get it done.

Bold now, he strode up the walk and directly to Sawney's door, where he knocked briskly, then set his heels and waited.

The top half of the door opened first, showing Sawney from the chest up. Dominic had forgotten about that, and could have groaned in frustration if he hadn't been knocked silent. Damn. Though he'd have thought it impossible, he'd forgotten, too, how pretty Sawney was with his chestnut hair and supple muscles. His wide eyes, even wider with surprise as he registered Dominic on his doorstep.

His lush mouth, lips parting in a smile. "Dominic?"

"Did it work?" Dominic blurted. He felt his face redden, and clamped his mouth shut.

Sawney cocked his head, his smile not fading. "Well," he said. The lower half of the door swung open and Sawney stepped back. He wore a light, thin shirt with a V collar, and there was no hiding how he'd changed. His scent was different too, richer and headier. "What do you think, Dominic?"

It'd worked. Before he registered what he was doing, Dominic had stepped forward and laid his hand on the gentle swell beneath Sawney's shirt. "Be damned," he breathed, as awed by the feel of it as he was by a nearly dizzying swell of relief. Relief? Why? He didn't know, and could only shake his head. "Look at you."

Sawney exhaled, and when Dominic looked up he saw that Sawney's eyes had fallen halfway shut. As if he felt the same odd, bone-deep relief as Dominic. He tilted forward and let his forehead rest briefly against Dominic's, the pressure a soothing counterpoint to the pounding of Dominic's heart. "It worked."

A shiver worked its way through Dominic's muscles, leaving him with the strangest sense of anticipation. He licked his lips, knowing what he wanted. What his body demanded as soon as Sawney made contact with him.

He wanted more. Skin on skin. Body on body. Consequences and strings be damned.

He might have asked for it, but for Sawney drawing back abruptly with a hand clapped over his nose and mouth. "I was going to ask where you've been, but oh, my Lord. I know where you're *going*, and right now."

Dominic couldn't help it. He guffawed. "Oh, come on. Four months at sea doesn't leave a man smelling *that* bad."

"Oh, yes, it does. I promise you. Shower. Now." Sawney stood aside, laughing behind his hand, hurrying Dominic along. "Go!"

* * *

Sawney

Sawney's heart was still pounding against his ribs as he shepherded Dominic to his bathroom, walking behind the Alpha to guide him along. He pressed a hand to his chest, wondering if Dominic's ears were keen enough to hear the rapid tattoo.

Four months. Almost five. He hadn't thought he'd see Dominic again.

And he'd been all right with that, he told himself. He had. Their arrangement was straightforward enough, and at no point had shared custody or visitation been mentioned. Sawney wouldn't say he hadn't been disappointed, but he'd accepted those terms as unspoken but understood.

Now here Dominic was again. Scruffy, disheveled, stinking so ripely of life at sea that it tickled the back of

Sawney's throat, apparently so keen to check in that he'd hit dry land running the first chance he got.

Sawney moved his hand from his chest to his face, where it felt cold against his hot cheek, and discovered he was smiling without knowing it. No, grinning. A big, boyish, delighted grin, one that shouldn't have gone well with the fire kindling in his libido -- but did, truly did.

Dominic glanced over his shoulder. "Something wrong?"

"Not at all," Sawney answered honestly. "Just through there. It's small, but there's enough room for an Alpha and his dirt."

Dominic chuffed, but then sniffed himself and grimaced. "Riper than I thought. It's hard to tell on board. Everyone smells the same after a while."

"Not out here they don't," Sawney said with a firm push to Dominic's shoulders. He chuckled to himself when Dominic saw the neat porcelain tiled stall and moaned in reaction. "Use all the hot water you want. I have a well."

"I'm kissing you later for this. Just so you know."

"Duly noted." Sawney turned his back discreetly while Dominic hurried out of his jeans and layers of flannel, all of them so stiff with salt they'd likely stand up without a person inside them. "Can I burn these?"

Dominic cranked the hot water, and groaned in bliss, but still had the wherewithal for naughtiness. He poked his head out and waggled his eyebrows. "As long as you don't mind me running around naked. I didn't bring a spare."

Sawney wouldn't have minded that at all, but he cleared his throat. "I have clothes in all sizes. I keep them for patients who need changes."

"Then I'd be obliged." Dominic shrugged and let the curtain fall shut.

And there they had it. Sawney crouched to pick up the fallen clothing, wondering at himself as he did. Amazed that it hadn't fazed him for a split second when Dominic stripped off. It must not have seemed at all odd to Dominic either. It'd just been... Comfortable. Easy.

How strange.

But that was how it often worked with Dominic. Sawney glanced down at the slowly growing curve of his belly, awed at the changes in himself. It hardly seemed real that one night -- even such a very good night -- could make such a difference. He stroked his stomach, the bump still small enough to fit against his palm, and sighed at the tingling of his body's reaction.

Did he imagine it, or did Dominic pause underneath the spray as if looking his way? He wouldn't be able to see Sawney. The curtain was a good, thick one. But perhaps, like Sawney, he had a good imagination.

"Tell me," Dominic rumbled, jolting Sawney out of his thoughts. "What it's been like for you."

Sawney didn't have to ask what he meant. "Strange," he said after a moment's thought. "Strange but good."

Dominic made an impatient noise, and Sawney chuckled.

"Sorry. It's hard to explain, though." Sawney leaned on the wall next to the shower, still stroking himself thoughtfully. "You're alone inside your skin. Then, suddenly, you're not. I was in bed, almost asleep, and I felt this sharp sting down deep. Implantation," he explained. "And there he was. I became two."

Sawney fell briefly quiet, still awed by the memory.

"And then?" Dominic prompted. The swish and patter of falling water made a soothing, almost hypnotic background to his baritone. "I missed it all."

"Through no fault of your own. I knew going into this that you were married to the sea. But if you want to know..." Impulsively, Sawney opened his shirt. He'd have to go up a size soon enough. His skin showed faint imprints from the buttons. He hissed between his teeth at how good the touch of his hand was on bare skin.

Dominic definitely paused that time. Did he catch his breath too? "I do. Tell me."

"I haven't been sick. Not once. It's so odd. Almost no one escapes that, but I've felt good. My skin is softer." Sawney drew his fingers up his side. "My hair is thicker. My joints are starting to loosen up just a bit, making room." He cupped his chest. "And here. It's so sensitive here. A breeze makes them hard." Pinching his nipples drew a low cry from the bottom of his throat. "Oh God."

He sensed, rather than saw, Dominic's lusty shudder. "More," the Alpha begged.

A light sweat from the shower steam and his own arousal made Sawney too warm. He had already given up wearing a belt, and so it wasn't hard to slide his trousers down his hips to pool on the floor, nor to step out of them. He sent his loose shorts directly after them.

Behind the curtain, Dominic stopped moving as he growled. "*More.*"

Sawney closed his eyes. This almost felt like the euphoria of assisting with birth. Maybe it wasn't so different, in its way. "Twenty-two weeks down. Eighteen weeks to go. Everyone will know, soon. They'll be able to see. I'll change by the week, by the day." He caught his teeth between his lips when he slid one hand around his cock; just as quickly, he had to let go. His libido was on a hair trigger these days. "And then..." No, he couldn't take it. "Dominic. Dominic, please."

There was a dreadful moment of silence in which Sawney thought he might have gotten this wrong. That Dominic didn't still want him.

But Dominic thrust the shower curtain back and held out a hand, his knuckles white with the strain of restraining himself, and so hard his cock jutted out before him. It made Sawney's mouth water even as his knees went weak with relief.

"Come here, Omega," he said roughly. "Now."

Chapter Four

Dominic

He'd thought Sawney looked good enough to eat before. Man, he hadn't known jack. Then again, Dominic guessed he'd probably liked vanilla wafers before he first tried chocolate.

All that smooth, pale skin of Sawney's. The curve of his abdomen. A sprinkling of dark hair on his calves and thighs and chest; his long, creamy throat. His stiff cock.

Dominic swallowed and felt it go all the way down to bottom out in his stomach. He curled his fingers. "I said come here," he ordered, hearing his voice thrum in a way it usually didn't. "I won't hurt you, but if I don't have you…"

Sawney's eyes fluttered briefly shut, giving Dominic a second's pause. Maybe it wasn't playing fair. He'd heard all the stories about hormones and how they drove pregnant Omegas twice as crazy with the need to be satisfied.

He wasn't vain enough to think Sawney needed him. Sawney was an intelligent, independent man who'd made it clear he wasn't looking for a mate. Same as Dominic wasn't, come to that.

But maybe it was playing fair after all. Dominic, as he was, might not be Sawney's mate, but he was an Alpha. He could damn well make Sawney feel good.

"Oh," Sawney said thickly. "Oh yes." He opened his eyes, took Dominic's hand, and let Dominic lead him into the shower.

Damn. Dominic groaned at the sight of Sawney under the warm, falling water, soaking it up like a seal, growing sleeker with every drop. If it'd been just a shower stall there wouldn't have been room for two full-grown men, but Sawney had the luxury of a tub and that gave Dominic space enough to back up and get a proper look at him. His groin tightened, making his cock jerk upward.

Sawney saw Dominic's reaction to that. He blushed and ducked his head.

"No, don't look away," Dominic said absently. He still had a soapy sponge in one hand, and on impulse reached out to draw it across Sawney's shoulders. Then, down his chest. Sawney's nipples already stood erect, but at the touch of sponge and soap they tightened into knots. He cried out, arching his back.

Who could say no to that? Not Dominic. He'd never had a chance at this before. Coming closer, careful not to let either of them slip, he crowded Sawney to the shower wall and bent his head to take one of those nipples between his teeth. The tissue beneath seemed fuller and softer, swollen yet yielding, and the skin tasted faintly of sweetness.

Fascinated, he drew the nub deeper, cheeks hollowing as he sucked.

Sawney moaned and dug his fingers into Dominic's hair. His hips moved in abbreviated half thrusts. "*Please.*"

Dominic let go with a twinge of regret, but only for a second. So Sawney liked sucking, hmm?

As Sawney watched him with huge, luminous eyes, Dominic went to his knees and guided the Omega's thighs apart. "This all right?" he asked, stroking the soft inner skin. "Say so, or say no."

Sawney whimpered, a faint cry like a puppy's bark, and nodded. "Please."

Dominic bent closer and breathed in the scent of the Omega's skin. It was different here, too, earthy in an unfamiliar but wholly luscious way. He had to nuzzle in beneath the new fullness of Sawney's stomach but he was a flexible man, and he could reach. He took Sawney's cockhead almost delicately between his lips and sealed them tight.

Above him, Sawney groaned and threw his head back. His fingers tightened in Dominic's hair.

He liked sucking, indeed. Dominic grinned wickedly to himself, and slid his mouth slowly, luxuriously, down the length of Sawney's shaft, not stopping until wiry hair tickled his nose. He breathed in through his nose and laved Sawney with the flat of his tongue, feeling him grow harder, longer, and only pulled off to get another look at Sawney's face.

Well worth the effort. His eyes were closed, and he rolled his head against the hard tiles in a desperate wave of sensation.

Dominic knew how he felt. His cock throbbed insistently, demanding attention, but that in itself was a sweet kind of torture, and Dominic wanted to enjoy it. It jerked, thrusting against the air, and released two, three drops that fell hot on his thigh.

He hollowed his cheeks and drew Sawney in, not playing now, and the reward was worth the effort. Sawney let out a wild shout and drew his nails against Dominic's scalp, a fierce sting that felt good in the heat of the moment. He rocked his hips harder, straining to get Dominic to take more in, but then stopped with a ragged groan of frustration.

"It's not enough," he panted when Dominic looked the question up at him. He grimaced down at Dominic. "It's -- almost, almost, but it's out of reach, and I can't --"

Dominic leaned forward to bite at Sawney's thigh. "Hush, then. I'll see you there."

Sawney shook his head, trembling with the energy it took to hover on the edge of coming, and pulled at Dominic's hair. "Please. Please, please."

Dominic shushed him with another bite to his soft inner thigh. "Pinch your nipples. Hard. Twist them."

"I can't."

"You can." He took Sawney into his mouth again, and that was good. He could taste Sawney's salty pre-cum on his tongue, swallowing it down, but he could feel the quaking in Sawney's muscles. He surged up as he tormented his nipples himself, coming closer but not close enough. Hard, so hard. He must have ached almost beyond bearing.

And that was good, but not good enough. An idea occurred, but Dominic wasn't sure. Would it be safe?

He'd have to trust Sawney to stop him if it wasn't. Mouth still full of cock, eyes closed, Dominic let his body guide him. One hand between Sawney's legs, tracing the path behind his tightly-drawn balls to the cleft of his ass.

Sawney keened, choppy with his struggle for breath, and then went utterly still.

Almost. Dominic unfurled his fingers and slid one, just one, up inside the Omega. He curled it, and pressed hard. Scratched ever so lightly. Then let Sawney feel the edge of his teeth.

And -- *there*, oh hell yes, *there*. Sawney's back curved into a tightly drawn bow, his stomach hard and thighs stiff as boards, loosing a wild thing's scream as he came. Dominic's hips jerked hard and he followed, as stunned as he was mad with the sweet relief. He caught himself in one hand and shuddered through it, panting hot against Sawney's thigh.

God, he loved his Omega. *His* Omega, full of *his* child… *His.*

Mine.

Water pattered down around Dominic, barely noticeable behind the shocked quiet that filled his head.

Wait.

Loved? His Omega?

Oh, hell. Dominic dropped back onto his heels, every bit of his skin prickling. Lord love a duck and save an old sea captain from a sudden heart attack, possibly literally.

What was he supposed to do with that bit of insight?

* * *

Sawney

Still wet, towels wrapped around them, Sawney led Dominic to his bed. Seemed like the place to be after a ground breaking epiphany like that, and if nothing else then lying down together was the safest way not to fall.

Again, that was.

Sawney lay on his back, propped by the quarter-mountain of pillows he'd taken to using lately, while Dominic sprawled on his side with his head resting on Sawney's chest. Their legs tangled together as Sawney sifted his fingers through Dominic's drying hair. He had a few threads of silver in his thick mane, Sawney discovered.

He'd turned his face away, and his body language said little. Sawney let his fingertips glide along Dominic's scalp as he worked up his courage to speak first. "Dominic?"

"Hmm," Dominic rumbled. He rubbed his thumb along the crease of Sawney's thigh.

Sawney swallowed. Even so small a touch made his skin tingle in a way it never had before. "What are you thinking about right now?"

Dominic chuffed. "Never had anyone ask me that before. I thought it was just in stories." He pressed his lips lightly -- but distractedly -- over Sawney's breastbone. "I'm thinking about something that needs more thinking time."

Sawney understood what he meant, every syllable of it down to his bones, but it wasn't good enough. He tugged lightly at a lock of Dominic's hair to make sure he was listening. "Is it what I'm thinking about too?"

Dominic exhaled, then turned his head to look up at Sawney's face. "Maybe so." He stretched one leg across both of Sawney's, and stroked his stomach. "I don't know, but maybe so. You hear stories from other Alphas about what it's like, but until it's you…"

"You hear stories from other Omegas, but until it's you," Sawney agreed.

He knew he should tell Dominic to stop touching. They'd be right back in the same fix if he didn't. But Sawney couldn't bear to. He found himself stroking the back of Dominic's neck, tickling up the short hairs and smoothing them down. "It isn't what we planned."

"No."

"What should we do?"

Silence answered him, but Sawney had no idea what to say to fill it any more than Dominic did. He could see the conflict, the struggle in Dominic, and it was an exact match to what Sawney felt inside his heart.

He touched his tongue to his lips and lay his head back, drawing Dominic slightly higher up his body so he could draw his fingertips across Dominic's shoulder blades. "Tell me what you love about the sea."

"Say again?" Dominic raised his head.

Sawney coaxed Dominic back down. "Tell me," he insisted. "I want to hear you talk about what you love."

Dominic made a *huh* noise, but the answer was already on his tongue, warm with his breath. "The sea can't be tamed. Can't be mastered. The Bering takes on all comers, and you can give it your best shot, but there's no victory guaranteed." His breath quickened as he spoke. It was the truth, then.

"I love how you never know what's coming," Dominic went on, raising himself on one elbow. "You think you know, but you don't." He stroked Sawney's thigh as he spoke, making Sawney's toes curl. "The Bering's a beautiful beast, as wild as all hell, as fierce as the devil, and sometimes as generous as a birthparent. I feel alive when I'm out there."

Sawney closed his eyes and shuddered with a rush of sensation. He was getting hard again. Dominic, too. He could feel the Alpha's cock against his leg.

Sawney cleared his throat before he spoke, but his voice still came out in a husky whisper. "Now ask me what I love about being a doctor."

"What do you love about being a doctor?" Dominic murmured, lowering his mouth -- deliberately this time -- to Sawney's collarbone.

Sawney hissed at the sensation of Dominic's teeth lightly scraping over his sensitized skin. "Oh. I -- It's the same."

"How?"

His brain wasn't working right, too torn between arousal and reluctance for coherent thought, but Sawney gave it his best shot. "It's a fight to be won. Always. No matter how well prepared, how educated, bodies and the way they work are so different. What you think you know is mostly wrong, and you adapt as you go. You fight, tooth and nail."

"Every victory's true," Dominic said, his lips at Sawney's throat now. "There's no games or second guessing."

"The losses devastate you."

"And yet you come back for more, and more, and more," Dominic rumbled. "You're either addicted or you were made for this, and sometimes you don't know which."

Sawney exhaled a long breath. "Yes." His eyes drifted open as Dominic moved. The Alpha lifted up so that he could look down at Sawney, and Sawney couldn't help but lift his hand to brush Dominic's cheek. "It wasn't supposed to be like this."

"Maybe we should have known better." Dominic leaned into Sawney's touch. He was so hard. His cock rutted against Sawney's thigh, grazing Sawney's erection with every other stroke. "Would you have done it anyway?"

Sawney couldn't answer that. But he could ask something else. "Is it enough?"

"You tell me." Dominic reached between them and captured both their cocks in one hand, squeezing them together, his gaze darkening when Sawney cried out in a mix of ecstasy and agony. "Too much?"

"Yes. Don't stop. It's like I've been skinned, and it's all growing back new." Sawney found Dominic's hips and cupped a double handful of his ass, squeezing. "What do we do?"

"I don't know," Dominic admitted. Then, he stopped and shook his head abruptly. "No, damn it, I do. We're not ones to dance around."

Sawney's pulse kicked into high gear. "Don't make promises you'll regret."

"You don't want those kind of promises from me?"

"I want them too much," Sawney admitted. "But would that be the right choice for us? Would it be wise? Would taking another big risk make us happy? Am I thinking with my body and not my mind?"

"One and the same if you ask me." Dominic rolled his hips, grinding their bodies together. "Sawney --"

He was going to ask. Sawney knew it, just as he knew what his answer would be in the heat of the moment, no matter what his doubts.

They barely knew each other.

That didn't stop you or Dominic from making a pup together.

This wasn't what they'd agreed on.

When did life ever go according to plan?

What if it didn't last?

But what if it does?

Dominic had moved fully over Sawney now, his mouth hot on Sawney's neck and his hand stroking with exquisite slowness. "Sawney…"

Sawney caught his breath.

Dominic opened his mouth to speak, but whatever he might have said was lost to the frantic, fierce pounding on the door that startled them apart.

* * *

Dominic

"Shit," Dominic groaned, as heartfelt a curse as he'd ever produced. He collapsed downward, landing across Sawney's chest.

Or at least that'd been the idea. By the time he touched down, Sawney had already popped up as if he had springs in his ass. Legs over the side of the bed, hands busy tying his hair up and back somehow in a bun that tucked into itself.

"One minute," Sawney called.

Dominic boggled at him. All business without a trace of the conflicted lover he'd been just seconds ago. If he hadn't had the same face, Dominic wouldn't have thought he was the same man.

"Doc? You there?" a man called from the outside. His scent was strong, clearly Alpha, clearly wound up tighter than a two-dollar clock. "Doc!"

Sawney elbowed Dominic in the ribs, then stood to whip a fresh set of scrubs off a shelf above his bed. He tossed a set to Dominic, then bundled every stitch of bedding off the mattress and snagged a fresh fitted sheet that he tossed on the bed like a pizza before tucking in the corners. It all happened so fast Dominic could barely track it.

"Get dressed," Sawney hissed. Then, louder: "Who's there?"

A moan answered him, this one just as definitely Omega and distressed. Sawney's eyes opened wide, but for all that he didn't panic, and he didn't visibly rush. He dressed himself faster than Dominic had ever seen, his limbs covered as quick as lightning. Dominic could only hurry to keep up, but he knew he looked as if he'd been dragged backward through a hedge while Sawney looked as cool and polished as a diamond.

"It's Matthias," the Alpha finally called back. "And Bree."

Sawney muttered a choice word under his breath, checked himself once in the mirror, and didn't look back at Dominic as he made for the door. Dominic, on the other hand, pressed a hand to his forehead and groaned. So much for secrets.

Dominic mentally gave himself a firm boot up the ass. This wasn't about him. He got to his feet and had his Captain's face on by the time the door opened.

Matthias it was indeed, with his pregnant mate in a bridal carry, the Omega's ridiculously long legs drawn up. Bree moaned again and pressed his face to Matthias's neck. Matthias had gone tomato-red in the face, and anyone could see he was frantic with worry. "We were on our way home," he said. He paused briefly to gape at Dominic, then shook his head hard and looked to Sawney. "And then..."

"And then," Sawney said. He addressed Bree directly. "How close together?"

Whatever held Bree in its grip eased. "Not long," he said. "I'm not -- I can't tell."

"Well, this is your second. They usually go faster." With a nudge here and a hand there, Sawney guided Matthias into letting Bree down. "Can you walk? Good. Come over to the bed."

Unaccustomed adrenaline made Dominic jittery. He rushed the double armful of used bedding into

Sawney's washing machine, but doctor and patient hadn't made it halfway across the room by the time he got back. Matthias hovered, hands raised helplessly, looking as rattled as Dominic felt.

"I wanted it to be born at home, like the last one," Bree protested before groaning.

"Men make plans, but life usually has other ideas." Sawney smoothed Bree's tangled red hair back, guiding him toward the bed one step at a time. He didn't look at Dominic as he spoke. "Out. You and Matthias both."

Dominic's jaw dropped, but Matthias was the first to speak. "I want to be in the room. I missed the first one."

"I need to get Bree settled first, and then I'll call you." Sawney looked over his shoulder. "Dominic, take him outside. Now. This is Omega business. Would you let a greenhorn drive a boat?" He managed to deposit Bree on the bed. "Go."

* * *

Somehow -- and it wasn't easy, Matthias put up a fight -- Dominic got him outside Sawney's house with the door safely shut between the Alphas and the Omegas. He blocked it with his body when Matthias would have tried to rush back in. "Let Doc do his thing. We'd just get in the way."

"I have to be in there."

Dominic pushed him back. "If Doc said he'll call you, then he'll call you. Stand still and catch your breath. I don't think it happens as quick as all that."

Matthias growled but made a visible effort to let go of his fight. "So. You and the Doc?"

Dominic raised one shoulder.

"Huh," Matthias said. He clearly didn't have the focus to spare and returned to his original point of obsession. "At least let me put my ear to the door."

"Long as you don't try and knock it down." Dominic stood on the knob side, just in case, and eyed Matthias from top to toe. "Thought you'd already be in your home by now."

Matthias shook his head. His face darkened, but with rue. "Fire while I was away. House isn't livable right now. Bree didn't send word because he didn't want me distracted out there."

"Damn."

Matthias rubbed at his forehead. "It is what it is. Bree's been staying with a friend. I was walking around town looking for temporary lodging. Someplace better for Bree and the pups before I go back out to sea."

Dominic frowned. "You need to be with Bree after this. I can give you some vacation time."

"Don't do that. I have to go." Matthias ran a frustrated hand through his hair, setting it on end. "It'll take every cent I've earned this year to fix the place up, and pups are a blessing but they cost, Dominic. They cost so much." He'd nearly plastered his head to the door, straining to hear. "We'll make it work somehow, but…"

A scrap of memory floated through Dominic's head. "Painter made me an offer," he said slowly. "For the summer months, a share in his boat while they're fishing lobster and tuna."

Matthias's head came up. A job like that paid well if they had a good season, and both of them knew it. "How long?"

"Four months," Dominic said. "Maybe five."

"I --" Matthias looked desperately torn.

Hell. Dominic's tough old heart twinged for him. Talk about a rock and a hard place. He rubbed his jaw, his stubble rasping against his palm.

There was a way to solve this problem. Less than a day ago, he'd have taken it without a qualm. He'd said it himself, hadn't he? He owed Matthias, and as the captain he was the one responsible for the man's welfare. By extension, his family's.

He could take the job himself, as Matthias's proxy. Send sixty percent of the money home. It'd see their house fixed and their pups provided for.

But he'd be away for half a year. There'd be a continent plus change's distance between himself and Sawney. He'd likely miss the birth of his own pup, and as for the rest of it, for what he and Sawney had almost become just now...

The door flew open and Sawney stuck his head out. He grabbed Matthias by the arm and nearly yanked him off his feet. "If you want to be there when it happens, hurry!"

With the Alpha tumbling behind him, Sawney disappeared back inside.

Whether by accident or design, he'd left the door open wide enough for Dominic to look inside if he chose to. And maybe it was a hell of an intrusion, but once Dominic glanced at the scene he couldn't have peeled himself away with a lever.

"God almighty," he breathed, rapt.

It wasn't Bree he watched, nor Matthias either, though there was a hell of a lot of action going on at that end. No, it was Sawney he couldn't look away from. Sawney looked as alive as Dominic had ever felt while riding the sea, fierce and joyous.

It was a thing of beauty. Something no one should strike asunder.

All right, then, Dominic thought. *No qualms to be had here after all.* Their mutual independence and passion for their work was the reason why they'd made their arrangement in the first place, wasn't it? Neither of them were free. Dominic belonged to the sea and his sailors, and Sawney to his craft and his patients.

He knew what he had to do.

Best get it done, and quick, before it's too hard. Don't think.

His back straight, his face guarded, howling inside at the loss of what could have been, Dominic walked away.

Chapter Five

Sawney

"Not long now, is it?"

"Hmm?" Sawney blinked out of the light daze he'd fallen into. Seemed to happen more and more often these days, and it got harder to snap himself out of it.

You hear stories, but until it's you...

Fortunately for him, Bree was the patient sort when it came to the foibles of pregnant Omegas. Experience, Sawney supposed. He crinkled his nose at Sawney, then reached out to snag the wolf puppy running around them in excited circles in the grass outside Sawney's house. Unseasonably warm, if not terribly sunny, it was the kind of long afternoon normally to be savored. "It won't be long now for you, am I right?"

Sawney looked down to his hand and what it rested on. He couldn't remember the last time he'd seen his feet. "I hope not," he said with deep fervency, making Bree laugh.

Actually, according to his dates -- and there was no chance he'd forget those -- it should be within the week. He didn't tell Bree that, though they'd become good friends in the nearly four months since Bree's youngest was born.

Since Dominic headed for the hills. The sea.

Sawney's gaze drifted sideways, toward the path that ran by his house, the one Dominic had always taken whether coming or going. He'd fallen into that habit, too, and couldn't seem to break it. It was as if some part of his mind insisted Dominic would come back.

Oh, he knew by now why Dominic had left. He even understood it -- logically speaking -- and besides that, it'd been kindness itself for Dominic to work for Matthias by proxy. It'd given Matthias the money to fix his damaged house, and time to spend with his family.

And yet. And yet. And yet.

Sawney shook his head to clear it, and opened his arms just in time to catch the wiggling wolf puppy as it escaped Bree. "You're very cute," he told the little wolf, who in his human shape was a toddler with a shock of red hair and a gap between his two front baby teeth. "Now behave."

"Babies have selective deafness when it comes to that word," Bree observed. He stood and gave Sawney a hand up, though at this point in the game it was more like two hands and a heck of a lot of pulling.

Bree's son thought it was hilarious.

With that done, Bree bent to scoop up his infant, too young to shift shape, and secured it in a sling. "Are you sure you don't want me to stay the night? You're so close."

"No. I'm too restless to settle, and I'd drive you crazy. Besides, those two need you."

Bree rubbed the soft puppy fur between his son's lopsided ears and laughed when he barked. "They're a handful, all right. Just call me if you need anything, all right? Anything at all."

To please him, Sawney drew an obedient X over his heart, then stood and watched Bree shepherd his small brood away until they disappeared around a bend in the road. Only then did he let himself blow out a breath of relief. Normally he enjoyed Bree's company -- Bree had expressed an interest in getting his LPN certification, and wouldn't that come in handy -- but he'd told the truth. He was as restless as if he had ants in his shoes, and couldn't settle for a hot second.

He took one last look at the road, clicked his tongue with impatience at himself, and stalked into his house.

Though once he was inside, Sawney had to admit this wasn't any better. When he'd bought the place, its diminutive size had seemed just right for a single doctor.

Bed, kitchen, bathroom; a window with a view of the glacier; what more could he have wanted?

Space. Lots of space.

Every inch of the place was packed to the brim. Sawney could sympathize. He wandered for a moment, running a hand over the crib and changing table and layette, all handmade by patients who'd banded together to surprise him. Everything was ready, everything set up to go at a moment's notice. Nothing for him to do. Not even any patients to see. No one to talk to, even if he'd been able to concentrate on a conversation.

And he was so damned horny.

Sawney pressed one palm to his face and growled in annoyance. Now that he could barely reach, his body had taken to clamoring for attention. Some Omegas had trouble with this, some didn't. Looked like he'd won the lottery. His skin was so sensitive a mere brush of cloth brought goosebumps, and if the wind blew the wrong way he'd end up achingly hard.

He drifted to the nest he'd arranged under his window view, a soft chair mounded with blankets to fit his kinks just right.

There was too much cloud cover to properly see the glacier. Figured.

Unthinking, Sawney let his hand fall to the top of his thigh. How good such a simple touch felt. It drew a light sweat from his skin and a simmering warmth that pooled between his legs. From there it was only natural to palm his cock, a light touch, feeling it grow eagerly stiff. He bit his lip and moaned, then closed his eyes and squeezed tighter.

Good. Oh, so good.

His breathing quickened as he drew his nails gently down the inside of his leg, imagining the prickle was that of stubble. *Dominic.* He hesitated, then impatiently twitched his scruples aside. Why shouldn't he think of

Dominic when he did this? Dominic was the cause of this current sensitivity, after all.

Fully hard now, his cock filled his palm as slow, lazy ripples of pleasure washed through his blood. He slipped a hand beneath his shirt to cup his breast, to draw his nails across the nipple, catching his breath at the memory of Dominic's discovering them.

And yet. It wasn't enough.

He needed Dominic inside him. Needed Dominic to fuck him, hard and fast and ruthless, to drive an orgasm four months denied out of him. He ached, needing to be filled. His fingers wouldn't be nearly enough. He might come, but he wouldn't be satisfied.

Frustrated, Sawney let go. Dominic wouldn't be coming back. They'd made their agreement, and the Alpha had stuck to it. He was only punishing himself with wishful thinking. Would he want Dominic for more than the satisfaction of his hormones, if he did come around?

Yes. Oh yes.

Dejected, Sawney opened his eyes.

Then popped to his feet faster than he had in months, catching his elbow on the windowsill and clapping a hand to his chest lest his heart pound free of his ribs. Was he seeing things, or was this real?

"You?" he breathed. "What are you doing here?"

* * *

Dominic

Everything Dominic had meant to say disappeared in an instant, leaving him with his mouth open and his feet rooted to the ground.

Look at you, he thought in astonishment. *You're the size of a --*

His hindbrain, concerned with matters of survival, choked the rest of that sentence into silence. He closed his mouth, but for all that he couldn't stop staring. Sawney's legs and arms were as slim as they'd ever been, but as for the rest?

Sawney's mouth quirked briefly. "You don't have to say it. I know. I look like I've swallowed a cannonball."

"Two," Dominic's traitor mouth answered for him. He grimaced and waved that aside. "No, that's not what I wanted to say. You look…"

Fierce. Fecund. Beautiful.

He shook his head in silence. How could he say any of that and have it come out sounding real? Even if he would have truly meant every word. "You look healthy," he said at last, his voice hoarse even to himself. He could taste interrupted arousal, familiar and spicy, on the back of his tongue. "Damn, Sawney. You look good."

"Thank you. You don't smell like four months on a boat this time."

"I showered before I came." Sawney seemed wary, for which Dominic couldn't blame him. He wrapped his arms around himself. "What are you doing here?"

Dominic ducked his head, studying his feet. He'd wrestled with that selfsame question for miles over land and water, and he still didn't have any answer but the truth. He ran a hand over his thick stubble and looked up. "I couldn't stay away."

Sawney made the tiniest movement, one Dominic couldn't interpret. "You seem to have managed so far."

"By the skin of my teeth. Can I sit?"

He could tell Sawney was considering saying no, but after a brief struggle the Omega sighed and gestured to a low ottoman that hadn't been there before, close enough to the window nest that neither of them would have to shout. Dominic crouched on the edge of the firmly padded thing and laced his hands loosely between his knees.

"I tried," Dominic said baldly, looking up. The sight of Sawney was like water in the desert to him. He couldn't stop drinking him in with thirsty gulps. "I tried my damnedest."

"Thanks."

"That's not what I meant either." Dominic rubbed his forehead. "I was trying to honor our arrangement."

"A few things changed, between then and now."

"And don't I know it." Dominic ached to touch, to run his palms over Sawney's smooth skin. "I called myself a fool half a dozen times before I left the path. Every day. I almost turned the boat around when I sailed off. Figured you'd be pretty pissed at me by that point, though, and I couldn't blame you."

Sawney frowned as he rubbed absently at his back. "I wasn't angry."

Dominic raised an eyebrow. "Sure you weren't."

"Maybe a little." Sawney kneaded his back a little harder, then sighed as he apparently hit the right spot, and relaxed. "I could have throttled you those first couple of weeks. Then..." He shook his head. "I don't know. I tried."

Had he, then? Dominic sat up straighter, wondering if he should test his luck, not able to resist it. "It's like a pull," he said. "Waking, sleeping, it makes no difference. It's just this tug that winds you tighter and won't let go. Everything else pales and fades away."

"Same here." Sawney studied him. "It's like that for Alphas too?"

"It was for this one." Dominic couldn't hold out any longer. He held one hand out, only arresting his movement at the last second when Sawney drew in a sharp breath. "I've got no right to ask, Sawney, but can I touch?"

Sawney weighed that for a moment before tilting his head to the side. "If you answer me one question."

"Ask it," Dominic said.

"I've thought of you more than I have of medicine these past few months. Did you think of me more than the sea?"

Dominic exhaled long and slow. "Every damn day, Sawney. From dawn till dusk, you were all that was in my head."

"That," Sawney said, "was the right answer." He raised his arms away from his body. "We'll talk about this later, using real and actual words, and we'll get everything settled. But for right now -- touch me, Dominic. Put your hands on me, and don't you dare stop. All right?"

"Damn, Omega. That's a promise. And the way you got under my skin? I won't be stopping any time soon." Giddy relief made Dominic feel lighter than air. He stood and took Sawney by the wrists, finding him heavier and more awkward to maneuver, but no less pleasant to touch.

Dominic pressed his palm to the curve of Sawney's stomach and felt a sense of peace seep into his bones. The restless itch that'd driven him for months ceased so abruptly it was dizzying, and from Sawney's sigh he thought it must have been mutual. He had to press his mouth to the soft spot between Sawney's neck and shoulder then, and take hold of Sawney's hips with an eagerness that made him clumsy.

"Oh, that's better," Sawney murmured. He laid his arms around Dominic's neck, giving him all the room he wanted to touch, and rested his head on Dominic's shoulder. He shifted his hips restlessly, his scent growing abruptly stronger. "Don't stop."

"I won't. Swear I won't."

It was an addiction, Dominic discovered, the way Sawney felt moving against him. The warm dampness of his skin, the way he parted his lips to let Dominic inside.

He pressed their bodies hard together, frustrated by how they didn't fit so well anymore, but at the same time wild to catalogue every change with his lips, his hands, his cock.

"You're the best thing I ever saw," Dominic said between deep, harsh breaths. He pushed Sawney's shirt up to take a nipple in his mouth, between his teeth -- to stroke every inch of new skin with greedy hunger. Sawney's stomach was hard, solid. Dominic had thought it would be soft or maybe squishy like a balloon, but that great mound was as tight as muscle.

And his hips. Those had changed, gotten wider, his movements seeming somehow more fluid. Still firm, though, yielding only to his kneading.

Sawney panted, light and shallow, his hands as busy as Dominic's. They were everywhere, sharp nails at his back, and his kisses full of bite. "And you," he said, gasping. "And you."

Dominic needed to be closer. Was it safe? He didn't know. Sawney would tell him, if it wasn't. He slid his fingers between the cleft of Sawney's ass and pressed against his entrance, highly gratified by Sawney's jerk and moan.

"More?"

"More," Sawney demanded, pushing into Dominic's touch. "Keep saying it."

Dominic wet his lips, tasting both of them, and traced a path from ass to hip to groin, finding Sawney hard enough to drive nails and creamy-wet. "I smelled you when I came in. Were you thinking about this?"

"Always. I couldn't stop."

"Me neither." Dominic felt Sawney's cock pulse in his palm. "Damn, you're close, aren't you?"

"In all ways." Sawney tried to raise one leg to hook around Dominic's hip, but he needed help, and he groaned when Dominic had to take his hand away to assist. He shuddered once, a wracking thing that seemed to vibrate in his very bones. "I can't get there on my own."

Dominic drew back to drink his fill of Sawney, shaking to pieces in his arms, wild for him. No wilder than he felt for Sawney, though, and had since the moment he'd walked away.

If it wasn't too late, he wouldn't turn his back again.

"You're mine," he said, taking Sawney's cock and not being gentle this time. "And I'm yours. You're the only thing I ever cared about more than the sea. *You.* You're the work of my lifetime."

Sawney came with a gasp, soaking Dominic's sleeve halfway up his forearm, but Dominic barely noticed. Sawney's quick, clever hand was on him, and somehow he kept his head together. Not that it took much; he'd been so long without that just the brush of skin on skin undid him. He drew his teeth across Sawney's shoulder as he fucked into Sawney's fist, ungentle and fierce.

They clung together, each breathing as hard as the other, the solid proof of their bond wedged between them.

"We'll talk," Dominic promised as soon as he could speak. "Talk until it's all settled. We've got time."

Sawney made no reply. Was he listening? Dominic couldn't be sure, but somehow he didn't think so. Sawney's fingers dug into his arms too sharply, and he'd gone too still.

"What?" Dominic shook him gently to try and rouse him. "Sawney, you in there?"

Sawney answered with a groan.

* * *

Sawney

Sawney tapped Dominic's shoulder to say *give me a minute*, then knotted his fists in Dominic's heavy flannel shirt and breathed.

He pinpointed the second that Dominic figured it out. The big Alpha flinched, then went still as a stone. After a beat, he cleared his throat and hesitantly put his arms around Sawney to help balance him. "Is this the orchestra warming up, or is this the real deal?"

"Showtime," Sawney said as soon as he could talk and stand. They were soaked with more than spunk and sweat, but a surprised Alpha wouldn't recognize that right away. "Curtain on the rise in a few hours, give or take."

He patted Dominic's chest absently. The restlessness and excitability made sense now. How many times had he seen Omegas acting the same way and thought *Ahhaa, I know what's happening*.

The things you never knew until it was you.

Over him, Dominic's jaw worked with a slight clicking sound, rousing Sawney's curiosity and a slight sense of worry. "Problem?"

"Mmm." Dominic didn't let go. "Trying to figure out if I could have timed this better if I'd tried, or if I could have timed it worse, and my hand to God I don't know which it is."

Sawney laughed and butted his head to Dominic's chest. "All of the above." When Dominic started to move away, he snagged a double handful of Dominic's shirt and dug in. "Don't leave me, okay?"

"Wasn't planning on it. Just needed to find my phone."

"No need." Sawney's head had cleared well enough to think. "I'm doing this myself." He didn't have to look up to be certain Dominic's jaw had dropped, and poked him in the ribs to get him to focus. "I know what I'm doing. I've delivered over a hundred pups."

"Yeah, but…"

"Even if I wasn't willing, there isn't another doctor within a day's hard travel."

"Wanna bet?" Dominic shot back, but Sawney could feel him coming to grips with the deal set before him. "Omegas can do that on their own? Really?"

"And have been since the world began, I promise."

Sawney had to cling to him again, and it was some few minutes until they were both in a mood to talk. By then he'd allowed Dominic to guide him back to his nest by the window, and to scrounge up a cool cloth for his hot face. "So," he said, as intent on his work as if he'd been building bombs, "I'm allowed to stay this time?"

He was teasing, Sawney knew, but despite that he caught Dominic's wrist and squeezed. "Yes. It's your right. And -- and it's what I want. You can't leave me now, Dominic. Swear it."

"Hand to my heart, I won't." Dominic started to dab the back of Sawney's neck, then stopped and dropped the cloth, seeming not to hear Sawney's surprised yelp as it tumbled behind his collar. He hunkered down to make direct eye contact. "Doc. Do you love me?"

"What?" Sawney took him by the collar and yanked. "What did you think all this was about?"

"Say it plain, Sawney." He grimaced, giving Sawney a glimpse of an uncertainty that melted the last crumbs of resistance. "Just so I'm sure."

Sawney might have given the collar an extra little twist, but only incidentally. He lifted his hand to cup Dominic's cheek. "I didn't expect to -- at all -- but yes, I love you." And because they were a fine pair, himself and Dominic, he bit the inside of his cheek before asking, "Do you love me?"

Dominic's eyes crinkled at the corners. "I'm not leaving. What's that tell you?" He noticed the sodden state of his jeans for the first time and went faintly green. "Though I may throw up at some point."

"Permission granted." He lifted his face for Dominic's kiss, given freely despite his nerves, a sweet kiss that deepened and grew hot, silky, sweet...

Only for a while, of course. But they could get back to the game later, and Sawney was sure of that now. He let go with a ragged breath. "Help me walk?"

"As long as you promise to be all right at the end of this." Dominic, so strong, lifted Sawney as easily as a packet of feathers, and set him gently on his feet. "I never thought I'd fall in love, and I won't lose you. Deal?"

Love. Sawney savored the word. That, above all else, would give an Omega strength. He pressed a haphazard kiss to Dominic's jaw, a promise for later. "You've got yourself a deal, Alpha. Let's do this, but fair warning. It might not be *too* many hours at that."

* * *

And, as such things went, it wasn't that many hours at all. Twelve-odd, average for a first-timer, and the rush of euphoria was so much stronger on this end that Sawney marveled at how anyone survived either side of the coin.

He strongly suspected Dominic had no idea either, but when he got in there at the big finish, he could see what the bliss looked like on another man's face, and that was good enough for him.

"Damn," Dominic whispered, eyes wider than saucers. "Holy damn, man."

"You're telling me," Sawney murmured. "Still love me?"

He closed his eyes when Dominic kissed the top of his head. "More than. Don't you ever ask it again."

Oh yes. More than good enough. Sawney kept his eyes closed, savoring the warmth of those words.

Love.

Epilogue

When he opened his eyes again, Sawney discovered that more hours must have passed. The light had changed, going from yellow-pink dawn to the blazing blue of midday.

He didn't speak at first, much preferring to watch Dominic. The big Alpha had done surprisingly well from what he could see, swaddling their clean smelling pup in several lengths of towel, holding him to his chest as he loitered in Sawney's doorway to show him the world.

"Job well done," he said when Dominic glanced his way, and was rewarded by a broad grin.

"Well done yourself," Dominic said affably. "You're never, ever doing that again, by the way. Just so you know."

Sawney laughed. He'd heard those words so many times. Usually about a year before the same Alphas came knocking on his door, frantic in the middle of the night. To his credit, Dominic rolled his eyes and grinned ruefully at himself, then padded toward him to lay the pup at his side. "You ought to have mentioned how heavy he was. Feels about equal to a king crab."

"Solid little thing," Sawney agreed sleepily, though he knew he wouldn't drowse off again for a while. He tickled the pup's nose -- this young, there was no telling which parent he'd look more like -- and tucked a hand under his cheek. "What do we do now, Dominic? What are our plans?"

"Rest. Healing. Maybe eating."

"You know what I mean," Sawney chided.

Dominic gave an expressive shrug, but sat on the edge of the bed and laid his hand over the pup's chest, as if too fascinated to stay away for more than a moment. "Well," he said after due consideration, "I always had a fancy to build ships."

Relief made Sawney dizzy enough to laugh, and to sock Dominic on the knee. "No you didn't."

"Hey, I could," Dominic said with another grin. "It's a thought. Or I might invest in Painter's tuna boats. Send out some proxies of my own."

Sawney covered Dominic's hand with his own. "I don't want you to turn your back on something you love."

"I'm not. That's the whole point."

The plainness of his speech wrapped around Sawney in an embrace. And if Dominic could give, then so could he. "Maybe short trips," he suggested. "Until the pup's old enough to swim. And I'll put the word out that I could use a colleague up here, to lighten my load."

Dominic gave up on trying to keep any sort of distance, and laid himself carefully down on Sawney's other side. He studied Sawney for a long, long moment, his smile never fading once. "It's the last thing I expected," he said at last, "And the most confusing. Damn me if it's not what I wanted most, though." He took Sawney's hand. "One more time for the form of it, Doc. Want to make a new arrangement?"

Sawney could feel the brilliance of his own grin as he stretched up for one more kiss. *Until it was you. And it was him, this time, at last.* "Captain," he said, tugging Dominic closer, "I think I do."

Fun and Games
Will Okati

Captaining a fishing boat's long, hard work, and when Sullivan brings his catch to the fishmongers he has his mind set on a strong ale and a hot meal in a quiet, family establishment where he's not likely to lose his wallet or his life.

The Fisherman's Friend looks like just the place, but once Sullivan sets his gaze on Ari, he knows he's found a lot more than he was looking for -- and exactly what he needs. For there's no scent on earth quite as alluring to an Alpha male as that of an Omega in heat.

Fun and Games

Sullivan

With the last of the catch unloaded and his deckhands paid, Sullivan took the opportunity to stretch until his back creaked. An Alpha wolf like him did get awfully cramped on board a ship. Hungry, too, with several appetites he wanted satisfied. He cast a thoughtful glance along the docks. Not much there. A roughneck bar and a general supply that charged three hundred percent on the dollar.

No classy, upscale establishments fit for fine folks. No fine folks around to take advantage of them, for one thing, which was just as Sullivan liked it. But a few streets back, good watering holes fit for hungry sailors on shore leave just waited to be found. Places where a man might go of an evening to find companionship with his supper, and zero risk of a brawl or a knife fight.

"Headed up to *The Fisherman's Friend*," he told his deck boss in passing. "Pass it on. If anyone needs anything, tell 'em it can wait until morning."

His deck boss guffawed and slapped Sullivan on the back. "Unless they're bleeding?"

"Even then." Sullivan stretched again. "Might go for a run first, though." He hadn't taken wolf shape in far too long, and his muscles itched to enjoy the change. "Ah well, I'll tell you what. If you can keep the crew out of bar fights until I get back, I might even let you lot come with me."

"Aye, aye, Captain."

* * *

Ari

Nothing ever tasted better -- ever -- than the first deep swallow of cold ale after a hard, hot day's labor. Ari tilted his mug back and drank in thirsty gulps. The bitterness of hops filled his nose as the liquid did his throat, but as good as they were together they didn't put out the fire.

He could feel it coming, deep in his insides, his groin. A rising rush of warmth that made his skin feverish to the touch and left his mouth dry. A growing urge that made him press his thighs together and rock to ease the craving.

Heat.

Ari could feel it coming, and it wouldn't be held back. His body cried out with need. He dropped his half empty mug on the battered bar top and let his head fall forward. Dark curls cut short for the summer tumbled over his forehead, his cheeks. He brushed them out of the way, then lifted the mug again to press its cold side to his face. *Better.*

Not best. *Best* would be a good thick knot filling him up, but -- that would come.

Ari had enough control over himself to sit up straight and breathe deep for a moment. He opened his eyes to look at the pub he'd chosen -- and not at random. Close to home, comfortably down-at-heels, and utterly safe, even for an Omega wolf in heat. They even rented rooms upstairs so men like Ari didn't have far to go if they decided they liked the looks of a particular suitor. Unattached Alphas on the prowl regularly stopped in, hoping for a chance at someone like him.

Ari's lips parted in a fierce grin. *Chance, hmm*? If he had anything to say about it, it'd be someone's lucky night. But as for who it'd be, that was Ari's choice, and he'd make it as wisely as he could.

Alphas had outnumbered Omegas four to one for the past hundred years. Sometimes not even that. Unattached Alphas occasionally grew coarse and cruel when too many chances passed them by, giving Omegas all the more reason to choose their mates with care. Neighbor had to look out for neighbor. Ari often thought that was why all along the northern coastline, packs chose to live in such tight, crowded groups.

True, there were small villages spread more widely apart in the sparsely populated tundra, but here, along the coast, when they were all knocking elbows with their neighbors, it was easier to forget they were so close to being very alone. The wolf packs would all have died out entirely by now if not for the Omegas. Some could even bear two pups at once if they were fortunate.

An Omega in heat was the best hope the wolf packs had of a future. Wise Omegas understood that power, and made good use of it.

Ari reached out to catch the sleeve of a slight man passing by. He wore a vendor's tray around his neck, and Ari had caught a whiff of candied ginger in the sweets he had for sale. When he turned, Ari saw that he was an Omega too, and heavily pregnant. He had a bright, clever smile. "Candy, mister?"

He nodded in approval as Ari plucked a packet of crystallized ginger wrapped in a twist of wax paper from the tray around the Omega's neck and replaced it with a coin. "Excellent choice. Those go fast."

Ari slipped the candy into his mouth and moaned. High quality, and real ginger. He always craved spicy things when he was on the verge of going into heat, and put down another coin for a second packet. "Your Alpha doesn't mind you being out at night?"

The Omega's grin widened. "He knows better than to try and stop me. Don't worry. He's never far away in case I *do* need him."

Ari laughed. "Good man." He watched the Omega wend his way through the crowd of after-work drinkers and early-night revelers in the bar. With every step, he drew avidly eager stares.

The rowdy musicians at the far end were all old, past breeding age, but even they paused to watch the pregnant Omega walk by. Rounded and fertile and beautiful, he was everything a man could crave.

Ari pressed the flat of his hand to his own stomach, flat now, but hungry, and moaned. Moisture made the insides of his thighs buttery-slick. He could feel the dull ache within of an empty womb that wanted to be filled.

Soon, he told himself. *Soon.*

Restless, he took up his ale and drank the last few swallows thirstily while scanning the room. Truth be told, he was almost spoiled for choice tonight when it came to Alphas. Tall ones, lean and eager, short ones, square and sturdy. Broad-shouldered bulls and sleek, silver-tongued seductors.

None of them were quite right, though. Ari rubbed his thighs together to ease the ache and pressed his fist into his belly. He knew what he wanted had to be close. He just had to find... And then -- he did.

A group of working class men burst in, sailors to the last man, laughing and joking, all rough and ragged after a full day on the job. Ari could smell the good clean sweat on them from where he sat, as refreshing as the air after a thunderstorm. Plain and simple men, the salt of the earth. Laughing and joking with one another, and craving nothing more than a drink and an eyeful of an Omega.

One of them, though... One of them -- a man with a full head of heavy, dark gold hair -- caught Ari's eye and kept it. That one held his head higher than the others, who looked to him as their leader. He had a firm hand and a brisk way about him, and an ass made for clutching in both hands. That one walked as if he had an Alpha's knot worth bragging about and knew how to use it -- yet he looked kind, too. He paused in his march toward a serving lad to reassure a nervous looking young fisherman who'd stopped to stare around him with wide eyes, clearly overwhelmed.

That one. You, with the golden mane. I want you.

Ari sat up straighter and kept his eyes fixed on the Alpha. He waited. He knew what would happen, and it didn't take long.

The Alpha's gaze drifted his way. He stopped to stare hungrily at Ari and whistled in pure admiration.

Ari crooked a finger at the Alpha to beckon him.

Catcalls and whoops went up, near-deafening. His fellow laborers pounded the blond's back and shoulders hard enough to leave bruises. The Alpha stared at Ari with an endearingly crooked grin, and pointed at himself as if to ask, *Me*?

Ari nodded and licked his lips.

More back slapping and jealous jeers sent the Alpha on his way. It would have been a fight through the crowd for anyone but an Alpha who'd caught an Omega's scent. The closer he came, the more Ari liked the looks of him. He walked with the steady confidence of a man who'd been born to command, to lead, to take control.

Perfect. Ari stood before the Alpha could come to a stop, or speak, and held out his hand. He could smell the waves of pheromones rising from his groin, his skin, and knew the Alpha would surely smell him, as well. Given a few more deep breaths, the fever that consumed him would enflame the Alpha, too. "I paid for a room upstairs when I bought my drink. It's all mine until midnight. Come with me."

"Did you, now," the Alpha said. He took the last fragment of ginger from Ari's unresisting hand, and slipped it into his mouth. Strong white teeth crunched down. "If I go with you, then you won't come out before midnight, and you won't come out unbred. Better be sure."

"I am." Ari leaned forward to breathe in the Alpha's scent. *Mmm*. It reminded him of the smoke from bonfires, of hot sand and stones, of fertile seas. "That's what I want." He had to go now, or he wouldn't be able to walk. He'd drop to his knees and beg the Alpha for his cock then and there. "Come with me. Come with me *now*. Please."

* * *

Sullivan

If there were any man -- Alpha or otherwise -- in any town along the coast who could say no to an offer like that, Sullivan had never met him. He sure as hell wasn't about to turn down a pretty Omega wolf reeking of his oncoming heat cycle, damp patches of slick already showing wet through the clothing that covered his inner thighs.

Sullivan followed at a distance of three steps to get a good look at what he'd let himself in for. He liked what he saw. Tall, with agile limbs and grace in the swivel of his hips. A tumble of soft black curls that fell over the Omega's forehead, and dark eyes with thick black lashes. A kissable mouth, and a way of looking over his shoulder to make sure Sullivan hadn't changed his mind.

The Omega's hands shook when he unlocked the small, plain door to one of the club's private rooms. Sullivan hadn't been inside one in years, and he took a good look at that, too, while the Omega shut the door behind them. Plain. No frills. Four walls, a lamp, and an iron-framed bed in the corner.

The room smelled intensely of sex, almost thick as a cloud, and the scent made Sullivan's head rush. His groin tightened and he reached for his cock. He'd gone hard when the Omega made his first move, and only gotten harder since.

The Omega kept three steps' worth of distance between them as he toed out of his simple shoes and padded barefoot to the lamp in the corner to turn it on.

He peeked back over his shoulder again and touched a hand to his cheek. "I could call for wine. Do you want some?"

"Not interested in wine," Sullivan said. He loosened his boots and stepped out of them. An Alpha's rut was nothing like the fever that burned this lovely Omega up from the inside, but he could feel it warming him. He licked his lips, tasting the Omega's pheromones on his tongue. "I told you what would happen if you brought me up here."

The Omega's eyes widened, dilated. He pressed a hand to his throat and nodded roughly. He said nothing, though.

Shy? No. Sullivan didn't think so. More like wanting to see what the Alpha he'd picked was made of.

Sullivan could do that.

"Take off your clothes," he said, almost mildly, but in the way he gave orders to his work crew. Not to be disobeyed. "Slow. First your shirt. Let me see you."

"Come and put your hands on me," the Omega begged.

Sullivan shook his head. "Do as I tell you."

The Omega let out a needy whimper, but put his hands to the buttons of his shirt and wrestled them loose. He shrugged his shoulders impatiently to shake off the wash-worn cotton, and laid his hands on his stomach. Silvery scars showed in lightning-forked patterns over the smooth, tight skin. He'd had at least one cub, then. Fertile. "Please."

Sullivan walked toward him, not stopping until his chest touched the Omega's. This close, he could see how his pupils had blown wide, leaving barely a ring of amber-brown about the rims. He took a deep, lusty breath of the Omega's scent, then took the Omega by his hips and pressed his cock forward to give him a taste. "What's your name?"

"Ari," the pretty Omega whispered. "Oh, please. Please, fuck me."

Sullivan laid a finger on the Omega's lips. "I'm Sullivan. Call me that. Not 'Alpha' as if I'm some walking penis. I don't like that."

Ari put out his tongue to lap at the tip of Sullivan's finger, teeth catching briefly on the soft pad. His hands moved, opening Sullivan's shirt, his trousers. "As long as you don't call me 'Omega', as if I'm just a walking womb."

"That is what drives you right now."

Ari purred. "Even so."

"Cheeky," Sullivan murmured. He ran his thumb across Ari's mouth. "I like cheeky."

With a moan, Ari drew Sullivan's thumb into his mouth and sucked. He squeezed his legs together, but he couldn't hold back the gush of lubrication dripping down his thighs. Truly in heat now, wasn't he?

Sullivan caught him by the waist and let Ari grind against him, soaking his thigh. "Need something, did you?"

Ari keened softly and put his hands to the fastening of his trousers. He undid the tie with shaking hands and let them fall to puddle on the floor. "*Please*. Fuck me. Breed me. I'm dying for it."

He was. The rush of hormones and scent nearly drowned Sullivan, and almost went to his head. He could have happily thrown the Omega down on that narrow bed and himself on top -- could have shoved his cock in and knotted Ari and been done with it, but Sullivan meant to make this last.

He ran his palm down Ari's chest, fascinated by the ghosts of the stretch marks left behind. Ari's skin burned with dry fever. His nipples stood up in tightly furled peaks, hard as pebbles. Sullivan put his mouth to one and bit, just once, just lightly, then cupped Ari's groin.

Mmmm. Ari had a respectably sized cock for an Omega, as hard as his nipples, and heavy in Sullivan's hand.

For now, they were still there, and they made Sullivan's mouth water -- but there was one part of Ari he wanted even more to see. He slipped his hand between Ari's legs to tease two fingers behind his sac; they came away soaking wet. He licked the fluid off, pleased when Ari watched with dilated eyes and moaned at the sight. "Open your legs. Let me see."

Ari parted his thighs and spread them shamelessly wide. Moisture dripped down Ari's bare thighs, slow trickles that smelled of salt water. Sullivan drew in a deep breath, remembering the last time he'd caught this scent -- when he'd been in the same room as an Omega giving birth -- and couldn't help imagining how very fine Ari would look ripe and rounded out with a belly full of pups.

Ari keened and pushed forward, then back, trying to get Sullivan's fingers in deeper. Slippery and tight, his channel gripped Sullivan and bore down. The Omega's stomach muscles flexed as his womb contracted.

Sullivan's cock ached with how hard he'd gotten. He growled low in his throat. "God, you are desperate, aren't you?"

The Omega was almost past speech by then. He nodded, quick and frantic. "*Please.*"

"Shh, then." Sullivan was an Alpha, but he was only human too. He squeezed his cock and relished the shock of sensation, then gave Ari's hip a good hard slap. "Turn around. Lean over the railing of the bed, and spread your legs again for me."

The Omega sobbed once, then sank his teeth into his lip and nodded. He turned clumsily, hobbled by the trousers tangled at his knees, but he turned eagerly just the same. He draped himself heavily over the railing and canted his hips up to present for Sullivan -- slick, swollen, soft.

Sullivan couldn't resist. He bent and pressed his mouth to the Omega's opening and thrust his tongue inside.

Only his weight kept Ari from bucking up, and the shout that tore from the man made the window rattle. Sullivan smacked his butt again, a warning to be silent, but didn't stop. He stroked the Omega's hole with the flat of his tongue, then formed a stiff point and fucked inside.

His face felt wet when he came up for air. Sullivan could feel Ari's moisture drying on his cheeks and chin. "Eager little thing."

"*Yes*," Ari said between gritted teeth. His cock hung heavy between his legs.

Too tempting. Sullivan stood and got his arm beneath the Omega, taking Ari's cock in hand. A hard grip, almost punishing, but not quite. It swelled in his palm, slick wetness easing the way there too.

"Please," Ari gasped. "Please. Sullivan. I want, I *want*."

So did Sullivan. He freed his cock from his trousers and eased it forward, teasing the Omega's opening. "Like this? Hmm?"

"Harder. Please, harder." Ari knotted his hands into fists. "Gods of heaven and hell. Please."

"Like this," Sullivan said. He slid two fingers forward, shallowly in. "Or harder than that?"

Ari cried out, pushing back. Thirsty and impatient, he caught Sullivan unaware and took him knuckle-deep in one hard, fast stroke. Sullivan groaned between clenched teeth and grabbed the Omega's hips hard to stop him moving again.

"No more of that," Sullivan chided. He withdrew his fingers, then thrust three in harder and faster. It wasn't rough as the Omega would want, but better than nothing, and with the promise of more.

"Yes," Ari panted, fucking into his hand. "Oh, yes - - oh -- oh, gods. Please. I'm so close. *Please*."

"If you're good," Sullivan said next to Ari's ear, "Then *next* time I'll give you my knot. I said I wasn't letting you go before midnight, and I meant it."

Fluid gushed from Ari, soaking Sullivan's hand, his trousers, the bed. Sullivan just barely managed to keep hold of Ari as he came. His inner muscles bore down so on Sullivan they almost trapped him. If he'd put his cock in instead of his fingers, Sullivan knew he would have stayed locked in there for hours, until the heat passed. But he hadn't, and he didn't.

Sullivan petted the Omega, soothed him, held him up until he could stand on his own. "You didn't think we were done yet, did you? No, pretty Ari. I have plans for you."

* * *

Sullivan

Ari's head hung as heavy on his slender neck as a broken flower would on its stem. His eyelids were heavy, and his mouth curved in a wide, lazy smile. "Oh, you are a bastard," he murmured. "You didn't come."

"Plans, love. Remember?" Sullivan licked salty liquid off his fingers. "But I know what a mating frenzy looks like. You left it too long."

Ari shrugged, loose and languid. "Maybe. And?"

"And I'll give you what you want," Sullivan said. "When I'm sure you want it too." He cupped Ari's ass and kneaded the tight muscle there. "Go lie on the bed. I'll come and be with you directly."

"That's what they all say," Ari remarked, but with an arch look at Sullivan he did as he'd been told. His knees weren't that steady, after all, and when he collapsed on the bed he groaned in relief. The heat fever still had a good hold on him, leaving his skin dry and hot to the touch. He ran a hand restlessly over his chest, his stomach, and tucked the other arm behind his head for a pillow. "You're too far away, over there."

Sullivan chuckled. "Shameless, aren't you?"

Ari licked his lips. "Yes."

Honest, too. That deserved its own reward. Sullivan refastened his trousers with one hand, and tugged at the braided rope hanging just inside the door with the other. Places like this often had them. Cheaper than a phone, and less intrusive than banging on the floor or shouting down the hallway. Though he couldn't hear a bell peal at its terminus, less than a minute later light footsteps pounded to their rented door and knocked.

"What are you doing?" Ari tried to look past him.

Sullivan waved him quiet, pleased when he obeyed, and gave instructions to the young man who'd answered his call -- a local who, like all boys his age, liked gawking at Omegas as much as they did earning tips. He slipped the teenager a few bucks to encourage him to hurry.

Ari waited for the door to close before clearing his throat. He looked amused. "If you don't want to make use of the bed with me, what *do* you want?"

"Oh, I never said I didn't want to throw you on that bed and not let you up until you begged for mercy," Sullivan replied. He cast a hungry eye over the Omega's lean body and cupped his cock through his clothes, showing Ari what he had to offer as his reward for Ari's patience. "I promise you that."

Ari hummed quietly, looking as pleased as he did intrigued.

The teenager knocked again. Sullivan tucked another five bucks in his hand in exchange for the pitcher of water, a tin cup, and string bag with a sponge in it that he'd brought, then closed the door and turned the latch.

Sullivan didn't see any chairs of any sort in the room, but a stepstool tucked in the corner would do. He kicked it out next to the bed; it looked about the right height for what he wanted, and the padding would wash.

Ari took the cup when Sullivan offered it and shivered, fine goosebumps running through his skin. "For me?"

"Plans." Sullivan shed his trousers in quick, economical movements before he sat. He wet the sponge and drew it up the length of Ari's slim chest, then ran the soft/rough stuff over Ari's nipples and blew cool breath over both. "I've seen how going into heat can affect an Omega's will, and I want you in your right mind."

"Doing that won't help."

Sullivan chuckled. "It might." He ran the sponge down Ari's stomach again, tracing it over the fine silvery stretch marks, as fascinated by them as he was Ari's constant pressing over the muscles, kneading at his side. "Lie still. How many cubs do you have?"

"Hmm?" Ari's eyes had begun to glaze over as the fever built. Taking the edge off as Sullivan had would have given him the ability to think clearly, but it wouldn't last for long. Longer if he kept his hands off, Sullivan admitted, but with a ripe Omega under his nose begging to be fucked, any man would think himself a saint for not already being balls deep in Ari's pert ass.

"Cubs," Sullivan repeated, stroking the scars with one fingertip. "Tell me about them. How many have you birthed?"

"Two," Ari said. He fidgeted, flexing the muscles in his thighs. To his credit -- strong-minded, that one -- he shook his head to try and clear it, and slid slightly more upright in the bed. "Seven and four years old. Both Omegas."

Two Omega children born in a row? Sullivan shook his head in amazement. It was nearly unheard of. "Where are they now?"

Ari stirred again, growing more restless by increments. "Safe. I could feel this coming on, so I trusted them to a care giver for the night. Another Omega. A good man. He loves children, and I work for a printer. I can afford it. I wouldn't leave them on their own."

"Hush, hush, I know that," Sullivan soothed. "Two cubs. And you want another one."

"Oh, I do," Ari said on a long breath that ended in a moan.

"Have that easy of a time with it, hmm?"

"God no." Ari laughed. "The first cub nearly killed me. I labored a full day before it came. I swore I'd never do it again, but it's true, what they all say. You forget. And the second was so easy. I barely had time to call the local doc before it was out and screaming." He shifted, and hummed. "I love being pregnant. I love it. To feel myself growing new life, to make bets with myself on what they'll be like. To see how big I get, and how long it all takes. I'm good at it."

Sullivan approved, but curiosity still compelled him to ask. "Any Alphas in your life?"

Ari cracked his eyelids to gaze at Sullivan from between the sooty lashes, a gleam of humor in the fever-bright depths. He drained the tin cup and cast it clattering aside before saying, "I'm looking at him."

"Nicely answered." Sullivan bent to retrieve the cup and filled it a second time. "Drink it all."

Ari grumbled but raised the cup to his lips. When his hands shook so that he nearly dropped the cup, Sullivan held it steady and watched Ari's throat work as he drank. He finished the water with a groan. "No more. Please."

"It's all right. You did well," Sullivan soothed. He caressed the Omega's arms and sides. "Why me?"

"What?" Ari's eyes weren't tracking him; the man twisted, straining his hips up.

Sullivan gave him a light shake to bring him back into focus. "Why me? There are hundreds of Alphas out there for the taking. Especially smelling like you do. You could have had any of them. That's my price. Tell me why you chose me."

Ari pressed his forearm over his eyes. "Your scent," he said after a moment, then slid the arm away to look at Sullivan. "It matches mine. It fits. And you were kind to the men you came in with. You have a strong back and I think you must have a good heart. You're fine to look at, and you're firm but you're fair. You're making very sure I'm not dehydrated, and that I'm willing. Is that enough?" He shifted his legs again, raising them slightly, and rubbed at his abdomen. When Sullivan tried to draw the sponge over him, Ari knocked it away. "It's like fire under my skin, liquid fire melting the clay I'm made of. I feel things shifting around, getting ready, but they're *empty*. Gods! I can't bear it. Fuck me, Sullivan, please."

Sullivan let the sponge fall. The heat beneath the Omega's skin evaporated the water before it could do any good anyway. Nothing would help him now except a good hard fuck. Sullivan slipped his hand between Ari's thighs and stroked low, between his legs. He'd soaked the sheets.

Ari moaned and shifted, parting his legs and raising his knees. His stomach clenched and flexed, the play of dim light in the room betraying faint shadows of the muscles moving beneath the skin. He put his own hands on his thighs to spread them as wide as he could. His channel wept clear fluid, the swollen tissues throbbing with the beat of Ari's pulse, his body demanding to be fucked and filled.

"Please," Ari begged, barely loud enough to hear. "Oh, please."

Sullivan gritted his teeth and made himself move off the edge of the bed. His cock jutted out before him, dark with arousal and the knot already forming. "Do you promise to do what I tell you?"

Ari nodded and reached up for him, trying to coax him down.

"Ah-ah-ah." Sullivan waited for Ari to settle, even if he did so impatiently, then rewarded him with a long, smooth stroke of his cock. "Move over. I want to see you riding me."

Ari moved. Not gracefully -- he needed help -- but the bed was big enough to do so without falling off, and once Sullivan had joined him, he was able to coax the Omega up and onto his lap to straddle him.

Not fucking him just yet, though. Sullivan slipped three fingers up and into Ari's body, through the throbbing opening, wetting his hand with the steady patter of clear fluid. He sank his teeth into his lip and groaned when Ari's inner muscles grabbed at his fingers.

"No more games," Ari said. He rested his hands on Sullivan's chest and arched his hips. "Have mercy. Give it to me."

Sullivan wasn't made of stone after all. He took the Omega by those hips, already red and tender from the marks his palms had left before, and lowered Ari onto his cock. Held him steady when he cried out and thrust down, straining for the lock that would knot them together. The musicians were in full swing in the club below, a steady drumbeat and a wailing trumpet filling Sullivan's ears.

He thrust up, in, and was there.

* * *

Ari

Yes. Oh yes. Ari pressed his wrist to his mouth and bit to keep his keening shout muffled. That was what his body craved, what it needed --

Almost. He sensed it coming the moment before his chosen Alpha withdrew, and was ready for it when Sullivan tugged at him, impatient, and tossed him down to the bed. He got his knees beneath himself and braced his knees, ready.

Sullivan had the willpower of an army general and the sense of humor of a demon. He took himself in hand to thrust just barely inside Ari's body. "Ask me sweetly, one more time. Let me hear you say 'please'."

Ari drew his knees beneath him and raised his hips to present himself. He knew what he looked like and he didn't care. "Please," he murmured, toes curled and fingers knotted. He panted, not able to get enough air. The fever would kill him if he didn't find relief, and he wanted another baby. He had wanted that even before the heat took over. He wanted to grow ripe as a plum; wanted to feel the movements inside him, to know he had created life. Wanted Sullivan, with his golden hair, to leave his maker's mark on the new cub so that Ari would see it every time he looked at their face. *"Please."*

The Alpha groaned behind him, and then -- finally -- slid properly inside Ari. All the way, not stopping till the rough hair on his thighs prickled, pressing against Ari's ass. He dug his fingers into Ari's sides, his hips, and held him there as the knot locked them together at last. Tight, and it hurt, but it was a marvelous sort of ache and it made Ari hard.

"Oh God," Sullivan said, hips working in short thrusts though he couldn't get any further in. "You feel good. So good." He ground his teeth audibly together. "Ari. You're sure?"

Ari nodded his head and braced himself. He reached back to stroke the man. "*Yes*. Give it to me, give it to me *now* --"

Sullivan's teeth raked his shoulder, and oh, oh, there it was. Ari keened at the feel of it, thick gouts of come inside him, soaking him. Sullivan's hips pounded his ass hard enough to leave bruises but he didn't care, didn't care. He arched his back and loosed a wild scream that hurt his ears and left his throat raw, but it was drowned beneath Sullivan's roar when his inner muscles grabbed hold and bore down, demanding still more.

"Greedy," the Alpha said, reaching under Ari. "Greedy enough for this?"

Ari could only nod and moan, thrusting back to take all Sullivan could give. So much come; it oozed out of him even around the knot and dripped down his legs, hot as molten silver. "More."

"All I have to give." Sullivan had Ari's stiff cock in his hand and worked it ruthlessly. "Fill you up, give you a cub to remember me by." His wrist strained with the effort toward stripping Ari's own climax out of him, and his thighs shook with the strain of holding himself up. "Almost -- almost --"

He jerked, sending them both down flat on the bed, the shock of jarring bones a bright-hot flash that nudged his knot deep, so deep. Ari buried his face in the soft bedding and came with a howl as loud as he ever made in wolf form. Deep inside, he could *feel* the Alpha's seed take hold.

God. Yes. At last. Ari shuddered his way to a stop and knotted his fists in the bedding with Sullivan flat on top of him, still locked within, until he too stopped and lay still, hot breath panting in Ari's ear, his body electric.

There. That's what I wanted.

* * *

Ari

Still lying on top of him, as wrung out as the sponge they'd abandoned to its fate, Sullivan began to laugh.

Ari reached back to slap lightly at Sullivan's thigh. "Stop that."

Sullivan didn't. His chest and shoulders shook with laughter, warm puffs of air heating a patch on Ari's back. "Can't help it."

Ari had to chuckle too. He dug his elbow up and back, nudging the Alpha. "At least you made it all the way to the end of the show before you broke character. Well done."

"Oh, thanks." Sullivan nuzzled the back of Ari's neck. "The look on your face when you crooked a finger at me from across the bar? I almost swallowed my tongue."

"I noticed." Ari nudged him again. "Push off, my love. I want to see you."

"Hold still, then." Sullivan was gentle, sliding out of Ari. His erection had gone down while the sweat on their skins cooled, but he could have been rougher if he liked.

But Ari had always loved that the Alpha he'd taken as his mate seven years ago could be so gentle. Ari had come to their mating ceremony naked, as Omegas did in the old stories, showing his six months of pregnancy proudly to the world. The look on Sullivan's face had been the same then as the one Ari had seen this night.

Sullivan was kind. A good father. Strong. He made his living as second in command on a fishing boat that went halfway down the coast and back. Clever, too, and willing to go along with whatever Ari cooked up to make their lives interesting.

Like pretending to be strangers meeting for a breeding fuck, for example.

Ari grinned so broadly his cheeks ached and pointed his toes in a good long stretch. It hadn't all been pretense, after all. When he laid his hand on his abdomen he could feel sub-seismic quivers inside, the sensation of being molded like warm wax shivering through its completion. His fever turned, beginning to abate. He sighed in contentment and laid his head on Sullivan's shoulder.

Sullivan brushed a fallen curl out of Ari's eyes. "You and your games."

"You liked it," Ari asserted smugly.

"That I did, love. Seeing you burning up with the fever and picking me out of a crowd? You might as well have tossed a lasso around my cock." Sullivan turned to lie on his side, and rested his palm over Ari's, atop his womb. "Did it work?"

"It did. I know it did. You'll see for yourself in a few months."

Sullivan bent to press his mouth to Ari's chest. "Suppose I will. And in three more years, we'll end up back here again, hmm?"

"Or something," Ari said with a hum of enjoyment. "Trust me. By then, I'll have thought of something even better. You wait and see."

"I will. Because, fun and games aside, you're all mine," Sullivan said. He lifted Ari's chin, and kissed him properly, deep and wet, drawing a zing of sensation deep in Ari's groin. "Omega to my Alpha. Mine."

"Yours, oh yes," Ari said, tilting up for a deeper kiss, and then one deeper still. "Always."

Tooth and Claw
Will Okati

Lewis, Alpha master of the Wasp Lake wolf pack, knows that finding his mate should be a joyous event. But former army ranger Jacobi isn't an Omega. Or even a wolf. He's a grizzly bear shifter, and Alpha to the bone.

Falling for an outsider is risky, especially given Lewis's secret. He yearns to be an Omega, not an Alpha, and has never met anyone willing to accept the man he really is behind the Packmaster's mantle. As for Jacobi, it's been a long time since he's been loved so well that it made him want to be a better man.

The pair try loving in secret -- for a while -- but know that's not going to be enough to satisfy them forever. When Jacobi adopts an orphaned lynx cub and Lewis becomes the toddler's second father, they realize something has to be done. But what?

Nature is red in tooth and claw -- but sometimes true love really does save the day.

Chapter One

Lewis

The wolves of the Wasp Lake pack didn't have a cafe or a diner in their community -- they were too rural for that -- but they did have the next best thing. One of the pack elders, a venerable wolf so old he'd run covert ops under Saigon moons, would open his door for any Alpha who wanted to drop by, pour themselves a cup of Joe, read the papers, and pass the time. Call it an open house, call it a village-sized town hall, it served its purpose.

Omegas were welcome to come if they liked, but from what Lewis's cousin Ivoire told him Omegas mostly had better things to do with their time, and better sense as well.

Lewis kept quiet when he visited the elder's cabin. Partly nature, partly common sense. If the wolves of his pack could forget their Packmaster was among them, they'd open up. He heard more by listening than he did by asking.

Sometimes things he wanted to hear. Sometimes not.

The job of Packmaster wasn't one that a wolf could survive into old age. It came with a target painted on the back and a ticking clock counting down to the day when a younger wolf would challenge him. Still. Lewis remembered the Packmaster that'd come before him, a vicious old bastard without a heart. He'd do the best he could in the time he had because it sure as hell beat the alternative, and hoped the pack would remember him kindly when he'd gone.

Which they wouldn't do, if they knew the truth about him.

He nursed his mug of coffee sip by sip, the brew spiked with nothing whatsoever, and kept his eyes open.

"Heard tell that bear's been sighted again," one of the oldest wolves grumbled as he warmed his hands by the wood range that worked as well now as it must have when it was new, a hundred years ago. "I'd have thought it'd be dead by now."

Lewis pricked up his ears.

"The skinny one?" old Boaz asked. "Hell, I thought it'd starved a while back."

"Nope. It's hanging on. I found bear sign out near my trap lines, and I saw it once, too. It's the same bear as last year." Abner slurped his coffee and made a face. The older wolves would much rather hunt for themselves instead of using traps, but they weren't as agile in either form as they used to be. "Somebody might ought to do something about the poor bastard, if it can't feed itself properly or sleep through the cold season. Hungry bears in the winter, well…"

Lewis could fill in the blanks for himself. Bears didn't often venture close to human habitation, or pack lands, but if one was awake and hungry enough in winter to be desperate, wolf cubs could be in danger. Valuable Omegas too. Anyone who hunted bear put themselves at risk, Alpha or not.

Which made taking care of the menace part of the Packmaster's job.

Though Lewis felt all the men watching him, he took his time about draining his cup, then stood as if he wasn't bothered. Part of him wasn't. "I'll see to it."

"Pretty dangerous, son," one of the elders said.

"Most things are."

"Ought to gather the enforcers, take them with you."

"For one bear?" Lewis fastened his coat and took a long look at his pack. Some of these wolves might volunteer -- they were good men -- but he wouldn't ask it of them. This was his duty, and his alone. He made for the door with his back straight, not even turning around when he said, "I'll be back before dawn."

* * *

When he'd said it, Lewis had meant it.

He still did now, slogging his way through snow that would be thigh-deep by morning. Would have gone faster on four legs, but a wolf couldn't carry a hunting rifle in its mouth. Lewis had been the one to order against that particular folly.

He was a good Packmaster. Lewis knew that deep down. He'd done good things for the Wasp Lake pack. Letting Bree leave to find his happiness. Bringing Ivoire in so he and Zachariah could learn joy. There were others. The Wasp Lake pack was growing by leaps and bounds.

Sometimes Alphas lay with Alphas. In times of need, or in case of scarcity. It wasn't talked about, even if it was tacitly understood as a necessary evil if there weren't enough Omegas around. That was permissible.

But for a Packmaster to crave only the touch of an Alpha's hand? To fall asleep restless as an ant hill, itching for the roughness of command, the peace of surrender; to dream about being dominated and to wake up hard? To wish -- sometimes -- often-times -- that he'd been born an Omega instead? No way in hell would that be allowed.

Lewis set his jaw and walked on, searching the elder's trap line for signs of the bear.

Somewhat to his surprise, he found plenty. A scrap of dark fur here, scratches on a tree trunk there. Clear footprints a few hours old. Traps that'd been popped wide open, with barely a whisker or drop of blood left to mark what they'd caught. Lewis stopped to pluck one of the tufts of fur from where it'd caught on a bush and frowned at it.

He doesn't care if he's found.

Smart enough to scavenge, crazy enough to have abandoned caution. It put Lewis on edge and made him take a more secure grip on his rifle. Bears didn't behave like this, not even those hungry enough to range about in the winter. He kept his eyes open and his ears pricked, searching the woods for a sign of the creature.

He didn't even realize he'd stepped into the open bear trap until it closed around his ankle.

Then he knew. Oh, he knew. Lewis shoved his fist into his mouth to stopper the roar of pain that nearly burst out of him, and breathed sharply through his nose. Agony burned below his knee, white-hot and fierce. He wasn't any kind of coward, but when he looked down his stomach churned and he had to turn his head.

With his eyes shut, he reached down, searching for the release. There had to be one, but his fingers slipped in the blood. He gritted his teeth and tried again, iron rust coarse and cold against his palms where it wasn't sticky-hot.

Too much blood. Lost too fast. Wolf shifters healed fast, and Alphas faster than Omegas, but if he couldn't free himself he'd die. It happened like that out here, just this quick. The third time he fumbled the release, Lewis stopped, trying to recover his self-control.

If he hadn't, he wouldn't have heard the bear's movements before it was too late. Even as it was, he caught the raspy sound of a ragged bellows just in time to look up and see the bear he'd been standing a dozen feet away.

Lewis went still, utterly still as he could.

It had to be the same bear the elders were talking about. Skinny as a rail, his coat dull and dry. Wide awake and watching him.

Lewis gritted his teeth until his jaw creaked, then pushed himself upright despite the burning agony in his pierced calf. If this was the end, then by God he'd meet it with dignity.

The bear didn't move. It narrowed its eyes at Lewis, but it stayed put for one breath. Two breaths. Three.

Then, it sighed, a startlingly human sound. Before Lewis even processed that, the bear shook itself and its animal form melted away, leaving behind a gaunt, naked man with shadowed eyes, old military tattoos, and -- strangely -- a gentle mouth.

Lewis stared.

"Well," the bear said, his voice as rusty as the old trap, "If the iron doesn't kill you, the irony just might."

* * *

Jacobi

Jacobi had stopped believing in angels long ago. Shame on him. Should have kept the faith.

He clicked his tongue at himself. This wasn't any kind of fallen angel. Just a man, even if he was a fine-looking example of the kind, and in damn certain danger of doing himself permanent damage. Jacobi knew from damage. He didn't want to see any more of it than he could help.

"Hold still," he said, not used to talking after a few months of silence. He dropped into a crouch to study the trap's mechanism.

To his surprise, the big blond Alpha he'd caught did as he'd been told. Went still as a statue. Jacobi flicked a glance up to see the Alpha staring down at him, lips parted. "Who are you?"

"Jacobi. You a screamer? Try not to. I don't do so well with loud noises."

"What?" The Alpha shook his head a couple of times. Shock would be setting in right about now, Jacobi figured. His leg twitched, and he grunted. "Oh. That. I won't scream."

Jacobi wasn't any too sure -- no one could step in or out of a bear trap without making some kind of noise -- but they didn't have time to argue the point. He piled snow over the trap to wash the Alpha's blood away, then pulled the pin that'd make the whole shebang come harmlessly apart.

True to his word, the Alpha clamped his jaw shut and groaned behind it as the trap came away, but nothing worse. Jacobi approved.

Trouble was, now that he'd been freed, he'd either bleed or freeze to death if Jacobi left him alone. Jacobi rubbed at his jaw, huffing as he thought. He'd been alone for a long time, a long damn time, and he liked it that way, but leaving an Alpha to die wouldn't do *him* any good either.

Besides. It'd be a shame to waste a fallen angel on a few snowflakes.

Jacobi wedged his shoulder under the Alpha's arm, taking most of his weight. "Think you can make it forty feet or so due west?"

The Alpha blinked, clearly struggling to form coherent thought. Definitely in shock. Jacobi gave up waiting for an answer -- he'd find out for himself soon enough -- and hauled the Alpha back the way he'd come, wondering who was poking around in the trap line.

Forty feet due west through dense timber brought them to the shack Jacobi had claimed for his own. It looked to have been built in the nineteen-sixties or so, then abandoned. No one else knew it was there, not even the old man who ran his trap line so near to hand. Even now the shack didn't look like much inside or out, but Jacobi had fixed it up well enough to keep off the wind and water, and it served its purpose.

He'd left a fire going in the potbellied stove, and breathed a heavy sigh of relief to find it still alight, crackling away and warming the shack. Good. One less thing to worry about. Though the Alpha was nearly limp weight by then, Jacobi got him wrangled onto the pile of blankets he used for a bed.

The Alpha weaved slightly as he watched Jacobi pull on a pair of pants, then retreat to dig through his supplies. "Who are you?" he asked again.

"Not important," Jacobi said, because it wasn't. He rumbled in satisfaction when he found the Canadian med kit he'd traded with a backwoodsman for, and lugged it back to the bed. Kneeling beside the Alpha, he cut away the wreckage of his pants on the trap-ruined side and took a good hard look. "Bad," he said. "I've seen worse. You allergic to penicillin?"

The Alpha shook his head. "Do you know who I am?"

"Should I?"

That made the Alpha chuff. "Guess not. I'm Lewis. Packmaster of Wasp Lake."

The information gave Jacobi a moment's pause. An ordinary Alpha could make life difficult for him, but a Packmaster would have the right to drive him out of this shack if he chose.

Ah, hell. He was in too deep now. "Hold still, Lewis."

Lewis didn't jump when Jacobi injected him, and though he gritted his teeth so hard his jaw creaked, he didn't make a fuss of any kind over having his leg cleaned. Only when that was over and done did he speak up again. "You're the bear that's been haunting this patch for a while now, aren't you?"

Jacobi shrugged. If Lewis already knew, what was the point in asking or answering? Instead, he looked up to study the Packmaster's face. White as a sheet, he judged, and nearly as cold as death.

A sweep of dark gold hair, wide set hazel eyes, a firm mouth. Broad shoulders. Narrow hips. Long legs, with sturdy muscles and strong bones. A well-turned ankle. Jacobi looked down to see he'd braceleted his fingers around it, idly stroking the fine bones there.

Bad idea. Lewis wore an air of command on his shoulders as familiarly as he would an old coat. An Alpha to the core. They didn't take kindly to approaches from other Alphas, not as a rule, and surely wouldn't from a worn-down wreck of an Alpha like Jacobi. They weren't even the same kind of shifter.

Jacobi bandaged up the wound, then made himself let go. "You'll live."

He wasn't sure Lewis had heard him. Seemed like he wasn't tracking quite right, his head still weaving slightly. "Did you open all those traps?"

"Yes," Jacobi said. No point in lying about it. "I didn't steal the meat. I let the animals go."

"Why?"

Jacobi rubbed at his nose, trying to find the right words. "I don't like suffering," he said at last. "I'd rather not see it or cause it if I can help it."

Lewis frowned at him as if too lost to follow that. He might well be. Shock took men oddly, and Jacobi would have to admit he had decent cause.

He pushed at Lewis's shoulders to make him lie down, and with an effort of will kept his touch distant, cool.

Of course Lewis fought him. What Alpha wouldn't? "What are you doing?"

"Can't go anywhere until morning," Jacobi said, nudging Lewis until he was properly in the bed, not just on it. He caught his breath at the sight. God, it'd been a long damn time since he had anyone in his bed, let alone an Alpha like Lewis. Trying to hide his reaction made him gruffer than before. "Rest. Get your strength back. Warm up."

"Not sure I can," Lewis said. His teeth chattered as he tried to pull himself together. "I'll do my best."

Shivering like that was a good sign, but Jacobi knew for himself how cold could go straight down to the bones. He wrestled with himself for a moment, then sighed. "Move over then."

"What?"

"Body heat," Jacobi said briefly. "I need rest too."

Lewis made an odd noise but slid to the side, making room for Jacobi. "You're supposed to be hibernating. I wondered why you weren't."

"Not sleepy."

Lewis shook his head, but shut his mouth. Two bodies under the blanket Jacobi rescued from the floor and tossed over them already made it warm as a burrow under there. The Packmaster's eyelids were heavy, and Jacobi could nearly feel his struggle not to doze off.

"I won't hurt you," Jacobi said. "I won't even touch you if you don't want. But rest."

"I…"

Jacobi put his hand over Lewis's mouth and held it there just long enough to make his point. "Rest," he said again. "Argue later."

He held that gaze, looking Lewis in the eye, until that eye slid shut. Good.

Jacobi shut his eyes himself, though he didn't expect to drift off. He never did…

Chapter Two

Lewis

Lewis came awake with a jolt.

What... He stiffened, not knowing where he was or how he'd come to be there. For a Packmaster to lose control like that was to invite his own ruin, but his sleep dazed brain refused to produce any answers for him.

Without moving any other muscles, he opened his eyes a slit and let his vision focus.

A dark room. Small. Lewis could sense the close proximity of the four walls that boxed him in. That wasn't unusual in the Alaskan interior. Smaller spaces held the heat better. He tilted his head to listen to the quiet crackling of a small hearth fire that smelled of pine and creosote. The floor underneath him had been softened by what felt like mounds and layers of Army blankets washed so many times they were as soft as lamb's wool, and someone had draped a surprisingly heavy quilt over his nude body.

His calf muscle cramped, surprising a grunt out of Lewis. When he flexed his knee and ankle and discovered the mostly healed wounds, he remembered the trap. A bear trap in the snow, yes, and...

And his rescuer.

Lewis exhaled, slow and long and careful. He remembered everything now, up to the point where shock and pain had stolen his wits. There was no forgetting how cold he'd been, or how hard the shakes had rattled him. Jacobi -- *yes, that was his name* -- must have stripped him out of his snow-wet clothes and wrapped him up.

And where was Jacobi now? Lewis lay on his right side, but rolled his left shoulder and drew his foot slowly back, searching through the quilt for what he knew he'd find. Jacobi. The bear shifter lay on his right side too, directly behind Lewis. A few inches separated them, but he'd likely fallen asleep the same way Lewis had, huddled together for warmth.

He was as naked as Lewis, the lean, hard muscles in his limbs and chest fairly radiating heat.

Lewis closed his eyes and bit savagely at the inside of his cheek as he went abruptly, achingly hard. His stomach muscles flexed, and he released a small groan.

It was taboo, to want an Alpha the way most Alphas wanted Omegas, but God help him, Lewis craved it. No one knew. They couldn't, not if he wanted to keep his position as Packmaster, and he did. He had too many lives depending on him.

He exhaled to the count of seven, then drew in a quiet breath and started again. Behind him, Jacobi stirred. Only a little, and it could have been the reflex motion of a man fast asleep, but Lewis could tell it wasn't. Jacobi tensed ever so slightly, then went as still as Lewis save for his breath. Warm puffs brushed slowly against Lewis's nape, as gentle as the brush of a hand.

The brush of a hand. That was a hand, sliding through the covers, coming to rest on Lewis's hip. A thumb, stroking the arch of Lewis's iliac crest.

A groan, quiet as could be, escaped Lewis.

"Shh," Jacobi murmured. He slid closer, the inches that'd separated them gone in an instant, and pressed his hips to Lewis's ass.

He was hard. As hard as Lewis was. Jacobi nestled his cock fully against the cleft of Lewis's ass and spread his fingers wide on Lewis's hip, waiting for either permission or denial. Lewis sensed he'd take either without a fuss, but...

Lewis's breath shuddered in his throat. He fisted a handful of the quilt, needing it for an anchor, and pressed back into Jacobi. *Yes.*

Jacobi made a quiet sound that encapsulated everything that needed to be said. He slid his arm around

Lewis's waist and stroked his stomach, then took Lewis's cock in hand and closed his fingers lightly around it. His chin rested on Lewis's shoulder, his mouth just beneath Lewis's ear.

Lewis closed his hand around Jacobi's and nodded once.

Jacobi tightened his grip and stroked the length of Lewis's cock, hard and slow, steady and relentless. He slid his knee between Lewis's to part Lewis's legs and give him space to work -- and all in silence broken only by the harshness of their breathing. Lewis cried out once, when Jacobi's cock bumped the exquisitely sensitive spot behind his balls, and let go of the quilt to reach back and seize Jacobi's hip just as hard.

He cried out again when he came, the orgasm a surprise -- so fast -- but so hard, his abdominal muscles cramping from the force of it, a pulse pounding hard in his groin. Behind him, Jacobi groaned in his ear and held him so still that he couldn't move, could only come, and not stop himself until he was emptied.

Lewis hadn't realized he'd held himself as tensely as strung wire until he collapsed, panting, back on his side.

Jacobi wasn't finished yet. He swiped his hand through the mess Lewis had made, coating his fingers, and rubbed it on the insides of Lewis's thighs. Like an Omega's natural lubrication. The thought made Lewis gasp, and made his cock try to go hard again as he imagined himself that way. He'd never spoken of it to anyone, not even his Omega cousin Ivoire, but he'd seen Omegas in heat and he'd wanted, he'd *wanted* --

"Shh," Jacobi crooned again, stroking Lewis's side. "S'okay. I won't tell."

Lewis believed him. Something in his voice, or in his body language, made him sure. And he wanted this too much to protest. He hadn't gone soft yet, and he could feel himself starting to climb toward a second orgasm.

He raised and bent his knee to give Jacobi the room he needed, ready to take him with nothing more than a little spunk to ease the way, but Jacobi shushed him and eased his leg down until his thighs were pressed together. "Like this," he breathed in Lewis's ear, and slid his cock through the slick between Lewis's thighs. He groaned and used the edges of his teeth on Lewis's neck, but still stopped long enough for Lewis to say "yes" or "no."

Lewis nodded, all he was capable of, and pushed back as Jacobi thrust forward. Sweat made them slippery as they moved together, muscles crushed one against the other, hard flesh sliding against hard flesh. Lewis gritted his teeth to keep from shouting, so tense that tendons stood out in his neck, but could feel the same bowstring tightness in Jacobi's muscles as he fucked between Lewis's thighs. Could feel the hard swelling of his knot rising, too, as if Lewis *was* an Omega begging to be bred.

A keening groan escaped him and he came a second time, almost dry; he hadn't finished shuddering before Jacobi stilled, thrust once more, and came with a deep, deep growl. His teeth scraped Lewis's shoulder once more before he pulled his head away.

Lewis -- couldn't move. Almost couldn't think or breathe. Oh, he'd needed that. Needed it far more than he'd imagined.

And a thieving bear had been the only one to see it -- the only one to give it -- with no judgment. Nothing but an understanding of Alphas.

* * *

Jacobi

Jacobi knew it was coming. He waited for it, and sure enough before the sweat had dried on their skins, Lewis went abruptly still. One tick of his head spoke volumes about how he wanted to look over his shoulder, to check and see whether Jacobi had gotten mad or wanted to pretend this had never happened. Jacobi had seen it before. Hell, he'd been the same himself once upon a time.

But the one thing he'd learned -- had to learn, to survive out here on his own -- was to not get so caught up in his head that he went rest of the way crazy.

He slapped Lewis once on the hip, casual as he could, then slid off the pile of blankets and got to his feet. Though he still wasn't much good at conversation, there were other ways to make this easier on both of them.

Coffee never hurt. Jacobi padded barefoot to the iron kettle on its hook by the hearth, which was as fancy as his cooking got, and lifted its lid to sniff at the contents. Leftover from earlier in the day, it'd almost boiled down to syrup. He tipped half of a canteen into the kettle and sloshed it around to thin the stuff out, then tossed a tin cup to Lewis.

Lewis caught it with a startled look.

"Good reflexes," Jacobi said. His voice still sounded hoarse to him, even though it'd gotten more use tonight than it had in months. He kept an eye on the coffee, waiting for the added water to heat up. "I didn't do that out of some sense of obligation. I'm not that good a host."

Awkward words, but they did the job. Lewis snorted quietly and sat up, feet planted flat on the floor next to the stack of blankets that made Jacobi's bed. He searched for words, then nodded.

It made Jacobi's heart, rusty though it was, go out to him. Like he said -- he'd been there, back when he still gave a damn about what the world thought about him.

The coffee had heated to boiling. Jacobi wrapped his hand in padding and poured for both of them. He grimaced at the first taste, as did Lewis, but after that they both drank in peaceful silence. Jacobi watched Lewis out of the corner of his eye, noting the improvement in the wolf's color and spirits with each swallow.

"This is awful," Lewis said, halfway down his cup. "Thanks."

Jacobi lifted his mug in reply. "Do what I can."

"Yeah, I see that." Lewis rested his cup on his knee and looked around, drinking the place in, everything from chinked log walls to hard-packed dirt floor and the stack of disassembled traps rusting in one corner under a ragged sheet. He shook his head as if what he saw confused him, but he met Jacobi's gaze then without hesitation. "Who are you?"

Jacobi chuckled. "Good damn question," he said after a moment's thought punctuated by a slug of coffee. "My name's Jacobi. I'm a bear shifter. I was a soldier." He stopped to touch his tongue to his lip. "Overseas."

Lewis made an *ahh* noise.

"Now that I'm not a soldier, I guess I'm a homesteader. I keep to myself. And I don't like to see anything hurting." Jacobi drained his mug and gave Lewis look for look. "And you're a wolf, and a Packmaster. What's that going to make us?"

"I don't know." Lewis wrapped both hands around his cup, though it couldn't still be warm now that it was mostly empty. "I don't want us to be enemies."

Jacobi raised one shoulder. "Then we won't be."

"You know it's not as easy as that."

Yeah. Jacobi did. And yet it rubbed him the wrong way clear down to his toes. He and this Alpha wolf fit together in more ways than one. In a good world, they could have been friends. Maybe more than that. The sense memory of Lewis rutting back against him made Jacobi's groin pulse.

"I'm not hurting anyone," he pointed out. "Pretty much the opposite."

"Except for the elders who can't hunt in either form anymore," Lewis said. "Who need the furs and the meat. I can't turn my back on that. But. But."

Jacobi, who had started to prepare himself for a fight, stopped at that. He waited curiously, wondering what Lewis was up to.

"You helped me when you didn't have to." Lewis made eye contact so direct it felt as if he were looking inside Jacobi's head. "So here's what I'll tell them. I found you, and had a word with you. You listened to me, and we came to an understanding."

Jacobi shook his head in admiration. That was a twisty bit of edited truth worthy of a lawyer. Lewis must run rings around the contentious members of his pack.

All right, then.

"Salmon will start running soon," Jacobi said after a beat, lips at the rim of his mug. "Then the growing season. Plenty for all."

The corner of Lewis's mouth quirked up briefly. "And this year the Packmaster's going to make damn sure everyone's well supplied for the winter. Maybe find some other source of income so traps aren't needed."

Jacobi grinned -- quickly, but still. He offered Lewis a hand up off the bedding. "No one offered me a deal, so I won't take it. But if they had..."

"If they had," Lewis agreed. He grimaced and swiped at the mess on his skin. "I must reek."

"I've smelled worse," Jacobi said with a shrug. "You want something to wipe down with?"

"No. My clothes are already wrecked with sweat and blood. A little spunk won't do any harm at this point. Besides." As he worked his way back into his clothes, Lewis looked at the door, then at Jacobi. "I need to get back."

Yeah, Jacobi had known that was coming too. A Packmaster couldn't stay gone without his absence being noticed, especially if his pack knew he'd gone sniffing into something dangerous.

It was for the best, of course. He and Lewis had needed what they'd given each other, and it would loan them both the strength to keep going.

It still rubbed Jacobi the wrong way. He didn't *want* to let the Packmaster go -- no more than he thought the Packmaster wanted to be made to go, the way Lewis's heels were dragging.

"Take care of yourself," Jacobi said, offering Lewis his hand again.

The Packmaster closed his hand around Jacobi's with another faint smile. "You too."

He almost spoke again. Jacobi saw it. And Jacobi almost spoke again. He could tell Lewis saw it.

When Lewis walked away, a tall, masculine shape moving silently through the snow, stopping only once to retrieve his rifle, Jacobi watched him until he disappeared into the darkness, then closed the door between them.

Too bad this was how it had to be, but Jacobi couldn't hold it against him. After all, what else could there be between an Alpha wolf and bear but two ships passing in the night?

Chapter Three

Lewis

Jacobi slid his arm around Lewis's waist and stroked his stomach, then took Lewis's cock in hand and closed his fingers lightly around it. His chin rested on Lewis's shoulder, his mouth just beneath Lewis's ear, and...

"How's that little cousin of yours?" The wolf elder hobbled under a heavy pine branch that Lewis held up for him, jostling him out of his daydream about Jacobi. He cackled a rusty laugh, as if fully aware he'd caught Lewis off guard. "The pretty little Omega one. Reminds me of my Ben, back in the sixties."

Lewis arched an eyebrow at the man -- *careful who you tease, hmm?* -- then let the branch fall harmlessly behind them. "Ivoire's well. Pregnant with a second set of twins. Zachariah's building more rooms onto their house, since it doesn't look like these will be the last."

The wolf elder smacked his lips in approval. "Good healthy young blood. That's what we need. You should take a mate of your own."

"Too busy," Lewis replied, clipped, but softened that by thumping lightly on the old man's shoulder. "I'm tied up taking your mangy hide out hunting, aren't I?"

That got him another wheezing laugh, but it got the elder to drop the subject too. *Good.* Lewis exhaled in relief as they walked on in silence.

After spending time with the bear -- with Jacobi -- he'd put his mind to solving the problem of the trap lines, and come up with a solution. The elders preferred to hunt. They only ran trap lines because it was their sole option. Meanwhile, Lewis had a pack full of bachelors loaded to the gills with hot blood, needing outlets for their energy until they found mates.

So why not send an Alpha or two out with an elder when they needed meat? The elder could move at his own pace and spot game that the young bachelors would chase down for them. They got out in the fresh air, the bachelors wore themselves into peaceable states, and no animals suffered needlessly in traps.

It'd taken some reminding the younger wolves that his word was law and if they didn't like it, they could either fight him or lump it, but Lewis had his way in the end. Might have helped that he didn't hold himself exempt from the new order, and spent at least one day a month treading the old game trails with elderly wolves.

And if walking those trails took him within scent range of Jacobi's cabin, warming those memories for him, that was no one's business but Lewis's.

He'd thought about going back. Thought long and hard, with his cock in hand and Jacobi's name on his lips. If he'd been an Omega, he would have dreamed about mating, but as it was…

Just seemed more like an invitation to heartbreak, dwelling on it.

"This is where you used to keep your traps?" he asked the elder, scanning the narrow winding path.

"Rabbit," the elder confirmed. He pointed one gnarled finger. "Sometimes things that hunt rabbit, too."

Lewis flexed his hands. The path was a familiar one to him. Just around that bend, he'd stepped into the bear trap meant for Jacobi. He held his breath and listened, not meaning to but not able to resist, and to his surprise heard a scrabbling, scratching sound. He shot a hard look at the elder. Old or not, the law of the Pack was the law, and he wouldn't be disobeyed. "You didn't sneak any traps out here again, did you?"

"Hell no! Why would I trap when I could hunt like a wolf should?" The elder spat on the snow, then scratched his nose. "Could be a hawk got a rabbit."

Could be. Lewis wrestled with himself, then shook his head. "I'll go and see. I trust your word. I don't trust all the bachelors to keep theirs."

"More balls than brains, these young Alphas," the elder agreed. "You go on. I'll come behind."

Lewis clapped him on the back a second time, making the old man beam with pride, before setting off down the trail. He kept his eyes carefully open. Arctic hares were white at this time of year, to blend in with the snow. If a hunting bird had caught one fair and square, that'd be one thing. If one of the bachelors was getting cute with him…

But it was neither. Lewis pulled to a stop, startled, when he rounded the curve in the trail. Someone had set a trap. Not a cruel one with metal teeth, but a rope snare that yanked its victim off their feet and dangled them in the air to starve and freeze wasn't any kinder. Nor was it specific.

The elder's stumping steps caught up with him. He whistled. "That a lynx cub?"

"Nearly isn't," Lewis said grimly. He carried a knife on his belt when he hunted in man shape, and took it out now to carefully cut the rope, his other arm ready to catch the mostly-frozen cub. It fell limply against him, too cold to fight his unfamiliar hold.

"Wrong season for their cubs," the elder said after a moment's frowning study. "Think it's just an animal cub, or a shifter? My eyes aren't what they used to be."

"It's not your eyes. I can't tell either," Lewis admitted. "It's hard when they're that young, unless they change." He took off his coat and wrapped it around the cub. The pitiful thing barely stirred, except to open its mouth in a silent meow. "Doesn't look like he's in the mood to let us know one way or the other."

The elder spat again. "Damn shame." He hesitated. "What do you want to do with it?"

A thought, like a lick of flame, kindled in Lewis's mind. "I might know someone," he said, careful to sound casual. "A backwoodsman, not pack, but he lives out this way and he's good with first aid. I'll see if he's willing to help, if he can tell whether this cub's a shifter or not. Go back to the pack. Tell them where I am and why, and keep an eye out for anyone who starts looking guilty."

Elderly or not, the old man was as tough as shoe leather and beamed with pride. "You're a good Packmaster," he said in approval. "Much better than the last one. I'll carry word. Think you'll be back tonight?"

"Late," Lewis said, already looking down the long, narrow trail that would lead him back to Jacobi. "Don't look for me before dawn."

* * *

Jacobi

"Hello, the house!"

Jacobi glanced up from his work. The heavy brush he'd been using nearly slid from his hand, but he caught it before it could tumble off the edge of his newly cleared roof. He thought that was the only sign of surprise that he gave, but truth be told he hadn't expected to see Lewis again.

Hoped for, but he'd kept his hopes realistic. Alphas might play around with Alphas. It happened. But they didn't set up housekeeping together. Even in the wilderness, where packs were larger, the wolves needed every cub they could get.

Yet here Lewis was, and God help him, Jacobi's heart leapt at the sight of Lewis, looking at Jacobi for one second as if he thought Jacobi had hung the moon.

He kept his external reaction to a nod. "Hello, yourself."

"Need your help," Lewis said. He held his arms crossed snugly over his chest, cradling something inside. "Come down."

It wasn't a request. Jacobi knew that tone of voice. Came natural to all commanders. Besides, Lewis's peculiar body language pricked his curiosity. He slid to the edge of the sloping roof and jumped down, landing lightly on his feet in a shallow snowdrift. "What've you got there?"

Lewis grimaced as he opened the first three buttons. "You tell me."

Curiouser and curiouser. Jacobi ambled closer, taking his time. Making sure Lewis meant him no harm, for one, and wanting a scent preview of what lay in store. He caught something unfamiliar, but that was a sniff next to the rich, ripe scent of Alpha that made him want to groan with lust.

He caught Lewis's blue, blue eyes, brighter against the winter paleness of his skin, and had to stop nearly mid-stride to compose himself. God, how he wanted this Alpha in his bed again. He --

Stopped, when he saw what Lewis had brought him tucked inside his coat.

"Where did you find him?" Jacobi refastened the bottom two buttons so the lynx cub wouldn't get chilled all over again. "No, don't answer that yet. Bring him inside where it's warm."

Lewis fell in step behind him. Jacobi approved. He held the door for both of them, then gestured at the fireplace. Lucky for him, he'd kept the fire going while he shoveled snow off his roof, and the inside of the shack was as toasty as an oven. With the wintry world safely shut outside, he opened Lewis's coat all the way and scooped the lynx cub into his arms to check it over.

Not dead. *Thank God.* Jacobi breathed a sigh of partial relief. Not dead, but nearly frozen to the core and it had a raw circle around one back ankle. The sight made him growl.

"I'll deal with the one who set the trap," Lewis said grimly. He still hugged his torso, arms around his middle, rubbing absently. "I don't know if the cub has a chance, but I had to try. Can you do anything? Do you know who he is?"

"One question at a time, and not until I say."

Lewis held his tongue impatiently as Jacobi examined the cub. It'd already started to revive somewhat, still weak from cold and no doubt hunger, but aware enough to hiss at him when he poked the sore spots to make sure no bones were broken underneath. It even tried to wriggle away from his unfamiliar scent.

"Food, rest, and time, and he should come around," Jacobi decided out loud. He tugged a blanket off his bed and wrapped the cub up like a burrito to stop him taking swipes with his sharp little claws. Once it was safe, he stroked the cub's head to familiarize him with the new smell. "And yeah, I know who this is. Some backwoodsmen were talking about the whole mess when they didn't know I was nearby, listening. His Omega parent ran away from an Alpha who liked to use his fists. They found the Omega frozen in the snow about a week back. Some said he'd been pregnant, but no one knew for sure."

"Then he is a shifter." Lewis gritted his teeth audibly. "There'll be reparation, I promise."

"Good." Jacobi blew into the cub's nostrils to check its response, then chuckled when the cub sneezed. A wriggle, a twist, and abruptly a human baby filled the wrappings instead of a lynx. He changed back a second later, but it satisfied any hint of doubt. "Tough little guy, aren't you?"

"A real survivor," Lewis agreed. He'd relaxed a touch, less ready to pick a fight with God in lieu of the wolf he really wanted to get his hands on. "What are you going to do with him?"

Jacobi frowned over that. He wasn't a hundred percent sure. From what the backwoodsmen had said, the Omega lynx hadn't had any family that could be found at the time of his death. Just a couple of concerned neighbors with a houseful of their own kittens to feed and clothe. They wouldn't be able to take this one in.

"I'll think of something," he said at last, though it was a puzzler. "Maybe keep him myself."

Lewis's brows drew together. "You? By yourself, without an Omega?"

"Why not?" Jacobi shrugged. "Main benefit to living out here alone, Lewis, I can do what I damn well please. There's been stranger families than bears raising cats."

Lewis gave a barking laugh. "Well…" He stopped and rubbed his forehead. "I wouldn't have thought of that."

"You're a Packmaster. You don't think about going your own way. Just not how you're wired," Jacobi said. His heart went out to Lewis, and he laid a hand on the man's shoulder.

That was a mistake. The feel of the Alpha's sturdy muscles and the heat of his body made Jacobi's entire body jolt like he'd come far too close to a bolt of lightning. He heard Lewis suck in a sharp breath, and knew it must have felt the same for him. When he looked up, Lewis's pupils were dilated wide and dark, and filled with raw hunger.

"Stay," Jacobi said without thinking. He refused to take it back, though. "Stay the night. For the cub's sake."

Lewis swallowed audibly, the dark circles of his irises growing wider, hotter. "For the cub's sake," he agreed, ragged voiced. "For tonight. I'll stay."

Chapter Four

Lewis

"Good." Jacobi cracked a lopsided grin as he stood with the swaddled lynx cub cradled in one arm. "If you're staying, you can pay back one of the two you owe me by lending a hand around here."

Surprised, Lewis looked up at him. "Yeah?"

"Yeah. If I'm going to have an active cub in here, I need to make sure it's safe. You don't think I hand out favors for free, do you?" Jacobi squeezed Lewis's shoulder.

Lewis let out a rough breath and rubbed at his face. He'd thought he knew how much he wanted to stay -- at least for a little while -- but he hadn't known anything until now. Felt like waking up the morning after a long illness, opening his eyes to find his fever broken and his body as light as a cloud. "I'd like that."

Jacobi didn't say anything in response, but Lewis could sense his approval.

The lynx cub wriggled in its bindings then, catching Lewis's eye and making him chuckle. "He's going to be a handful. Reminds me of my -- I call them nephews, because it's easier. My cousin's pups. They have a houseful and there's more to come."

"That so?" Jacobi cocked his head thoughtfully, then without any further ado decanted the lynx cub directly into Lewis's arms. "Then that's how you can help. Keep him out of trouble while I square away everything a cub could get into trouble with."

"You don't want help? I could lend a hand." Lewis made a grunting sound. The cub had taken a swipe at his nose and nearly connected. "I could start by trimming this little man's claws."

Jacobi chuckled as he waved that off. "I know where everything is. Besides." A flicker of heat entered his gaze as he turned it toward Lewis. "I like the way you look, holding that cub."

Answering heat rolled through Lewis. He exhaled slowly, raggedly.

"Thought so," Jacobi murmured. He traced one fingertip along the line of Lewis's jaw. "Stay there and let me look at you while I take care of needful things first."

All Lewis could do was nod. Anyway, if he stood up before he cooled down he was almost sure to shame himself.

The thought only made him harder.

He gritted his teeth and filled his mind with pictures of snow, ice cold and shocking to heated skin, until he could take a clear breath again and focus on the cabin around him. His first glance was casual, but his second look was immediate and startled. "It wasn't like this last time, was it?"

"Hmm? No."

Jacobi hadn't needed to reply. Lewis could see the changes for himself. Before, the cabin -- shack -- had truly been a shack. Four walls, a roof, and a packed-earth dirt floor. Two windows blocked by sheets of heavy paper. A stack of blankets for a bed. Junk everywhere and a pile of disassembled traps in one corner. The blanket stack was still the same, but nothing else remained unaltered. The windows were clean, letting light inside; the dirt floor had been swept until it was hard and smooth as poured concrete. He'd made a rough seat out of stacked logs near the hearth, and put up a fire screen made of those broken traps stacked together. Coffee bubbled in the kettle on the hook, but there was a cast-iron Dutch oven tucked at the back of the fire that smelled like it had stew inside. A loaf of bread rested on the mantel. The tidying Jacobi needed to do was minimal, mostly stowing his carving knife and scouring the corners for any random trinkets.

Lewis whistled in honest amazement.

A faint hint of pink touched Jacobi's cheeks. He scrubbed at the back of his neck. "Figured it was about time I started making this place more like a home."

Had he done it thinking Lewis might come by again? Lewis couldn't be sure without asking... but maybe he didn't have to.

The lynx cub, tired of all this inactivity, finally wriggled fully free of its swaddling. Wobbly-legged, it balanced foursquare on Lewis's knees, dug its baby claws in, and mewed at him.

Lewis winced at the claws, but he knew that particular noise, no matter what species it came from. "He needs to eat."

Jacobi took that in his stride. He opened one window and thrust his arm outside regardless of the snow under the eaves, then came back with a plastic jug he placed near the fire. "Goat's milk. One of the backwoodsmen keeps them, but they're hellions for getting loose. I took this as payment for herding them back home with no one injured." His smile was wide and surprisingly boyish. "Can't beat serendipity."

Serendipity, hah, Lewis thought, hiding his own grin. *You were hoping you'd find this little fellow and wanted to be prepared.*

A cool head; a warm heart. Proof of both only made Lewis like Jacobi all the more. Lewis rocked the cub absently in his arms as he fed it with the corner of a new looking, clean smelling washcloth dipped in milk. The cub sneezed at his first taste, startled, then went after it with the intensity of the recently starving.

When Lewis was too slow rewetting the cloth, the hungry baby tried to chew on his wrist. Slowly, mouthful by mouthful, the cub satisfied its hunger. It fell asleep the way Ivoire's children sometimes did when they'd had enough, between one swallow and the next, belly rounded and limbs going lax. Lewis had only watched that from a distance before, chewing on his envy of Ivoire's ability to provide for his pups, and never known what it felt like.

Now he did. A powerful sense of yearning filled him, too strong to ignore; he had to close his eyes tight and breathe through the moment.

Before he'd finished, Jacobi was at his side, his hand warm and strong on Lewis's shoulder. He kneaded gently, providing strength and comfort.

"I don't know why I'm like this," Lewis said. The words burst out of him. "I'm an Alpha. A Packmaster."

Jacobi scooped the cub deftly out of Lewis's arms and carried him across the room. Though Lewis had been too occupied to notice what he was up to, he'd restocked some of the logs in a rough bin shape and padded them thickly with blankets for a makeshift cradle. He laid the cub inside and stood looking at him for a long moment.

Then, he came back to Lewis and waited for Lewis to look up at him. "Nothing wrong with you," he said, his voice rough and raw. "I like you the way you are, Lewis. Maybe more than I should. And I think maybe you feel the same for me, Alphas though we are. Is that true?"

* * *

Jacobi

Look at him. Eyes the size of his head.

Jacobi let his fingertips rest on the sharp edge of Lewis's cheekbone. The big tough Alpha trembled under his touch, his throat moving as he swallowed hard, his fists knotted in his lap.

"You're not the only one, you know," Jacobi whispered. "It's not just you."

Lewis's eyes drifted closed. One more hard shudder racked him before he went lax.

How long have you wished you were born an Omega? Jacobi wouldn't ask, because he knew the answer would be *always*. He didn't know a single Alpha who hadn't wondered at least once, especially when they saw the power Omegas had. Alphas could fight. Omegas brought life.

And they were beautiful, so beautiful, so desirable. Jacobi traced the lines of Lewis's face, seeing beauty there too. He rested the pad of his thumb on Lewis's lower lip, tugging it slightly down. "Open your eyes."

Lewis obeyed him, eyes drifting open. He gazed at Jacobi, pleading in his stare. "You're sure," he said roughly. "Sure this is what you want, too."

Jacobi took Lewis's hand and brought it to rest at his groin, molding Lewis's palm around the aching stiffness of his cock. "Even if I were to be damned for it, I'd want it."

Lewis's hand flexed, gripping Jacobi almost too hard. "What do you want me to do?"

"Nothing you don't want to." Jacobi braceleted his wrist and gave it a return squeeze. "Take me out and suck me."

Lewis's breath escaped him, and with it went the last of his resistance. He pushed himself off the bed and onto his knees, careless of his own hard-on, and pressed his face hard against Jacobi's groin. Opening his mouth, he sucked through the denim, but only long enough to make Jacobi groan and curse. He drew down the zipper then with hands that shook a little, and coaxed Jacobi's cock out.

The cold air was a shock; the hot, wet enclosure of Lewis's mouth a revelation. Jacobi braced himself with both hands on Lewis's shoulders. Took all he had not to thrust into the tight seal of Lewis's lips, to see how deep he could get before Lewis fought back.

Inasmuch as he could think past the shuddering sensations consuming him, he marveled at Lewis's delicacy of touch. Teeth covered, lips hard, tongue sleek and nimble.

"You thought about this," Jacobi said, lifting Lewis's head to coax him off. His lips were swollen pink. "Didn't you?"

"Couldn't stop," Lewis said, already a little hoarse. "I tried. Didn't work."

"It's like I said. You're not the only one." Jacobi rubbed the backs of his knuckles along Lewis's jaw, then at his nape. "Get undressed. Lie on the bed, face down."

"The cub --"

Jacobi checked just to be sure. "Fast asleep. He won't wake up before he's hungry or wet."

Seemed that wasn't what Lewis had worried about. His face went dull brick red, but either he couldn't or wouldn't explain himself.

And that, in itself, was explanation enough. Jacobi understood Lewis now. Knew what he wanted, what he needed. Not just to be ordered, so that he didn't have to be the one in charge for a change. He needed, just for a few minutes, to have all his yearnings satisfied. To pretend the cub was *theirs*, maybe even born in this bed, drawn from Lewis's body.

Jacobi couldn't make that be true, but he could sure as hell pretend for a while. Jacobi tugged Lewis's arms up in the air and tugged his shirt over his head. Before Lewis recovered his composure, Jacobi had bent and fastened his mouth to Lewis's right nipple, sucking as hard as Lewis had nursed at his cock. When he'd left a wet red mark there, he gave the stunned Lewis a push backward on the bed.

"Lie down, Omega," Jacobi said. He had to grip himself hard until the shock of hearing it passed. "Lie down and spread your legs for me."

Lewis made a choking sound, and even inside his jeans his cock visibly jerked. He scrabbled at the fastening of his jeans with unsteady hands, too thirsty for it to take his time with buckles and zippers, and when he did manage to wrestle himself free he slithered over onto his stomach, hips canted, face down.

Jacobi groaned. An Alpha like Lewis, this eager for *his* cock... *Damn*.

He crawled onto the bed. Wishing wouldn't produce an Omega's natural lubrication, but Jacobi had time and willpower on his side. He spread Lewis's ass cheeks and put his face between them, a mouthful of saliva at the ready.

Lewis cried out and bucked up against him.

Ready for that, Jacobi spanked his hip once. "Lie still," he said. "Going to get you wet." He licked long, lavish stripes between every word. "Get you wet enough to take me."

Lewis tried, but he couldn't keep himself from moving. He writhed on the bed and burned with an inner fire that made his skin flush nearly as hot as an Omega's when they were caught in the grip of their heat cycle. Desperate for an Alpha's cock, reduced to begging. The saliva Jacobi added made the illusion almost complete. He couldn't be harder, he thought, until his body proved him wrong. He ached, and he burned almost as strongly as Lewis did by the time he was ready to thrust inside Lewis's willing body. Didn't make it long after that -- the clutch of Lewis's body grabbed him and held him the way an Omega's would -- but by God, he made it count while it lasted, slamming deep, bruising hard, and pinning Lewis down when he came.

But he stopped Lewis before Lewis could start to grind against the bed, seeking his own satisfaction. Stopped him and flipped him over, so that he lay face-up and startled. When Lewis tried to reach for himself, Jacobi stopped him.

This had to be said.

"I don't want this to be just once," Jacobi growled. "I don't give a damn what anyone would think or say. They don't matter to me. But you? You're mine. You understand that?" He hadn't laid claim to anything in years, but the shack and the cub. "Say it, and I'll let you come."

A rasping breath shuddered out of Lewis's throat. "I am yours," he said with a groan. "Have mercy."

"Oh, I will." Jacobi reached between Lewis's legs. Giddy with relief, with pride, with things he didn't have names for, he swabbed up every drop of his own spunk that he could gather. Then, he knelt above Lewis and made sure the Alpha could see what he was doing before he slipped his messy handful between his own legs.

Lewis's groan wracked his entire body. "Jacobi," he breathed.

Jacobi let Lewis's hand join his, working to open him up for Lewis's already-knotted cock. "Like I said. It's not just you. And we're nowhere near done here, Alpha."

Chapter Five

Lewis

Oh, they should have ended it. Lewis wasn't a fool. He knew they were playing a dangerous game. Never mind that they were Alphas. They were a bear and a wolf. What kind of future could they have together, even if their secret never came out?

It would have been smart to stop before they got too badly burned.

Lewis guessed that made him a fool -- and God help him, when he was with Jacobi, he couldn't be sorry about it. He forgot everything that weighed him down when he and Jacobi spent evenings trading war stories in front of his fire, kept watch over the active lynx cub, and especially times like now, when their Alpha energy demanded release and they plunged outdoors, eager as boys, whooping like wild birds.

Sometimes -- like now -- wrestling. When that happened, the winner took all.

The forward momentum of a leap brought Jacobi to a hard, slamming stop against the outside of the cabin, his cheek and his palms pressed to the weatherworn wood. Jacobi turned his head halfway, giving Lewis a look at his fierce, savage grin. "Is that the best you've got?"

"Not by a long shot." Lewis crowded against Jacobi from behind, molding his front to Jacobi's back. He rolled his hips to let Jacobi feel how hard he'd gotten.

Jacobi's lips parted. He pressed back, grinding his ass to Lewis's cock. "So that's how it is?"

Lewis chuckled as he put his mouth to Jacobi's nape. "That's how it is," he whispered, hot beneath Jacobi's ear. "Out here. Right now."

"Big talk, no action," Jacobi gibed. He reached backward to clamp his hands to Lewis's hips. "What do you want?"

Lewis knocked Jacobi's hands away from him, and caught Jacobi's hips for himself. He leaned forward, pressing them both harder and tighter against the wall, and ground his pelvis to Jacobi's ass. "This. I want this."

Jacobi responded with a laugh, dark and triumphant. He raised his arms and spread them wide, fingers splayed against the cabin wall, and canted his hips. "A gentleman would lend a hand."

"I'm not feeling gentle right now."

"Good." Jacobi snapped his teeth on thin air, biting it in half, then licked his lips. "Then give it to me hard."

Lewis set his teeth hard. He could do this for hours -- had, before -- losing himself in heat and pressure and the fire that burned in his gut when he was with Jacobi. He covered Jacobi's hands with his own to pin him in place and thrust against him in short, choppy shoves. When he put his tongue to Jacobi's neck, he tasted salt and sweat and smoke, male musk, the fragrance of coffee stewed deep black.

And Alpha. Jacobi tasted of Alpha, dominant and hard as stone. Yielding for Lewis, making the same growls he would when mounting a willing Omega.

When Jacobi wrestled one hand free and reached for himself, Lewis knocked his hand away. He thrust his hand down the front of Jacobi's jeans, the denim stiff from being hand-washed and dried in the cold air, and took the surging heat and weight of Jacobi's cock into his palm. Alpha slick coated his fingers, making a slick tunnel for Jacobi to rut into, driving Lewis half wild with lust.

They didn't often let their Alpha natures take the lead at the same time. They liked playing Omega, and they could be gentle with each other as few Alphas ever were to their fellows. But when the stars aligned and they did take the gloves off --

He should have stopped, but he couldn't, no more than he could choose to stop breathing.

Lewis bit Jacobi's neck, breaking the skin and tasting sharp copper when he came, knowing they were bruising each other, savoring the idea of making marks that would last. Jacobi roared, a full-throated bear's shout, at the feel of Lewis's teeth. Pain, pleasure, or a mix of both; it didn't matter. He came with a groan from the center of his body and rattled their bones with the way he shuddered in Lewis's arms.

When Lewis let go to draw deep, hungry breaths of the freezing air, and the roaring in his ears subsided, he heard Jacobi laughing. Rusty, wild, free. Though his head lolled slightly on his neck he turned to look sideways at Lewis with a devil's grin on his lips.

Lewis returned it, though he knew his smile was weary. He patted Jacobi's hip. "All right?"

"If you have to ask the question," Jacobi said, shaking his head. "Yeah. I'm good."

He looked it too. The bear shifter had put on weight since they'd started meeting in secret, remembering to eat, and taking in extra calories from what Lewis brought every time he visited. Junk food for treats, butchered meat, butter and cheese. Lewis couldn't count his ribs in man shape or bear form anymore.

Jacobi cocked his head, listening. Lewis did the same and picked up the small sounds of the lynx cub waking from his afternoon nap.

"Better go and feed him," he said, reluctantly peeling himself away to let Jacobi stand on his own. "How're those bottles I brought? And the formula?"

"He likes goat milk better." Jacobi's shoulders straightened with pride. "He recognizes me now. He watches me like I'm a TV show."

Lewis laughed. Though still an infant, the lynx cub had personality to spare in both forms. "You should name him already."

Jacobi raised one shoulder. He scooped up a handful of snow to clean himself with, cursing breathlessly and fluently as he did, then offered Lewis the same. Lewis grimaced, but as unappealing as scrubbing himself with snow was, even less did he want to walk around all day with a gummy mess drying inside his jeans.

As Lewis took his turn, Jacobi watched with his hands in his pockets. "Was thinking after the cub's had his fill we could go walking the old trap lines. Just to make sure."

Lewis frowned -- he'd made sure his pack knew he meant business about trapping, and almost no one had complained. "We don't need to."

"Maybe not, but I want to," Jacobi said. He had a stubborn set to his chin. "You can come or not. Up to you."

"Oh, I'm coming. I just don't think it's necessary."

Jacobi opened his mouth, clearly having plenty to say to that, but before the words came out a deafening *crack*! made them both jump half out of their skins. Lewis threw himself in front of Jacobi, heart in his mouth, but then exhaled gustily as his senses filled in the rest of the picture. Just an old tree, overloaded with more snow than it could handle, finally giving way. His ears caught the rustle of falling branches and the indignant calls of displaced birds, and his nose picked up the scent of raw pine resin from the broken branch.

He turned to check on Jacobi, and if he'd reacted any slower than a Packmaster's baseline, would have lost an eye for his pains.

Jacobi roared at him with a bear's voice in a human throat. "Back!" He sliced at Lewis with bear paws attached to human wrists. "Back!"

"No." Lewis made a grab for his wrists, absurdly narrow next to the width of the bear's paws, and squeezed as hard as he could. "Jacobi! Snap out of it."

The bear bellowed in Lewis's face. Jacobi's eyes were fully brown and wild, the bear snarling in their depths.

PTSD. A flashback. He's not seeing me.

Beyond that, Lewis didn't think. Only acted. He raised his arm and delivered the sort of blow he would to a misbehaving wolf, one that knocked Jacobi to the ground and left him gasping for breath. It was as hard to give as it was to receive, and Lewis stood over his Alpha lover with his arm numb from impact, gasping for breath as Jacobi did.

But Jacobi's eyes were human again when he lifted his head to stare at Lewis. He said nothing.

Neither did Lewis.

* * *

Jacobi

Humiliation made Jacobi's head pound as he walked behind Lewis, an ugly throb behind his forehead and temples. Pissed him off all the more because it *should* have been a good time. Winter was losing its grip on the interior, and all around them the snowmelt dripped like easy spring rain. Harder packed, the trails weren't so slushy yet that snow threatened to slosh past his ankles and into his boots. The lynx cub rode in a makeshift pack on Lewis's back, facing outward so he could take it all in.

That should have cheered Jacobi, if nothing else. The baby lynx had eyes the size of dinner plates, staring around himself. If he remembered any of this trail from his time alone, it didn't bother him. He babbled baby talk and pointed to every bird that flew past, squealed with excitement when an Arctic hare starting to turn spring gray darted across their path.

He smiled -- a little -- but the smile faded to a scowl. Lewis was right. He should have named the lynx cub by now. Why hadn't he?

Speaking of the devil, Lewis kept glancing over his shoulder at Jacobi, and he didn't like what *he* saw. His forehead creased in concern, but did he pipe up? Nope. Kept his trap shut.

Finally, his silence irritated Jacobi to the breaking point. "If you're going to keep staring at me, you at least want to tell me what you're looking at?"

Lewis's mouth thinned into a firm line. "Okay, fine. How often does that happen? The PTSD."

"It's not PTSD." Jacobi had seen PTSD. He wasn't that badly off.

But Lewis wouldn't be dissuaded. "Call it a panic attack, then. Bear attack. I don't give a damn what you call it, but how often does it happen?"

Jacobi's hackles rose. "Not often. This is the first time in months. I'm not crazy."

"I never said you were." Lewis stopped to turn sideways, giving Jacobi his profile. "Have you seen a doctor about it?"

"Hell no."

Twin puffs of air huffed from Lewis's nose. "Why not?"

Jacobi gave him a disbelieving look. "Maybe 'cause I don't care for the way they decorate psych wards these days? Or being tried for murder, if the bear went mad when it took over?"

"So you locked yourself away instead," Lewis said. "Out here, with no one and nothing to hurt or help."

"Have you ever met any of the backwoodsmen? They could put me down if they needed to."

"Jacobi..." Lewis rubbed the bridge of his nose. "That's not what I mean at all. I'm worried. I want to help. Do you see that?"

Jacobi did, and it made his face burn with shame just as it made his tongue sharp. "I'm not part of your pack, Packmaster. If I don't want your help, I'm not obligated to take it."

That shot sank home. Lewis narrowed his eyes and swung back around to face forward, the length of his stride increasing until it made Jacobi's hamstrings ache with the effort of keeping up with him. A stab of guilt made him growl. He oughtn't to take his temper out on Lewis, but a man -- an Alpha -- could only bear so much.

He tried to shake his mood as they walked on, down one trail and then another. Tried to let the sunlight and the soothing patter of meltwater, and the laughter of the cub, lift his spirits. Might have worked, if the crack of branches didn't sound every few minutes and shake him back to square one.

By the time they reached the trail where they'd found the lynx cub -- damn it, he needed a name! -- Jacobi was ready to burst at the first provocation, and it wasn't long in coming. They hadn't seen a single trap so far. Not one.

Until now.

They had barely turned the curve when the wicked glint of steel and the ugliness of rusted iron caught Jacobi's eye. He stopped in his tracks and cursed louder than the cracking branches. "Damn it, Lewis! That's a bear trap. I thought you said you had it under control!"

Lewis's hands fisted. He took three deep breaths. "I thought I did."

"Some control," Jacobi scoffed. "Some Packmaster." He shouldered past Lewis and went to his knees heedless of the wet snow to dismantle the trap.

He snarled at Lewis when Lewis pulled him away. "If you can't take care of it, I will," he warned the Packmaster.

Lewis had a face like thunder and when he spoke, his voice was tight with fury. "Oh, it'll be taken care of. If you let me get a look at the trap before you pull it to pieces, so I can figured out who put it here. I'll have that wolf in my sights tonight or know the reason why."

Jacobi saw the sense in that, and he would have listened if anger hadn't taken the reins. "The hell you say." He knew how these traps worked by now, and a couple of fierce blows from a bear fist twisted the ugly iron jaws beyond repair. He hurled them one after another into the highest branches he could swing for, where they caught and dangled like gibbets.

A muscle jumped in Lewis's jaw, and Jacobi thought for sure the fists would start flying now. He welcomed it. Almost.

Lewis didn't take a shot at him. Almost calmly, he unstrapped the cub and pressed him into Jacobi's arms; startled, Jacobi took him. Only then did Lewis speak. "You can't keep doing this."

Confusion didn't lighten Jacobi's mood. "Can't keep doing what?"

"This!" Lewis waved one arm at the woods. "Hiding yourself away, like that's going to solve your problems. Avoiding people, or driving them off. Maybe it works for now, but what about when the cub is old enough to want more than milk or mush? What about when he's school age? Are you going to keep him locked up here with you? It doesn't have iron teeth, Jacobi, but it's still a trap."

Jacobi's ears rang; his hands were numb, and so were his lips. "Maybe I'm hiding," he said despite all that. He wrapped both arms around the cub. "Maybe that's true. But that makes you one hell of a hypocrite, Packmaster Omega. Doesn't it?"

All the color fled from Lewis's face. He stood upright as if he'd been shot or struck by lightning. "You bastard."

Jacobi knew Lewis would never look at him the same way again. And that it was no more than he deserved, even if he couldn't shut himself up. "Go to hell."

"If I do, I'll see you there," Lewis retorted. His fists flexed. "That cub needs more of a life than you've allowed yourself. Or that I've let myself have. So this is your one warning, Jacobi, and even if I'm not your Packmaster I am *a* Packmaster, and my word is law. The cub gets medical care. It gets schooling. It gets a name. If you don't allow it any of those things, I *will* take it from you in due time. Do you understand?"

Jacobi did. Humiliation, hurt, and shame flared up one last time. He bared his teeth.

Lewis shook his head slowly. He looked as weary as he had the first time Jacobi had met him, save for the slow burn of anger that kept him on his feet. "Goodbye, Jacobi."

He turned to walk away, head held high.

He didn't look back once.

Chapter Six

Lewis

"You should have everything you need in here," Lewis said. He stood in the doorway of his sparse but clean spare room, eyes fixed on his pregnant cousin perched on the edge of the bed inside. "Do you need me to show you where it all is?"

Ivoire crinkled his nose at Lewis. "I think I can navigate my way through one little room, Lewis. Besides, you've already gone over everything once. I promise I don't need an encore."

Had he? Lewis's face warmed, but he kept his external reaction to a shrug. "Just making sure."

"I'm eight and a half months gone, Lewis, not addled." Ivoire rested a palm on his bulging belly. One of the unborn twins responded with a kick that made Ivoire's hand bounce, and made Lewis wince for him. Ivoire shook his head and put his hand to the small of his back instead, digging in with his knuckles. "I'm due for some peace and quiet, though."

Lewis had seen pregnant Omegas nearing the end of their terms before, and knew a rest would do Ivoire good before he delivered. When he'd begged the loan of Lewis's spare room for a long weekend, Lewis had been willing to let him have it. Even so... "You think Zachariah can keep up with your older twins and the singleton for three whole days?"

"He'd better, if he knows what's good for him." Ivoire gave him a cheeky grin. "I love him, and he knows that."

So did Lewis. From the moment he'd heard about the widower in need of someone to help him move on, and learned his pregnant cousin was coming to join the Wasp Lake pack, he'd seen how they would fit together -- and they had. There wasn't a better matched pair in the pack.

"He also knows which side his bread is buttered on," Ivoire finished, patting his belly. Then, he cocked his head. "Are you all right, Lewis? Don't shake your head at me before I've even finished asking the question. You look like you haven't slept in weeks."

Lewis didn't doubt that. Since walking away from Jacobi two weeks previously, and not hearing a word or whisper from him since, he hadn't gotten a solid night's sleep. An hour here or there was all he could manage before he started dreaming about Jacobi. Missing him. Wanting to be with him again.

All true. But what could he do about it without crawling?

Not a damn thing, that's what.

"I'm fine," Lewis lied in answer to Ivoire's question. "Don't worry about me. Get some rest."

Ivoire sized him up frankly, then surprised Lewis by hopping off the bed and standing on his tiptoes to kiss Lewis's cheek. "You forget I know you, cousin. I don't know what's going on, but whatever it is, don't be so stubborn about it that you miss out on life and love. Isn't that what you made such a point of with Zachariah and me?"

Lewis touched his cheek where Ivoire had kissed it and stared at his cousin, who only beamed back at him before giving him a light push. "All right. Omegas only in here, starting now. Goodnight, Packmaster."

He closed the door politely but firmly in Lewis's face. Lewis stared at it. "What if these twins are going to be Alphas?"

Ivoire only laughed. "Good *night*, Packmaster."

Lewis blew out a gusty breath as he walked the short distance from his spare room to his bedroom and shut that door behind him. What the world was coming to, when an Omega thought they could boss an Alpha Packmaster around like that...

Even when they were right.

And yet... Lewis gritted his teeth. As much as he wanted to see Jacobi again, he'd never be able to bridge that gap. Not without abasing himself more than a Packmaster could bear without losing face and sacrificing power. With the sacrifice of power, trap lines would go back up. Ivoire wouldn't be safe. And if he *did* find a way to reunite with Jacobi, and the pack found out their master had taken another Alpha as his lover...

Rock, meet hard place. And be damned if Lewis didn't wish there was some way around all of them.

Growling, he rubbed his face hard.

Crack!

Lewis looked up at the small but sharp, splintering sound. *What the...*

Crack!

The window. Two spider-webbed lines radiated out from chips in the glass where it'd been smooth and clean just minutes before. Lewis set his jaw and stalked to the window to raise the pane. If this was pack teenagers trying to get cute, he'd haul them home by their scruffs.

It wasn't. Down below, just inside the spill of light from his window, Jacobi crouched with a pebble in his hand. His eyes looked like two burned holes in white sailcloth, and he hadn't shaved in a few days. He swallowed when Lewis fell silent.

"I know I don't have any right to be here," he said, his whisper as harsh as it'd sounded back when he rarely spoke. "But I'm not here for myself. It's Ray -- the cub. He's sick." He opened his coat to show Lewis what he carried inside, next to his skin.

The lynx cub -- Ray? The name suited his sunny nature -- didn't stir. His eyes were glazed with fever and his cheeks had lost their chubbiness. Lewis felt the shock of it clear down to his bones.

"He needs help," Jacobi rasped. "I don't care what you do with me. Help *him*."

Lewis didn't question it. Not once. He reached out of the window. "Take my hand and climb in."

Thinner or not, Jacobi was still a significant weight to lift, but he helped Lewis lift him and the cub inside, and winced but didn't protest when Lewis closed the window. His focus was all on Ray as he unwrapped the lynx from its swaddling inside his coat. "I don't know what's wrong. He started coughing this morning, and then his fever went up."

Lewis hissed when he touched the back of his hand to Ray's forehead. Sizzling hot, and dry as old leather. He glanced up without thinking and met Jacobi's eyes.

Jacobi swallowed again. Pleading and panic at being so enclosed warred with pride in his face, and in the end they both gave way to a simple shake of the head. "Help."

He wasn't just asking for himself. Lewis could hear it. The Packmaster inside him would have given the same answer the man did. He pressed his lips to Jacobi's forehead, and his palm to Jacobi's cheek. "All right," he said. "I will. I swear. Stay here. My cousin's come for a visit. He has three children, almost five. He'll know what to do. I'll wake him."

Jacobi went paler and shuddered, but he held his ground. "Go get him. I'll be here." The corner of his mouth turned up, and he caught Lewis's hand to squeeze it slightly as Lewis would have withdrawn.

"I promise. And Ivoire will know what to do."

He hoped.

* * *

Jacobi

Ivoire did know what to do. Lewis's cousin made him proud with the Omega's reaction to his guests. One blink at Jacobi, one at the cub, then a firm nod and Ivoire was all business.

"Let me have him," Ivoire ordered, taking the cub from Jacobi with a force of personality that Jacobi plainly wasn't prepared to resist.

Lewis raised one shoulder at Jacobi and stood back, beckoning for Jacobi to do the same. Ivoire barely noticed they were still in the room. "There now, there now," he murmured to the cub, who began to stir as Ivoire unwrapped his swaddling. "Warm as a little coal. Has he been pulling at his ears?"

"What?" Jacobi visibly pulled himself together. Lewis's heart could have burst with pride. "No."

"Coughing? Sneezing?" Ivoire asked.

Jacobi shook his head.

Ivoire laid the back of his hand on the cub's forehead, then bent his head to press his ear to the cub's chest. "I'm not a doctor, but his heartbeat is steady and his lungs sound clear. It's likely just a fever. They happen, and the first time is always the worst." He touched his fingertips to Jacobi's arm and smiled at him. "You should have seen how panicked I was the first time the twins came down with a cold. Lewis?"

Lewis snapped to attention. "What can I do?"

"Run a lukewarm bath. *Not* cold. That would shock his little system. We'll lower the water temperature if we have to. I'll give him a baby dose of fever reducer."

"Is it safe for lynx as well as wolves?" Jacobi asked in a bear's deep thrum. His hands shook, but they stayed human-shaped and the rest of him was as steady as a rock.

Ivoire raised an eyebrow at him and then at Lewis, made a *hmm* noise, then patted Jacobi's hand soothingly. "Should be. The bottle's in a pocket of my coat -- lucky for us I never clean those out -- so you go get that and look it up while Lewis runs the bath. We'll figure out something else if we have to, but I think we'll be all right."

"He'll --" Jacobi had to stop and clear his throat. "He'll get better?"

"I think he will," Ivoire said. "I promise I'll take care of him as if he were my own." He bounced the cub gently. "Well? Let's get started."

* * *

Lewis

Near dawn, the cub's fever finally broke. Safe and sound, he slept securely in a temporary cradle made of an emptied, well-padded dresser drawer tucked in the corner of Ivoire's room. Ivoire had chivvied them out without taking no for an answer.

"I'm used to it," he'd said frankly, with another of his impossible-to-resist smiles. "Besides, after keeping up with three that are mobile, this is still like a vacation for me. I'll come get you if anything changes, but I don't think it will. Right now what we all need is some sleep."

Lewis couldn't deny the wisdom of that, but as for himself he sincerely doubted sleep was going to happen. Nor would it come easily to Jacobi, who'd started to tremble as soon as they knew the cub was on the mend and hadn't stopped since.

Closing the door to his room, Lewis turned to face Jacobi. "Are you --" he started to ask.

He didn't get any further before one hundred and fifty pounds of solid, leanly muscled bear shifter collided with him, filling his arms. Words didn't matter then, and Lewis closed his arms as tightly around Jacobi as Jacobi clutched him.

"He's okay," Jacobi said over and over, all the emotion he'd kept at bay during the crisis flooding out in a steady stream. He dug his fingers into Lewis's back and held tight. "He's okay, he's all right."

Lewis rubbed Jacobi's back, murmuring wordless reassurance in response.

Finally, Jacobi shuddered one last time, then let go. His eyes were red, but he didn't seem to notice that. "Your cousin," he said, gravelly again. "That's one hell of a spitfire Omega."

"With sugar on top," Lewis agreed. "When Ivoire puts his mind to something, he makes it happen."

Jacobi snorted wetly. "I noticed." He cleared his throat and stood straight, studying Lewis eye to eye. "I owe you both for that."

Lewis started to wave that aside, but Jacobi wouldn't allow it. He shook his head and took Lewis by the shoulder to make him stand still and focus.

"I'm a lone shifter," Jacobi said. "I'm a bear who's had no pack and no master, by my own choice. But it's not just me now."

He let go of Lewis's shoulder, and dropped to one knee with his head bowed. "I owe you a life for Ray's life. If you'll have a bear in your midst, then I'm yours to command -- Packmaster."

Lewis drew a sharp breath. The words hit him dead center, a shock to the system that made heat flare in his groin and in his heart.

"I mean it," Jacobi insisted. "I won't take it back."

Slowly, Lewis moistened his lips with the tip of his tongue. "I know you meant it," he said, "and I'm not asking you to take it back. I'll accept you into my pack, but with one condition. I'm not your master." The more he spoke, the more he felt the rightness of it. *Yes. This is the only choice I could make.* He took Jacobi by the arm and raised the bear to his feet. "You're an Alpha, and you're my equal. And you're my lover, if you'll still have *me*. If you still want me."

Now it was Jacobi's turn to look as shocked as Lewis had felt. "Your pack won't like that."

"I know," Lewis said steadily. "That's not my concern. My word is law in the pack, and if I have to fight for it I will."

"You…" Jacobi turned his head slowly side to side, but the beginnings of a smile made the corners of his mouth curl. "It must run in the family. All right. I accept your word. And… God, Lewis. Still have you? Still want you? I don't want anything *but* you, and Ray to raise as my own. That's all I could ever need."

He turned, but caught Lewis's hand as he did.

"What?" Lewis asked, puzzled.

"Packmaster, can I make it any more plain?" Jacobi tugged at Lewis's hand, leading him to the bed. He glanced over his shoulder, and his smile widened. "Come and be my equal."

Lewis pulled back, the surprise of it bringing Jacobi stumbling into him. He barely had his arms around the bear before he couldn't wait a second longer, and kissed him.

Chapter Seven

Jacobi

Jacobi led Lewis by the hand to his bed -- no, it'd be their bed now, wouldn't it? His heart pounded in his throat and a curious sort of shyness made him keep his head down. He glanced back over his shoulder once and saw that Lewis looked the way he felt inside. As if this was more than sex.

Well, it was.

Jacobi let go of Lewis's hand, his fingertips trailing over Jacobi's palm, to climb on top of the bed. He lay on his back and watched Lewis hesitate at the edge, unsure of his next move. Yeah, he felt it too.

But they didn't have to let that stop them. Not now, and not ever again.

"Come here," Jacobi said, a quiet murmur of sound. He curled his fingers to beckon Lewis. "Be with me."

Lewis's throat moved as he swallowed. A rush of pride erased at least half of Jacobi's unaccustomed bashfulness. *He* had done that. He, Jacobi, had that effect on a Packmaster.

Pretty powerful stuff.

Lewis's mouth tipped up in a grin. He shook his head at himself, and followed Jacobi onto the bed. He didn't stop there, though, but crawled over Jacobi and brought himself down to rest lying half on Jacobi, one leg slipped between both of Jacobi's, and half on the mattress. "This all right?"

"You don't have to ask." Jacobi brought his hand up to ruffle through Lewis's short hair. "But yeah."

"Good," Lewis breathed, warm and tingling on Jacobi's lips, and kissed him.

Jacobi melted into the kiss. He wrapped his right arm around Lewis's neck and brought his right leg up to curl over the back of Lewis's thigh. God, how that Alpha could kiss. It made him melt inside as if he really were the Omega they both sometimes ached to be. Made him feel liquid and hot in every pocket of his body, a deep hunger driving him for more, more, more.

Lewis didn't stop there either. He moved down Jacobi's neck, over his collarbone, and unbuttoned Jacobi's flannel shirt to get at his breastbone. He stopped with his lips over Jacobi's heart. "I can feel it beating," he murmured. "So fast."

Jacobi touched his fingertips to Lewis's neck. "Not the only one."

"I know." Lewis captured one of Jacobi's flat nipples between his teeth and bit gently, tugging at the nubbin.

Jacobi groaned and raised his hips in a rush, only for Lewis to press him back down into the bed.

"How do you want it?" Lewis asked in Jacobi's ear. "I mean… What do you want?"

Letting his eyelids drift open, Jacobi looked up at Lewis and studied his face. So earnest and eager and sweet, in a way only he -- Jacobi -- ever got to see.

It was a question that required due thought before answering. They'd played at being Omegas, and they'd indulged themselves as Alphas. They'd switched every way that they could, enjoying their games, and Jacobi didn't regret a single one of them, but…

"I think I want us to be who we are," Jacobi said, sweeping his palm in light circles over Lewis's back. They were still mostly clothed, yet he felt utterly bare, and no longer even a little bit hesitant. "The Alpha body. The Omega heart. Just ourselves."

Lewis's smile dawned bright and easy. "I think we can do that."

Though neither had said what they wanted, they both knew. As one, they turned on their sides, facing each other as if they were brackets. Jacobi lifted his hips to let Lewis ease his jeans down far enough to free his cock, and did the same for Lewis in his turn. He nudged closer, so that their cocks brushed, and captured them both in the circle of his fingers.

Lewis drew in a sharp breath, then covered Jacobi's hand with his own. "This," he said on the exhale of that gasp. "Oh yes. Like this."

They pressed their foreheads together, Jacobi's to Lewis's, and slowly but surely they moved together. Jacobi fed the fire burning inside him with the hard press of Lewis's cock to his, and with his mouth pressed to Lewis's until it tingled, too numb to kiss but still moving one against the other. He thrust his free arm beneath Lewis's neck for Lewis to rest his head on, and moaned when Lewis used his legs to bring them closer, tighter, to grind their bodies in a slow, inexorable rhythm.

They came together, or seconds apart -- Jacobi couldn't tell who was the first, and it didn't matter -- as gently as the pull of the moon that guided their shapeshifting. Lewis groaned into Jacobi's mouth, and Jacobi muffled his shout against Lewis's breast, and for one moment he seemed to forget which of them was which. Who was the bear, and who was the wolf.

It didn't matter. Tied together in a lover's knot, they breathed each other's breath, and let their bodies make promises of forever.

And it was good.

* * *

Lewis

Just past dawn, the scent of brewing coffee brought Lewis sniffing out of his room and into his kitchen, where he found Ivoire bundled up in a borrowed robe and drinking his own cup of herbal tea. His hair stood up in all directions and his eyes were puffy, but he still cracked a grin when he saw Lewis come in. "I thought that'd get your attention."

"It's almost like you know me," Lewis said, deadpan. "We could be related."

Ivoire chuckled and gave him a light shove. "Drink up."

He didn't have to tell Lewis twice. Lewis filled two mugs, meaning to take one to Jacobi, but lingered for a moment to start sipping his and to assess Ivoire. "You're supposed to be sleeping."

"You try sleeping with two active cubs tucked inside your skin, and see how much rest you get," Ivoire said with a grimace, but waved off Lewis's rueful response. "I'm used to it. I'll sleep the clock around after they're born, and Zachariah can manage all five of them until I wake up."

Lewis grinned. "How's the cub? Ray?"

"Doing well," Ivoire replied with a promptness that reassured. "The fever reducer worked like a charm. He's fast asleep, and purring."

Lewis was familiar with those sleep purrs, and they never failed to fascinate. "I'll check in on him before I take this to Jacobi," he said, gesturing with the mug. He started to leave, but stopped when Ivoire put out a hand to halt him. When he looked at Ivoire, Ivoire was nibbling his lip.

"Something wrong?" Lewis asked, old habit making him alert.

"Lewis…" Ivoire shook his head and smiled. "No, nothing's wrong. I just wanted to say I'll have your back. I won't ask for the whole story if you would rather keep the details to yourself -- you've always been private -- but I can put two and two together as well as anyone else, and all I care about is that you're happy. Are you?"

"So much," Lewis said, his throat thick. "So much, cousin."

Ivoire nodded decidedly. "Good. And Lewis?" Stroking the sides of his mug, then the bulge of his belly, he sized Lewis up for another moment before going on. "I've been thinking. If you'd like to be in the room when these two are born, I'd be honored."

So Ivoire did understand him. The kindness and compassion of his cousin nearly made Lewis's knees buckle, and he had to clear his throat twice before he could speak. "I'd like that."

"Then it'll happen." Ivoire set his mug down with a sigh. "But that's not the real reason I made coffee to tease you out of your room. You've got company waiting for you outside."

Lewis frowned. "Why outside?"

"One of them said he preferred the open air. The other one, I didn't invite." Ivoire's lips thinned briefly. "One of the pack elders and his grandson. An enforcer."

Ahh. Lewis grimaced. He could understand Ivoire's distaste for the enforcers, who'd hunted him for sport before he joined the Wasp Lake pack. He only kept the ragged gang of toughs because ancient pack law dictated their necessity -- but all kinds of things seemed to be changing. Perhaps that should be one of them.

Glancing up, he saw that either the scent of coffee or the quiet hum of conversation had coaxed Jacobi out of the bedroom. Jacobi held back, but raised an eyebrow at Lewis to ask *what's going on?*

"Come with me," Lewis said. It was an impulse, but he refused to reconsider, and instead held out a hand for Jacobi to take.

Jacobi took it, but as he did he asked, "Are you sure about this?"

Lewis squeezed his hand in answer.

He led Jacobi outside as Jacobi had led him to the bed earlier, and though he had to let go of Jacobi's hand to open his heavy cabin door, he made sure Jacobi stood side by side with him once past it. It was a right traditionally given to the Packmaster's mate, and no wolf would fail to recognize the significance of the gesture.

It certainly wasn't lost on his visitors. Lewis could see that right away. The pack elder, a seamed and wizened Alpha, made no comment. His grandson, one of the more brutish of the enforcers, started to sputter.

He shut his mouth when the elder jabbed him in the ribs. "Quiet, you," he ordered in his cracked old voice, then bowed his head to Lewis in the old traditional way. "Packmaster."

"Boaz," Lewis replied. "Why have you brought this wolf to me?"

"Because he's a damned fool," Boaz said frankly. "One who doesn't have the respect due his Packmaster or the pack's laws, old or new. I found half a dozen jerry-rigged traps stowed under his cabin."

Jacobi bristled, but kept silent.

Lewis bit back his first response, full of heated words, and fixed the enforcer with a hard stare instead. Though he was a big man, with shoulders like hay bales and biceps like beer barrels, he shriveled under Lewis's gaze until he seemed smaller than any of them.

"I am the master of this pack," Lewis said then, quiet and steady. "And my word is law. Your punishment is mine to decide. Do you understand?"

Boaz jabbed his grandson in the ribs again, but that didn't stop the young fool from opening his mouth. "I needed the money for this year's Arctic Man festival! Dude, there are so many Omega hos just ripe for the picking there. You can't make me quit trapping anyway, you're not the boss of --"

A bear's roar thundered out of Jacobi's throat, a sound so fierce it made Lewis's hair stand on end even as he voiced his own snarling howl. "Aren't I?" Lewis walked down the three steps that led to his cabin door, never once taking his eyes off the enforcer as the sulky beast shriveled again. "Wrong. If you don't like it, you can fight me. *If* you think you can take me. *If* you think you want to be master of the pack. Is that what you want?"

The enforcer couldn't meet Lewis's eyes. He stared at the dirt instead.

"Then this is your punishment." Lewis stopped barely two feet away from the enforcer, well within striking range. "For your grandfather's sake, I won't cut you off from the pack. But you will leave for at least one year. And since you like traps so much, then that's what you'll do with that year. Find a crab boat and sign yourself on as a deckhand. Half your pay comes back here, to help your grandfather in your absence."

The enforcer started to protest, but Lewis's sharp cuff cut him off. "I could kill you for disobeying," he said, low with menace. "And you damn well know it. So count yourself lucky, and get out of here before I change my mind. *Now!*"

Jacobi's growl was subsonic, but it got the point across. Though stormy with anger, the enforcer rounded on his heel and stalked away.

Lewis knew this wasn't over. A year at sea might cool the enforcer's head, but it might not. If he came back carrying a grudge, it could spell trouble. Yet they had enough difficulty keeping up their numbers with limited Omegas in their pack, and could ill afford to banish this wolf for keeps.

Lewis pushed that aside for the moment. They'd wait and see what happened, and deal with consequences in their own time.

The enforcer's grandfather lingered a moment longer. He narrowed his seamed eyelids at Lewis, then at Jacobi.

Lewis steeled himself. If there was going to be any fuss over his taking Jacobi as a mate, it would start here and now, but out of respect for the wolf's age, he held his tongue.

"I remember the old Packmaster," Boaz surprised him by saying. "And the Packmaster before him, and the one before him."

Frowning, Lewis nodded.

The old man cracked a wry smile. "I remember those Packmasters too well. So when I look at you and think 'times are changing,' well. Sometimes they change for the better."

He turned to stump after his grandson, his steps slow but steady and sure to get him there.

Lewis's breath escaped him in a great puff, and he was grateful for Jacobi's sturdy shoulder to lean against.

When he turned to look, Jacobi's fury had melted into silent laughter. He shook his head as he chuckled, but just before Lewis would have asked him to explain, he turned that sweet smile of his full on Lewis and took his hand. "Well done, Packmaster."

Lewis lifted Jacobi's hand to kiss it out in the open, where anyone could see, and felt nothing but free. "It's a good start."

Epilogue

"Are we ready?"

Jacobi glanced up at Lewis, then down at his boots, then chuffed quietly. He nodded at the boots' trailing laces. "More ready than you are for walking the old trap lines."

Lewis made a face at his feet. "Figures," he grumbled, dropping to one knee.

Before he could reach the laces, a lynx cub beat him to it. Ray darted out of the corner where he'd been hiding in his animal form, tail twitching to and fro with excitement. Jacobi had seen him. He didn't know if Lewis had.

Did it matter? Lewis knew the appropriate response when being stalked by a babe in arms. He pretended to yelp and fling himself backward, ass over teakettle, and flung an arm over his eyes. "Help, Jacobi, help. I'm being attacked by a lynx."

Jacobi burst into full throated laughter. "Sorry, babe, you're on your own."

"Cruel, cruel world," Lewis intoned soberly as Ray tried to drag him off by his laces. He sat up and swooped Ray into his arms, tickling him until he shifted back into toddler shape -- all the better to squeal and pretend to wriggle away. "There you are. I thought it might be you under all that fur."

"Daddy!" Ray gave Lewis his best two-year-old impersonation of Lewis's Packmaster face. "Silly."

Jacobi chuckled to himself. "Don't look at me. I said you were on your own."

"Nope." Lewis rolled easily to his feet and brought Ray along with him, bouncing him lightly in his arms. From there, he gave Jacobi a look of such surpassing sweetness that it nearly took Jacobi's breath away. "I haven't been alone in a long time."

Jacobi rubbed at his mouth, but couldn't hide the way it curved in pleased answer. They'd come a long way, the two of them. Three of them. And they had just as far to go, hand in hand.

"Good answer," he told Lewis, knowing his own face reflected as much love for his Alpha as his Alpha did for him. "Very good answer."

"I know." Lewis balanced Ray on his hip, and held out his hand to help Jacobi up. Like he always did, except when it was Jacobi's turn. "Come with me."

Jacobi knew that, but took one more moment to bask in the perfect peace and pleasure of just being -- and of not being afraid. Not needing to hide. Not ever again.

Of loving, and being loved. He drew a deep breath, knowing it was good.

Then, he took Lewis's hand and got to his feet. He kissed Lewis lightly on the lips, and Ray on the cheek. "Let's go, Alpha. The world is waiting."

Have and Hold
Will Okati

Former bad-boy pack enforcer Alpha Scott knew he had to change his ways if he wanted to see his thirtieth birthday. He's worked hard to remake himself, and now that he's bought the *Fisherman's Friend* he's within inches of achieving his dreams.

Six months ago, Scott had a one-night stand with Maccabe, a feisty Omega. Maccabe didn't know he was on the verge of going into heat, but when he realized he was pregnant, he figured it out. Maccabe hasn't had an easy life either. As a teenage runaway, he spent a few years making bad choices before he turned his life around.

Neither of them are ready to be parents. Neither of them expects to fall in love. But that's what's happening. And now it's up to them to make the right choices.

Chapter One

Scott

"You won't regret this. No sir! You'll work and you'll sweat and you'll forget there ever was such a thing as spare time -- and if you're ever in the mood for a little something-something, forget it! With a little hard work, you'll have her open again in no time. Then, my boy! Then you'll serve beers by the keg load to fishermen fresh off the sea all night long and be too busy to go to bed with anyone but your own right hand. It'll eat you alive and you'll love it to death, sure as shooting fish in a barrel."

Slapping Giles, his old friend and the former owner of the *Fisherman's Friend,* gently on his once-beefy shoulder, Scott laughed. "You don't have to sell me on it, my man. Or is it someone else who's already got my cash in his hand?"

"Damn right, and it's already burning a hole in my pocket." Giles pounded Scott on the back in return, then sighed. "It's not easy to let this place go. If I could still keep up with all the repair work... But I can't, especially not after all the storm damage we took last winter. Fixing up a place like this is a young man's game."

Giles trailed off, resting his arthritis-gnarled hand on the scarred old bar top and gazing around, drinking the place in.

Scott let him. He knew love when he saw it, and he knew -- he'd learned the hard way -- how to tell when it was time to say goodbye.

Giles cleared his throat, then thumped the bar top gently. "Anyhow. You serve this place right, and it'll serve you until you're as old and gray as I am."

"Planning on it." Scott offered the old Alpha his hand for a shake. "I'll do my best by the place." He winked. "Even if I never get laid again."

Delighted out of his brief melancholy, Giles cackled at him. "See that you do, boy." He dug a set of keys from one pocket of his overalls and tossed them over handed to Scott. "Hit the ground running, boy. It's all yours. I won't say goodbye. I've never been too good at it."

Scott nodded. He could understand that. Big changes weren't ever easy. He honored the gray wolf's wishes by watching him go in silence, and waiting for the front door to shut behind him before he let *his* feelings out to play. He pumped his fist in the air, jumped a good foot off the ground, and let out a quiet but heartfelt whoop of joy.

His! All his. Scott turned in circles to take it all in. It'd break his back and finish emptying his pockets fixing up the place, but he owned a *bar*, by God. Him. And more than that. He'd make it more. He'd get the kitchen open again. And the rooms upstairs. Once they were cleaned up, fixed up nice, he'd make it the kind of place Alphas could bring their Omegas. Homey. Safe.

Ten years ago, he'd have laughed at anyone who suggested such a thing might ever happen -- that was, if he hadn't been too full of himself to take notice of what anyone else was saying. He'd been an enforcer for a big wolf pack in the rugged Alaskan interior, and one hell of a son-of-a-bitch.

Well, things had changed. He'd pulled himself up and sorted himself out one grueling step at a time. Gone fishing for crab, and saved his cash instead of throwing it to the wind. Hunted in wolf shape every time he got restless and sold the furs he caught.

And look at what he'd done for himself. A business, an honest to God business, of his own.

He'd do right by the place, Scott vowed. Come hell, high water, or whatever else may.

Movement caught his eye, and he looked right just in time to see a slight man shade his eyes to peer past the *CLOSED* sign on the door.

Scott knew he should have sent the man on his way -- they weren't open yet, after all, and wouldn't be for a good few days. And yet -- this was his first customer, not even five minutes after he'd taken over the business. It felt like a good omen, so Scott waved at the man to beckon him in.

Opening the door, the small man stepped inside. He blinked in the semi-darkness of the room as he took off his hat. "Are you sure you're open? You look pretty closed to me."

Scott chuckled as he circled around to stand behind the bar. He'd worked hard to train himself on all the taps and the ancient cash register too, and the confidence he felt buoyed his steps. "Open as a hippie's mind, at least for you. Flip on the switches as you pass 'em if you want more light. What'll you have? It's on the house."

"The natural light is fine, and I'll have a screwdriver without the vodka." The man -- from the petite size of him, he had to be an Omega -- didn't come any closer. He stood with his hands in the pockets of his heavy, puffy winter coat, kept his head cocked to one side, and studied Scott like he was something new and fascinating.

Truth be told, Scott liked what he was looking at too. He'd worked hard over the past few years, but he hadn't lived like a monk and he did appreciate a pretty Omega. This one sure fit the bill. A soft cap of dark sable hair, eyes so blue they were striking even in low light, and skin that would have been smooth and pale as cream if the sun hadn't kissed him on every limb. He had a gamin, angled face that made him look like a wolf even in his human shape.

The only odd note was that coat of his. The weather was far too warm for a winter coat, and he'd zipped it nearly up to his chin. Scott couldn't help but wonder why.

"Virgin screwdriver it is," he said, finding the right glass. "Want me to bring it to you?"

"Mmm." The Omega narrowed his eyes, thoughtful-like. "You don't remember me at all, do you?"

Uh-oh. Scott's movements slowed, though they didn't stop. He took a second, more careful look at the Omega, and then a third. Hell had no fury like an Omega scorned, and like he'd said, he hadn't denied himself the pleasures of the flesh while he worked and saved to turn his life around. A smart Alpha would lie and say *of course I remember, great to see you again, how are you doing*?

But one of the things Scott had always taken pride in was not being a cowardly dog. He wouldn't go changing that now. "Sorry. I don't," he said at last, with a rueful grimace. "Though the way you're asking that makes me think I should. Come a little closer, would you? Maybe once you're up close…"

The Omega snorted. "I can't say I'm too surprised. We didn't exactly do a lot of *talking* last time we met. The only time we met, actually. It was just over six months ago. You know what? Never mind the screwdriver. All I want is one question answered."

Before Scott could process that, the Omega walked toward the bar with long, powerful strides. He stopped just outside of arm's reach. Taking the zipper on his parka in hand, he jerked it all the way down, shrugged the coat off his shoulders, and stood with his chin up and his shoulders squared. Underneath, he wore a summer-weight blue T-shirt several shades darker than his eyes, a pair of jeans, and nothing else. He had the sweetest hips Scott had seen, and better legs than Bettie Paige, made for painting on the side of a fighter jet.

'Course, that wasn't what made Scott stop and stare. *That* honor went to the unmistakable curve of a pregnancy well underway. The Omega laid his hand over his bump, and fixed Scott with a fierce stare as he asked his question.

"Did you do this on purpose?"

* * *

Maccabe

No. He hadn't done it on purpose. Even before the Alpha spoke, the thunderstruck look on his face gave Maccabe his answer. Scott couldn't have been more surprised if Maccabe had squatted and given birth right then and there.

Three more months to go before Maccabe had to worry about that.

Hallelujah for small mercies.

"Okay," Maccabe said, taking in a deep breath. He laid his coat on a barstool and leaned his forearms on the bar itself. "I'll take that virgin screwdriver now."

Scott had opened his mouth, though soundlessly, as if searching for words. He shut it now to give Maccabe a long look. Finally, he pushed the glass of orange juice across the bar to Maccabe and took a couple of steps back. "I'll ask you not to throw that in my face, and I swear I'm sorry, but I'm racking my brains and I don't remember you. Are you sure it's --"

"Yours? I am." Maccabe tried a sip of the juice. His eyebrows shot up in surprise. Low acid, sweet, and cold. Delicious. He folded his hands around the chilly glass as he went on. "I hadn't been with anyone for almost a year before that, and I haven't been with anyone else since. Do you at least remember going to a party up in Fairbanks?"

He could see Scott recalled the event itself. "Someone passed around a jug of homemade -- they called it wine, but it wasn't, was it?"

Maccabe grimaced. "It was not. None of us there knew how strong it was until after the fact, but that's beside the point. You were there, so was I, and we both had a few shots of might-as-well-be-moonshine. There was a bonfire and dancing and... Well. Like I said, we didn't do a heck of a lot of talking. It took me weeks of asking around to find someone who even knew your name."

Scott had listened to that whole speech with a deepening frown, rubbing at the back of his neck all the while. "I remember the bonfire," he said. "And the rest, in bits and pieces. I was only passing through."

"Maybe so, but you sure left something for me to remember you by," Maccabe replied.

"Hell. Give me a second, would you?" Scott started back around the bar, headed for the door, explaining himself over his shoulder as he went. "I figure we need to talk, and I'd as soon not be interrupted. Unless you'd rather not be locked in?"

The man's consideration surprised and touched him in a way Maccabe hadn't expected. He stood a little straighter as he watched Scott come back, considering him with new eyes. "I don't mind. I might be an Omega, but I'm tougher than I look. No Alpha's ever forced me to do anything I didn't want."

"Which answers the next question I was going to ask," Scott muttered. He seemed more relieved by that than Maccabe would have imagined, a big tough Alpha like him.

And he was all that -- big, with shoulders wide enough to balance kegs on, and a nose that he'd broken at least twice and had set badly once. He wouldn't have looked out of place in black leather and on the back of a Harley.

Just the way Maccabe usually liked them. Scott had appealed to him more than most by the light of the bonfire. Lit a flame in him that wouldn't be quenched until they'd fucked themselves raw and aching-sore.

Maccabe cleared his throat. "I didn't know I was in heat, by the way. I didn't do this to *you* on purpose either. I've never been regular -- comes of being so skinny, usually -- so I had no idea it was coming."

"Didn't think you would, but I appreciate that all the same." Scott inclined his head somewhat awkwardly, maybe a little shyly, a suspicion confirmed by the way he shuffled his feet in their size-fourteen-or-more boots. "Begging your pardon, but what happens now?" he asked simply. "I've never been in a fix like this. What do you want me to -- what can I do to help you?"

The last thin rime of wary ice in Maccabe's heart melted away at that. He meant it, didn't he? Every word. Such a big, rough-looking man to have such a surprisingly gentle heart. Maccabe sighed and propped his chin on his hand, and found his mouth curving up at the corners. "You know what? I think we might have gotten off on the wrong foot. I'm Maccabe, and it's nice to meet you, Scott. Again."

Scott's grin was a surprise too, boyish and almost bashful. He inclined his head. "Same to you. But that doesn't answer my question. I don't have a lot of money. Just spent it all buying this place from the previous owner. But if you want me to -- to mate with you --"

"Whoa! No." Maccabe held up one hand with the palm out. "Not meaning to shout at you, but no." His back ached slightly. It would, he thought, be worth the effort of boosting himself onto the bar stool. Even at six months, it fascinated him how his center of gravity had changed. He could see it fascinated Scott, too, the Alpha's gaze tracking his every move.

Once he'd settled, his smile didn't want to fade, so Maccabe didn't try to make that happen. "I don't want a mate," he said as gently as he could. It'd never been one of his strengths. He liked rough and tumble, and wild and free, and he'd made plenty of bad choices in the past before getting his life turned around. "I do need some help, but not the kind you're thinking. I want to get to Seattle."

Maccabe could see that'd thrown Scott for a loop. "Say again?" he asked.

"I've got a friend down there who's opened up a food truck. I know how to cook, so they're willing to give me a job. It'd be a fresh start."

Scott frowned as he processed that. "And the pup?"

"Adoption." Maccabe kept his chin up as he said that. "I'm not ready to have a family, and if you just bought this place with your life savings, I'd dare say it isn't the right time for you to get tied down with a mate and a pup either."

Though he'd been easy to read so far, this time Maccabe couldn't tell what Scott was thinking.

"You're sure?" he asked.

In perfect honesty? No.

When Maccabe had first realized he was pregnant, he'd been incandescent with fury at the Alpha who'd knocked him up and left him without a word. Morning sickness hadn't helped his wrath, but once his body started to adjust he'd found his mindset altering subtly day by day, too. And when he'd felt that first flutter of movement just a few days ago the sense of protectiveness, of territoriality, nearly knocked him off his feet.

But that wasn't the point, was it? What he wanted and what he needed were so often different things. It'd taken Maccabe far too long to understand that, and he'd had to learn it the hard way.

"It's the right thing to do," Maccabe said to Scott at last. "We're strangers, you and me. We don't even know if we'd get along without a bonfire and some moonshine."

Scott chuckled. "So far so good."

"True," Maccabe had to admit. "But seriously, Scott. I want this pup to have its best possible chance at life. There's a packmaster with some experience at blending families who lives on the Puget Sound. I'd have work there. I could keep an eye out."

Scott frowned as he listened to that, but he was still listening. It was more than Maccabe would have expected from most Alphas. "What's my part in it? I offered to help you, and I meant it."

"I need to get to Seattle, but I don't have a way there," Maccabe said. "I hitched rides from Fairbanks out here, but I'm out of money and I don't know anyone else around these parts."

"That's it?" Scott asked, dubious.

Maccabe nodded. "That's it."

He could see Scott wrestling with himself, but the man stuck to his guns. "All right." He put out his hand. "I made myself a promise not long ago I'd never harm or hinder an Omega ever again. So if you swear that's all you want -- really swear -- then I'll make sure you get it, Maccabe. Shake on it, and we'll call it a deal."

Relieved, Maccabe put out his own hand and clasped the Alpha's.

He realized half a second too late what a mistake that was.

Chapter Two

Scott

Once, when Scott had been young and randy and too dumb to be let out in public, he'd tried to impress an Omega by picking a burning coal out of a camp stove with his bare hands.

Touching Maccabe again brought the way that had felt right back to him.

A shock of sensation. Licking tongues made of fire and light. The *thump* in his breastbone as the air was driven out of his chest. And from the way Maccabe started forward slightly, eyes going wide and dark, Scott thought he must feel it too.

Slowly, carefully, Scott folded his fingers around Maccabe's. They were so small his enveloped them. He half expected to find their shape burned into his palm when he opened his hand again.

"Now I remember you," he said, with the little breath left him.

Maccabe licked his lips, one quick swipe of his pink tongue. "I -- Yes."

Scott knew better than this, honest he did, but his brain didn't appear to be in charge of his body. He lifted his free hand to brush Maccabe's hair out of his eyes, to tuck a stray lock behind one ear. To trace the pad of his thumb along Maccabe's cheekbone.

Maccabe drew in a sharp breath. His eyelids drifted closed.

Scott had worked hard to use his willpower for good. It was one hell of a wrench to let go of Maccabe's hand and take a step back, but he made it happen. The tension cracked just wide enough open to let them breathe, though Maccabe looked a little dazed and Scott bet he did, himself, too.

"Might be best if we don't let that happen again," he said with a grimace.

Maccabe's throat worked as he swallowed. "Might be you're right." He shook his head as if to clear it, then cracked a rueful grin at Scott. "Maybe it wasn't all the moonshine. But you're right."

Scott laughed quietly to himself. Maybe it wasn't all moonshine, at that. He'd always liked Omegas with a sense of humor. Too bad they hadn't met in some other way, some other place and time. They could have been good for each other, him and Maccabe.

But it was what it was. Scott straightened his shoulders and jerked a thumb at the closed door. "Tell you what. I'll walk you back to wherever you're staying while you're in town so you can put your feet up for a while, and I'll work on the details of how to get you to Seattle."

Maccabe crinkled his nose. "You can walk me there, sure, as soon as I figure out where *there* is. I came straight here. Is there a motel anywhere nearby?"

Oh. Scott had assumed -- though he wasn't sure why -- that Maccabe had relatives or at least friends in this neck of the woods. But if he didn't...

Looking at his face, Maccabe sighed. "There aren't any motels, are there?"

"Not a one." Scott gestured around himself. "This is about the only game in town." He gnawed thoughtfully at the inside of his cheek, then blurted out, "Stay here."

Maccabe brought his head up. "Say again?"

"Stay here," Scott said, meaning it. "There's rooms upstairs. They might need a little tidying up, a few licks of paint, but it's better than digging a burrow out in the woods and sleeping in your wolf skin." He risked taking Maccabe's hand again, only for a second, to capture his attention. "The rooms all have locks. I'll give you both keys."

Maccabe glanced down to where Scott's hand rested on his arm. He gave an almost silent whistle, but

Scott could see him buck up. When he looked up, it was with that endearing lopsided grin of his. "All right, innkeeper. Lead the way."

Seven-odd minutes later, Scott found himself heartily regretting his offer -- but mostly because he didn't know what he should do if a pregnant Omega kept on laughing so hard he was likely to end up pissing himself.

"Oh, my lord." Maccabe wiped tears of mirth from his eyes and spread his arms wide to gesture at all the mess at once. "Scott. Did you even take a look upstairs before you handed over your cash?"

Scott grumbled under his breath and kicked the toe of his boot against the floor. "I knew fixing up the place would take some work. I just didn't think it'd be *this* much." The rooms were trashed, and not just from storm damage. "I've been up here before, and it didn't seem that bad at the time."

"Uh-huh. Did you have an Omega you wanted to take to bed with you when you were last here?"

The blood heating Scott's face to boiling point answered for him.

Maccabe snorted, but as he did he socked Scott's arm gently. "I don't expect I'd have noticed the mess myself under those circumstances." He ruffled his hair back. "Lord help, though, Scott. You need more than a few licks of paint up here."

Scott had to admit Maccabe wasn't wrong. He looked around, taking it all in. A broken bed frame braced on bricks, a crack in the window, strange stains on the walls and floor that he did *not* want to shine a black light on, and gaps between the floorboards nearly stuffed full with dust and dirt. And that was only one room out of six.

"Shit," Scott said with deep feeling. "Shit. *I* don't have anywhere else to sleep tonight!"

Maccabe hooted. His eyes sparkled with mirth, but even so he was already rolling up his sleeves. "Come on, you. Let's check the other rooms. The old owner used to live on the premises, right? Maybe his personal room will be better."

"Giles was an elderly bachelor Alpha. I doubt it."

"Well then, worst come to worst, we'll run a load of blankets through the washer with some bleach, scrub the bar floor, and bunk down there." Maccabe shrugged. "I've slept on worse."

So had Scott. But -- if worst did come to worst, he vowed he'd see to it they did shift into their wolf shapes and find a cozy spot in the woods. He could dig a decent burrow for Maccabe, and stay awake to guard him through the night.

Truth be told, something in him liked that idea. He was almost disappointed when the third door opened proved to be Giles's room. It surely wouldn't feature in a good housekeeping magazine any time soon, but Maccabe probably wouldn't catch foot and mouth disease from sleeping there, either.

"I'll make myself a pallet down in the bar," Scott said firmly. "You'll get both keys to this room, like I promised."

Maccabe's sharp-angled face softened a little at that. He reached to lay a hand on Scott's arm again, only drawing back at the last half-second, so that Scott could feel the warmth of the almost-touch on his skin. "I'm not afraid of you, Scott. You don't have to."

Scott shook his head stubbornly. "I made a promise. I'll keep it."

Maccabe's smile flashed out. "You know what? I think I believe you, Scott." Still smiling, he reached out a second time, and laid his hand on Scott's wrist.

The shock was no less potent, no less immediate. Scott drew in a sharp breath, echoed by Maccabe's quick gasp.

Maccabe swallowed, a rough gulp, and shook his head. "I --"

Bang!

The sound nearly made Scott and Maccabe jump out of both sets of skins. Maccabe's feet even cleared the floor, but when he came down he was spitting mad. "What the hell?"

Bang! Bang! Bang!

"Open up!" a full-throated bellow came from outside, directly below the window. "There's a couple of thirsty sailors here who want a drink!"

Scott groaned. He recognized that voice. "Hellfire and damnation."

Maccabe cocked his head. Now that he'd gotten over being startled, he was back to wry amusement. "I've never worked in a bar before so I'm not sure, but I'm guessing that's not the usual reaction to paying customers."

"Paying customers would be one thing. These assholes are a whole 'nother deal." Scott turned, meaning to go down the stairs as fast as he could and deal with Painter and Jimmy before they cranked their teasing up to eleven. He paused on the threshold to look back over his shoulder. "Stay here. Please."

He hurried on before Maccabe could reply. Explaining Painter and Jimmy would have taken too long, and there wasn't any excusing the two of them. By the time he reached the front door and wrestled the lock open, Jimmy had already moved on to caterwauling, "Little pig, little pig, let me in. I'm thirsty!"

Scott wrenched the door open and glowered at the men he usually called friends. Just at the moment he wasn't any too sure. "I know you can read. Sign says *Closed*."

Jimmy grinned at him, wide and white and cheeky as hell, enough to blind, before he hauled Scott into a headlock and rubbed his knuckles across Scott's scalp. "And yet here you are, so who's laughing now? Ha!"

Two steps behind him, Painter chuckled. He kept his hell raising to a lower key these days, mostly telling stories dirty enough to singe a full-grown Alpha's eyebrows off, but only an idiot would let that fool them for a hot second. "Better do like the ugly wolf says. He's already had a few."

Scott hesitated. What should he do? He didn't want them catching a whiff of Maccabe. Maybe if he poured them a free shot and beer and sent them on their way --

But he was already too late. Painter's nostrils flared. "Holy hell. There's a pregnant Omega in here."

Jimmy drew up sharp and sudden. "Wait, what? Where?"

"You lay one finger on him and I'll have your balls for breakfast," Scott warned. "And back up out of here, would you? I just bought the place today. It won't be open again for a while, not until it's in fit shape. *Out*."

As Painter and Jimmy protested, Scott caught a flicker of motion in his peripheral vision. He swore inside his head. Curiosity killed the cat and the Omega. Maccabe had tiptoed down the steps and was busy dropping eaves.

"Come back then," Scott insisted, trying to close the door.

He'd have succeeded if Painter hadn't shoved his boot in the crack. "No, seriously," he said, industriously sniffing. "I won't hurt him, I promise. I'm just curious. Who is it?"

Scott shut his mouth and shook his head, mulish.

"Wait." Jimmy visibly put two and two together. "First he buys a business, and the next thing you know there's a pregnant Omega on the premises." He punched Scott joyously in the chest. "You dog. Moving at the speed of light! Or is he here to be the entertainment?"

"Jimmy, don't show your ignorance any more than you can help. I can smell that the pup is his." Painter's forehead furrowed. "Damn, friend. What have you been into? And with someone so new I've never caught a whiff of him on you before?"

All right, that was it. Enough, the end. Scott opened his mouth, ready and willing and able to tear strips off both shifter's hides.

But Maccabe beat him to it.

Cool as anyone could please, he glided down the steps and as smoothly as silk to stand by Scott's side. He gave Jimmy and Painter the kind of look that could have rendered lava barely lukewarm, and turned his gaze fully on Scott. "Is there a problem, sweetheart?"

Jimmy shut his mouth with an audible *click*.

In the blessed silence that followed, Painter looked to and fro between Maccabe and Scott. Scott had no idea what he saw, but he started to laugh soundlessly to himself.

Before Scott could ask, Painter took a couple of steps back, catching Jimmy by the collar and hauling him along. "No problem at all," he told Maccabe, serious as a wet Sunday afternoon. "We'll do our drinking elsewhere tonight. Sorry to bother you."

Maccabe held his ice-cool pose, giving Painter and Jimmy another long, unimpressed stare, until Scott shut the door and threw the lock again.

Maccabe grinned as brightly as the sun, and held up his fist for a pound. "Not bad, huh?

Scott couldn't help it. He really couldn't. He caught Maccabe up in his arms and whirled him around, once-twice-three times, and when he let the Omega stand on his own two feet again, it was only natural to bend his head and kiss him.

Only natural.

And even though he knew better than to test his resolve like this, it was only heaven...

Chapter Three

Maccabe

Oh. Maccabe melted into Scott's kiss. He found himself bringing both arms up to drape around Scott's neck, his lips falling apart, his body rocking forward. *Oh, I've been here before.*

There wasn't any magic to it, the way his body responded to Scott's. Not beyond the gifts that made them Alpha and Omega, made them men and wolves at the same time. But be damned if having the breath kissed out of him didn't feel like falling into a spell.

Scott tore himself away and pushed Maccabe back. His eyes were wide, his lips dark from moving against Maccabe's, and his chest heaving. "Sorry," the Alpha rasped. "Shit. Maccabe, I'm sorry. I gave you my word."

"I'm not," Maccabe said. He closed the gap Scott had put between them, and took Scott's chin in his hand so he'd have no choice but to make eye contact. Giving it a gentle shake, he went on. "I know I should be, but I'm not."

Scott was a stubborn one. He dug in his heels. "I promised."

"And I'm giving you permission to break that promise." Being so near to him made Maccabe ache inside, a low sweet burn very like being in heat, but without the mindless urgency that drove him. The kind of arousal that took its sweet time, but exploded in an arching crescendo at the finish. He stood on his tiptoes to bite Scott's lower lip. "You want me, and I want you. True or false?"

Scott tried to hold out, but in the end he nodded. "True."

"Good." Maccabe bit the edge of Scott's chin for good measure, then laughed. "For God's sake, man. You can't get me pregnant a second time. So what are we waiting for?"

Scott's grin dawned slowly, but it was like watching the sun come up -- if the sun had mischief and mayhem in mind. "Not a damn thing."

"Now *that* was the right answer." Maccabe brushed his lips across Scott's, slow and deliberate, then came down off his toes and turned on his heel to walk away. He glanced back over his shoulder to see Scott staring dumbstruck after him. "Well? There's only one decent bed in this place, and we just established I'd like to share it."

"Oh hell no," Scott blurted, making it Maccabe's turn to stop in surprise.

"Excuse me?"

Scott's cheeks colored, but he shook it off and made for a closet recessed in the wall. When he flung it open, it proved to be full of what could charitably be called linen -- worn but serviceable blankets and towels, all in faded blues and greens. He pressed one to his nose, grunted, then tossed it on the floor.

Maccabe blinked at him. "What are you doing?"

"Not taking you to an old bachelor Alpha's nest, that's what," Scott said firmly. He sniffed another blanket and added it to the pile. "I know the floor's clean in here, because I helped him wash and sweep it this morning before he handed the keys over." He grinned, lopsided and roguish, at Maccabe. "I'm making us a bed to lie in."

If anyone else, anywhere else, had made an offer like that, Maccabe would have unleashed the dogs of war and hell on their presumptuous ass. But this was *Scott*, and in the *Fisherman's Friend* it was possibly the sweetest gesture anyone could have made.

And that made his decision easier still. Maccabe drew the blinds at the front windows to make sure no one would peek in at them, then strode to the growing pile of linen. It smelled faintly of sunshine and detergent, the scent stronger when he knelt beside it to arrange it in a better shape. "I'll help."

Scott's gaze darkened so that Maccabe was amazed he didn't begin to smolder like banked coals. "Then I'll hurry," he murmured.

Heat pulsed low in Maccabe's groin. "That's the right answer, too. And here's my reply."

Maccabe had once been a hell raiser too, and he still knew the moves. He stood beside the growing bed and waited till he was sure he had Scott's full attention, then put his hands to his waist. It was the work of seconds to slide his jeans off his hips; he'd been wearing them a bit big and loose, allowing for room to grow. Then, Maccabe took the hem of his shirt in his hands and pulled it, cross-armed, over his head.

He wore nothing underneath but his skin, big belly and all, and he laid his palm on the curve of that. Scott stared at him as if poleaxed. Maccabe could see the lump of his Adam's apple jump wildly as he swallowed.

"Well?" Maccabe tilted his head. "Still want to lie in the bed we made?"

Again, Scott swallowed. "More than anything."

The sweet simplicity made Maccabe weak in the knees. He lowered himself to the floor a second time and lay on his back in the soft pile of linens, and opened his arms. "Then come here. I'm waiting."

And Scott did.

His clothes came off with less grace, but more efficiency, cast carelessly aside to land behind the bar and making Maccabe laugh -- but only for a second before Scott, gloriously nude, was in the bed with him. His skin was so warm that it made Maccabe's prickle in response, and his cock already hard enough to drive nails through rock. He lay halfway on top of Maccabe, careful not to compress his belly, and reached between Maccabe's legs to cup and massage Maccabe's erection.

Maccabe cried out. Sensitive! He hadn't realized his responses would be so heightened.

Neither had Scott, apparently, who looked first surprised and then wickedly pleased. He'd taken his hand away in a flash, but now brought it back and slid it deeper between Maccabe's legs. Work-hardened fingers traced a path behind his balls and through his crack until they circled his entrance. They glided through the natural slick Omegas produced, letting him slip the tip of his thumb inside.

When Maccabe keened again, he hesitated. "It's not -- it won't hurt the pup, will it?"

"No. And neither will this." Maccabe tugged at the big Alpha, wanting Scott's weight and warmth fully covering him. He wrapped his fist around Scott's cock and gave it a rough, hard stroke that brought beads of liquid to the tip. "Fuck me, Scott. Fuck me good and hard and don't you dare stop until we've had enough."

Scott dropped his head and sucked in a ragged breath. "Omega, you're going to be the death of me. You know that?"

"Then we'll go happy. Please, Scott. Please." Maccabe had managed to haul Scott fully over him, and shamelessly parted his legs to allow him access. Gravity and instinct brought him down, his cock sliding through their mixed lubrication, and only sheer willpower must have held him back -- even when, especially when, Maccabe canted his hips and wrapped his legs around Scott's hips. He felt -- wilder, now, not quite crazed but thirsty as a sailor set adrift on the sea. "Please."

Scott groaned as if he were being killed when he slid his cock inside Maccabe. He held still, shaking in every muscle.

So did Maccabe, the breath gone from his lungs once more. The weight and thickness of him stretched Maccabe as far as he could be stretched. He bore down, squeezing, to see what Scott would do, but the delicious pressure made *him* sob and clutch tighter.

Scott started to move, slowly at first, panting Maccabe's name. Maccabe clung to him, not able to move much in this position but fully capable of feeling the power behind every thrust. He dragged his blunt nails down Scott's sweat-slick shoulders and dug his heels into Scott's back, amazed at his own recklessness and reveling in it.

But why not? He *couldn't* get pregnant a second time, and being fucked like this satisfied a bone-deep craving Maccabe hadn't even known he had before now.

He cried out again when he came, high and thin, helpless to do anything but ride through the shudders that racked him, so right it was only just this side of wrong. He dug his fingers in, urging Scott toward his finish, and when Scott groaned from his core and filled Maccabe, it felt like coming again himself.

They lay together, sheened with sweat and panting for air as if they'd run for miles in their wolf shapes, Scott too heavy now but Maccabe too boneless with pleasure to push him off.

He satisfied himself by nudging Scott until Scott went back to his original pose, mostly on his side with his head on Maccabe's shoulder. Maccabe nudged fallen strands of wet hair off Scott's forehead with the tip of his finger. "Was it like that last time?" he whispered.

"Best as I recall." Scott captured Maccabe's hand and pressed a kiss to the back of it, then laid it over his heart. "Feel that. Beating like a drum."

Maccabe did. His fingers flexed, combing through Scott's chest hair.

Oh, it was a shame they hadn't met some other time, some other way, some other place. They could have been so good for each other. Really, so good.

Scott must have been thinking the same thing. He stirred restlessly. "Are we all right, Maccabe? Did we do right?"

"We're not wrong," Maccabe said after a moment's thought. "We're just doing our best. And I'll keep on doing my best if you will."

Scott's smile was as relieved as it was endearing, and even after all that just the littlest bit shy, and it went straight to Maccabe's heart. It wasn't new. Maccabe recognized the feeling now, even if he didn't want to give it a name.

Oh. Maccabe shut his eyes. Oh no.

He was in love with the father of his child.

Oh, he really was in trouble now.

Chapter Four

Scott

Scott whistled to himself as he wielded a dry mop along the corners and edges of the ceiling in the main room of the *Fisherman's Friend*. He never had been able to carry a tune so it was less of a song and more of a collection of flat notes, but that didn't bother him.

Had he ever slept as well as he did last night, curled up next to Maccabe? Not since he'd been a pup himself, snoozing where he dropped in a pile with his playmates.

He and Maccabe had moved to the ex-owner's bed for actual resting, which Maccabe had made up fresh and crisp before they bunked down. Maccabe had slept curled up in a little ball as if guarding the unborn pup in his dreams. Though Scott had been a gentleman and nodded off on his side of the bed, he'd woken spooned around the Omega.

It was a thing he could have gotten used to. Easily.

Best not, Scott warned himself, poking at a stubbornly sticky spider web in the upper corner nearest the bar's tiny kitchen. Maccabe had made it clear he didn't plan to stay. He'd been let off easy on one promise, which meant he'd best make sure he kept his word on the rest. Otherwise Maccabe wouldn't trust him again.

And that mattered, to Scott. Mattered a hell of a lot, what Maccabe thought of him.

He glanced up at the sound of slow, shambling footsteps dragging their way down the stairs, and chuckled to himself at the sight that greeted his eyes. Maccabe's hair stood up and out every way hair could go, nearly defying gravity and almost completely obscuring his line of vision. He clung to the stair rail with both hands and took each step one at a time, treating it with suspicion until he'd gotten safe purchase.

"Not a morning person?" Scott asked, amused, as soon as Maccabe came close enough he wouldn't have to shout.

Maccabe peered blearily at him. "Nrrfff. Coffee."

He'd take that as a yes. "Kitchen." Scott indicated the direction with a jerk of his chin. "Wasn't sure if you could have any while you're carrying, but I wanted a cup and it wasn't any harder to make enough for both of us."

"'So long's just one. S'okay." Maccabe shuffled past him, weaving slightly but making a steady beeline for the industrial-sized coffeemaker. Scott had left a mug out for him. Good thing, too. He doubted Maccabe was capable of rummaging through cabinets just then. He poured without spilling, held the mug to his face to breathe deeply of the steam, and moaned like he'd just orgasmed after his first sip. "*Coffee.*"

Scott's laughter might have become audible then, and Maccabe might have flipped him the finger.

It didn't bother him. Felt good. Felt like things falling into their natural places.

Careful, he warned himself again.

Once he'd gotten halfway down the mug, Maccabe pushed his hair out of his puffy eyes and grinned crookedly at Scott. "A morning person's the last thing I am. Looks like you are, though." He carried his mug out into the bar and boosted himself onto a stool, then squinted up at the ceiling. "You dusted."

"Am still dusting," Scott said with a one-shouldered shrug. "I never knew ceilings could get dirty. Seems like the dust and all would fall back down."

"Static electricity. Makes it cling. And everything that people breathe out rises up, too."

Made sense to Scott. He carried on for a few minutes, until the last drop of coffee went down and Maccabe looked as bright-eyed as he had the day before, then cleared his throat to get the Omega's attention.

"About what you asked for yesterday. Help getting to Seattle."

Maccabe stiffened slightly. "What about it?"

See? He's worried you'll break your promise. "Got updates for you," Scott said hurriedly, to ease Maccabe's concern. "I woke up so early most folks hadn't gone to bed yet, so I made some calls."

"Oh yeah?" Maccabe laced his fingers around the mug. He pressed his lips briefly together. "And?"

"And…" Scott laid his dust mop down so he wouldn't get distracted. "I've got a fisherman friend -- heh, yeah, I know, ironic -- who anchors his boat on the Puget Sound during summer. Says he's too old to give a damn about fishing for anything but crab, and that's in winter. Anyhow, he'll be heading down there in a couple of weeks. He'll be glad to give you a lift."

Maccabe's eyebrows had drifted toward his hairline, disappearing in the tangled locks falling over his forehead, as Scott spoke. "Seriously?"

"Mm-hmm." For the price of a free round for captain and crew next time they stopped by the bar, but Scott had expected to pay more, and in any case Maccabe didn't need to bother with the details. "Only problem is he's all the way down in Homer."

Those eyebrows of Maccabe's lowered and furrowed together. "We're nearer to Nome here. I don't know if I can run that far even in wolf shape in two weeks."

"Not without wearing yourself to a shadow, so hell no," Scott said firmly. "I've got another friend who owes me a couple of favors, so he's loaning me an ATV. I'll drive it down with you riding behind me, and then I can bring it back. *And,*" he went on, "I have a cousin who opened a boarding house on the outskirts of Seattle. Real nice guy, what they used to call a gentleman. He's a widower and he's got a soft spot for pregnant Omegas.

He'll give you a room rent-free until you've got your job settled."

Maccabe's mouth had fallen open somewhere during Scott's speech. He blinked, looking stunned. "You did all that for me?"

"Well…" Scott hunched his shoulders. He waved at Maccabe's midsection. "Seems only fair, on account of I did that to you. Just paying toward my part of the bill."

Maccabe shut his mouth with a quiet click and looked down, shaking his head slightly.

Scott frowned. "Did I get any of it wrong?"

"No," Maccabe said, looking up. His eyes seemed a little shiny, but that might have been a trick of the light, for he smiled at Scott as he propped his chin on his hand. "No, you got it all just right, Scott. I couldn't have asked for any better. Now. I'm not good at just sitting around idly. What can I do to help?"

* * *

Maccabe

Scott had done all of that -- for *him*? Two weeks later, on the eve of their departure for Homer, Maccabe still couldn't wrap his head around it. When he'd come to town, at best he'd hoped for a *do what you want with the pup as long as I don't have to pay for it* and a ticket down the coast. Not this.

Scott kept on surprising him.

On the one hand, that was a fine thing. Wasn't it? Thanks to his kindness, Maccabe had everything he could have asked for and more. He'd tried to repay Scott for his kindness by working side-by-side with him, whipping the *Fisherman's Friend* into shape one room, one floor, one window at a time.

And sometimes, when Scott looked at Maccabe with fondness, Maccabe almost thought the Alpha cared for him as much as he cared for Scott.

But...

Maccabe had been born to an Omega whose Alpha used him as a punching bag and a chew toy, depending on his whim. The Omega who'd birthed him had been a pitiful thing by the time Maccabe was old enough to be self-aware, so thin his bones showed through his skin and so fearful he cringed at every sound no matter how slight.

Maccabe had done his best to take care of his Omega parent until he died, and considered it a mercy when he'd passed. Then he'd packed up every last bit of his goods and gear and hit the road, and never looked back.

How he hadn't been killed or ended up as an Alpha's plaything himself, Maccabe still didn't know. He'd been so green back then, with nothing but the wariness and willingness to fight for survival that'd helped him survive his childhood to keep him safe. Yet somehow he'd managed. He'd made bad choices but he'd U-turned out of them in time to get his life back on track. To learn the culinary trade.

The most reckless thing he'd done in a few years was to sleep with a roguish Alpha at a bonfire without triple-checking his birth control.

He'd cussed himself pretty good when he'd realized what'd happened.

But now... He wished he could be different. That things could change.

Sometimes, Scott made him think it was possible.

Maccabe clicked his tongue impatiently. *Don't read too much into it*, he scolded himself. *You've seen for yourself how much work this place is going to take, and he just dropped his life's savings on the deed five minutes before you walked in the door. He's got a kind heart but what he doesn't have is the time to spare for starting a family. And with an Omega he barely knows? Please.*

No, he wants you gone. He's just being gentlemanly about it, and you're not used to that. What you're seeing is wishful thinking.

Stick to the plan. The one thing you can count on in this world is yourself.

"Lunch," Maccabe said after a glance at the clock behind the *Fisherman's Friend's* bar. He slipped down off his stool and made for the kitchen, actually able to see where he was going now that the caffeine had taken hold in his bloodstream. Boy howdy, had it. In his belly, the pup wriggled and danced. Maybe he ought to switch to decaf. "I would offer breakfast, but it's past the noon hour. Why don't you wake me up when I sleep so late?"

"I thought about it," Scott said with another of his careless shrugs. "But I figure you need your rest, so I let you lie."

There it was again -- that kindness, that consideration. Maccabe shook his head in puzzlement as he made for the kitchen.

There, he studied the range thoughtfully. It was a hideous old beast, but after a few grumbles it'd bowed to his will. "Behave," he warned it as he fetched bread and cheese and bacon, and butter too, from the refrigerator, and two cans of tomato soup from the pantry. It wouldn't be haute cuisine, but Maccabe had never met anyone who didn't like grilled bacon and cheese sandwiches with a side of soup.

Scott worked quietly while Maccabe clattered around in the kitchen, and sniffed appreciatively once the odors permeated the air.

"Almost ready," Maccabe said.

"Good." Scott's stomach rumbled. He stuck his head through the kitchen door to grin at Maccabe, exactly the way he had approximately fifteen minutes before the first time they'd slept together. The sight made Maccabe's knees wobble and sent a pleasant pulse of warmth through his groin. "Make plenty."

Maccabe waved him off with a faux-irritated click of the tongue. From the way the Alpha chuckled as he withdrew, he could tell Scott saw right through his bristly ways.

And liked him anyway.

It was such a shame that they hadn't met when they were both in a better place. Maybe then they could have had something. Could have built a life together. Where was the justice in fate bringing them together when all they could do was pass like ships in the night? It wasn't fair.

And this kitchen! Bigger, better, and nicer than anything a food truck could offer - or at least it would be once it'd been properly scoured from top to bottom. If Scott were willing to let him stay, then he could cook here. Maybe come up with a menu that'd bring in a lunch crowd as well as the all-day drinkers. Maccabe wanted so much to stay, to put down roots, that he could have tipped his head back and howled with frustration.

But Scott, with all his quickly made plans for Maccabe's departure, clearly didn't want him to linger any longer than he had to.

Maccabe stabbed angrily at the four browned sandwiches ready to come out of the pan, and made a face at himself. Life wasn't fair. No sense in crying about it.

Instead, he poured the soup into freshly rinsed bowls and plated the sandwiches, neatly cut into triangles, then brought the whole kit and caboodle out to the bar. "Eat up," he said firmly, to Scott and to himself. "We've got work to do, and we'll need our strength."

He didn't have to tell Scott twice. He'd barely put the plate down before Scott stuffed an entire triangle of sandwich in his mouth, making Maccabe splutter with unexpected laughter. He tossed a napkin at Scott. "My God, man. You are such an Alpha."

Scott grinned at him with a crumb of toasted bread caught in his stubble. He palmed that away. "Can't help it. It's good. Oh, did I tell you -- Jimmy and Painter left apology notes pinned to the door early this morning. Painter likely gave him the idea, but I think Jimmy's sincere enough. He's a decent guy. Just has a habit of jamming his foot in his mouth." He stopped abruptly and frowned. "Are you all right? You flinched."

Maccabe grimaced, embarrassed. "I shouldn't have drunk my coffee so fast this morning. The pup's tap dancing on my liver. It feels weird."

"It's moving?" Scott's eyes widened. "I didn't know that happened this early."

"I promise you, it does." Maccabe rubbed the side of his stomach, trying to soothe the pup into calming down. "At first I thought it was gas, but now I'm starting to be able to tell what's a foot and what's a hand. Feels like he's got his butt halfway up under my ribs."

Scott hooted with amusement, but then stopped. He swallowed once and made a tentative reach for Maccabe. "Is it -- could I --"

Maccabe blinked. He hadn't thought Scott might want to, but he should have, shouldn't he? He turned to face Scott, beckoning as he did. "Give me your hand."

Scott reached out again, letting Maccabe take his big Alpha mitt and guide it to the pup's favorite pummeling spot. He startled back at the first sturdy *thump*, then abruptly blazed out a grin that stretched from ear to ear, and placed his other palm on the opposite side of Maccabe's belly. "Be damned," he murmured. "I can feel it."

He slid his palms gently around, almost playing a game with the pup. The light brush of his hands made Maccabe draw in a quick, shallow breath and close his eyes.

Scott glanced up. "This still all right?"

"Mmm." All Maccabe could do was nod until he got himself and his libido back under control. Thank God the smells of cooking clung to him and would camouflage his scent.

He rested his hands just barely atop Scott's, amused at how the pup seemed to have figured out this was a game and started playing his own side. Scott chuckled in delight. "He's feisty, isn't he?"

"He comes by it honestly, I'd say."

Maccabe tilted his head, gazing at Scott through half-lidded eyes. He licked his lips, not sure if he should ask what he wanted to, then abandoning caution and just going for it. "Were you always like this, Scott? Kind. Gentle."

Scott gave a small snort. "I'm not either of those. Better'n I used to be, but I've still got a ways to go. I spent most of my life as a real son of a bitch. Too much balls, not enough brains."

"You're smart enough," Maccabe said, ruffling Scott's hair back, resisting the urge to linger. "And I'll be the one to say you're gentle enough to suit me. What changed?"

He watched Scott try to find the words, but fail to. It didn't matter. Maccabe understood.

"One day you woke up and you decided you wanted better," he said, still watching Scott. "And from somewhere, you found the strength to start making it happen. That about the size of it?"

Scott nodded in plain relief, still bent over the mound of Maccabe's belly.

Maccabe sighed once, and gave in to the urge to stroke Scott's head. He couldn't stand in the way of this good man putting his life back together. He just couldn't.

He would have to keep his word, and go.

Scott had made his decision, and Maccabe knew better. But he still kissed Scott anyway.

Chapter Five

Lord help, how this Omega melted him.

Scott put his arms around Maccabe's slim shoulders, his hands finding their natural resting places on Maccabe's back before sliding, hungry, down the elegant line of his backbone and over his hips, small soft curves that invited caressing. Maccabe parted his lips with a soft moan to let Scott in, and clung to Scott as if Scott was the only thing in the world keeping him from falling down.

Oh, he could get used to this. So easy. *Too* easy.

Scott wrenched himself away, though he couldn't go far. Couldn't bear to pry himself loose of Maccabe, or Maccabe loose of him. When he looked down into Maccabe's dazed, half-lidded eyes, the beauty of them made his groin pulse with eagerness.

He brushed his thumb along Maccabe's kiss-swollen lower lip. "Better stop me now if you want this stopped."

"I don't." Maccabe looked drunk, drugged, but blissed out with it. His pupils drowned out his irises. "So don't stop."

"I didn't do all that arranging because I expected you to pay me back," Scott warned. He doubted Maccabe thought so, but he had to be sure.

Maccabe reassured him in his inimitable way by punching Scott sharply in the ribs. "I know you didn't. *That's* why I want to."

And that was a horse of a wholly different, fully pleasing color.

"All right then, darlin'." Scott bent his head to Maccabe's again, and let himself be kissed until he barely knew which moving mouth, which lusty tongue, belonged to who.

Somewhere in there -- though he couldn't have said whose idea it was to begin with -- he found himself lifting

Maccabe, coaxing Maccabe's agile legs around his waist. Belly full of pup or not, Maccabe barely weighed more than a dandelion and Scott had no trouble holding him up. He turned them so Maccabe's back was to the wall, and rolled their hips together in a rhythm that let him know he'd better find them a bed fast, or they'd undo all his hard work cleaning the bar.

Maccabe must have been thinking the same thing. He laughed wildly, breathlessly, when Scott let go and was immediately distracted kissing down Maccabe's fine throat and delicate collar bones. "Where? Here? It'd do me fine."

"Not me," Scott said firmly. "Hang on tight."

One of the advantages to carrying Maccabe like this was being able to choose which way they went. He could still walk -- he thought -- without doing his oversensitive cock an injury, though each step and the friction that came with it was an exquisite kind of torment.

Maccabe tried to twist at the waist to see where Scott was taking them, and when he couldn't do that he kicked playfully with his heels. "You'd better not be headed for the great outdoors. Not unless you did go and dig me a real den out there."

"One day," Scott promised, and meant it. Maccabe would come back and visit from time to time, wouldn't he? Maybe they could hunt together, and they'd want a place to rest.

But for the moment...

With no arms free, Scott had to shove the door he wanted open with his boot, but since he hadn't locked it that was fine. Once inside, he hit the light switch with his elbow. A lamp he'd prepared, one with a soft tasseled crimson shade, filled the small room with a warm, inviting glow that softened all the still-rough edges and made the shadows gentle.

He let Maccabe down, careful not to jostle the Omega, and turned him around to see.

Maccabe's reaction was everything he could have hoped for. His mouth fell open in surprise as he turned in circles to take it all in.

It wouldn't look like much to anyone else. Just a bedroom, but one that'd been made as neat and comfortable and appealing as an Alpha who'd never done this before could manage. A brass bedstead, polished until it shone, with the best two mattresses in the joint piled on top. Thick blankets that smelled of fresh sunshine and detergent made those mattresses soft. He'd swept the floor and rubbed in enough wax to make the boards shine, and though they were covered by plush sea-blue drapes, he'd washed the windows until they sparkled.

"Scott," Maccabe breathed, still turning around and around. "You did all this? For me?"

Scott toed the floor, feeling as bashful as he was pleased. "I think it was meant to be where the barkeep slept, but he'd been using it for storage. You like it?"

"Like it?" Maccabe asked incredulously. A big, beautiful grin transformed his face, edged with heat and want. "Alpha, get on that bed and I'll show you how much I like it."

Sounded like a *yes* to Scott, who couldn't help but grin back at the Omega -- his Omega, even if only for a couple of weeks -- and do exactly what that Omega said.

Off with the boots. Off with the jeans, and over his head with the light jersey he wore. Maccabe laughed at the way he tossed his clothes in every direction, but Scott barely bothered to notice for Maccabe was shedding his clothes just as fast, and just as eagerly.

He stepped out of his jeans and stood naked, ripe and round and unashamed, looking up at Scott through the heavy fringe of his eyelashes. "Thought I told you to get on the bed, Alpha."

Scott shook his head and whistled. "Not sure if I can move right now without embarrassing myself."

Maccabe laughed. "Oh, is that so? Well, how about I show you how it's done?"

He climbed onto the bed -- climbed being the right word; double mattresses made it tall -- and stopped in the middle, braced on his hands and knees, to glance back at Scott with a wicked smile. "Your turn."

Scott breathed a silent prayer, and started counting backward from ten in his head as he walked toward the bed. By the time he reached it, he'd calmed down just enough to wrestle back an ounce or two of control. If they were leaving in the morning, this day would be his one and only chance with Maccabe, and he meant to make it count.

He slapped Maccabe's bare hip lightly, awed at how sensitive the Omega's fair skin was. The tiniest nudge made him color up a beautiful red. "As I recall, we've gone at it like animals before," he murmured. "At the bonfire, you were just like this. But I want to see your face. Roll over."

Maccabe did. As shameless as before, he lay on his back with his legs spread and his thighs shiny-wet with lubrication. Scott knew he'd have to wash those blankets all over again, and he one hundred percent did not care. Especially not when Maccabe dipped a hand between his legs and began to stroke himself, letting out small and breathy cries.

Yet it still wasn't quite right. Scott gritted his teeth until a wave of sensation passed and he thought he could hold off his orgasm at least a little longer, then caught Maccabe by the wrist and stilled his hand. "Not like this either," he said roughly. "Scoot over. Let me in. I'll show you."

"Demanding," Maccabe said in a purr, but he must have been in a malleable mood. He slid to the far edge of the bed and lay, pressing his legs rhythmically together, watching Scott climb into the bed and lie on *his* back. He didn't say anything but only watched curiously until Scott reached for him.

Then, as Maccabe let Scott guide him astraddle, the penny visibly dropped. "Ride me," Scott said, taking both of Maccabe's hands in his own for a brace. "Slide me inside you, and ride like you've never been broken to saddle."

"I haven't," Maccabe informed him. He caught his lip between his teeth and bore down as he moved, easing Scott into the ecstasy of his tight, slick-soaked channel, and lowered himself until he rested fully against Scott's hips.

They both let out long, shuddering breaths.

Before Maccabe could move, Scott stopped him by squeezing Maccabe's hands. "Stay for just a minute," he managed to say. "Just let me look at you."

Maccabe's channel tightened around Scott in a vice, then eased up as Maccabe gulped and nodded. He tilted his head back, eyes closed and lips parted, breathing in quick pants broken only by bitten-back moans. "Big," he whispered once. "Feels bigger than last time."

"Too big?"

Maccabe shook his head. He freed his hands, laying them on his own body, letting his knees do the work of holding him up.

Suited Scott fine. He wanted the pleasure of touching Maccabe's body one last time. The Omega's shape was changing day by day, fascinating Scott endlessly, and he wanted no barriers between them tonight.

Maccabe's skin invited him, soft and smooth and nearly hairless save for a few downy curls over his chest.

The jut of his six-month belly was large enough that it rested against Scott's, satiny and startlingly hard. He'd thought it would be soft, but it was firm. When he ran his fingertips up the sides, Maccabe cried out and brought his own hands to his nipples, pinching and rolling them.

"Scott," Maccabe breathed his name like a prayer. He flexed the muscles in his thighs, but otherwise didn't move. "Oh Scott, please. Please."

Scott *wanted*.

"Hold still," he whispered, easing a hand between them to give Maccabe something to thrust his cock against. Then Scott moved his hips the slightest fraction. Just enough to press up, to stay as long as he could bear, then to lower himself. He could feel his orgasm coming on like a fighter jet, not to be denied this time, and he could feel the tension winding tight-tight-tight inside Maccabe, could hear his quiet cries building to a frantic pitch, could feel the way his channel clenched as fast as a heartbeat.

"*Scott*," Maccabe sobbed as he thrust against Scott's palm and came.

Scott didn't know what he said -- if it even had words -- as the grinding and panting built to a pure white pinnacle inside himself, but he knew he'd dug his fingernails into Maccabe's sleek thighs, and that he'd started fucking high and hard as his body could. He just knew that when the top of his head came off, he was looking into Maccabe's eyes.

Then, everything was pleasure, was just *yes*.

Maccabe caught his hands, mumbling things that sounded half like prayers, and half like laughter.

If only they could stay this way, Scott thought, wishing it with all his heart. If only Maccabe would stay, they could run the *Fisherman's Friend* together. Make it a home as well as a thriving business. Put down roots and make their mark on the place. It wouldn't be half as much fun alone.

They could be so good for each other. They could. If only he hadn't given his word...

But -- he had.

Chapter Six

Maccabe

"Are you ready?"

"Hmm?" Maccabe blinked out of a mental fog to find himself standing on the walkway leading to the front door of the *Fisherman's Friend*. He looked back over his shoulder at Scott, who had just locked that door.

The big Alpha stood with the keys still in his hand, one eyebrow cocked at Maccabe in question. "Did you hear me?"

"Not really," Maccabe admitted with a sheepish shrug. His thoughts insisted on wandering, distracted with wondering *how* could he stay? There had to be a way.

Trouble was, he hadn't found it yet -- and here they were, ready and set to make the trek down to Homer, where the captain of a ship waited to carry him and the pup away.

"Hey." Scott had moved from door to walkway while Maccabe zoned out a second time. The warm, sturdy touch of his hand on Maccabe's upper arm was as soothing as it was jolting, drawing sparks of yearning from his heart and between his legs. "Maccabe. Are you okay?"

No, Maccabe thought. "Sure," he said out loud. He shook his head briskly, attempting to clear it. "Just pregnancy brain. I've heard about it before. Too many hormones make it hard to focus."

Scott frowned, but seemed to accept that. He opened his mouth as if he wanted to speak, then exhaled and shut it again. "We'd best get started. It's a long haul down to Homer, even with the ATV." He chuckled. "You ever talk to someone from the lower forty-eight who's only ever seen Alaska floating off to one side of the map?"

Maccabe surprised himself by laughing. "Yeah. They think it's only about as big as Texas."

"Alaska could eat Texas in one bite and still have room left over for North Dakota through Kansas. They never get how big and wild it really is up here, unless they get dropped in headfirst." Scott thumped Maccabe's back companionably. "All right, then. Let's get going."

Offhand comments, but they stuck in Maccabe's head like burrs to a wool blanket as they roared their way across the tundra on their borrowed ATV. He clung to Scott's waist, his head pressed against Scott's firm back. His eyes were closed, but his mind was busy.

He'd never lived anywhere but Alaska. He'd been born there, though much farther inland, almost at the Canadian border. This was where he'd learned how to run and taught himself how to hunt. So much land it almost seemed endless.

Maccabe loved it, with all of his heart that wasn't taken up in loving Scott and their pup.

He didn't want to leave them, and he didn't want to leave this place. Seattle had seemed like a good idea when he had no other options. Now? Not so much. Maccabe almost wished he'd never come to challenge Scott.

Only almost.

He racked his brain as the miles thundered past beneath the wheels of the ATV.

I could climb up a tree and refuse to come back down again until he says I can stay.

Maccabe snorted.

I could run into the woods and all the way back to the coast. I've done it before.

Yes, and the thought of doing it again made Maccabe's spine curl. He was closer to seven months now than six, and seemed to get bigger with every day that passed. In the two weeks he'd spent with Scott, he'd started to notice aches in his pelvis that he'd been warned most Omegas had trouble with in later pregnancy. The joints were loosening, making the room he'd need later, but throwing his gait off in the present.

That wouldn't work.

Maccabe growled under his breath. *I could... I could...*

Nothing came to him -- at least not anything less ridiculous than the notions that'd crossed his mind before.

Maybe it's not meant to be. Maybe what I want and what I need aren't the same thing here and now.

He thumped his fist against Scott's ribs in frustration.

Scott wore enough layers he shouldn't have been able to feel Maccabe's fist land, but he did. He glanced back, then pulled the ATV to a stop in a natural clearing and killed the engine. Taking his helmet off, he gestured for Maccabe to do the same. "Need a break?" he asked as soon as the engine vibrations died down enough to hear speech. "Want to stretch your legs?"

Maccabe almost said no. He'd done enough making himself miserable for one day already, but the part of him that would have refused a break was drowned out by the part that leapt at the chance to make his time with Scott last just a little longer.

"Break sounds good," he agreed gruffly, carefully climbing off the back of the ATV. "Five minutes."

Scott raised one shoulder. "We could go wild and take ten, if you want."

Maccabe's mouth quirked. "Maybe. We'll play it by ear."

He shook his hair out of his face, put his hands at the small of his back to ease the ache there, and scanned the horizon. The clouds were low and the light poor, but it seemed as if he could still see for miles. Mountains loomed in the distance, their peaks still covered with snow. The air smelled fresh and cold and clean.

Scott ambled to his side, lingering there, taking in the view. "You know this place?" he asked offhandedly.

Maccabe didn't. "I've never been down this way before."

"I have, a couple of times, running with a pack. This used to be homesteader land." Scott kicked at the dirt as he indulged in his memories. "Back in the early 1900's. I don't know who they were."

Whoever they had been, they'd left a long time ago, but now that Maccabe knew how to look, he could see the places where those homesteaders had tried to make their mark on the land. *There* was where they'd laid the foundation for a house, and *there* a handful of planks once long ago painted barn red. Tangled weeds in a more-or-less rectangular shape indicated there'd been a garden, too, once upon a time.

Maccabe wondered why they'd given it up, but he thought he knew the answer. Alaska didn't take kindly to interference, and only the tough survived; only the toughest thrived.

He decided he'd rather look up and out, at the view. It might be harsh, but it was still beautiful.

Beside him, Scott did the same. "My grandfather used to say Alaska was God's country." He dropped his arm casually across the top of Maccabe's shoulders, heavy but so warm. "When I was a kid, I would have argued with him on that. Now, though. Now I think the old man knew what he was talking about."

Maccabe thought so too.

It seemed to him in that moment he couldn't take another second of this. Of being near a man like Scott, of drinking in a view like this. Not if he had to leave it all behind just because he couldn't figure a way out of the deal he'd made.

"Let *go* of me," Maccabe snapped, ducking out from beneath Scott's arm. He gave the Alpha a push to make sure he got his point across. "We're going to be riding for hours pressed up together like sardines in a tin. Can't I get five minutes of breathing space?"

Scott's initial confusion shifted sideways into annoyance. "Excuse *me*, then. All you had to do was say so. You don't have to shove me around like a pup on a playground."

They might have been all right if Scott had stopped there. If his reaction hadn't taken another left turn into concern.

"You shouldn't get all upset," he went on, laying his hand atop Maccabe's belly. "It's bad for the pup. Didn't you know that?"

The top of Maccabe's head didn't literally blow off, but Maccabe would swear it sure felt like that. He snarled, sounding very much like he did in his wolf shape, and knocked Scott's hand away. "Who's the one carrying this pup? I know a hell of a lot more than you about what I should and shouldn't do. Like going to bed with you at all, let alone more than once. That was something I shouldn't have done."

"You wish you hadn't?" Scott's surprised hurt went straight to Maccabe's soul and rankled there.

But Maccabe couldn't let up now. If he couldn't think of a way to stay, if he had to leave, he had to make the break as clean as possible. "Damn right I shouldn't have," he said, each word clipped off sharply. "I need some air."

"All of Alaska doesn't have enough air for you?" Scott growled back.

Knowing he was mad now didn't help ease the hurt or the frustration. Maccabe glowered at the Alpha and turned his back, meaning to stalk away and cool his head. He'd dunk it in a stream if he had to, though now that he came to think about it, Maccabe didn't see any water sources on the old homestead. Maybe that was why they'd left. No one could live anywhere for long without water. If it'd been him, he'd have cut his losses and moved on too.

He took half a dozen frustrated strides forward, and then let out a strangled yelp of surprise as he scrambled for something to grab onto. There was no more ground under his feet. Nothing but sudden darkness, cold clammy stone, and then a splash at the bottom. When Maccabe looked up, the sky was a weed-choked small circle fifteen or twenty feet above him, and he had to tread water or sink.

"You've got to be kidding me," he said, his teeth already chattering. That water was *cold*.

He heard his name being bellowed, and a stab of guilt shot through him. *Scott*. Scott must have seen him disappear. "Here!" Maccabe shouted back. "Down here!"

Scott's head popped into view at the top of the ground. He must have been lying on his stomach, Maccabe thought. If there had been stones or a well cover at any point, they'd disappeared as long ago as the homesteaders. "Maccabe! You okay?"

"Been better," Maccabe said, shivering almost too hard to speak. That was good, though. If he got too cold to shiver, then he'd be in real trouble. And -- the pup. Maccabe drew in a sharp, shocked breath. If cold like this could kill a grown wolf, what would it do to a pup? "Get me out of here!" he begged. "Hurry, Scott."

He'd known Alphas before who would have scoffed at him, told him if he was so all-fired crazy to be on his own, he could rescue his own ass. But not Scott. Though his face was pale and his jaw tighter than drawn wire, he only nodded once. "Be right back."

All Maccabe could do was trust that he'd keep his word. His teeth chattered together as he trod water the best he could with an altered center of gravity, and to keep from panicking he started to count back from one hundred. He slapped his own face when the first wave of sleepiness washed over him. No. If he drifted off, he'd never wake up. He'd drown, and the pup with him.

My pup. *Mine.*

He knew then he'd never give this pup up for adoption. He couldn't. He'd find a way to make it work, because the alternative was unacceptable.

As he thought that, the light coming from the top of the well darkened. Scott peered over the edge. "Still with me?" he called, visibly as tense as a coiled spring, but still keeping himself in control. "Catch this. I'm going to pull you up slowly. Understand?"

Maccabe managed to jerk his head in acknowledgment. He paddled back to allow room for the long rope of -- were those clothes, his and Scott's, all tied together? -- to drop down the well and splash into the water, then wrapped the end of the makeshift rope around himself and clung tight with both hands. "Do it."

"Don't try to help," Scott warned as he backed away from the hole. Maccabe could see him wrapping his end of the rope around his arms. "Just let me take care of you."

The dizzying sensation of being lifted made Maccabe's head spin, and he had to squeeze his eyes shut or be sick. Or maybe that was the adrenaline. He couldn't be sure.

But he was certain of one thing. Just as he'd never give up his pup, neither would he leave this man behind. He'd be a fool to even try.

So he couldn't think of a way to get out of his promise? Fine. Maccabe would keep that promise. He'd let Scott chauffeur him to Homer, and he'd get on a boat that took him to Seattle.

There, he'd make his apologies to the wolf who oversaw adoptions. He'd tell his friend with the food truck that he couldn't take the job for keeps. Just for long enough to earn a little cash.

Then he'd get his ass on the first boat he could buy a ticket for, one that would take him up the coast and back to Scott.

Scott hauled Maccabe over the lip of the well, and didn't stop pulling until he'd wound Maccabe into his arms. Maccabe huddled into his warmth with a cry of relief.

"Shh now, shh now," Scott said. Maccabe could feel the violence of his shaking now that he'd gotten him back onto dry land. "You'll be all right. I've got you."

Damn right you do, Maccabe replied inside his head, while he pressed himself flush against Scott's body heat. He pulled back long enough to manage his way into dry clothes.

And if I have anything to say about it, you always will.

Chapter Seven

Scott

And then, there they were. One more hill crested, and the harbor they wanted lay below Scott and his quiet, withdrawn Omega.

"Right down there," Scott said with a nod. "Maccabe?"

Maccabe didn't budge from his place on the back of the ATV. "I can see it."

Scott shook his head silently. He'd grown more worried about Maccabe with every passing mile. He'd not heard a peep out of the man for three or four hours, and if it weren't for Maccabe's constant firm hold on his waist, Scott would have bypassed the harbor and taken them straight to the medical center.

The terror that'd seized him when he saw Maccabe disappear down that deep dark hole -- hell. Scott had never felt anything like it before, and prayed to God he never would again.

He shuddered.

Maccabe must have noticed, for he squeezed Scott in light question.

"I'm fine. Goose walking over my grave," Scott said, reaching down to pat the back of Maccabe's hand. He half-expected Maccabe to swat him for it -- he liked the Omega's normal feistiness -- and that he didn't get that reaction now worried him even more.

Something didn't add up. Throw in Maccabe's unusual savagery right before that whole clusterfuck with the well, and it was an odd equation, one that Scott couldn't wrap his head around.

But here was the thing: he didn't give a damn. Not anymore.

He'd made up his mind, lying on his stomach next to that well and peering down into the darkness at the Omega he thought he'd lost. He wouldn't -- he couldn't --

let that happen. He'd not be able to bear surrendering Maccabe for keeps.

They'd be good together, him and Maccabe. So good. Scott could see how their lives could knit together just so if they gave it a proper try. They had a home already, ready-made and waiting for them at the *Fisherman's Friend*. He could run the bar, and Maccabe take over the kitchen, and between the two of them they'd lick those upstairs rooms into shape. They could expand that innkeeper's quarters at the bottom, maybe put on an addition to let their family grow into. Raise their pup together and maybe give him a few brothers along the way.

Grow old together.

He'd be the gentleness Maccabe needed. Maccabe would be the fieriness that made life fun.

They could do it if they wanted. They really could.

So if Maccabe didn't see that now, if all he wanted was to run and to keep running, why then it would be Scott's job to convince him. He'd even come up with a plan. Since Maccabe was so determined to take the ship waiting for him, then Scott would see him safely on board.

Then he'd keep on driving his ATV, trading it in for whatever he needed along the way, until he reached the Puget Sound and found Maccabe again. He'd do whatever it took, there, to coax Maccabe into coming home. To win Maccabe's heart.

Did he think that would be easy? Scott snorted. Hell no. But nothing worth fighting for was ever easy.

Scott glanced over his shoulder at Maccabe, though he couldn't see anything past the curve of the Omega's head. "You want to stop? Take five, maybe run for a bit and stretch our legs?"

Maccabe moved his head from side to side, his nose bumping the spot between Scott's shoulder blades. "No. Let's just get it done."

Like I said. Not easy. Scott fired up the ATV's engine. *But worth it -- I hope, in the end.*

They left their transport at the far end of the harbor, Maccabe claiming he wanted to stretch his legs after all, and Scott willing to indulge him. Taking an ATV onto a busy harbor would be tantamount to either suicide or murder, anyhow, and Scott had left his taste for taking risks back in his old life.

He kept pace with Maccabe, who walked as if his joints hurt him and no wonder after all their adventures in getting there. Even so, Maccabe didn't voice a word of complaint. He kept his jaw locked and his chin held stubbornly high.

Scott had to admire that. Just another aspect of the Omega he'd fallen head over heels in love with.

He cast an eye over Maccabe's bump. Unless he was mistaken, Maccabe had gotten bigger during the days they'd spent together. It fascinated him still. He wanted to spend the last couple of months before their pup came measuring all those changes with his hands and his lips, to worship Maccabe's body with his own.

In time, he promised himself. *In time.*

Meanwhile, Scott kept one protective arm firmly around Maccabe's shoulders. The sight and scent of a pregnant Omega drew plenty of attention from the fishermen and processing plant workers that crowded the harbor, swarming on and off boats. To anyone that slowed down to cast a lustful eye over Maccabe, Scott gave his fiercest glare.

Most backed off. Some looked thoughtful, as if weighing their chances.

"I could take 'em," Maccabe murmured, surprising Scott. More so when Maccabe nudged him gently in the side. "I've fought off Alphas before."

"Darlin', I have no doubt you could." The endearment slipped out before Scott could catch it behind his teeth.

Maccabe must have heard it. He colored up a pretty pink, but then shook his head and said nothing. Just looked more miserable than before.

Winning his heart might be harder than Scott imagined -- not that he planned to let that stop him.

The ship they wanted had docked at the far end, because that was their general luck. Scott breathed easier once they were past the other fishing vessels. He trusted Captain Morrisson, who was old enough to be his grandfather, and who had never stood for a single drop of nonsense even when he was young.

Scott waved when he caught sight of the silver-haired Alpha directing traffic on and off his boat. "Permission to come aboard?"

Captain Morrisson rolled his eyes, but he was grinning too. "Depends. This the passenger you asked me about?"

Scott nodded. Beside him, he felt Maccabe take a deep, steadying breath.

"Then they're welcome." Captain Morrisson gestured for Maccabe to approach. "Better hurry, though. You nearly missed us. Five more minutes and we'd have been on our way out."

Perversely, Scott wished they'd taken those five minutes to run in wolf form back when the harbor first came into view. Would have made their lives less complicated -- or maybe more.

Still, he had his plan. He'd stick to it.

He gave Maccabe a gentle push. "Go on. You'll be all right. The Captain's a good man."

"I can see that." Maccabe took another deep breath, but it didn't seem to help. He took the bag stuffed with his clothes, still knotted together, that Scott had carried for him, and slung it over one shoulder as he turned to look at Scott. "Scott, I…"

He stopped there, looking troubled and lost for words.

Scott knew the feeling. "It's fine," he said, trying to ease Maccabe's tension. "You don't have to say anything if you don't want to."

"But I do want to," Maccabe said, more frustrated still. He raked at his hair. "I just don't know how. Or if I even should."

Pregnancy brain again. Sympathy moved Scott's heart. Though he would rather have had a kiss, he put out his hand for Maccabe to shake. Asking for more would be cruel when the Omega was overwrought with hormones and exhaustion.

"It's been a pleasure, Maccabe," he said when Maccabe stared at his hand in seeming incomprehension. "But if you don't want to miss the boat, then it's time."

Maccabe bit his lip. "I know."

Scott hadn't been sure Maccabe would take his hand, yet he was still startled when Maccabe didn't. Mostly because instead of a simple handshake, Maccabe swarmed him. Stood on his tiptoes and flung his arms around Scott -- pressed to mouth to Scott's in a hot, hungry kiss that took Scott's breath away -- and didn't stop until Captain Morrisson's boat horn blew a sharp blast.

Then, Maccabe settled down on the flat of his feet and gave Scott a look that defied interpretation. Something wild, something wistfully yearning, something hungry.

The Captain blew his horn again.

Maccabe bared his teeth in a snarl, then went back up on his tiptoes to press his mouth to Scott's ear. They moved, words less audible than their shape on his lips was tangible, and then Maccabe tore himself away and fled to the ship.

As Scott watched, hand pressed to the memory of warmth on his ear, a deckhand helped Maccabe onboard. Maccabe took up a position near the bow, at the railing, his duffel at his feet and his gaze fiercely fixed straight out to sea.

The words he'd said -- Scott's skin buzzed where they'd been spoken.

Not a goodbye, as he might have expected. Not a thank-you, either.

Only this: I love you.

"I will be damned," Scott said out loud, lost beneath the noise of the boat engine. Maccabe didn't want to leave him any more than Scott wanted to be left, did he? They'd both changed their minds, and been too stubborn to say so. "We're a pair of fools."

But it wasn't too late to change that.

The boat hadn't taken off yet; Scott didn't care. If it had, he'd have swum out to meet it. As it was, a good run-up over the dock gave him the momentum he needed to jump across the narrow gap between safety railing and the ship itself, where he landed in a tangled heap of limbs very nearly at Maccabe's feet.

"What the hell?" Maccabe yelped, quick hands busy helping Scott back to his feet. When Scott's head stopped spinning, he could see Maccabe looked mad enough to chew nails and spit bullets, and that meant Maccabe loved him.

Without a word, Scott bent his head to kiss all the words out of Maccabe's mouth. To say, with that caress, everything he hadn't been able to before.

And Maccabe understood. Scott knew it for sure when Maccabe let out a small cry and melted into his arms, only the bulge of the pup separating them from fusing together.

Maccabe punched him in the ribs, a love tap that Scott saw for what it was now. "I thought I'd have to get all the way down there and come back before you understood."

"I thought I'd be there waiting for you, hoping I could make you understand." Scott kissed Maccabe's sweet lips one more time, then rubbed noses with him. "We're not that bright, Maccabe, you and me."

"Maybe not," Maccabe said, his grin bright and brilliant. "But that's all right. We get there in the end, Scott, same as always. Now come on. The captain's laughing his ass off at us right now, and I want to get started."

Scott cocked his head. "Started on what?"

"Getting back on that damned ATV and heading back home." Maccabe nuzzled his chin into Scott's chest and exhaled a happy breath. "Back to our home, Scott, if you'll have me."

"Have you? I'll have you and hold you," Scott promised. He fired off a salute at the captain, then scooped Maccabe up into his arms. "Just you watch, Omega. Just you see."

Epilogue

Scott

"I'm going to kill you." Maccabe knotted his fingers in the sheets covering their bed and groaned. "I'm going to kill you so slowly and so painfully you'll beg for death, I swear to God. *Oh*."

Kneeling beside him on the bedroom floor -- Maccabe never did seem to do anything the traditional way, Scott reflected -- Scott chuckled under his breath and pressed a cool cloth to Maccabe's forehead. "No, you won't. You love me."

Maccabe bared his teeth at Scott and snarled. Not having enough breath left to do more than pant, he let his glower speak for him. He wouldn't really kill Scott, no, but just at the moment making threats was infinitely satisfying.

He dropped his head to the edge of the bed and groaned. Scott switched his attention to Maccabe's back and pressed two knuckles to the very lowest part, just where he'd been told the extra pressure helped. Maccabe's groan rose to a yelp, and then a slump forward in relief.

"Maybe I won't kill you if you keep doing that," Maccabe muttered behind his crossed arms.

The doc, just as comfortably settled on the floor as Scott and Maccabe, grinned as he watched them. He'd been in the area visiting friends when Maccabe went into labor, and hadn't minded being called in. What was his name? Scott couldn't remember. Sawney. Right, that was it. Scott had been distracted enough during their introductions that he figured he could be forgiven for forgetting.

"Don't worry. Alphas who don't get death threats at about this point are rarer than hen's teeth." Sawney knelt to do some mysterious sort of checking that Scott couldn't make heads or tails of -- and suspected his not being able to was for the best. "Not long now. Three more pains is my guess."

"You sure it's okay, his being on the floor like this?" Scott asked with a worried frown. He'd swept it and mopped it and swept it again before laying down sheets when Maccabe made his wishes clear halfway through the whole ordeal, but it was still a floor.

"I've delivered pups in stranger places," Sawney promised. He lifted his chin to Scott, directing him to help support Maccabe through the next pain. "I'd be more concerned about all that racket outside."

Maccabe shook his head hard, stubborn to the last. "No. I like the noise. This is our place. We worked our asses off getting it fixed up. Besides, they're taking bets." He laughed breathlessly. "Jimmy already lost. He bet it would happen almost an hour ago."

Scott made a razzing noise of amusement. Jimmy never did learn. One day he'd find an Omega who'd whip him into shape, though. Scott hoped.

As for the noise? Scott liked it fine, himself. They had a whole taproom full of rowdy Alphas and sympathetic Omegas cheering them on out there. Couldn't be a much better birthday than one that would be celebrated by a hundred-odd whoops of delight.

Maccabe cried out and went as tense as a board, the massive bulge of his stomach hard as stone.

"Maccabe?" He didn't answer, so Scott turned on Sawney. "What's happening?"

"Hush, Scott. Maccabe? Pant now. Like you're blowing out a candle." Sawney's hands were busy doing things Scott couldn't see, but when Maccabe flipped him off the doc laughed out loud. "That's right. Stay mad at me, as long as you do what I tell you. Now just a little, just a very little -- there."

Maccabe kept the middle finger of one hand jutted up at the doc, but seized Scott's hand with the other and squeezed so hard Scott could feel bones grinding together. He gritted his teeth and bore it.

A long, breathless moment, and then -- a cry.

"There we are," Sawney encouraged. "That's what I like to hear."

It was what the barroom liked to hear too. Those shouts and howls of celebration nearly deafened the lot of them, and drowned out their new pup's cries as Maccabe gathered it to him in shaking arms, but it was worth it. All worth it.

Because he let Scott come up behind him, and hold Maccabe to him, helping hold him up.

"To have and to hold," Scott said in Maccabe's ear -- the words they considered to be their marriage promise. "I'm yours, Omega."

"You're damned right." Maccabe's smile was tired, but exultant, and he found the strength to knuckle Scott in the wrist. "For now and for always, Alpha, all three of us. Now what are you waiting for? Go tell everyone!"

And Scott did.

Chapter and Verse
Will Okati

Put aside by his former mate for his inability to bear children, Omega Lane retreated into the Alaskan interior and has lived there alone ever since. He's a lone wolf and a hermit, not part of the world and no longer wanting to be.

Until Carey comes across his path. Younger, and also an Omega, Carey's on the run from an Alpha who won't take no for an answer. Though Carey thinks at first he might be pregnant, he soon learns that isn't the case -- instead, he's going into heat.

Carey doesn't want or trust an Alpha anywhere near him. Lane, who has kept his preference for Omegas hidden for years, is the only one Carey chooses to trust. But can Lane let Carey into his life after living alone for so long?

And what if Carey decides he doesn't want to leave?

Chapter One

Lane

The entire point of living as a lone wolf in the interior of Alaska was the blessed solitude of it all. Lane hadn't seen a face he didn't know, and hadn't been bothered by any familiar acquaintances for almost five years.

Until today.

Alaska boasted the only whistle-stop trains still in existence in the United States. With a line running through the heart of the wilderness, would-be passengers who likely didn't have piped water, much less Wi-Fi, could wait by the side of the tracks and flag down an oncoming train if they needed to go to town. Lane kept his visits to a strict quarterly schedule -- biannual if he could manage it, and sometimes he could. But no matter how well anyone planned, they would eventually run out of essentials like coffee, and a trek couldn't be avoided.

Of course, not knowing exactly when the train would come could mean hours of waiting in thigh deep snow, but those were the breaks.

Lane had just wrapped his fleece-lined coat more snugly around his narrow shoulders when there came a racket he hadn't heard in years. It was so unfamiliar that at first he pricked up his ears in confusion, unable to identify the noise.

But when the Omega struggled free of his tree line, it all came flooding back. Lane's lips parted in shock at the sight of a stranger on his property -- and a clumsy one at that, clearly unused to walking in snow this deep, stumbling every other step and showing signs of having fallen flat on his face several times in recent hours.

So surprised was he that he couldn't speak a word until the stranger had come within arm's reach of him. The Omega stopped there and searched Lane's face with desperate speed, then let his breath out in a puff of -- relief? "You're not an Alpha," the Omega said. He had a sweet voice made ragged from exertion. "You're *not* an Alpha, are you?"

Lane's teeth ached from the cold, and he finally remembered to close his mouth. "No. I'm not."

The sound of his own voice was strange to him after three solid months of silence, but the words came out as they always had. Clipped, cool, precise. Emotionless. He knew how he must look, returning stare for stare with the Omega. Too tall, too thin, and too wiry for any kind of beauty, with a Madonna mouth and blue eyes like chips of frozen sky.

There wasn't any way to avoid the impression of a disapproving monk, so he usually didn't bother. He folded his hands in front of him and lifted his chin. "Who are you?"

"It doesn't matter. I'm sorry. I know that was rude. But I had to be sure," the Omega said in a rush, with an embarrassed shrug. "You look like an Alpha from a distance."

"You don't."

The Omega paled and looked down at his boots. "Oh."

Why is that a bad thing? Lane wondered. It was true. Small and slim and delicately shaped, this one shouted *Omega* from the second he came into sight. True, he would be better described as "cute" than pretty, with a spray of freckles across his nose and cheeks -- and his hair! It looked like he must have worn it long, then tied it up in a ponytail and cut it off just above the band with a pair of kitchen scissors. Dull ones. "And you didn't answer my question. Who are you?"

"I did answer. I said it doesn't matter." The Omega lifted his head, strong emotion giving his skin color despite the cold. "Where are you going?"

Lane considered not replying, but the old habits of politeness ran deep. "Talkeetna. For supplies."

The Omega's lips moved in what looked like a silent *thank you*. He made a sudden movement that culminated with his pressing a bundle of folded bills, mostly ones and fives, into Lane's hand. "Buy my ticket for me with that. Please."

Lane didn't close his fingers around the money. "What on earth?"

"Please," the Omega begged, casting a wary glance toward Lane's tree line. "*Please*. You look like an Alpha from a distance."

Yes, and being reminded of his failures wasn't exactly winning him over to the Omega's side. "It's not the 1800s anymore. Omegas are allowed to buy their own tickets."

"I know, I just -- please." The Omega tried to close Lane's fist, his fingers slim and cold. No gloves? If he wasn't a shifter, he would have succumbed to frostbite hours ago. Even so, he had the luck of the devil.

Lane pressed his lips together. "Who are you?" he asked for the third time. "What kind of trouble are you in?"

The Omega shook his head. "I can't -- I mean, I'm not -- I'm not in any trouble. I swear I'm not."

"Yes, you are, and you're a bad liar on top of it." Lane rubbed at his forehead. Oh, this one was trouble walking. Anyone could see that. And yet… Lane knew a few things about wanting to run away from your worries, and your worse-than-worries. Hadn't he done exactly that? Looking at the Omega's huge, pleading eyes, how could he do anything besides help?

The train was coming. Lane could hear its great engines roaring and chugging in the near distance. He had a minute, or less, to make up his mind. He let out a long breath that puffed white vapor in the frigid air and closed his fingers around the Omega's money. "On one condition. You tell me your name."

The Omega sagged with relief. "Carey. I'm Carey. Thank you. I owe you."

"Hmm," Lane said. He guided the Omega -- Carey -- a few steps back as the train drew nearer. "You can pay me back by telling me who or what you're running from."

A false gale, whipped up by the oncoming train, tossed Carey's ragged-edged locks into wild disarray around his face, but he shook his head stubbornly. "I can't say."

"Can't, or won't?" Lane wanted to know.

"Same difference in the end, isn't it?" Carey cast a worried glance at the money in Lane's hand. "You won't change your mind? About the ticket."

"Can't, or won't?" Lane asked again with an arched eyebrow. "No. I said I would, and I will. But that's it, do you understand?" He'd chosen to live alone in the wilderness for a specific reason, and getting enfolded in a stranger's business wasn't part of the plan. "No more favors. You get on the train, and what you do after that isn't any of my business. Agreed?"

"Yes. I just…" Carey licked his lips, and to Lane's startled surprise the Omega flashed a bashful smile at him. "Thank you. I heard there was a medical clinic in Talkeetna. I'll go straight there and not bother you."

Lane frowned. Carey looked healthy enough to him. Before he knew he was going to, he'd opened his mouth again. "Are you sick?"

"Umm." Sharp white teeth nibbled the curve of Carey's lip, and his face flashed deep crimson for a moment. "I… might be pregnant," he said so quietly that it was a wonder Lane heard him at all.

But hear him he did, and the bottom fell out of Lane's stomach. His lips were numb as he replied. "I see."

"I don't know, is the thing," Carey went on, his speech gaining speed now, like sweet blush wine flowing from an abruptly uncorked bottle. "I think so, but I've never... I don't know how to be sure. But I think so."

The wash of words flowed over and around Lane without sinking in. He looked down to see he'd pressed a fist over his own barren womb, its emptiness having cost him everything he'd once cherished, and that it was the hand with Carey's money clutched in it.

Carey stopped speaking with a blink of concern at Lane. "Are you all right? You went pale." He reached for Lane, who dodged his touch.

"I'm fine," Lane said, not feeling his mouth move despite hearing his own voice. He could have wondered why a pregnant Omega wanted a stranger to buy his train ticket, or why he couldn't see a doctor without running to a strange town, or what he was afraid of, but it wasn't his business. None of this was, and he needed to remember that.

So he didn't ask. He moved his lips into the shape of a smile instead. "Well. Congratulations."

* * *

Carey

He has such sad eyes. Did I say something wrong? Carey thought he must have, though he didn't know what. He'd seen the curiosity light up in the other Omega's eyes, and seen it die in an instant just as the train pulled in. The second they were onboard and moving down the tracks, Lane had shut his mouth with a *click* and kept it shut until they reached Talkeetna. He wouldn't even look at Carey. Just kept his arms crossed over his middle, his sad, pale blue eyes staring at something about a thousand miles away. When they disembarked, he didn't look back once as he walked away.

Carey faltered, one hand pressed uncertainly to his breastbone. *If he'd said what I did wrong, I could have...*

But did it matter? Carey bit at his lip, but in the end had to shake his head. He could go back and forth with himself all day long and not be any closer to the truth when the sun went down. He'd do better for himself if he kept his focus.

It wasn't easy. His stomach lurched and grumbled, unhappy with the motion of the train and empty besides. Carey couldn't remember when he'd last eaten. Game had been scarce and wily along the way, and he hadn't dared light a fire to cook anything even if he'd caught it.

He swallowed down a sudden mouthful of thin saliva at the thought of food and felt at his pocket. The train ticket had taken almost every cent he could call his own. Maybe twenty dollars left, maybe ten. He wouldn't know without counting. If the clinic doctors wouldn't agree to send him a bill he could pay by installments, he'd be screwed.

Again.

A hysterical laugh rose in Carey's throat. He covered his mouth with one cold hand until it subsided. The last thing he needed was for someone to tackle the crazy Omega and haul him away for his own good.

Clinic, he told himself firmly. *Now. Find out if you're alone inside your skin, or if that... Alpha... did leave you pregnant.* Carey broke out in a cold sweat, making him shiver with the chill and shudder with revulsion at unwanted memories. He hadn't wanted... hadn't asked for, no matter what he'd said...

Not that what Carey had said mattered to the Alpha. He'd just...

Carey wrestled himself back under control. *Find out before you freak out. And if you are pregnant, then you can have something to eat while you figure out what to do next.*

Even though he knew better, Carey found himself scanning the people around him, searching for a glimpse of Lane's battered hat and sturdy coat and long, slim legs, but he'd disappeared. It was a shame. Carey had liked him. He wished he'd --

Enough of that. You're wasting time. Go.

* * *

Only it wasn't that easy. Really, by now Carey knew he shouldn't have expected anything to be easy. He found the clinic all right, a small cinderblock square of a building painted in cheerful primary colors, but no lights were on and a handwritten sign was taped to the door.

CALLED OUT. BACK BEFORE FIVE. SORRY AND THANK YOU.

And that was that. Carey stared at the sign, hoping against hope the words would change and the lights inside would spring on, but no such luck.

He checked his watch. Okay, nearly four in the afternoon. That wasn't so bad. He could wait an hour. *And if the doctor doesn't come back on schedule? What then?*

He would find somewhere to den up for the night. Under a porch, in a doorway, as long as it was sheltered from the elements.

Except every Alpha who walked by could sense he was an Omega. Could smell his giveaway pheromones, and more than a few of them stopped to take a long, considering second glance. They probably weren't planning anything bad. They likely just wondered what he was doing there.

Maybe.

Carey shuddered again, and tucked his hands in his pockets, turning to walk away. Maybe he wouldn't wait for the clinic to open. If the general store sold pregnancy test kits, that would do just as well. If he paid cash, there would be no way to trace his identity. His uncle couldn't track him down and insist he marry that Alpha to save the family's honor.

Honor. Carey spat on the ground, his face flaming hot with embarrassed rage. Store, pregnancy test, take the test, wait for it to give a result, then maybe dinner. *Maybe, if he had enough cash left over for a burger or an energy bar.*

His stomach roared with impatience. It didn't care about scheduling. It wanted food *now*.

Carey bit at his lip. He didn't know how much a pregnancy test would cost. If he'd so much as looked at one -- before -- his uncle would have torn strips off him, demanding why he wanted to know about that, calling him a slut. A slut, when he'd never so much as slept with an Alpha until --

He counted his money with shaking hands. Slept with an Alpha? No. While all the other Omegas around him were finding mates, he'd never understood the appeal. They all reminded him of his uncle. Alphas were loud, rude, and often cruel, and the Omegas they caught were tied down with cub after cub until they wore out. Carey did want babies, he did, but someday. With someone he loved, or could grow to love.

And he'd never met an Alpha he thought he could fall for. They left him cold. He'd learned how to take care of business for himself when he was in heat, and he liked that fine. He still did. It'd given him comfort during the long, freezing cold nights on his journey from home to here.

Before that night, he'd started to wonder if there was something wrong with him, some reason he wasn't drawn to Alphas. Maybe he was broken in some way. He didn't know. That was why he'd agreed to go for a drive with that Alpha in the first place. Just to see if he could get over himself and give him a fair chance.

But then...

Impatient now, Carey counted his money a second time. Thirteen dollars and forty-three cents. Might not even be enough for a pregnancy test.

Food, his stomach demanded.

Carey tried to fight it. The general store was right across the snow-covered street, packed hard with snow machine ruts. He could see people going in and out.

Trouble was, it stood right next door to a restaurant that smelled like heaven, that made his mouth water and his stomach twist. Frying meat, bacon grease, *coffee* --

He stood very, very still, struggling with himself, but when a pair of older Alphas lingered nearby to argue about the weather, it seemed almost like a sign. One of them had his back turned. Carey could see the outline of his wallet in his back pocket. A thick one. The edge of it peeked out of the pocket.

If he kept arguing, if he stayed distracted…

Carey edged forward, reaching slowly. He'd never done this before. Seen it on TV before his uncle decided television was too much of a corrupting influence and thrown it out, but he thought he remembered how it went.

Almost. He almost had it.

The Alpha's hackles near visibly rose. He jerked around, and he wasn't as old as Carey had thought before, his hair salt-and-pepper but his face smooth and unlined. His companion *was* old, and bristled as if someone had just insulted his ancestors when he saw Carey's hand still outstretched.

"He take your wallet?" he barked.

The Alpha Carey had tried to steal from clapped a hand to his pocket. Almost absently. His nostrils twitched, scenting the air. "No," he said slowly, still sniffing. "You need money, little Omega?" His mouth cocked up at the corner. "You want to earn some? Because I know of a thing or two I'd gladly pay you for -- "

"And what might that be?"

Carey nearly jumped out of his skin at the voice and at the accompanying touch on his shoulder. He glanced down to see the hand was bony but smooth and smaller than an Alpha's, then looked up into glacially-blue eyes over a mouth pressed firm in disapproval.

Lane kept his hand on Carey's shoulder, but kept his gaze fixed on the Alphas. "Correct me if I'm wrong. Did I hear you propositioning my cousin? My married cousin?"

"Well -- I --" the younger Alpha sputtered.

Lane ignored him. He squeezed Carey's shoulder hard, a clear warning to keep his mouth shut. "Because if that's the case, I'd like to know your names. I'll need to know who his husband will want to beat the shit out of."

He waited for another fit of Alpha spluttering to cease. "Or," he said, fixing them both with a look so hard he could have driven nails with it, "You could both turn around and walk away right now, and we'll forget this ever happened. The choice is up to you."

Carey could feel his heartbeat pounding in his ears, a roaring that made him feel dizzy. He couldn't hear what the Alphas had to say for themselves, but it didn't matter, it didn't, because they were walking away. Almost running.

Lane waited for them to turn the corner before giving a decided nod. Finally, he took his hand off Carey's shoulder and turned to face him. "Are you all right?"

"I thought you said it wasn't your business," was all Carey could think to blurt out.

Something fleeted through the cool blue of Lane's eyes. "It's not, but I'm not going to stand by and watch someone like that eat you alive, either."

"You were watching?"

Lane raised one shoulder slightly.

"I... thank you." Carey shook his head. He wanted to ask why, but his stomach chose that moment to loose a mighty roar that made him turn scarlet.

The corner of Lane's mouth lifted so briefly that if Carey hadn't been staring, he would have missed it. "Come on. I'm hungry too. My treat."

Chapter Two

Lane

How long would it have been since Carey ate anything?

Two days, Lane decided, watching the other Omega tear into a platter of bacon, eggs and wheat toast meant for two or more to share. Two days of hunger would create an appetite like that. Maybe three. If he thought he was pregnant he wouldn't have risked shapeshifting into his wolf form, to make hunting easier. Unless he'd been trying to miscarry, that was, and perhaps he had; Lane didn't know his whole story yet. But Omega instincts tended to go deeper than that. Alphas would prefer to think they ran even deeper, but what Alphas didn't know wouldn't hurt them.

Lane diligently picked away at a bowl of fruit salad, not hungry but not wanting to make Carey feel self-conscious about his appetite. As it was, Carey snuck occasional wary peeks at him between bites, then went back to his plate with red cheeks, but he couldn't stop himself.

Nor should he have.

Nor did Lane let that stop *him* from assessing Carey in equally quick, stolen peeks. Hunger was one thing, and shabbiness quite another, but Carey had his fair share of both. His clothes looked worn, their hems ragged and caked with snowmelt and dirt. The light in the diner was kept warmly bright at this time of day, a replacement for the sunlight Alaskan winters were so stingy with, but as a downside it wasn't easy to hide anything in shadows.

Carey had a bruise on his temple. Fading now, but it would have been a messy eggplant-colored thing when fresh. Before he could stop himself, Lane had reached out to brush his fingertips against it.

Carey froze.

Damn. Lane quirked his lips in an attempt to be reassuring. "This looks nasty. What happened?"

"You have the saddest eyes," Carey blurted. His own went promptly as wide as saucers, and he buried his gaze in a spray of toast crumbs on the tablecloth. "I'm sorry. That was --"

"True, as far as I've ever heard and seen in the mirror," Lane replied. "I was born this way."

Carey frowned as if he doubted that, but aside from a shake of the head kept his opinions to himself.

Somehow, that rubbed Lane the wrong way and made him feel prickly inside. Why would Carey suspect him of lying?

"I'm sorry," Carey said again, letting out a sigh as he stacked his fork and knife in an X on his cleaned plate. He met Lane's gaze so frankly that it made Lane ashamed of his temper. "I'm not used to trusting -- well, anyone." He brushed the backs of his knuckles against the fading bruise, perhaps unconsciously. "It's been a long time."

Lane tucked his fist under his chin and rested it there. He regarded Carey openly for a long moment, careful to choose his words before he spoke. "I don't know your story, but you don't have to tell me if you don't want. I think I get the gist of it."

Carey's blush deepened to a rose red. He hunched his shoulders and kept silent.

"Who was it?" Lane asked, deliberately casual. "A relative? A pack member?"

"Pack member," Carey said in a whisper. Then, he straightened and in the same fluid motion caught Lane's free hand and held it, startling Lane into silence. "I haven't told anyone about it. No one at all."

"You don't have to tell me," Lane repeated.

Carey shook his head, his chin stubbornly pointed out. "No. I want to. I don't want you to think the worst of me. I..." He faltered. "I..."

Lane couldn't bear it. "My mate set me aside," he said as calmly and plainly as he could, though he had to press his hands together white knuckled tight to keep his control. It was an old wound, but a deep one, and still raw. "That's a very old fashioned way to say it. I think it's the most accurate."

Thank God. He'd distracted Carey, who now stared at him in chagrin.

Lane could take that. "I couldn't have children, you see," he went on. "We tried for several years, but nothing ever came of it. He blamed me. Omegas and their notorious fertility, right? He was positive I had to be doing something to stop it happening. I wasn't, but he wouldn't be convinced. Not even by doctors." He raised one shoulder slightly. "So he found an Omega who was more fertile. And I came here."

Carey had brought his fingertips up to cover his mouth while Lane spoke. "I'm so sorry."

"It was a long time ago."

"I'm still sorry." Carey seemed to realize he still held Lane's hand, and he gave it a tiny squeeze. "But I envy you a little too. Is that wrong?"

To his amazement, Lane produced a genuine smile. "All things considered? Not really."

Carey smiled in return, then made a rueful gesture at his temple. "That was my uncle. He -- I never liked Alphas. I still want to tell you. Is that okay?"

Lane nodded. Maybe Carey needed to get it out to someone who wouldn't judge. God knew he understood that urge.

"I thought I just needed to -- to acquire the taste. So I tried it. I found someone who said he'd be fine with taking it slow. But when we went out for a drive, he... He wouldn't take no for an answer."

Carey had moved his gaze to the tabletop again, but Lane had to admire the stubbornness that pushed him on, and gave Carey's hand an encouraging squeeze in return. He had such fine, delicate hands. Beautiful, really. "And your uncle?"

"Tried to make me marry the Alpha." Carey's jaw set. "He said I'd brought shame on the family."

Lane scoffed without prompting. "Then your uncle is a fool."

Carey looked up in plain surprise. "What?"

"A fool," Lane said. Reluctantly, he withdrew his hand. He could feel curious stares starting to pepper them from other diners. Omegas of their age were almost all mated, not eating cozy meals together without an Alpha in sight. He cleared his throat. "And so you think you're pregnant."

"Maybe. I don't know what it feels like. I never have been before."

He'd been kept hungry, shabby, and ignorant, then. They were meant to be living in a more enlightened age where Omegas weren't kept barefoot and pregnant and submissive, but every Omega knew it still happened. And it made his blood boil.

Carey, not privy to those thoughts, started to fidget with his napkin. "I'll pay you back for the meal as soon as I can. I just don't have enough right now. But if you give me your address, I'll send a money order."

If he did, Lane would send it right back, but they could cross that bridge later. In the meantime… Well. There wasn't much Lane could do about Carey's current situation, no. But he'd be damned if he didn't do what he could. He stood and offered a hand up. "You can pay me back by helping me at the grocery store."

Carey stared at him. "What?"

"I'll divide my list down the middle, and you can help find things. They change their displays too often to memorize them."

The tiniest of smiles dawned on Carey's lips. "I can do that." He took Lane's hand, and rose lightly to his feet.

His hand against Lane's was electric. A shock that went through Lane like a slender bolt of lightning, a crackle from scalp to sole. Lane only just resisted catching his breath. He'd given away too many secrets for one night already.

His preference for Omegas would have to stay locked in the closet for now.

"Good," he said instead. "Follow me."

* * *

Carey

It was a small world, but a new one, and Carey was dazzled.

He'd never been anywhere like the Talkeetna grocery store before. Oh, he knew in the lower forty-eight this wouldn't be considered a big deal. It probably wasn't any bigger than a corner store, but they sold in bulk and packed in the goods nearly wall to wall. He couldn't stop looking at all the *variety*. And fresh vegetables, at this time of year!

His uncle prided himself on being a self-sufficient homesteader. The very few things he couldn't make or barter for were always mail ordered, and picked up by one of his cousins. Carey hadn't given it much thought before, but now he wondered why he'd been kept so isolated.

Were they trying to protect him? Or were they ashamed to have an Omega in the family? If one encounter with an Alpha was enough to make them look at him like an abomination, then what had they thought of him before?

"Are you all right?" Lane stopped in the middle of a densely crowded aisle to look sideways at Carey. He kept one hand on the cart, but reached out to steady Carey with the other. Only then did Carey realize he'd been so lost in thought that he'd nearly veered into the packed shelves. "You look a little lightheaded."

"I'm fine," Carey promised, though he tugged at his collar to bring a draft of cooler air down his unaccustomedly warm front. Lane had insisted on picking up a heavier coat for him at the front of the store, saying he could just add the cost to his tab, and Carey hadn't put up a fight. He *did* need something better, and Lane was a formidable opponent. Not in the way his cousins or uncle were, with their stony glares denying any possible response, but Lane had a backbone of steel.

Carey liked that. He'd never known Omegas could be just as strong as Alphas, inside or out. He *was* hot, though. Watching Lane in his peripheral vision, he unbuttoned the coat and opened his collar one more button.

And all Lane did was remark, "They do keep it warmer than it needs to be in here."

Dazzled.

The heat got better, though still simmering warm under Carey's skin, once he had the coat open. The lightheadedness and attendant clumsiness didn't, baffling Carey. Maybe it was the big meal, and a blood sugar spike, or just the stress of running away finally catching up with him. If he'd been home, he would have snuck out and gone for a long, long run in wolf shape. The thought of that filled him with a sudden sharp yearning, and yet if he was pregnant, then he didn't dare change forms.

He nearly tripped over his own feet when he tried to help fill Lane's bags at the cash register, earning him a blatantly nosy frown from the checker.

Before the checker could open his mouth, Lane stepped in. He steadied Carey with a quiet murmur of reassurance, then fixed the checker with the longest, coolest stare Carey had ever seen. Lane's lips were faintly quirked up at the corners, perfectly pleasant, and yet under the weight of his gaze the checker shriveled up like a slug that'd just been doused in salt.

Carey made himself a promise: he *had* to learn how to do that!

But he couldn't learn it from Lane. That realization made *him* deflate. Lane had already been generous -- more than -- and Carey couldn't expect more than he'd gotten. Lane would take his groceries home, and Carey would take his pregnancy test behind the next convenient bush, and their paths would lead them in different directions.

"You can help me carry everything to the train stop," Lane said abruptly. He strode off, walking tall and fast despite being laden down with bags, leaving Carey to grab the rest and hurry behind him.

Was Lane angry?

No, the look on his face didn't seem like anger. More like preoccupation. "Is something wrong?" he asked when he'd caught up.

Lane shook his head, then crinkled his nose. "It's nothing."

The train stop wasn't far, and the path through the snow to it well trampled down. Carey was only just barely out of breath by the time they reached it. He set his bags down and massaged his arms, unused to carrying that much weight, and gave Lane a rueful smile.

Lane returned it with a curving of his lips that wasn't too different on the surface from the smile he'd given the grocery checker, and yet somehow it made Carey want to duck his head and blush. "Thank you." He cleared his throat. "I suppose we'd better go ahead and say our goodbyes. The train's due any minute."

It would be the right thing to do. Yet somehow Carey couldn't make the words come out of his throat. Strange. He should have gotten chilled, being out in the snow after sweating in the grocery store, but his skin felt dry and tight, burning hot.

Lane pulled his gloves off, frowned at them, then tugged them back on one finger at a time.

Carey kicked lightly at a chunk of snow that'd frozen into a chunk. He wanted to pick up some fresh fallen snow and rub it over his chest, but it was all dirty this close to the tracks.

"You'll be all right," Lane said abruptly, looking away. "You're smart, and you're adaptable."

Carey nodded, though he wasn't sure he agreed.

"You are. Look how far you got on your own already."

Well, that was true enough. Carey tugged at his collar again. He'd disliked sweating in the store, but now he wished he could. His skin felt like he'd gotten sunburned all over, and it was dry as desert sand. When the train whistle sounded in the not-too-far distance, he turned in relief to face the blast of wind it kicked up in its path.

He could smell himself, which embarrassed him deeply, though it wasn't a *bad* smell as such. More like the ocean, salty and clean, with the earthiness of sand and shell beneath. And -- he was wet --

Lane sniffed the air curiously. Half a second later, his eyes grew round as saucers while Carey clapped his hands to his mouth in horror.

He wasn't pregnant. He was in heat.

"Oh God," Carey whispered. "Oh God." Not a curse, but a prayer; there were so many Alphas around, and if they smelled him, they'd -- he wouldn't have a chance!

He surprised himself by laughing, though it was a broken and terrified sound. "At least we know I'm not pregnant."

"It's not funny." Lane's eyes flashed blue fire, though the rest of his face was still set in a mask of dismay.

"I know. I know." Carey bit down on a cry of fear. "Oh God."

The train rolled in, a great black iron beast that stank of diesel and oil and grease. The smell was strong enough to choke Carey, but it was strong enough to cover the smell of an Omega in heat. Thank God. But it wouldn't last long, and then --

Lane looked at the train. Then back to Carey. Then to the train again. His jaw hardened. He caught Carey hard by the wrist to get his attention, then put his mouth to Carey's ear so he could be heard over the noise of the train. "Do you trust me?"

Baffled, Carey nodded, but Lane's nearness made him moan as well. Lane wasn't an Alpha, but he was strong and kind and gentle and --

"No." Lane shook his head. He feathered his thumb lightly over Carey's wrist. "Do you *trust* me? To help you? If you want me to, I can. But only if you say so."

Carey gasped, startled back far enough to search Lane's face. He couldn't. Could he? When he was an Omega too?

His heat surged, not caring about that. It wanted warmth and a body to cover his own. If he didn't take Lane's offer, it would throw him in the path of Alphas worse and less careful than the one he'd run away from, and he knew it.

And Lane was kind. Lane was… Carey liked him.

Hesitantly, Carey nodded.

"Then come with me." Lane pulled him, guiding him by the wrist, leading him to the train. "I'll take care of you."

Chapter Three

Lane

Afterward, Lane didn't remember much about the train ride back to his home. It was strange. The return journey always seemed to take forever, every turn a cause for worry about his supplies falling out or being broken, but this time it passed in a flash. He had his arms full with holding Carey tightly against him, cushioning his overheated body from the bumps and jounces, and mixing his scent with Carey's.

For once, he didn't mind being mistaken for an Alpha from behind or from the side. No one would question an Alpha holding his Omega as close as this.

By the time they reached his home, Carey was nearly insensible, and yet they couldn't leave the bags unattended. Lane had left a hand-drawn wagon by the side of the trail before, knowing he'd need it. If there had been room, he would have made Carey ride in it. Every movement drew a moan from him, his body overstimulated and in desperate need of relief.

Lane set his jaw grimly as he guided Carey toward his cabin. He'd never done this with an Omega in heat. With an Omega he barely knew. Carey had said he trusted Lane, and Lane wanted to believe that, but…

Though it took a strength of will Lane wouldn't have thought he possessed, somehow he got both Carey and his groceries inside, and locked the door behind them.

There he stood for a moment, panting lightly and out-of-sync with Carey's ragged breathing. God in Heaven, could he do this? With an Omega so far gone that he doubted Carey would understand the meaning of consent?

Lane kept two guns handy in his cabin, ready-loaded despite the safety risk. Bears and the like generally wouldn't wait for a man to unlock his gun safe and load a few rounds. One, a rifle, hung on the far wall. He kept a pistol tucked in the drawer of an end table by the door, too.

Maybe he should tell Carey about them. Just in case he wanted to change his mind at any point. That'd make him feel stronger about it.

He looked over his shoulder to find Carey had found Lane's bed in the corner of the one room space and perched on the side of it. Lane had solar panels and a generator set up to power his home, giving him a measure of warmth to return to after a long day, but it wasn't muggy by any means. Yet Carey looked as if he was ready to melt. His collar was open so far that the shirt barely clung to his shoulders, and his jeans were plastered to his skin, his hair soaked with heat perspiration and sticking to his cheeks in curling tendrils.

But his eyes were open, and though they were wild around the edges he looked directly at Lane.

Lane's cock, already hard, ached stiffly between his legs, making walking difficult. The scent of ripe Omega filled his cabin in a heady perfume. He stalked toward Carey and allowed himself only the luxury of reaching down and pushing Carey's wet hair away from his face.

Carey pressed his cheek into Lane's palm, never once looking away from him.

"Are you sure?" Lane asked, only just out loud. "Are you *positive*?"

Carey pressed his lips against Lane's fingers. "I'm sure." He hissed and doubled over slightly, a wave of heat and contraction passing visibly through him, before he looked back up. "Please, Lane. Please."

"No." Lane put his fingertips to Carey's lips. "I mean, I'll help you. But don't beg. You don't ever have to beg me. Do you understand?"

To his astonishment, Carey smiled. A wavering thing, as quickly gone as it'd come, but it couldn't be mistaken. "I don't know. You're not already on me. Do I have to beg you for that?"

Lane's mouth dropped open. He covered it, and his startled laugh in response. Then, he bent and touched his lips to Carey's. "No," he murmured. "You don't have to beg for that either. Lie down."

"Too hot with these clothes on," Carey protested.

Lane shook his head. "Shh. I'll help you with that, too."

And he did, piece by piece. He couldn't go faster, with the damp fabric clinging stubbornly to Carey's limbs. At that, the scent of aroused Omega made him feel as if he'd set off a box of Roman candles inside his head. His cock throbbed in time with the rapid pulse in his temples and wrists, making his hands shake as he peeled Carey's jeans off.

He was so wet. Clear slick coated his thighs, dripping in fat beads onto Lane's once neat bed and into the quilt he'd pieced himself one long winter. He raised his knees and spread them apart, moaning at the caress of cooler air. His cock lay thick and dark against his belly, drops pearling at the tip. He reached for his small, flat breast tissue and cried out at the touch of his own fingers.

Lone wolf or not, Lane's wolf howled with wanting a taste.

He compromised by skinning hastily out of his own clothing, pausing only for a moment to rummage in a rarely used trunk before he crawled onto the bed with Carey. "Shh, now, shh, now," he soothed, stroking Carey's stomach and marveling at the flexing muscles that rippled smoothly beneath his soft skin. He'd been in heat before, technically, but never reduced to this sort of state. "I said I'd take care of you, and I will."

Carey only moaned in reply, but his eyes were open and fixed on Lane with a trust that floored him.

Or would have, if he'd had the brainpower left to consider such things. As it was, he was in barely better condition than Carey. His body screamed out with the need to *fuck*.

But he had made a promise. Still murmuring soothing nothings, Lane guided Carey's legs wide apart and settled himself between them. He looked up one last time, waiting for Carey's nod, before he gave in to the howling hunger and closed his lips around Carey's cock.

Carey surged up, legs clamping around Lane's shoulders and hands diving into Lane's hair as Lane laved his cock with tight, wet friction and caressed his pretty little balls with gentle strokes. He had to stop every few strokes to breathe, to avoid drowning in Carey's juices, but he took air in through his nose and blew it out over Carey's shaft, addicted at once to the maddened and maddening noises he made.

"Lane," he panted. "Lane --"

His body arched in a bow as he came, keening out his pleasure -- but not for long, his shout ending in a strangled, frustrated sob. He didn't go soft; if anything, he was harder and larger, almost too big for Lane's Omega mouth. Pressing his hands to his eyes, Carey almost wept as he stammered, "I can't -- it's not -- I'm still --"

Lane had known this wouldn't be enough, even if he'd hoped. He shushed Carey again, stroking him to calm him, and reached for the thing he'd had the foresight to bring with him. This was *not* an item commonly found in the possession of mated Omegas, and might even be illegal. He hadn't bothered to care when he'd ordered it. His heats were weak compared to Carey's, but they did still require satisfaction.

He brought the model of an Alpha's phallus to Carey's opening, pressing it lightly against the rim. "All right?"

Carey was beyond answering with his voice, but after one gasp he nodded frantically and spread his legs wide, so wide that Lane had to stop and squeeze his own cock hard to keep from coming at the sight and scent of Omega heat.

He brought his mouth back to Carey's swollen cock, and slipped the false phallus inside Carey's body. A small button concealed in the shaft, when pressed repeatedly, drew air into a reservoir and inflated a knot as slowly and gradually as a real Alpha's cock might.

It wasn't enough -- until it was. Carey's wild scream, a wolf's mating call, made Lane's ears ring. Something like savage pride made him keep moving, thrusting the phallus into Carey until Carey's body spasmed, then clamped down around the false knot.

He sobbed, cries of relief and ecstasy, as Lane inflated the knot as far as he could -- and reached for him, frantic, as Lane's self-control deserted him and he swarmed up the length of Carey's body to lie on top of him. Carey's arms went around Lane's back, his nails sharp on Lane's skin with a blissful sting, and their sweat mixed together as their legs tangled. Lane took their cocks in his hand, rutting in time with Carey, and when Carey's mouth opened wide in a soundless O Lane's control abandoned him in a bottomless leap. He came as Carey did, spunk mixing with slick and the doubled scent of Omega completion almost too thick to breathe.

Even so, he stroked Carey's hair and murmured to him as he wept with relief. "There's a good Omega," he said over and over again. "There's my good Omega."

As he said it, he knew he meant it. Which begged the question Lane had been trying to avoid.

What was he supposed to do now?

* * *

Carey

Had that really happened?

Carey kept his eyes closed as he drifted awake. Waking on his own time was another new experience for him. He'd always been on edge in his uncle's house, alert long before dawn, straining to hear the first sounds of Alphas stirring so he could start breakfast cooking.

Not here. He patted the bed beside him and found it empty, only just the faintest bit warm. Lane had gotten up, but not woken him.

And that was wonderfully new, too.

Among other things. Eyes still closed, Carey stretched his legs and pointed his toes, then stretched his arms as wide as he could. He brought them back to lay his hands gently on his torso, just beneath the breast tissue in his pectorals. They felt a little tender, but pleasantly so, and his skin reminded him somehow of a plum's. Tissue thin, bursting with sweetness, so sensitive that his own breath made him shiver.

He touched his forehead and his cheeks. Warm, but not burning. Still in heat, but in a lull. It was always like that, peaks and valleys. The peaks had never been so high as last night's, but the lull felt comfortingly familiar.

And yet… different. Had that really happened, the night before? It had. Carey's body held the sense memories of Lane's touch. The other Omega had known when to be rough and when to go easy, where to dig in and where to barely brush the skin. And that toy he'd used! Carey's face bloomed hot, but only with bashful glee. He'd heard stories about false phalluses, but never seen one in person. He'd half assumed they were made up.

But they weren't. Lane had known how to make his body sing. And why shouldn't he, after all?

He was an Omega too. He knew how it all worked.

Carey rolled languidly to one side, the better to lazily rub his thighs together. A little slick, not enough to make a mess, just enough for the friction to be pleasurable.

He let his eyes drift open.

Was it still night, or morning? Carey couldn't tell. Lane's curtains were both thick and tightly drawn, and he'd had lit a candle rather than turn on a light. He stood in what passed for a kitchen in the one room cabin, absorbed in tending a kettle on a camp stove set up by the basin sink. His cabinets were the type that had no doors, giving Carey a view of simple staples like flour and sugar and pasta, and stacks of soft blue plates and bowls beside them. A tendril of blond hair, longer than Carey would have thought when Lane kept it all tied up, had slipped free and fallen over Lane's cheek.

He had his inscrutable expression firmly in place again. He'd be hard to read, if Carey hadn't started to learn his ways. The calm was a cover for concern, and the distance he'd put between them Lane's attempt at kindness. If Carey had chosen to sneak out of the cabin, if he had been that horrified by what they'd done, Lane would have let him go without once looking away from the kettle.

But he wasn't. He wouldn't be.

Carey never wanted to leave.

He slipped his legs off the side of the bed. He noticed in a vague sort of way that he was still naked. Good. His bare feet made little sound on the floor, and Lane didn't seem to pick up on it, standing motionless by the kettle.

Or was he only pretending?

Pretending, Carey decided when he padded a few steps closer. Lane had frozen, and the blue eye Carey could see through that fallen lock of hair was fixed on him.

Carey couldn't imagine what he looked like. *His* hair was awful, the victim of the terrible trim he'd given himself, and tangled into Elf knots after heated lather and solid sleep. His skin was flushed rosy warm, and he could smell the rich Omega musk on himself as if he'd bathed in a tub of the stuff. He probably had cum dried on his stomach, for pity's sake.

He didn't care. And as he came near enough to reach out and touch, Lane's eyes held steady on his face.

Carey smiled at him, not in the least bit shy for once in his life, and took the Omega who'd rescued him as boldly into his arms as Lane had done the night before.

Turnabout was, after all, the fairest of play.

Lane's first startled gasp melted into a shuddering sigh as Carey slipped open the buttons on his plaid flannel shirt. It hung a size or two too large for him anyway, and was easy to push aside once opened. It fell almost unheeded to the floor. Carey had better things to do. He bent his head to Lane's beautiful pale breast and took the rosy nipple between his teeth.

The soft cry Lane gave made a wave of heat tingle beneath Carey's skin. A small peak, one he knew he could manage -- and so much better, wasn't it, not to be alone? He bit down gently on Lane's nipple, laved the soft skin with his tongue, sealed his lips around it. Sucked.

Lane thrust his fingers through Carey's wretched hair. He keened softly and rolled his hips against Carey. He was hard.

Good again. So was Carey. Carey had sometimes wondered what this felt like... and he had no reason not to try now. He slipped his thigh between Lane's legs, giving him something to rut against, and giving himself the same -- and all the while, kept his mouth fastened to Lane's breast, nursing like a cub, like an Omega. He knew how it all worked too, after all.

Lane shut his eyes and tipped his head back. He breathed in fast, ragged gulps and let his air out in rough sighs. "Carey..." he whispered. "Oh, Carey."

Carey could taste the sweetness of Lane's skin, of his natural Omega flavor. He wondered what breast milk would taste like, whether it was earthy or savory or maybe a little like honey, but it couldn't be better than this.

His skin prickled with heat and a light dew of sweat, and Carey could feel his climax rolling gently but inexorably toward him. He urged it on with the rhythm of his hips, but held back at the very edge until Lane bit his lips savagely and shuddered.

Then, he let go. Not the kind of orgasm he'd had the night before, where the world had stopped and flung him into space, but he thought he liked this kind better for its easiness, for the sweet relief of it that left him feeling as if his very bones were humming in satisfaction.

He opened his eyes to meet Lane's, dazed and bluer than ever, staring drunkenly into his. Lane's mouth curved into a smile, the one that Carey could already recognize as the real deal with nothing forced about it. "*I* was just going to offer you some coffee."

Carey laughed out loud in delight.

* * *

Lane

Lane frowned up at his cabinets. He'd unpacked the supplies he'd bought the day before, and filled all his shelves to bursting. Enough staples to last a couple of months, even with two mouths to feed.

The trouble with staples, though, was that they all had to be made into things before they could be eaten. Unless you craved a handful of raw flour, and if you did, you likely had more problems to consider than simple hunger. Normally he didn't mind, and could get by on just coffee in the mornings.

Normally, he didn't have guests. Actually, he never had guests. Carey was the first. And he didn't feel like a guest at all.

Lane shook his head at his foolishness, warning himself to be careful about thoughts like that. Even if he would have liked it -- and he would -- Carey couldn't stay. It wouldn't be fair to lock him up in the middle of nowhere, with no one else for company. After his life of near seclusion, Carey deserved to roam as far and wide as he possibly could, and see all the things there were to see.

Besides, it was risky enough for one Omega to carve out a homestead and live there. Two Omegas sharing the same house, without an Alpha in sight? They might as well roll out the red carpet and post gilded invitations to come harass them. It wouldn't matter that Lane wasn't fertile. Carey clearly *was*.

Idling beside him, wrapped from chin to toes in one of Lane's old robes, Carey at least seemed content to munch on the bread slathered in butter and drizzled with honey that were the only things ready-to-eat that Lane had, and to drink coffee sweetened with more honey too. He leaned comfortably against Lane, peaceful as a child, and occasionally beamed up at him with honey on his lips.

I'd better be very careful. "Hunting," Lane said out loud.

Carey blinked up at him. "What?"

It was a good idea. A quick examination from all angles confirmed that. "Hunting," Lane said again. He balanced Carey against the sink and put some distance between them, heading first for the rifle he kept on one wall -- bears were too big for single wolves to tackle on their lonesome -- then changed his mind, and shrugged the shirt off.

He almost laughed at how Carey's eyes immediately glazed over at the sight of his bare chest. It was just the hormones guiding Carey's reactions, of course, but it was awfully nice to be thought appealing for any reason. "Hunting," Lane said for a third time, firmly now. "Of a sort. You haven't spent any time in your wolf form since… well. Have you?"

Carey shook his head, but his dazed satiation had started to give way to genuine interest. "I didn't think it was safe. Just in case I was pregnant."

Lane bit the inside of his cheek hastily and covered it by raising one eyebrow. "Now we know you're not," he pointed out as calmly as he could. "I think we could both use a good hard run. If we scare up any game, and since there are enough ptarmigan over the ridge to drown in their feathers, we assuredly will, then so much the better."

Carey's face was alight now. He hurriedly chewed and swallowed the last of his bread, washed it down with the last of his coffee, and started untangling himself from the heavy swathes of Lane's robe. "Running in my second skin," he said worshipfully. "Yes. That's exactly what I want right now. What are we waiting for?"

What, indeed. Lane sighed. Waiting for nothing. More like putting off the inevitable.

But as long as it *could* be put off, he'd be damned if he wouldn't.

* * *

And it was everything Lane had ever dreamed of, running with another Omega. In his wolf shape, he was the picture of a lone wolf, a natural outcast from the pack. His coloring was pale blond, a far cry from the natural timber shadings of the group he'd been born into, and his legs were just as long and lanky. His tail was an absurd short fluff.

Carey was small, gray-white-silver, and had a tail like a plume that arched over his back -- when he wasn't wagging it wildly with wolfish excitement. No doubt he'd never had the chance to run as freely as he liked, and he made up for lost time now by bounding everywhere, worse than a pup on a sugar rush.

When he misjudged a jump and landed in a drift so deep all that could be seen of his was a pair of startled eyes, he made Lane laugh. As a wolf did, his tongue hanging out of his open mouth, but still. A real laugh.

Lane trotted to the snowdrift and helped Carey dig his way out. Carey licked Lane's mouth then, nuzzling under his jaw -- then barked a bright puppy yip, nipped at his flank, and took off in a bounding run.

Oh, so that was how it was, was it? Lane chased after Carey, his longer legs making short work of catching up the lead. As soon as he could, he tackled the smaller wolf and sent them both tumbling ass over teakettle.

Carey popped up right away and sneezed, then shook the snow off his muzzle and made a play bow, his rump in the air and his front paws stretched out before him. He bounced a couple of times, inviting Lane to keep playing.

He shouldn't. But he couldn't resist, either. And he didn't want to.

He could have this stolen moment.

Lane followed where Carey ran, sometimes in circles, sometimes forward for as long as his wind lasted. They caught a couple of ptarmigan, no more than they could carry in their wolf jaws, and it was Lane's suspicion that it wasn't hunting skill but rather the birds' astonishment at their behavior that made them easy prey.

When they were too out of breath to run any farther, Lane nuzzled Carey to direct him home. Nights were long in the winter, and it would be just as well for them to be safe inside once darkness fell.

A slow pace brought them there in the end, just as the sun began to sink. Carey dropped his ptarmigan carefully on Lane's stoop, and with an artless grace shifted back into his human shape. Naked but clean-washed with snow, he looked like an Elf and he smiled like the sun itself as Lane changed to join him.

Carey surprised Lane by leaning over to kiss his cheek. It was strangely sweet, with the both of them naked, and yet it went heart deep and warmed Lane from the inside out. "That was the most fun I've ever had," Carey said simply. "Thank you."

Lane's throat closed up. He couldn't speak, but nodded his response, and Carey didn't seem to mind. He patted Lane's shoulder. "I'll go clean these poor birds, and roast them for lunch. I know how."

"Carey?" Lane called as Carey's footsteps padded away behind him.

The sound of movement stopped. Lane could easily imagine Carey turning to look over his shoulder, as naturally as if he'd always been there.

Lane looked over his own shoulder and smiled. "It was the most fun I've ever had, too."

Chapter Four

Carey

"Hold still."

"Sorry." Carey resettled his shoulders and dropped his head forward to allow Lane clear access to the back of his neck. Scissors clicked together in a slow, hypnotic swishing, and bits of hair tickled their way down his back as Lane trimmed them free. Carey couldn't remember ever feeling as peaceful as this, tucked up in a snug log cabin by a crackling fire while Lane nestled behind him, taking care of him, but he bit his lip all the same. "You don't have to do this, you know."

Lane gave a dry chuckle. "Yes, I do. Anyone who saw you as you were would know you'd hacked off your hair in a hurry, and then they'd wonder why. I did."

Carey let his head hang forward a little farther, enjoying the pleasant burn in his muscles. He was near the end of his heat, at the place where his skin still felt as thin as a ripe cherry, but every sensation was drowned in drowsy bliss. "You did?"

"Mm-hmm."

"But I can trust you." Carey reached behind himself to stroke Lane's calf.

Lane went briefly still, then clicked his tongue quietly and readjusted Carey's position. "Try and hold still. I don't do this much, and I don't want to accidentally leave you with a bald spot."

Carey sighed and fell silent for a moment, listening to the fire crackle until a thought drifted across his mind. "Do you cut your own hair?"

"Only the ends. I meant to unbraid it for you earlier."

But he'd been distracted. Carey smiled to himself in satisfaction.

Lane could just about read minds. He nudged Carey's shoulder and made another sound of amusement. "Anyway. I've been letting my hair grow since I moved out here. It's down to the small of my back now. I want to see how long it'll get." He moved as if raising one shoulder in a shrug. "And I figure there's no reason why I can't amuse myself as I see fit, out here all alone."

All true, Carey thought. *And I could get used to living like that. I would enjoy it! But you keep pushing me away and I don't know why*. Oh, Lane didn't do it openly. He might not even be aware of it. But he always caught himself whenever he and Carey got too close, and then there was the haircut. Why insist on trimming it up so it would look nice to other eyes besides Lane's?

Because he was planning to end this, and soon.

Carey's contentment seeped away like air from a balloon with a slow leak. He sighed and crossed his arms on his knees, pillowing his cheek on them. Lane didn't follow him with the scissors or correct his posture, which in Carey's mind only confirmed the conflict Lane must be feeling. Carey thought Lane didn't *want* him to go, as such. He just thought he *should*.

Why?

Carey liked it here. He liked Lane. Could someday soon more than like him -- he was sure of it.

Lane must have read his body language again. He put the scissors away with a clank of metal, then began to sift his fingertips through the freshly trimmed ends of Carey's hair. "We need to talk about it, Carey."

Carey shook his head stubbornly. "My heat isn't over yet. It can wait."

"No," Lane said. "It can't."

Carey looked back over his shoulder to see Lane pale but resolute, the ever-present sadness in his blue, blue eyes mixed with stubborn resolve. "Please."

Lane wouldn't give in. "For what it's worth, I'm sorry. It's not safe for you to stay here long term, Carey. Alphas leave me alone, yes, but I'm older. On a pheromonal level they can probably smell I'm different, not worth bothering with."

"You don't smell any different from other Omegas to me."

That seemed to fluster Lane. He blinked twice before regaining his composure. "That's not the point. I'm trying to protect you, Carey. Alphas might turn a blind eye to Omegas living with Omegas in big cities, where there's more choice of breeding partners, but not out here where the ratio is three to one. And it's illegal, besides."

Carey stuck out his chin. "Name me one person who's been arrested for it."

"That's not the point either." Lane narrowed his eyes. "I don't want you to be the first. That's not the worst that could happen, either. There's a family with three unmated Alpha sons living a few miles away, plenty close enough to catch your scent. It wouldn't be safe to go outside any time you're in heat. I saw them in town, or I'd have stayed awake guarding the doors with a rifle instead of sleeping by your side. Carey…"

He cupped Carey's cheek, so achingly tender that Carey choked on a sob. Instead, he pressed his face into Lane's work worn hand and closed his eyes. "I don't want to go," Carey said as soon as he could speak.

"For what it's worth, I don't want you to either. But you deserve a *life*. That's the most important reason of all. You've been deprived of so much. I'm not going to hold you prisoner here with a bitter old divorcee who's got nothing to offer. You should go to Paris. Omegas who love Omegas are supposed to be so common there you can't turn a corner without tripping over one or two."

Despite himself, Carey chuckled. "That's a ridiculous mental image."

"But it might be your happy ever after."

Carey shook his head, but kept silent. He knew very well when arguing was pointless. He'd learned that lesson early, living with his uncle and cousins. Lane was as unlike them as it was possible to be, but so stubborn he should have been an ox shifter, not a wolf.

But that didn't mean Carey considered himself defeated. He didn't want to go to Paris. Not without Lane, anyhow. He loved Alaska, anyway, and especially out here where it was so peaceful and the world seemed so much more gentle.

He would just have to think of a new argument. A better one, one that would work. And in the meantime...

Though his heat was nearly at an end, Carey could still feel the storm of urges and arousal simmering beneath his skin. He could have taken care of himself and satisfied the craving.

He didn't want to do that either. Instead, he rose to his feet and turned to look down at Lane. "If you want me to go," he started, then had to stop, swallow, and steady himself. He wasn't committing himself to leaving, after all. "If you want me to go, then I want one more thing."

Carey held out his hand, willing Lane to take it. "I want one more time, Lane. Come with me."

* * *

Lane

"Carey --" Lane started, ready to argue his point. Going their own ways after Carey's heat was over would be hard enough already. Why add more fuel to the fire? But Carey wasn't listening. He stood with his hand outstretched, his attitude suggesting he'd stand there patiently until Judgment Day if that was what it took.

Lane recognized donkey-stubbornness when he saw it. He'd looked at it in the mirror often enough, after all, and he knew when he was beaten.

For now.

He took Carey's hand, and let Carey raise him to his feet. "Where?"

Carey shook his head, and crooked one finger for Lane to follow. Still without a word, he shrugged to let the borrowed robe he'd been wearing slide off his shoulders and walked, proudly nude, toward the bathroom. Without waiting to see if Lane was obeying orders, he left the door standing open but the lights off, finding the shower spigot by touch and starting water pattering down like rain on the porcelain.

Lane had seen that sort of mood in Omegas before. Words weren't quite good enough, because they never fully expressed what an Omega in that state wanted to say. *Determination. Focus. Breathlessness. The sense of standing on the edge of a cliff.* Omegas gained that sort of unearthly concentration when they were in labor, ready to deliver, when nothing else existed beyond the boundary of their bellies.

A pang of envy and jealousy shot through Lane.

Then he shook it off. If wanting *him* had brought Carey to that state, the only way past was through. And beyond that, it was... Flattering. Enough so that it made him smile, and his cheeks pink up, as he undressed and followed Carey into the bathroom.

Carey had already gotten into the shower stall and stood beneath the spray. He blinked slowly at Lane through beads of water that made his eyelashes cling together in spikes. His own mouth quirked slightly as he beckoned a second time.

Lane stepped under the water.

His shower wouldn't have fit an Alpha and an Omega, but there was just enough room for two slender Omegas to stand together without risk of suffocation. He'd picked out the tile himself, a pretty pattern of deep blue and mellow ivory squares. Laid it himself, too, floor and walls and ceiling. It was rare enough for a cabin out here to have its own well, let alone indoor plumbing, and he'd meant to enjoy every last drop he could milk out of the thing.

Though he'd never expected something like this.

Carey searched among the small array of toiletries stored in a built-in niche, took one out for closer study, then nodded and handed it to Lane. Lane recognized Carey's choice by touch: shampoo. When he clicked open the lid, Carey sighed like a sleepy child and bent his head forward.

The directive seemed clear enough, and simple -- on the surface, and in theory. In practice was an entirely different matter. Standing behind Carey, rubbing shampoo through his newly-cropped hair, the limitations of space ensuring that their bodies brushed every time they breathed... Well, that wasn't simple. Not in the least. He was hard in an instant.

Oh, he ought to put an end to this. He knew that.

And yet he couldn't seem to stop running his fingers through Carey's hair, unable to cease even after the last of the soap suds had washed away and his hair was so clean that it squeaked. Carey's skin was warm, so warm it toasted Lane with reflected heat. Of course, he told himself that could just be down to the excellent water heater he'd splurged on after he set up his cabin's solar-powered heating and plumbing system.

Or not.

Carey shivered once and moaned, dropping his head farther forward still, arms coming up to brace himself against the wall with. Hips canted up. Legs parted. His opening on display. He glanced halfway over his shoulder, lips parted in pleading. Heat that had nothing to do with the shower darkened his skin, and when he moaned again it went down bone deep.

Lane's heart sank.

"I can't," he said, his whisper somehow jarringly loud as it broke the silence. He feathered his fingertips down the neat, trim line of Carey's bare back.

In answer, Carey looked archly over his shoulder and moved his hips, nudging them against Lane's stiff cock. "You can."

"Not like you want." Lane swallowed hard, and couldn't keep his hands steady. They settled lightly over Carey's sleek hips. The scent of Omega arousal, doubled, was a dizzying perfume that made his head swim. "It wouldn't satisfy you. You need to be knotted. I can't do that."

"I don't care."

"Carey --"

"Don't *care*," Carey insisted. He leaned heavily against the wall. Bent forward so, Lane could see the gentle, insistent pulsing of his channel, and see the heavy drops of slick rolling down the insides of his thighs. "I don't want a knot. I want you."

Oh God. Lane struggled with himself for an endless heartbeat. He could go and get his toy. That might help.

He didn't move.

He could just get out of the shower, and leave Carey to deal with the problem himself. No doubt he had, when he'd been in heat without any Alphas around.

He couldn't make himself move.

Be sensible, he ordered. *Don't do this. It isn't kind, in the long run. He has to learn, if he's to be set free.*

Lane had almost convinced himself of that when Carey let out a breathless, desperate whimper and thrust back. "Please," he keened. "Oh please."

And with that, Lane broke. His cock was in his hand, and he was guiding it forward. Bracing Carey's arms more firmly against the wall. Telling him to hold still, so harshly he didn't recognize his own voice, then soothing Carey's small, desperate cries with soft caresses and light kisses.

And then -- *inside* --

Both of them groaned, Lane just as loudly as Carey. He'd forgotten how *good* it felt, being surrounded by tight, wet heat. He could count on one hand the number of times he'd gotten to experience it before, and none of them were from the last ten years. Mostly just the games unmated Omegas got up to, when they'd had too much to drink.

This was beyond different. This was Carey, moving in harmony with Lane, opening for him, bearing down, begging for more. More than Lane could give, anyway, until Lane stopped and thrust two fingers inside Carey along with his cock.

Carey jolted forward, then held still, fine shivers working their way through him. "Yes," he said, panting. "More. Like that."

Lane could barely see through the haziness of arousal, but he could feel every quiver in Carey's limbs and every spasm of his channel. Slowly -- so slowly, as if it were an act of worship; and in a way it was -- he curled his fingers tight, exactly as a knot would form.

And it worked.

Carey loosed a full-throated wail and bowed his back in an arch, then slapped his palms against the shower wall. Slick soaked Lane's hand, thicker and stickier than the water raining down on them. He wanted to savor Carey's orgasm, to take hold of his cock and guide his past the point of pleasure to the fine sharp edge where bliss lived, but no one could bear that and not come themselves.

He felt himself empty deep inside the Omega, and *that* he never had done before. He didn't know any Omega who ever had. It left him wrung out, balls aching from emptiness, panting with his face pressed to Carey's back.

There would be a price to pay for this. Lane knew that. Saying goodbye would be all the harder, when tomorrow came.

But just in this moment -- just this once -- he refused to consider the cost. Some trades were worthier than others, after all.

Chapter Five

Carey

Carey's heat was over when he woke the next morning.

Even half awake, he frowned and tossed his head on the pillow, straining for any hint, as if it were a scrap of a good dream he wanted to go back to sleep and finish.

Nothing.

He opened his eyes and stared up at the ceiling. Nothing remarkable about it, but staring at a fixed point helped him prick up his ears and listen better. As seemed to be his habit, if you could have a habit after only a couple of days, Lane had woken early and gone to putter in the kitchen while he waited for Carey to finish sleeping.

Carey could smell fresh coffee as Lane measured it into a press. No doubt Lane could smell the chemical changes in him that signaled he wasn't in heat any longer.

Not in heat, and free to go.

The hell he would. Carey's jaw firmed up and gave his chin a stubborn point that he didn't need a mirror to be aware of. Once he got out of bed, this would be his one chance to change Lane's mind -- and good luck to him with that. He wasn't used to standing his ground. But when there was so much at stake...

He had to try.

Carey slipped out of bed and reached for the robe Lane had left draped over a chair. The sheer kindness in the gesture nearly floored him, and as he lifted the robe to his nose, it gave him hope. Lane wouldn't do all these little things if he didn't care. Would he? Bringing him home in the first place, for heaven's sake. That spoke of a loneliness and a need for companionship that touched home in Carey's heart. Of course, living all the way out in the middle of nowhere spoke to an equally strong contrary nature. That'd be the sticking point.

Rather than don the robe, Carey laid it back on the chair. He held his head high and walked softly on bare feet to the kitchen area, where Lane calmly finished measuring ground coffee before glancing obliquely at him. "You're awake. Good."

Before Carey could reply, Lane barreled on, speaking awfully quickly for someone who kept their expression blank and tranquil as a still pond. "I've been putting a few things together for you to take with you," he said. "Some food, mostly things that will keep like crackers and jerky. I can buy more the next time I go into town for supplies. Some clothes too."

"Lane, don't."

Lane darted a glance at him, then made the clear choice to misinterpret him. "I know you don't have the means to pay me back right now. I didn't expect it. We'll settle up in the future, once you're back on your feet."

"Lane…" Carey resisted the urge to roll his eyes; it would've been satisfying, but wouldn't have accomplished anything. Instead, he took a deliberate seat on Lane's single kitchen chair, pulled up next to his doll-sized table-for-one. He crossed his legs and folded his hands demurely on his knee, and fixed Lane with his best imitation of Lane's implacable expression. "Look at me, please."

Lane didn't want to. Carey could see that, plain as plain. But in the end, he did.

They gazed at each other for a long moment.

To Carey's surprised, Lane broke first. He cleared his throat and crossed his arms. "You're not going to try and argue me out of it? I expected that."

"I know. That's why I'm not arguing." Carey quirked his mouth up at one corner. "I'm just not going to go. That's all."

Lane's mouth fell open. *Score one point for my side!* Carey thought, pleased. He'd managed to gain the element of surprise.

Which meant he had to follow up, and fast. Even if it wasn't playing fair at all, he had a high card up his sleeve. "If you make me go when I don't want to and you don't want me to, not really," Carey said, gaze locked with Lane's. "If you make me go, if you *put me aside*, then how are you any better than the Alpha who abandoned you?"

He watched that point sink home like a dagger to the heart. Lane paled abruptly, white as a ghost. Hadn't thought about it that way before, had he?

Carey had to keep going, before Lane could think of a counter. He reached out to capture Lane's cold hand and enclose it between both of his. "You don't love me. Not yet. And I don't love you, not yet. But I *could*, and so could you."

Lane's hand flexed between Carey's. He shook his head several times before he managed speech. "You don't know me, Carey. Not really. I snore."

"Only a little," Carey reassured him. "So do I."

Lane's lips twitched. "I... bite my toenails."

"You do not." Carey clicked his tongue. "Besides, even if you did, you've seen me in the throes of heat. I doubt we *could* gross each other out at this point."

Lane tugged at the end of his braid in frustration. "I'm older than you."

"Do you think I care?"

Lane huffed wryly through his nose, but he wasn't giving up yet. "It's dangerous. Two Omegas living together? Everyone would know."

"We'd think of a story to tell them. And as for dangerous? So is life. I'd rather take a chance." Carey tugged gently on Lane's hand, though it was like trying to coax a cement block toward him. "It feels like I've known you for years already, we fit together so well. I want to stay, and see how we do grow together over time. Let me stay. We could be happy."

"I can't give you children," Lane said, resisting Carey's pull. "You'd never have cubs with me. And you should see the world. You've never been anywhere and never done anything."

"I. Don't. Care." Since Lane wouldn't come the rest of the way, Carey did it for him. He stood and put his arm around Lane's waist, feeling how his body immediately melted against Carey's before his mind recalled its duty and stiffened away. Rather than retreat, Carey followed. "I don't care. I'd rather have one person I loved than a trip around the world and a whole litter of pups. I'd rather have *you*. Don't say no." He pressed his lips to the corner of Lane's mouth. "Let me stay."

Lane opened his mouth. Carey could see him wavering, almost on the edge. "I…" he started to say.

He didn't get to finish. Between one breath and the next -- *BANG!*

And then again -- *BANG!*

A meaty fist hammering on Lane's cabin door, and a rush of scent that Carey recognized. One that froze him to the spot in unthinking terror.

His uncle. The Alpha. They'd found him.

* * *

Lane

The men stunk.

It'd be a pretty poor Omega who couldn't accurately scent an Alpha even through a sturdy wood door, but even so these two were beyond the pale. Lane heard Carey gag, and felt the gorge rising in his own throat. *Stink* wasn't a strong enough word. They reeked -- not only of Alpha rutting but of long unwashed dirt, sour body odor, and enough cologne to drown a muskrat.

And illegal home-brewed liquor. *Can't forget that,* Lane thought with a shudder.

Carey's strangled whimper snapped Lane out of staring at the door as if he were a deer and it a set of headlights. "Don't move," he said, barely parting his lips. "Let me think."

He wasn't given long to even try.

BANG! The door jolted, hinges protesting, at the force behind the Alpha's swing. "I know you've got Carey in there," a whiskey-roughened voice bawled like an angry bull. "I can smell his whorish Omega hide. Open up!"

Lane gritted his teeth.

A younger man laughed, sounding even drunker than the first Alpha. "Hello, sweetheart. I've come to bring you home."

Carey went stiff, utterly frozen with fear. When Lane glanced at him, he found him white to the lips.

"That's him?" Lane murmured. "The Alpha who raped you?"

Carey managed the tiniest of nods, his eyes showing white all around the irises. "That's him."

BANG! A kick this time, one that nearly popped the bottom door hinge loose from its frame. Looking at that, listening to jeering howls from the Alphas outside, sent hot flames of anger down Lane's spine. He'd bought those hinges and installed them himself, one at a time, not knowing how but keeping at it until the job was done. *His* hinges. *His* door.

Lane's mind didn't want to turn over, torn between rage and terror, but he clenched his jaw and made it happen anyway. What he came up with might not work, but it would be better than nothing. He hoped.

"They'll break it down if I don't open up?" he asked Carey, still quiet as a mouse.

Carey, past speech by now, nodded once.

"All right." Lane gave his braid a firm tug to settle it down the line of his back. "Do you trust me?"

At first he thought Carey wouldn't manage a reply, but then Lane felt the ghostly brush of cold fingertips against his. "Yes."

"Do you promise?"

Carey trembled, but nodded again. "Yes."

Lane shut his eyes briefly and shot a prayer skyward. "Then follow my lead. I won't let them hurt you. Do you understand?"

"You can't stop them," Carey said. Unheeded tears made his lashes dark and spiky. "They're too strong."

So am I. "Follow my lead," Lane repeated. "And get behind me."

He opened the door.

As he'd hoped, the bigger, older Alpha was standing back, letting his younger compatriot do the hard work with fists and boots. He'd be lazy, then, not used to challenges, and like all bullies a lily-livered coward under all that blubber bulking out his middle.

Lane ignored the young buck Alpha, who gaped at him in confusion, to fix the older Alpha -- Carey's uncle -- with his coldest blue stare. It'd made Alphas cut and run before, and it even made Carey's uncle flinch briefly.

Lane waited for him to realize it, and to flush with enraged shame, before he opened his mouth. "Speak your piece."

The Alpha regarded him narrowly. "You know why we're here. That's my property in there. Law says so, plain and simple."

Did he think Lane was stupid? "Those laws were changed almost a hundred years ago. Try again."

Narrow scrutiny shifted sideways into cunning. The Alpha tucked his thumbs into the belt beneath his overhanging belly and produced what he must have thought was a jovial grin. "Oh, I can see how this might have happened. A little runaway sees a kindly older gent and thinks 'Aha, here's my free ride.' You don't know him. He's a freeloader and a burden, but I took him in all the same when his folks died. He owes me for the years of room and board, you see, and he's been working it off for a while now."

Lane could feel Carey shivering behind him, and it only made him cooler with fury. "Those laws were changed too," he said, mild as milk on the outside, deliberately needling the Alpha with his lack of response. "A guardian is responsible for a child until he turns eighteen. Before then, they're obligated to provide basic necessities. Even if you *had* done that, there's no question of repayment due."

The younger Alpha gaped stupidly at him, but the older one set his jaw in rage at the sly insult Lane had slipped in there -- and why not? It was a true insult. Carey and his rags had more in common with Orphan Annie than Cinderella.

"He's my kin," the older Alpha said, belligerent now and crowding forward to try and intimidate Lane with sheer bulk. He looked absolutely stymied when he failed to budge an inch, not even when he could count the pores on his nose. "He's mine."

"He's his own," Lane replied. He set his heels, and prayed Carey's nerve held out through what had to come next. "Say I did give him over. What were you planning to do with him?"

The younger Alpha brightened as far as such a dim bulb could. "He's gonna be my mate. We already had our wedding night, or as good as, and he's probably got my pup inside him right now. So I'm gonna take him to my place."

"He didn't consent to that," Lane commented.

"Doesn't have to," the older Alpha countered. He'd truly lost his patience by now. "If he's got a pup in him, then don't the father have his rights?"

"I'm not pregnant."

Everyone blinked at that, but pride blossomed in Lane as Carey peeked over his shoulder. "Did you hear me? I'm *not* pregnant. You don't have any rights. You never did."

"So?" the older Alpha blustered. "He's shamed us by playing the whore, and now he's going to make up for it. Now either you move your ass, or I move it for you. Understand?"

Lane smiled at him, showing all his teeth. "Make me."

Old and fat he might be, but the Alpha moved fast. His meaty hand flew out, the back of it cracking against Lane's cheek in a blow that nearly rocked him off his feet. Carey cried out in alarm and caught Lane, keeping him from falling.

Lane exhaled quietly. He patted Carey's arm, then gave him a gentle push to send him back inside.

Then, he lifted his rifle off the wall -- loaded, in fact, for bear -- and pointed it directly at the old Alpha's nose, fully justified by the laws of the land and the packs by the bruise blooming on his cheek. "Get off my property."

He sneered at Lane. "You expect me to think you've got the balls to use that, Omega?"

In answer, Lane lowered the barrel and squeezed the trigger. The explosion of the shot nearly deafened him, but both older and younger Alpha yelped and jumped away from the shot he'd aimed between their feet.

"You're fucking crazy!" the younger Alpha declared in horror. "Man, this isn't worth it."

Lane smiled, and took aim a second time. "No, it isn't. I appreciate your concern, gentlemen, but I'm afraid you've wasted your time. There's only one Omega here. Me. I live alone."

The younger Alpha cocked his head in confusion. "I can see Carey right behind you."

"I live alone," Lane repeated. "There's no one here but me. Your eyes are playing tricks on you."

The younger Alpha clearly still didn't understand, but the older one was getting the picture. He raised his hand again. It might have made other Omegas quail.

"I live alone," Lane said instead, still smiling. "I've been here for years, and everyone knows that I'm a lone wolf. There's no one here but me, and my property is clearly marked. *Trespassers will be shot on sight.* I'll give you until the count of three. One -- two --"

He took his second shot half a blink before the older Alpha would have leapt at him.

The younger Alpha had plainly had enough. He jumped away from the bullet that landed near his feet and tore toward Lane's tree line, kicking up snow and panting as he ran.

The older Alpha wasn't so easily broken. He sneered, breathing liquor fumes over him. "You think you're so smart. All you Omegas do, leading us Alphas around by the balls unless someone teaches you your proper place, and all the time you're dumb as your cunts. That's a two shot rifle, little Omega, and now you're fresh out of ammo. Did you ever think of that?"

"Oh, I knew it only had two bullets," Lane said, showing him his teeth. He took one step aside. Just one. It brought him within reach of the old table with its recessed drawer, and the revolver he kept tucked there. He lifted it to sight between the Alpha's eyes. "How lucky for me I have six more on hand. I'll tell you one more time, and the law will consider I gave fair warning before I shoot. *Get. Out.*"

An extraordinary dark purple swept over the Alpha's face. "Have him," he barked. "Useless as hell anyhow. But I won't take him back when you're tired of him."

Lane only smiled, and took the safety off his pistol.

"Damn all Omegas," the Alpha snarled. He looked as if he'd like nothing better than to hit Lane again, but only feinted at it before turning on his heel to stalk away.

Lane had his pistol ready and aimed when the Alpha stopped halfway to the trees, clearly thinking about a sneak lunge at his house. "Keep walking."

He didn't lower his gun until he was truly gone. Not even then. He waited for the acrid stench of Alpha to clear before he finally relaxed his arm. More tired than he could ever remember being, even after his mate had put him aside, he set the safety back on the revolver and stowed it back in the drawer.

Warm Omega battened itself to his side. Lane looked to see Carey staring up at him with eyes like stars. "You..." he said, sounding stunned. "He ran away."

"He did." Lane's limbs had started shaking, flooded with too much adrenaline, but it made him laugh. "I did."

"Oh, Lane." Carey surged up on his tiptoes and pressed his mouth to Lane's, winding his arms around Lane's neck at the same time. "Thank you, Lane, thank you."

Lane wrapped his arms around Carey's waist. He started to speak, but a sob came out instead, and then another wild laugh. "You're mine. He couldn't have you."

Carey kissed the laughter away as well as the tears, and clung to him as sweetly as a rose vine to a rock. As determined as vines that grew through rock, Lane thought, and just as hardy. Someone who'd found his unusual way and would cling to it, come what may.

As he would too.

"You're not making me leave now," Carey said, settling briefly on his heels and searching Lane's face. "Are you?"

"No." Lane cupped Carey's cheek. "No, I'm not. You're staying here with me, if you'll have me."

"Have you? Lane!" Carey bit the point of Lane's chin. "You just watch me stay. I mean to make you fall in love with me, Omega."

Lane lifted Carey's hand and kissed the knuckles. "Can't do what's already been done."

Carey's lips parted in surprise, then curved in the widest and happiest of smiles. "Oh, Lane. You just wait and see."

Epilogue

Were such things possible? They weren't meant to be.

But that didn't mean they couldn't happen.

Careful not to wake Lane, who lay peacefully asleep in the hotel bed's crisp clean sheets, Carey tiptoed to the plate glass window on the far wall of their suite, and tweaked back the curtains. Outside, dazzling lights glittered and twinkled as far as the eye could see.

They hadn't made it to Paris, as Lane still insisted they ought to one day, but Vancouver wasn't at all bad for starters.

Carey fingered the simple silver ring he wore on the third finger of his right hand, still awed at the smooth coolness of the metal. Lane wore one just like it, and Carey had put it on his hand himself. And no one, not a single wolf, had given them so much as a second glance when they checked in for their week's vacation in the city. Nor had anyone come around to bother them at Lane's -- their -- cabin, during the long winter and the spring thaw. And if they had? Well, Lane still had six shots loaded in his pistol.

Somehow Carey didn't think he'd have call to use them.

The world was changing, he had decided. Laws could change and no one would take any notice, but when people's hearts altered, that was what made the difference.

And he and Lane would be right there in the thick of it.

Behind him, Lane stirred drowsily. "Can't sleep?" he murmured.

"Too excited," Carey said, looking over his shoulder. The sight that greeted his eyes made his smile even wider, and yet softer. A fox cub, still crinkled and red and new to the world, lay in the warm hollow next to

Lane's body. Theirs, now, to love and to raise. "Is he still out?"

Lane had smile lines now, and they showed at the corners of his eyes. "Out like a light, but he'll get cold soon. Come lie back down. We can see all of the city there is to see tomorrow. You, me, and him."

"A family," Carey said, satisfaction warming him down to his toes. "Tomorrow, Vancouver. The next day, the world?"

"Anywhere you want," Lane promised, sweeping back the covers for Carey to tuck himself beneath.

Carey slipped between the sheets, on his side facing Lane, and laid his hand over the fox cub's tiny ribs, breathing in time with him. "I told you, Lane," he murmured, leaning across to kiss his lover -- his mate's -- nose. "You wait and see. Didn't I say so?"

"And so I did," Lane said, kissing him in return. "And so I will. For now, and for always. My Omega. My own."

Will Okati

Will Okati (formerly known as Willa) has lived through a few Interesting Times, but come out the other side a little grayer, a little wiser, and ready to get writing. Still as passionate about coffee, cats, and crafts as ever, but knowing that to your own self you must be true. Also still one of the quiet ones to watch out for, but life -- like storytelling -- is always a work in progress.

Will at Changeling: changelingpress.com/will-okati-a-213

Changeling Press E-Books

More Sci-Fi, Fantasy, Paranormal, and BDSM adventures available in E-Book format for immediate download at ChangelingPress.com -- Werewolves, Vampires, Dragons, Shapeshifters and more -- Erotic Tales from the edge of your imagination.

What are E-Books?

E-Books, or Electronic Books, are books designed to be read in digital format -- on your desktop or laptop computer, notebook, tablet, Smart Phone, or any electronic ebook reader.

Where can I get Changeling Press e-Books?

Changeling Press ebooks are available at ChangelingPress.com, Amazon, Barnes and Nobel, Kobo, and iBooks.

Changeling Press, LLC

ChangelingPress.com